Something LIKE NORMAL

Something Like NORMAL

International Bestselling Author

MONICA JAMES

THE MONSTERS WITHIN DUET
Bullseye
Blowback

DELIVER US FROM EVIL TRILOGY
Thy Kingdom Come
Into Temptation
Deliver Us From Evil

IN LOVE AND WAR
North of the Stars
Fall of the Stars

REVENGE IS SWEET SERIES
Crybaby

HEART MEMORY TRANSFER DUET
Heart Sick
Love Sick

STANDALONE
Mr. Write
Chase the Butterflies
Beyond the Roses
Someone Else's Shadow

I've always been a fuckup.

When I arrived two weeks early, interrupting my father's monthly poker game, I was a fuckup.

When my mother walked out on my father and me, leaving without a word, I was a fuckup.

When I tried to hide my father's drug stash in my Malibu Barbie's beach house, I was a fuckup.

When I failed my senior year because I was too busy fixing my father's "problems," I was a fuckup.

But when I pulled the trigger of my Colt 911 and shot my father, I wasn't a fuckup.

My name is Mia Lee, but that person died the day she shot her father in cold blood and felt nothing.

One

"**G**ood morning, miss. Where to?" singsongs the clerk.

Who the *hell* is so chipper at three o'clock in the morning?

"Anywhere but here," I mumble to myself while rummaging blindly through my backpack, looking for my wallet.

My hand passes over my flick knife, my Colt, and finally, my wallet. The quicker I get this over with, the quicker I can blow this town.

"Where can I go with this?" I ask, sliding my money toward her. The money I stole from my dad's hidden stash as he lay unconscious and bleeding on the basement floor.

The woman counts my cash while I nervously take in my surroundings, afraid I have been followed.

This Greyhound bus depot is like all the others. It is

artificially lit, and no matter how many coats of paint are applied, the bright colors that coat the walls make it look outdated and lifeless.

But it's the smell that gives me the creeps.

It smells of desperation.

"Any preferences to where you want to go?"

"Somewhere boring and quiet. Someplace I would blend in."

Her hazel eyes widen, making it more than obvious she's taking in my not-so-inconspicuous appearance.

My straight black hair is long, and I've worn it this way for as long as I can remember. However, one day I decided to highlight my thick tresses with bright red, hoping to experience a kaleidoscope of jovial emotion with the change. I liked the color, but sadly, it failed to modify my miserable existence.

My blue eyes are always dressed up with the blackest mascara, and you'll never see my upper lids lined with anything other than dark kohl, giving me a—what did *Cosmopolitan* call it again? That's right—seductive cat eyes. Seriously, who comes up with this shit?

As a kid, my nickname was Cindy, thanks to the small beauty spot above my lip. I've been told it's my best feature. But growing up in my world, it was best not to have any "best features" and just fade into the background.

I have a small silver hoop in my nose and two piercings in both my ears. All piercings, even my tragus, was of course done by me. The pain was a reminder that I was alive.

What wasn't done by me is the moon tattoo I have inked on my inner left wrist. This ink holds much symbolism, and I've never regretted the day I got it at age fifteen. The horse tattoo in the middle of my back is something else I hold close to my heart. I dream of being wild and free because it's something I'll never be.

"You could probably get to South Boston, Virginia, on this. Scheduled arrival is in two days, thirteen hours, and fifty minutes," she says, tapping away on the computer keys.

I have no idea what they do in South Boston, and honestly, I don't care. All I know is that it's a small town in Halifax County, and it sounds perfect.

"Sure, that's fine. As long as it leaves tonight."

"You mean this morning?" she chirps with a smile.

I eye the ballpoint sitting in its perfect little pen holder on the counter near me and contemplate jamming the writing implement into my ears, as the pain is more appealing than having to listen to this woman for one more second.

She must construe my expression for someone who gives a flying fuck.

"You know, 'cause it's three a.m. and all, so technically, it's morning."

I drum my black-painted fingernails on the countertop, impatiently waiting for her to stop talking and give me my ticket so I can get the hell away from her.

Of course, she doesn't get it, and when I raise an unimpressed eyebrow at her, she continues staring and smiling, waiting for me to remark on her lame-ass observation.

I don't.

"Ticket," I remind her.

"Oh right, of course, sorry," she stammers as she nervously taps away at the keyboard.

Glancing around the small terminal again, I see two other people waiting for a ride, and I wonder if they're escaping, just like me.

A little girl holds a ragged pink teddy. She clutches her

mother's arm, her large eyes flighty and frightened as she studies her surroundings. When the frayed teddy slips from her fingers, she reaches for it quickly, as it, no doubt, is her security blanket and savior.

Judging by the shiner her mother currently sports, these two are definitely like me.

They're runners.

The young girl notices me looking at her and shyly hides her face against her mother's side.

I turn away quickly, not wanting to bother the kid because I see myself in her. I, too, was once that scared little youngster. But I was forced to grow the fuck up because, in my world, being scared fated you to become a victim.

Something I refuse to be ever again.

"Miss Cassidy?"

"What?" I snap, lost in my thoughts.

"Your bus leaves in ten minutes." She smiles uncomfortably as she finally hands me my freedom.

"Super," I reply, snatching the ticket and shoving it into the back pocket of my denim shorts.

"Enjoy your ride with…"

Turning away before she finishes her sentence might seem a little rude, but I have given her enough of my time, and my time is finally mine. And I am not a people person.

I plop down onto the hard plastic green seat and slouch low, crossing my feet at the ankles as my eyes drift over my plain attire. My black Converse high-tops have seen better days, but I don't have the heart to throw them away since I've had them for years.

I stand at five-foot-three and have always been underweight. I can thank my father for my gaunt frame because eating nutritiously in my household was unheard of, so after a while, you just forgot you needed food to survive. But in my line of "work," you had to be tough, so I worked out. Yes, I may be skinny, but I can kick the ass of a two-hundred-pound creep any day. Trust me, I speak from experience.

I've been pale all my life, and I know when contrasted with my black hair and blue eyes, I sometimes resemble the living dead. But if you're considered a freak, no one seems to fuck with you and leaves you the hell alone. And that's how I like it.

I frown as I peer down at the bag sitting at my feet, realizing I didn't have much to pack. My whole life fits inside this tiny, tattered backpack—my whole life, which I packed in haste.

But that doesn't matter. When I get to South Boston, I will blend in because I want to be like everybody else. I want to be normal.

But I know I won't ever be normal, so I'll settle for something like normal.

The singsong voice jolts me out of my head, but thankfully, this time around, I am semi-happy to hear it since it's announcing my ride has finally arrived.

Looking out the smudged window, I huff a deep breath of relief when my bus pulls into the lot.

Freedom.

All but springing out of my seat, I push open the double glass doors, anxious to make Los Angeles a distant memory.

Los Angeles, population three million eight hundred thousand, and growing by the second, is now minus two. I used to call a little house in the suburbs my home, but now, now it's my prison, filled with bitter memories and broken dreams.

Who am I kidding? It was never my home.

However, I used to feel safe there. Well, that was until my mom left me in the care of my father when I was three. And honestly, if I had a choice, I'd rather be alone.

Searching through my backpack, I find my black sweater and pull it on quickly as I suddenly have a chill. But this is nothing new—thinking about my father always has my blood running cold. Slinking into the hood, I rearrange the sides so my face is practically hidden underneath it.

I like anonymity. This is my new life now.

I am no one.

"Miss?"

My head snaps up, and the chubby bus driver, with a friendly face and warm smile, extends his hand to me.

"What?" I ask, confused.

"Your bag." He smiles, looking down at it.

I snatch it up from where I dropped it and clutch it closer to my chest, squeezing it for dear life.

When I don't budge, he clarifies, "Can I take it for you?"

"Can I keep it on board with me?" I ask, not wanting to part with it.

"Of course, you can. Welcome aboard."

Giving him a polite nod, I make my way over to the bus. However, before I ascend the first step, I look up at it with childlike eyes. I feel hope and optimism, something I haven't felt in a very long time. And that's because my nineteen-year-old eyes have seen things a person my age should never be exposed to.

Actually, regardless of age, no one should be subjected to the shit I've seen.

But that's in the past. The past I shot down—literally.

As I take my first step toward freedom, I feel my mouth tip up into a foreign gesture. One I haven't been familiar with

in a long time.
    I smile.
    Well, here's to new beginnings.
    'Cause the past fucking sucked.

Two

I awake, totally aware I'm drooling out of the side of my mouth, but I don't have the energy to move. Only when my neck creaks in protest as I attempt to shift do I wipe the spittle off my chin with the back of my sleeve.

My eyes drift over the boring landscape. It's not much to look at, but the farther we drive, the farther away I am from my past. I could be riding into hell, and that would be better than the alternative of staying in LA.

Rolling my eyes, I tell myself to harden the fuck up because, yes, my life sucked. And yes, my father made every villain look like Santa Claus. But I won't let that fucker dictate how I live my new life. I won't give him the satisfaction of being in control of me ever again.

Leaning my head back on the headrest, I close my eyes. Being alone with these thoughts should be daunting, but funnily enough, they aren't. They're simply a reminder of what I went through to get here.

Do I feel guilty for shooting my dad in cold blood? No.

Do I feel guilty for leaving his body to bleed out on the floor? No.

Do I feel guilty at all? No.

No, no, and no.

Did my dad feel guilty when he came home high or drunk and beat me every day with the belt I got him for Father's Day? No.

Did my dad feel guilty the first time he traded me to his drug dealer, Big Phil, to pay for his drugs? No.

Did my dad feel guilty the day he decided he could use me to pay off his drug debt in ways no nineteen-year-old girl ever should? No.

That day was only two days ago, and that was the day I'd had enough.

That was the last day of my old life.

So the fact I have no remorse for what I did to my father doesn't make me a bad person. It makes me a survivor. And in my world, where it's survival of the fittest, I had no choice. It was either him or me.

And for once, I chose me.

"Okay, folks, we're here. Thank you for choosing Greyhound to get you safely to your destination. We hope to see you again real soon."

I don't know how many hours have passed. Come to think of it, I don't even know what day it is since I've slept like the dead. But none of that matters because I've done it. I'm away from him, and I can start afresh.

It's dark outside, and storm clouds pass over the murky sky.

Grabbing my backpack and eagerly making my way toward the front of the empty bus, elated to start my new life, I'm stopped by the driver on the way out.

"You got someone to pick you up, miss?" he asks, head bowed while writing in his logbook.

Why does this stranger want to know my life story? Back home, no one asked me anything unless they wanted something.

"Yup," I reply dismissively and descend the steps as quickly as possible.

Sinking into my hood, which is a habit of mine, I arrange it to cover my face and blend into the darkened night. I look around at the unfamiliar sights and take it all in.

"Sorry, miss. I didn't mean to scare you earlier," someone says from behind me.

Jumping back, I'm startled when I feel a strange hand rest on my shoulder. I swallow the bile in my throat as I hate being touched by people I don't know.

"Back off," I snarl, spinning around quickly, ready to wage war.

The man, who I recognize as the bus driver, raises his hands in surrender, looking a little pale.

"Sorry, I mean no harm. I just thought you looked like you needed a place to stay, that's all. There's a motel not too far up the road. I know the owner, Hank. We go way back. You tell him Bertie sent ya, and he'll fix you up a room till you find your feet."

Narrowing my eyes, I ask, "What makes you think I haven't found my feet already?"

Bertie shuffles uncomfortably and chooses his words carefully.

"I've been doing this job a long time, miss, and well, you

get to know people."

"No offense, Bertie," I sneer. "But you know *fuck* all about me. So I'd appreciate it if you just mind your own fucking business."

Bertie's face drops, and damn, I feel a pang of regret for being so rude to him.

"Oh, I'm sorry, miss." He averts his eyes, and suddenly, a profound sadness overtakes him.

I know that feeling all too well.

"You just remind me of my daughter," he clarifies, clearing his throat.

As much as I hate to blow him off, I'm not here to make friends or owe anyone favors. And I certainly don't want to be reminding anyone of their daughter.

"Well, in that case, go bother her," I bark angrily, about to leave this awkward scene behind me.

I never used to be this way. But growing up among drug dealers and users hardens you up fast.

Watching Bertie's face drop further, I tell myself to walk away because I don't have time for this shit.

"I would, but she passed about a year ago."

The look on his face touches something inside me that I thought was long dead.

I feel guilt.

"I'm...sorry...about your daughter," I offer when Bertie meets my uncomfortable gaze.

Bertie nods and wipes his teary eyes.

"Thank you. Anyway, if you change your mind, the motel is about a mile up the road. You can't miss it. It's a big, ugly building with a red flashing cat. It's called Night Cats."

When I can see the tacky, buzzing cat sign, I stumble toward it, thankful the rain has held off.

Looking around the parking lot, I search for Norman Bates because this motel is a dead ringer for the Bates Motel.

The wraparound walkways are weather-worn and in desperate need of a good coat of paint. I think the original color was yellow, but it's hard to tell due to the heavy rot. A sad-looking basketball hoop is tucked away toward the back of the motel, and it's fair to say it's seen better days.

A flashing red arrow zaps loudly, pointing in the direction of the office, which offers twenty-four-hour check-in.

As the digital clock sitting under the fluorescent crimson motel sign ticks over to one twenty-four a.m., I rub my eyes with the heels of my hands. Only then do I realize how dog-tired I am, regardless of how much I slept on the bus.

I can't wait to crash, so I quickly make my way through the deserted parking lot, the gravel crunching loudly under my Chucks. My heart begins to beat faster when I hear a loud howling echoing in the distance.

Quickening my step, as I do not want to meet the owner of that ominous yowl, I charge into the tiny reception area, which smells of stale cigarettes and coffee. A TV with its volume close to being mute is humming from behind the maroon curtain, and I can't help but think it's just background noise for whoever sits in front of the screen.

A silver bell sits on the long, wooden counter, which I ding twice.

As I wait for someone to come out, I look around the

room and its minimal offerings. The reception desk takes up most of the space, and behind the counter, I eye the keys lined up neatly, attached to the back wall.

Leaning to the left in an attempt to peer through the gap in the curtain to see if anyone is back there proves to be futile because I can't see anything. Just as I'm contemplating whether to ring the bell again, an older gentleman comes strolling out, wiping the sleep from his tired eyes.

"What can I get for you, miss?" he asks kindly, giving me a crooked smile.

If I had a grandfather, I would want him to look like this old man. With his thinning gray hair and weathered skin, I automatically like him.

"How many days can I stay here with this?" I ask, reaching into my backpack and sliding my minimal offerings across the counter.

Grandpa, as I've dubbed him, counts my money and scrunches up his brow.

"Probably four, five days," he says, separating the bills from the coins. "Is this all you have?"

"Yes," I answer, wiping a hand down my exhausted face.

I know it's not much, but I'll be out job hunting as soon as first light breaks.

"Are you staying or passing through?" Grandpa questions kindly.

For some reason, I don't find his questions to be invasive. That might be because there's only kindness behind his crinkled eyes.

"Just passing through. Once I get a job and save enough money, I'll be out of here and looking for my mom," I confess openly, which surprises me.

This is the first time I'm sharing my plans with another

living soul. Saying them aloud makes what I am doing, and more importantly, what I have done, all the more real.

"Oh." Grandpa's mouth dips, and I see it. I see pity in his aged, wise eyes.

I hate that look, and I instantly regret the overshare.

"So can I get a room or not?" I ask, attempting to steer Grandpa away from asking any more personal questions.

"Of course," he says quickly, and the pity look fades.

His shaky fingers tremble as they reach for my room key, and I wonder if he has someone here to help him out. Someone younger and less frail.

Grandpa should be in bed or on some seniors' cruise, sailing the Bahamas, not manning this reception desk at this ungodly hour.

I watch with interest as he pulls out a leather-bound logbook from where he keeps it tucked away under the counter. He's in no real hurry as he reaches for his silver-rimmed glasses, which are hanging loosely from a linked chain around his neck. And as he perches them on the tip of his narrow nose, I can't help but examine the wrinkles on the back of his hand.

I look down at my hands, which are youthful and wrinkle-free, and it's hard to believe that Grandpa's hands once resembled mine. How age can change one's appearance baffles me. Will my hands look like Grandpa's when I get to his age? Or the better question would be *if* I ever get to his age.

He slides the key across the counter, snapping me out of my haze. As I look up at him, there is that damn kind-hearted look in his eyes again. I quickly snatch the key so I can get the hell away from his compassionate gaze.

Before I can flee, Grandpa asks, "Is there anything particular you're looking for?"

I raise my eyebrow at him, not following.

"I mean, job-wise," he explains with a smile.

"Anything that pays and is relatively legal."

Grandpa looks at me and lets out a loud, hearty laugh. He wipes the tear that has escaped from the corner of his crinkled eye.

My mouth tips up into a small smile, but it's gone before I can second-guess it.

"Well, if you're interested," Grandpa says, leaning forward onto the counter casually, "I have a job available here."

"You do?"

"Now before you get too excited, it's working in the kitchen to prepare breakfast for the guests and then cleaning out the rooms once they check out. I can offer you cheap accommodation in one of the rooms, and the pay, well, it's nothing flashy, but—"

"It's perfect," I interrupt. "Can I start tomorrow?"

Grandpa smiles broadly, revealing a few missing back teeth.

"Is that a yes?" I ask, mentally crossing my fingers and not bothering to amend his comment.

Grandpa smiles, and his kind, gray eyes give me all the confirmation I need.

"I'm Hank, by the way," he says, extending his hand.

Internally thanking Bertie for sending me this way, I look down at his weathered, wrinkled hand, and shake it firmly.

"I'm Paige. Paige Cassidy."

The pseudonym rolls off my tongue easily.

But that's who I am now.

Mia Lee was a victim.

But Paige Cassidy is a survivor.

Three

"**D**addy, I don't want to go with him. He's scary."

My father, Thomas Lee, is a tall man with black hair and blue eyes. I've watched my dad go from a healthy man to a skinny, sick man. And I know it's got to do with the white powder my daddy smokes, or sometimes, I see him put it up his nose.

Daddy crouches down and rests on one knee, looking me in the eyes.

"You be a good girl and go with Phil, okay, baby? He won't hurt you."

"But I don't like him," I reply, looking over his shoulder at Big Phil.

Big, fat Phil.

He looks scary, standing with his arms crossed. And even though he's wearing dark sunglasses, I know he's looking at me and making an angry face. His big, round belly sticks out like Santa Claus, but Santa doesn't look as mean as Phil does. And I don't think he's as fat.

Looking back at my father, I see his jaw moving back and forth quickly, and he shivers like he's cold. I wonder what's wrong with him.

"Daddy, are you sick?"

Daddy shivers once again and softly grabs my upper arms. "Yes, Mia, I'm sick. You have to go with Phil to make Daddy better."

I bite my lip and look over his shoulder once more. Phil takes off his sunglasses and gives me a small smile. My arms get funny bumps on them. I don't like him smiling at me.

"Okay, Daddy, I'll go," I say, nodding, and am happy when I see him smile at me.

"Good girl, Mia. You're my princess; you remember that. That's why you're called Mia," he says. "You'll always be mine."

Daddy told me that my name means "mine" in Italian. I like knowing that I'll always belong to my daddy.

"Okay, Mia, take this bag," he says, slipping my pink Tinker Bell backpack onto my shoulders. "Phil will take you to lots of different places, and all you have to do is give the little bags to the people who need them. Can you do that for Daddy?"

I nod. "Yes. But what's inside? Why can't he do it?"

Daddy closes his eyes and lets out a big breath. "It's candy for grown-ups. Once you give the candy to the grown-ups, Daddy can have his. Go now, Mia. I'll see you later."

I'm a big girl now. I'm eight years old, and big girls don't cry.

"Okay, I love you."

I give Daddy a big hug, and he feels sweaty and shaky. I

have to do this for him because I want my daddy to play catch with me again and make me food like he used to do before he got sick.

With my heart pounding, I take a step toward Phil, who has walked over to his white van.

"Mia!" Daddy calls out to me.

"What, Daddy?" I ask quickly, running over to him.

Maybe he's changed his mind, and I don't have to go with Phil.

"I promise, baby, it'll only be this one time. Daddy will get better."

"Okay. Bye, Daddy," I say, looking into his sleepy red eyes.

I walk toward Phil, and with every step I take, I look over my shoulder, hoping my daddy will stop me.

But he doesn't.

And that day I realized…my daddy was a liar.

Jolting awake, I attempt to catch my breath.

As my eyes take in my surroundings, my heart rate begins to slow to a semi-normal pace. I can see through the thin, frilly curtains that it's still dark out.

Holy shit, I hate dreaming.

I always wake this way, and it takes me several minutes to think straight. I know from experience that I have no hope of getting back to sleep, especially after having that particular dream. It was the day my faith in my father diminished. It was the day my father traded me to Big Phil for drugs.

It was the day I became a drug peddler.

Mia Lee, drug dealer at age eight.

No longer able to sleep, I decide to get an early start on the day.

I spend twenty minutes coloring my skin to a bright red while standing under the shower spray. Only then do I stop shivering.

I hate that my dad still has this effect on me. Whenever I think about my father, I hate that I transform into that scared little eight-year-old—the eight-year-old who became Big Phil's number one drug dealer.

I had the pleasure of being Big Phil's top employee for eleven years. In eleven fucking years, I've seen things that would make the toughest motherfucker cower in fear.

I've seen mothers get high and ignore their crying babies, too strung out to notice their child is dirty and starving. I've seen junkies pry needles from the arms of their fellow junkies to shoot up, desperate to get their next fix. I've seen kids no older than me addicted to their drug of choice and do anything, and I mean *anything*, to get a hit.

And I stood by and watched. No, I stood by and *helped* these individuals destroy their lives with every hit they took. I'm as much to blame as Big Phil. And my dad.

Big Phil is the biggest drug dealer in Los Angeles. Whatever you wanted, Big Phil could get. He dealt in coke, heroin, weed, meth, speed, prescription pills, and everything in between.

But Big Phil never got his hands dirty as he hid behind the ruse of being a hippie herbalist. He owned a small shop front downtown and was the perfect social chameleon. His business, Happy Herbs, sold remedies to "cure" everything from the common cold to cancer.

It was all bullshit, of course.

His "remedies" were cheap imports and usually only

cured people who wanted to believe in a miracle cure. He was a fraud on all accounts and couldn't care less when his miracle remedies fell short of achieving what they claimed to do.

But somehow, he evaded the police and continued his illegal dealings, making a name for himself among the lowlife scumbags of LA. But looking at Phil, you would never pick him out for what he is—a parasite. He blended into society in his nice suits and fake smiles, and you wouldn't look twice if you walked past him on the street.

On the outside, he's your average American with nothing special or memorable about him. But on the inside, he's a ruthless murderer with greed fueling his every emotion. And that's what makes him a dangerous predator. He'll attack when one least expects it, blindsiding his victims and catching them unaware.

The fear he induces in people makes him untouchable. This fact alone fuels his sadistic ways, making him feel invincible and unstoppable.

So how did I get involved in all these illegal dealings?

It all comes down to one man, of course.

My father.

When my mother left for Canada, she took a piece of my father with her. I don't know why she left, because we were happy. Well, I thought we were.

My dad worked for a successful manufacturing company and had just been promoted to shift manager. My mother was an art teacher at the local high school, and her art was on display at a gallery downtown, which was her dream come true.

But then one day, my father picked me up from kindergarten, and he told me my mother was gone and never coming back. I remember that day clearer than any that have passed since. I had drawn her a picture of an off-center butterfly, its wings streaked with bright greens and pinks and blues. I was so proud of my picture because it was similar to the one I had seen her submit to her art show.

I remember crying like I had never cried before when my father told me she had left us, and it was only him and me from now on.

I held that picture tightly to my chest because it was the last thing I would ever draw for her.

My father saw me gripping that piece of paper like it was my lifeline, and he angrily asked what it was. When I told him I had drawn it for my mother, my father flew into a fit of rage and tore the picture from my tiny fingers, tossing it out the open window.

The scream that ripped from my throat left my voice raspy for three days. I recall seeing my artwork fly into the wind like a balloon, and I closed my eyes tight, wishing it was all a bad dream.

But when I reopened them, sadly, it was real.

My childhood ended that day, and I was forced to become an adult quickly because my dad started dabbling in drugs soon after. But it wasn't until I got to age eight that his drug use got out of control.

I never understood why my dad became agitated and angry because he was usually such a placid, happy man. Now I know my father was a drug addict. Well, more specifically, he was a meth addict. He would abuse the drug over and over, and now I know this misuse is called a "run." He would inject the drug every few hours until he ran out of his stash or just got so fucked up he couldn't continue.

It started about a year after my mother left and escalated as time passed. Soon, my dad raked up a drug debt so big, he couldn't afford to pay it, so that's when I started "working" for Big Phil to pay for my dad's drug habit.

My dad lost his job and burned through his savings quicker than expected because his habit was getting out of control. Any help from the government was blown on his addiction, and it still wasn't enough to pay for his habit. So that's where I became useful to my dad and to Big Phil.

My dad and Phil came to an agreement. I would work for Big Phil whenever he needed me to deliver drugs, as no one questions an eight-year-old roaming the streets with a Tinker Bell backpack who appears to be on her way to school. And that's because no one could fathom that her backpack would be filled with drugs.

Big Phil used to fill my bag with a cocktail of drugs, and I would deliver his goods and collect his money, no questions asked. In return, he would give my dad cheap drugs; the cheaper the drugs, the bigger the addiction. Therefore, I ended up working for Big Phil full-time.

As I got older, I knew what was happening, but I was still that scared little eight-year-old whenever my father begged me to help him, promising it was the last time.

It never was. And that's how I ended up in the situation I'm in now.

I don't know if anyone has discovered his body because he had no friends or family. It was just us. Big Phil was supposedly coming over, but what if he never did? Is my dad lying dead and undiscovered? That thought turns my blood cold.

So why did I shoot my dad?

I ended his miserable life because he deserved it. I shot him because being a drug dealer wasn't good enough anymore.

I hate myself for ruining so many people's lives, but in the end, they had a choice. No one held a gun to their head to get high.

On the other hand, I did have a gun pointed at my head—literally.

The day my father pointed a gun at me and threatened to end my life if I didn't become a "working girl" for Phil to pay for his increasing drug debt was the day I had enough.

As I said, it was either him or me.

I just regret I didn't do it sooner.

"Holy fuck!" I screech as a beetle the size of a small child crawls out of room 9.

I scamper out of the way as the lazy bug is none the wiser that it has just scared the bejesus out of me.

This is the third room I've cleaned that has had some bug out of Arachnophobia creeping out, ready to attack me.

Pathetic, I know. After all the shit I've seen in my life, you wouldn't think a tiny bug would give me the creeps—but they do, as they're one of the only things I fear.

There's a reason for my phobia, and that reason can be found in my shitty childhood.

"Paige, you've done a wonderful job," Hank says with a smile while looking into the room.

Today, he looks the perfect Grandpa part in his gray trousers held up by navy suspenders. He has on a loose white T-shirt with a coffee stain on the front, and to the left of that stain is something that looks like jelly.

"Thanks," I reply, wiping my hands on my white apron as I rearrange the cleaning products on my silver cart.

"What are the plans for today?" he asks as we stroll down the walkway to the office.

I shrug because I haven't given it much thought. After the crappy sleep I had, I was hoping to catch some shut-eye. Apart from that, I have no other plans.

"Oh, c'mon. After all the hard work you've just done, you should go out and explore."

Raising my eyebrow at him and pursing my lips, I'm about to tell him I don't plan on staying here for longer than a month, but he gives me a lopsided grin, reading my thoughts.

"Yes, I know, you're not here to stay, but you're young. Go out and have some fun."

Fun? I don't see how I can have fun in a town like South Boston. I looked up the population in the little welcome brochure in my bedside dresser, and it's pretty measly. Pulling in at just over eight thousand one hundred people, I'm pretty certain no fun will be found in the city streets.

"I don't even know my way around. I'll get lost," I reply as we reach the office.

Grandpa unlocks the door, and I wait as he shuffles inside.

"I'll tell ya what. I don't need my truck today. How 'bout ya take the Old Girl for a spin? My neighbor gave me her old GP something or other, and God knows I have no use for it. All these modern gadgets are too complicated for my old brain," he says, reaching behind the counter and handing me a set of keys hanging off an old Dodge key ring.

I peer down at the keys like they're from outer space. Is he really lending me his truck? For the first time in forever, I'm shocked.

"I…can't take your truck," I say, shaking my head.

Grandpa lets out a warm laugh. "You're not taking it. You're borrowing it. There's a big difference. Go on."

I don't know what to do, as this is a circumstance where someone is being nice to me without wanting anything in return.

As I continue to hesitate, Grandpa reaches for my hand and places the keys into my palm. His hand clasps over mine, and when I would normally flinch or pull away, I involuntarily squeeze his hand in gratitude.

"Thank you, I…thank you," I stammer, looking into his gray eyes.

Grandpa removes his hand from mine and waves it off like it's nothing, but little does he know how his kindness has touched me.

Four

'm avoiding going out into the real world. So I've decided to waste some time and attempt to look semi-human.

I've brushed my hair, but taking a closer look at the red in it, I realize it's time to touch up my highlights as they're beginning to fade and look tacky.

My black jean shorts, which show off a bit of leg, are my favorite. However, I didn't buy them for that reason. I actually bought them because if I needed to hightail it out of a sticky situation, I could run like the wind in them.

My white T-shirt sits loosely on me, and I slip on my black motorcycle boots. Again, I dress for practicality and not for style. I hide my flick knife in my right boot. Seeing as my boots are knee-high, I can conceal my weapon in them without being detected.

A girl can never be too safe in an unknown neighborhood.

After one last look in the bathroom mirror, I'm ready to go, but the question is, where?

When I left LA, I had no desire to visit anywhere in particular. So now that I'm here, I don't know what to do.

I decide to listen to Grandpa and use the GPS to choose something for me to do.

Locking my door and shoving the keys into my pocket, it's showtime.

Seeing Grandpa's "Old Girl" parked out front, with the driver's side window wound down, warms my heart.

From the condition of the faded blue Dodge pickup, I'd say it was built in the mid-eighties.

Some may see this car as a rust bucket, but to me, it screams personality and character. Looks like the Old Girl and I will get along just fine.

Arriving in downtown South Boston takes less time than originally anticipated, and funnily enough, I don't hate what I see.

There's an old, antique feel to the shops, but it's also modern in what it has to offer. From services such as cardio kickboxing to yoga classes to traditional diners and a movie theater, the downtown is not what I expected.

It's nice. And it looks safe.

Pulling into a parking space, I take in the tree-lined streets and the beautiful Victorian architecture, and suddenly, I feel my heart thump in…excitement.

I can't believe I'm here and can't get out of the truck soon enough. I leap out, being sure to lock it. Although looking around at the friendly, happy faces of the townsfolk, I doubt anyone would look twice if it was unlocked. I'm in awe of the high antique buildings and can't stop looking at them.

As I walk past a florist, the fresh flowers can be smelled on the light summer breeze, and it's a scent I haven't smelled in, well, ever.

My mouth waters as I glance into the window of an ice cream shop. The endless flavors on display flip my stomach into a somersault, and I honestly can't remember the last time I ate.

Continuing my observation and being enchanted with all there is to see, I'm thankful I ended up here. And even though I won't be staying, it's a nice stopover.

My nose leads me toward an old diner across the road, and when I smell waffles, my feet head there before my head has a say.

The aged light-green building has red block letters that read Bobby Joe's. I love the fifties feel to this place, and I haven't even stepped inside yet. A Help Wanted poster is tacked onto the front window, and I wonder if it was a coincidence I decided to eat here.

Pushing open the glass door, I'm greeted by Elvis Presley playing softly in the background. I was right. The fifties feel continues inside.

An old-school diner sign hangs above the long counter, flashing in a bright fluorescent light. Red leather booths are positioned around the diner, and stools run alongside the lengthy counter, offering patrons the chance to chat with the pretty servers behind the counter. If that doesn't give it enough of a fifties feel, the floor is the traditional black-and-white-checkered print.

Servers walk around, happily topping up empty coffee

cups with a smile. The smell of coffee has me picking up a menu by the door and heading quickly to a booth down the back.

Looking over the menu, I exhale a relieved breath when I see the affordable prices. With what little money I have leftover, I should be able to afford to eat until Grandpa pays me.

"What can I get ya?" asks a bubbly voice.

I haven't decided what I want to eat, but I know I want coffee, and lots of it.

"Just a coffee for now, please."

The redhead, whose name tag reads Tabitha, smiles broadly and gives me a quick nod, which results in her long ponytail bobbing up and down. She picks up the coffee cup in front of me and pours me a cup from the glass pot she's holding.

"I haven't seen you in here before. Are you visiting family or friends?"

I instantly shuffle in my seat uncomfortably.

"Um, neither. Just passing through," I answer, being as vague as possible without rousing too much suspicion.

Tabitha smiles, and her face lights up instantly. "Oh, that's what they all say, and before they know it, they're here to stay."

I offer her a polite nod, but my stiff upper lip exposes my uneasiness.

Tabitha reads me loud and clear, and her smile fades. "Okay, well, when you're ready to order, please give me a holler."

Thankfully, she strolls off when another customer raises their hand for service.

Sinking into my booth, I berate myself for being so rude to someone who was just trying to do her job. Tabitha looks similar in age to me, and I wonder if she's working here to pay for college, or maybe she's saving for something special.

Either way, the next time she's over here, I'm going to try to act normal. Well, something like normal, because that's what I want. I just want to be normal.

After looking over the menu, I decide on the waffles.

"You ready to order?" Tabitha smiles, her sparkling green eyes reflecting nothing but kindness.

"Yes, thanks. Could I have the American waffles with all the sides, except for bacon, please?"

Tabitha nods, writing it all down. "Is coffee still okay? You didn't want any juice? Tea?"

Shaking my head, I reply, "Coffee is good, thank you."

Tabitha places her pen and paper into the front pocket of her black apron and smiles. "Not a problem. That shouldn't take too long."

Before she has a chance to turn around, I quickly ask, "Um, is that job advertised in the window still available?"

Tabitha gives me a big smile. "Yes, I'm pretty sure it is. I can find out for you."

"Only if it isn't any trouble."

I'm baffled at how friendly Tabitha is, but everyone in this town seems to be high on happy drugs, and for once, these are the drugs I don't mind being around.

"Oh, no trouble at all," she says, shyly gazing at my nose ring. "Did that hurt?" She makes a pained face.

Unable to help myself, a tiny laugh escapes me, and it actually scares me because I haven't laughed in a long, long time.

"No, not really. I just put a bit of ice on the area to numb it and then pushed the piercing straight through."

Tabitha's hands fly up to her nose, and her face scrunches

up in pain. "Oh my God, ouch! You're so brave. I can't even look at a needle without fainting."

"It was fine. My tattoo was worse," I answer, flipping up my wrist to show her my ink.

Tabitha's eyes widen in shock, and her lips part in surprise. "Wow, you're so cool."

I don't know how to respond because I've never been called cool before. Freak. Goth. Bride of Frankenstein, yes. But never cool.

"Thanks," I reply softly and lower my eyes, unsure of what else to do.

Tabitha picks up on my discomfort. "I know cool when I see it because you know, you're looking at the Queen of Cool."

I know Tabitha is taking a dig at herself. I instantly jump to her defense.

"I have no doubt you're the coolest girl in town. I mean, your hair color is amazing, as you can see," I say, lifting a tuft of dyed red hair between my fingers. "Mine comes from a bottle, but yours is naturally awesome," I finish, hoping she takes my comment as a compliment.

Tabitha's eyes tear up, and something inside me warms— slightly.

"Thank you. No one has ever said that before."

I nod like it's no big deal.

"Oh, I'm Tabitha, by the way."

"Paige."

"Well, Paige, how about I stop talking and go get your waffles and a job application?"

I raise my coffee cup in salute to her. "Thanks."

She's back a minute later, sliding the application across the table with a smile.

While I wait for my waffles, I quickly fill it out.

I really hope I get the job, as the hours are perfect, and so is the job. It's waiting tables in the afternoon and into the dinner rush. I could work in the morning at the motel and then grab a couple hours of sleep before starting my shift here.

Completing my form quickly, I hope skimming over some minor details won't be an issue since I can't exactly divulge that I'm a fugitive on the run. That thought sends a shiver down my spine, but I tell myself to breathe and not make a scene.

Totally engrossed in my own little world, I fail to notice a pair of eyes watching me closely from the booth across the aisle. As I become aware, my body demands I steal a look at the mysterious stranger.

Attempting to be subtle, I want to sneak a peek at who has my skin prickling in awareness, but it's difficult as my neck is crooked at an odd angle, so to hell with being sneaky.

Turning to the right, I see a pair of emerald eyes set off by dark, arched eyebrows examining me closely. Suddenly wishing I'd gone about this differently, I spin away quickly while nearly gagging on my own saliva, which refuses to go down my throat.

Now I look like a total freak. I scold myself for thinking something so inconsequential. Regardless of how hot he is, I'm not here to make friends or to check anyone out, but from my glimpse, he was intoxicating.

His tousled dirty-blond hair was tumbling into his eyes, but as he brushed back his long bangs with his fingers, that intense stare almost set me on fire. He had a predominant jawline sprinkled with a light dusting of dark stubble, giving his face a hard, almost harsh look. But I like it. He looks like someone who wouldn't put up with shit and isn't one to shy away from trouble.

However, it was the small, silver hoop snugly hugging his well-defined lower lip that had me fixated. He was running his straight white teeth over the piercing and tugging at it while watching me closely with those eyes.

"Here are your waffles."

Looking up at my savior, I'm greeted by a young man, who I'd say is similar in age to me, and I can't deny he's easy on the eyes.

He has a lighter hair color to Mr. Emerald Eyes, and his eyes are a vivid blue. The piercing in his septum draws my eyes to the fullness of his pink lips.

I'd say he stands at over six-foot, and even though he's slender, he's brawny. He might appear slightly skinny to some because of his height, but I can tell that underneath that leanness is a well-toned body.

He reminds me of Kiefer Sutherland in The Lost Boys.

I know I'm staring, but between him and Mr. Emerald Eyes, I'm at a loss for words.

"Have you finished the job application?" he asks, jutting out his chin toward the form in front of me.

"Yes," I reply, thankful to have found my voice.

"I'm Tristan," he says as I pass him the application.

He looks at my form and gives it a quick read, his soft eyes scanning over my info.

"And you're…Paige. Nice to meet you, Paige," he says, lifting his eyes to meet mine.

"Likewise. Do you have any idea when they'll make a decision regarding the job?"

If I focus on what's important, maybe I can forget about the two hot men I just laid my eyes upon in the span of a minute.

"Yeah. You're hired."

I'm slightly confused, and it shows on my face.

Tristan smiles, which reflects in his warm eyes. "We had a staff meeting, and you're hired. When can you start?"

Just to make sure my wires aren't crossed, I ask, "So I've got the job?"

Tristan nods, and his lopsided grin returns.

"Thank you so much. I can start today. Actually no, I can't," I correct quickly, making an apologetic face when I remember I have Grandpa's truck and want to return it as soon as possible.

I don't want to abuse the privilege of him lending me his vehicle for the day. I know he said he didn't need it, but I want to return it to him sooner rather than later.

"That's fine. You can start tomorrow if you'd like. Tabitha can go over the basics with you. I'm pretty sure you'll pick things up quickly, though."

"Thanks again."

"Don't thank me just yet. I'll catch ya tomorrow," Tristan says, shooting me a wink over his shoulder as he heads for the kitchen.

Giving Tristan a small wave goodbye, I sit back, taking in everything that has just happened. I got a job. I can't believe I got *two* jobs that I don't hate. And two jobs that are *helping* people—not destroying their lives.

When I look down at my waffles, my appetite instantly spikes.

Picking up my fork, I'm about to dig in when I remember Mr. Emerald Eyes. I'll attempt to be less obvious this time because, for some unknown reason, I'm drawn to look. Massaging the base of my neck, I turn my head to the right, and to onlookers, it would appear I'm just rearranging my position to give my aching muscles a chance to uncoil.

Growing up around shady people has taught me a thing or two.

My eyes bypass his table, and I'm slightly disappointed when I see that he's gone. He must have left while I was talking to Tristan.

Oh well, that's a good thing, as I have a niggling feeling that Mr. Emerald Eyes would prove to be an expensive distraction.

One I most definitely cannot afford.

I'm happy driving back to Night Cats. Looks like being normal isn't as difficult as I originally thought.

Gazing at the sleepy landscape ahead of me, I can't imagine what my life would have been like if I had grown up in this town. Would I be happier with the reflection staring back at me? I know my childhood wasn't at all conventional, but I like the fact that I can look after myself. It just sucks that I had to learn the hard way.

I park the truck close to the office, ensuring I lock the doors—old habits die hard.

Hank sits behind the front counter watching TV while chewing on a bagful of nuts. He mutes the TV when he sees me walk in.

"How'd it go?" he asks, smiling broadly at me while hooking his fingers through his suspenders.

Sliding him the truck keys, I give a noncommittal shrug.

"Fine. I got another job," I announce while leaning over the counter and stealing a handful of nuts.

"That's great, Paige. Where?" he asks, switching off the TV to give me his full attention.

I don't know what it is about him, but I feel like I can trust him.

"At Bobby Joe's," I reply, jumping up onto the counter, my feet dangling over the edge.

"When do you start?"

"Tomorrow."

"You make sure you don't wear yourself out, ya hear? If you need to cut down hours here, you just tell me, all right?"

My feet stop swinging, and I jump down from the counter in a hurry, feeling a sense of panic creep into my belly. Why is he being so nice to me? I can't help but think he wants something. But as I look into his genuine eyes, I know Hank wants nothing. There really are good people out there, I remind myself. I just have to remember to remind myself a little more often.

"Okay, cool, thanks. I'm going to take a shower," I reply, making a quick exit.

I know bailing on someone who's trying to help you is not considered normal, but I can't help it. I'm still learning the dos and don'ts of society, so I guess I'm allowed to slip up occasionally.

Locking the door behind me, I peer around my room, which has minimal furnishings, and I don't intend to change anything about that. I won't be staying here long enough to add any personal items, and even if I did, what would I add?

Back home, my room was plain, but it was mine. That's all I cared about. To have one single place I could call my own.

Stripping out of my clothes feels wonderful, and I make sure to hide my knife in the top drawer of my bedside table. There's a path of my basic clothes, like a trail of breadcrumbs, leading to where I intend to be for a long while—the shower.

The scorching hot water feels amazing against my skin,

and I swirl my big toe in the plughole, watching the water whirl down the drain as I wash away my sins for the day. Turning into the water spray and relishing the hot water tickling my skin, I fail to notice someone's eyes on me for the second time today.

Well, on my naked back, to be precise.

Spinning around so fast, I'm surprised I haven't fallen flat on my ass. Due to the mist fogging up the shower glass, I can't see who's currently standing just outside the bathroom door.

Covering up my pink bits with my right hand, I wipe down the glass with my left, leaving behind an angry streak with the movement.

As I take in those green eyes, the ones I saw earlier at the diner, my mouth speaks before my foggy brain can play catch-up.

"Can I help you?" I ask loudly to be heard over the pounding water.

I really should be more embarrassed that a strange man is in my bathroom, but funnily enough, I'm not.

Mr. Emerald Eyes leans against the doorjamb, crossing his arms over his broad chest with a smug smile.

"Practicing already?" he asks in a deep, rough voice.

"Practicing for what?" I ask, annoyed.

"For your job." He chuckles, toying with his lip ring.

I then realize he must have heard me inquire about the job. But why was he listening? And more importantly, why aren't I cussing his ass out for walking in on me naked?

"So is there a reason you're standing in my bathroom? Or are you just a creep who gets off on watching strange women shower?" I ask, my eyes challenging his.

He shrugs, and the momentum causes his upper torso to undulate, showing off his impressive physique. Judging by where he measures up to on the doorway, I would say he's around six-three. He's toned but not grossly massive with bulging muscles and protruding veins. His tight Misfits T-shirt has seen better days, with a few small holes around the hemline, but somehow, it works well with his snug black jeans and black Chucks. His unkempt, longish hair, which flips up at the back, is styled into a disheveled mess. Somehow, I know he's done absolutely nothing to keep it this way. It just naturally falls that way. The whole ensemble is set off by that silver hoop through his lip. Everything about him screams "bad boy," and I know I need to stay away from him.

But as I meet his piercing stare, which is also challenging me, I know I'm in trouble.

"So?" I ask again. "What are you doing here?"

He pushes off the doorframe and strolls into the bathroom, not bothered that I'm naked and in the middle of showering. He's acting as if having a conversation with a random person in her birthday suit is normal behavior.

Who knows, maybe it is? I'm still learning the normalities of society. However, I somehow doubt this is classified as normal.

As Mr. Emerald Eyes strolls farther into the bathroom, he finally speaks.

"I'm here to fix the shower door."

That's it? That's all he has to offer?

"O-kay, well how about you wait outside or something?" I say, not feeling so brave when he's only a few feet away from me and my nakedness.

"And where's the fun in that?" He smirks at me with a mischievous look in his eyes.

I open my mouth, about to shoot him a smart-ass comment, but I come up dry. And that's troubling because

I'm never short of sarcasm.

"Well, if you insist on standing there, can you at least pass me a towel?" I huff, feeling way too vulnerable under his unreadable stare.

He reaches behind him and latches onto a fluffy white towel hanging on the rack. He takes two steps closer, and I take one back. With nowhere to go, I feel the cold shower wall press up against my ass. I cringe as I hate being cornered.

He must be able to sense my panic as something in his cocky demeanor shifts. He turns his head and blindly passes me the towel over the top of the shower without a word.

I shut off the water and snatch the towel from his outstretched hand.

Drying myself off at Superman speed, I wrap the cloth around my vulnerability because I suddenly feel really, really naked around him.

"By the way, there's nothing wrong with the shower door," I say, attempting to sound nonchalant while tucking the towel under my arms, ensuring all parts are covered before I exit.

When I'm satisfied I'm not about to flash Mr. Emerald Eyes, I push on the shower door, which sticks. I push a little harder with one hand, as the other holds up my towel, but it still won't budge. Frustrated that the door has decided to malfunction and make a liar out of me, I push on it with all my force, and it falls open.

And of course, I fall with it.

Mr. Emerald Eyes has his back turned, but he obviously hears the commotion because he quickly spins to stop me from doing a face-plant.

I trip into his arms, and he ends up catching me awkwardly.

Thankfully, my towel has somehow remained tucked around me, but it has slipped, showing off the top of my breasts. Mercifully, no nipple has been exposed, but still, one wrong move, and it'll be a whole different story.

To make matters worse, I'm mere inches away from a pair of lips that look way too inviting when a set of perfect white teeth begin tugging on a lip ring.

My eyes snap to his, and I see them not-so-subtly looking at my chest.

I clear my throat.

"My eyes are up here," I say, rolling them.

But he doesn't meet them and continues his obvious appraisal of my upper torso.

"I know where your eyes are," he replies, and then meets them with a playful glimmer in his.

My skin instantly tingles at his forwardness. But I need to snap the fuck out of this because this isn't me. I don't ogle guys, and I most certainly don't end up in the arms of one, all damsel-in-distress-like.

I wiggle out of his hold, and he complies by dropping his arms. But he holds his hands out to the sides, just in case I'm going to fall again.

Slapping his hands away, I take a step away from him, and I can't believe when his full lips turn up into an amused smile. He actually finds this funny.

"I don't need you saving me," I retort childishly, clutching my towel.

"Oh, I beg to differ." He chuckles that annoying laugh.

"It was the shower door," I say with sarcasm.

"Yup, I know. That's what I said," he replies, rubbing his chin, attempting to hide his smile.

I suddenly have the urge to right-hook his self-righteous face, but I refrain—only just.

"Well, knock yourself out," I reply, sweeping my hand

toward the shower door.

As I attempt to make a quick exit, he shuffles out of my way, but I still have to touch him to get past because he's so freaking huge and taking up the whole doorway.

"No, that would be you." He smirks, and I notice a silver flash inside his mouth.

Tongue ring?

"Whatever," I toss over my shoulder as I shove past him, running into the safety of my bedroom.

"I'm Quinn, by the way," he mutters, but thankfully doesn't follow.

I'm a little unsettled by our strange encounter, but I find my reaction to him even more puzzling.

I've never had a boyfriend because I never had the time for the trivial drama of relationships. Therefore, I just didn't date, which means I'm still a virgin. It seemed way too much trouble, and I had enough trouble in my life without adding any more.

Again, I reinforce the whole 'too busy being a drug dealer to worry about boys and sex.' After the shit I saw, it was hard to get in the mood and have sex with a random stranger I had no emotional ties with.

Rifling through my backpack, I pull out mismatched clothes, not caring what I grab, as I need to get away from the boy who makes me feel…something.

Five

There aren't many rooms to clean today, so I finish my shift early. I decide to hang out with Grandpa until I'm due at the diner because, quite frankly, I enjoy his company.

Strolling into the office, I see him up on a stepladder, wobbling as he tries to change a light bulb.

"Hank, get down!" I screech, running around the counter and standing near the ladder, looking up at him.

"Hey, Paige," he says, looking down at me with a big smile.

Looking up at him with scolding eyes, I demand, "Get down from there! You're going to fall."

Hank waves me off, which, in turn, causes him to wobble slightly.

"Oh my God, down!" I command and pull on his belt loop to coax him to come down.

"I won't be a minute. This damn light keeps flickering,

and Quinn isn't in today, so I'll do it myself."

That has my interest spiking.

"Quinn?" I ask, attempting to appear nonchalant.

Hank nods and wobbles again.

Thankfully, he listens to me and begins to descend the ladder slowly. As his two feet touch the floor, I exhale a breath I was unaware I was holding.

I snatch the light bulb from his hands and climb the ladder.

"So who's Quinn?" I ask while unscrewing the bulb.

"He's the handyman around here. Well, he does odd jobs for me, chores these old hands can no longer do."

Glancing down, I see him looking sadly at his widely spread fingers, the melancholy clear in his voice. I quickly screw in the bulb and am down the ladder in the span of a minute, feeling the need to console him.

"Well, in that case, you should wait for Quinn to do things like this," I say, passing him the old light bulb. "That's what you pay him for, right?"

Hank laughs and places the light bulb in the trash.

"What's so funny?" I ask, confused.

"I don't pay him. He does it to help me out. He's been doing so for years."

"Oh, well…regardless, you shouldn't be climbing ladders. You need anything done, you tell me," I say stubbornly.

Hank laughs, sitting in his favorite brown leather seat. "You sound just like my wife, God bless her heart."

I freeze because I don't know what the right protocol is. And in an instance when I wouldn't normally care what happened, I find myself…curious as to what happened to Hank's wife.

I'm about to ask what her fate was when the phone rings,

startling Hank and me.

Giving him a small wave as he answers the phone, I decide I'll walk to work because it's a nice day, and I could do with some sunshine.

As I walk down the road, a road I have memorized after only one drive, I know I'm heading in the right direction. That's because that was my job. I remembered which routes were the quickest or not patrolled by the police, and I guess a good sense of direction stayed with me.

My mind begins to wander to my dad as the long walk looms ahead of me. Surely, someone has found him by now, and I wonder if they suspect me.

It surprises me that I feel no remorse. Does that make me a bad person? I remember watching one of those crime shows where a psychologist talked about different personality types. Studies have shown that some people with personality disorders don't experience "normal" reactions to death and pain. At the moment, I'm really questioning if maybe something is wrong with me because I feel absolutely nothing when I think about what I did to my dad.

Lost in my own little world, I'm not watching where I'm walking and stray a little too close to the road. I'm walking a pretty deserted stretch and haven't passed a car in a while. But that changes when a carful of college kids in a red Jeep speed down the road, driving too close to the shoulder and scaring the bejesus outta me.

I jump to safety but trip, falling ass-first into a patch of grass.

The Jeep beeps at me, and the cocky male driver sticks his head out of the window, yelling, "Watch where you're going, freak!"

They're gone before I can come up with a creative

comeback. But I memorize the license plate, which is *BRAD1*, just in case I ever see them again, and know whose tires I'll be slashing.

Thankfully, despite my little mishap, I'm not late for my first day of work. I walk up the sidewalk and bless the laws of physics when I see the offending Jeep parked illegally in a handicapped space not too far up ahead.

I'm so tempted to reach for my flick knife but refrain when I see a lady holding the hand of a child licking an ice cream. Most of it is spilling onto her pink sweater and tiny hands, and as they walk toward me, I can't help but wish I had a mom to hold my hand when I was her age.

Giving them a small smile, I make my way to the diner because normal people don't go around slashing tires.

Setting those thoughts aside, I push through the diner's doors and am confronted by a bouncing Tabitha.

"Hi, Paige!" she says excitedly, and I'm afraid she'll hug me.

I quickly slip my backpack off my shoulder and flip it to my front, covering my chest so I'm hug proof.

Tabitha ignores my stupidity and links her arm through mine, chatting away animatedly as we begin walking.

"Tristan told me to show you the ropes, and I can't wait. I've been working here for years, since I was sixteen actually, and I'm nineteen now, so wow…that's a long time."

Nodding while attempting to keep up with her rambling, I'm not listening to her because I feel ridiculous. I'm hugging my backpack to my chest and awkwardly trying to walk while she's linked arms with me like it's something I'm comfortable with.

"So for the first half of your shift, you'll work with me." She smiles widely, and I can see that her two bottom teeth are a little crooked, which makes her smile all the more friendly.

Tabitha has such a pleasant, welcoming face. I wish I could be like her and not feel like a total phony. Maybe if I hang around her long enough, her friendliness will rub off on me.

Looking at her high ponytail bouncing with each energetic step she takes and how her eyes light up when she looks at me, I doubt it.

"You can leave your bag back here," she says as we enter a small locker room and bathroom.

She pulls open a small gray locker, which is too high for her short frame because she has to stand up on her tippy-toes to reach it.

Standing off to the side, I keep my backpack clutched to my chest.

Tabitha looks down at my bag, then up at me, smiling.

"It's okay. It'll be safe in here. It's a combo lock, and no one but you, me, and Alice come back here."

I give her a small nod but don't budge.

"What's inside there, anyway? Your most prized possessions?" she jokes.

Oh, you know, just my gun, Mace, and real ID, I ad-lib in my head, but instead, I reply, "I brought a pair of jeans and a T-shirt because I didn't know what the uniform was."

Tabitha looks me up and down, taking in my blue denim shorts, black Harley Davidson T-shirt, and scuffed boots.

"Well, you can leave on your shoes and shorts, but you have to wear..." She leaves the sentence hanging as she reaches into a small cupboard behind her, producing a white T-shirt.

"This," she finishes.

Sitting on top of the shirt is a name tag that reads Paige.

"Oh, this is mine?" I ask, looking at her confused.

Tabitha wrinkles up her nose and giggles. "Yes, silly, your name *is* Paige, right?"

Well…

I leave the question unanswered as, for some untold reason, I feel awful lying to her.

I give her a small nod while placing my backpack into the locker and shutting the door, making sure to lock it afterward.

"Thanks," I say as she places the T-shirt and name tag in my arms.

"No worries. Go change, and I'll meet you outside," she says cheerfully, then leaves me to do my thing.

Taking off my worn T-shirt, I can't believe I'm slipping on a fitted white T-shirt that reads "Bobby Joe's" in bold red letters.

I look…normal.

Who would have thought Mia Lee could do normal?

I remind myself that my name is not Mia. The slipup with Tabitha could have been costly if she wasn't so trustworthy.

Looking at myself in the full-length mirror, I frown as I pin on my name tag. I feel like a total impostor when the name "Paige" stares back at me.

Brushing those thoughts aside, I walk out of the locker room, looking at my feet because I can't face the people I'm about to serve. If I was to admit why, it's because I'm nervous.

Actually, I'm petrified.

Delivering drugs to junkies, businessmen, and doctors was never an issue because it was a transaction we both wanted over with as quickly as possible. But waiting on tables and pretending to be *normal* is much scarier than dealing with drug addicts.

What if my customers look at me? Like *really* look at me, and see that I'm a fraud? What if they look at me and smell my desperation to fit in?

With those unsettling thoughts plaguing my mind and my eyes staring at my scuffed boots, I fail to see where I'm going and clumsily bump into a hard chest.

"Shit!" I cuss, lifting my eyes, meeting a pair of amused bright-blue ones.

Tristan.

"Hi," he says, his hands supporting my upper arms, which he thankfully drops once I've steadied myself.

"Sorry," I reply, making a face.

"Hey, no harm, no foul," he replies with a smile, and I'll be damned, he has a dimple.

I give him a small nod, thankful I'm not getting fired right now for being a klutz.

"You been out there yet?" he asks, gesturing with his head through the double swing doors to the diner.

"No, not yet."

Removing my black hair tie from my wrist, I secure my hair back into a messy bun because I'm suddenly flustered. I'm aware of Tristan watching me, not in a sleazy way but just observing. It's not unnerving, and I find myself wondering what he sees when he looks at me.

After a few seconds of silence, he says, "Well, if you need anything, just let me know. But you're in good hands."

He smiles genuinely as we hear Tabitha cackling just outside the doors.

How does she do it? How do I be human without showing people too much of who I really am?

"Tristan!"

We both turn to look toward the kitchen, and Tristan gives me a lopsided grin.

"I better go before I get flamed on an open grill," he jokes and looks as if he's going to reach forward and touch me.

I know it's a friendly gesture, but I still flinch at the thought.

Giving me a strained smile, he seems to want to say something but decides not to as he heads down the narrow hallway to the kitchen, and I breathe out a sigh of relief.

The double doors swing open, and in comes a flustered Tabitha.

"Everything okay?" she asks, hands full of dirty dishes.

Nodding, I take a deep breath, and reply, "Yup. So where do I start?"

Bobby Joe's is insanely busy, and Tabitha said this is nothing compared to the dinner rush.

I follow her for most of the afternoon and have quickly learned the ropes. I'm a quick learner, and on the plus side, I don't need to write anything down due to my photographic memory. I have Big Phil to thank for that.

It's the only good thing I can take away from my old "job." I only had my memory to rely on, ensuring I knew what each junkie wanted, how much, and when. That was it. No writing it down or rereading what they requested once they placed their order.

Looking at the cash register and then at Tabitha, who's telling me how to work the thing with way too many buttons,

I feel like I've woken up in the twilight zone.

Who would have thought I'd be standing in a small, sleepy town, learning how to bring up the total of a double cheeseburger with extra cheese and curly fries?

"Got it?" Tabitha smiles, taking a pen out of her bun and giving it to the customer to sign his credit card receipt.

"Yes."

This is the easy part. The hard part is dealing with people.

At first, I watched Tabitha take orders, reciting the special of the day by heart. But when it was my turn to serve a table of four, I freaked.

My happy voice came out kind of creepy, and I even cringed when I asked if they wanted a top-up of their coffee. But Tabitha was behind me the whole time, encouraging me when I was ready to give up. Quitting is not an option, as this is not long term. This is just a means to an end.

"Will you be okay on your own for around thirty minutes?" Tabitha asks, untying her black apron while we walk to the counter.

I nod even though I think I might choke without her.

"I'm just going on my break. It's usually dead at this time of the day, so you'll probably just need to refill the sugar pots and prep for the dinner rush. If you have any problems, let Tristan know," she adds, reaching behind the counter for her bag. "See you soon."

She gives me a small wave and is out the door, leaving me alone.

Thankfully, the two occupied booths have ordered their meals and seem quite content eating them without disruption.

Walking behind the counter, I begin searching for the sugar to refill the pots, but after a fruitless search, I come up empty. However, I do stumble across the ketchup in a huge refill bottle.

Dropping to my knees, I slowly shuffle the container out from under the ledge because it's damn heavy. Wrapping both hands around the bottle, I drag it out, but my fingers slip as there's ketchup running down the sides, and it drops onto the floor. The top pops off, resulting in a red river of ketchup staining the checkered floor.

"Fuck," I mumble, looking around for something to mop my mess.

I see a dishcloth sitting on the counter and blindly reach for it. I quickly wipe up the messy puddle but just make more of a mess by spreading the ketchup over a wider area. My name tag is digging into my boob, so I rip it off and shove it angrily into my pocket.

"Motherfucker!" I curse under my breath, wiping my forehead with the back of my hand, annoyed.

Slapping both soiled hands on the edge of the counter to pull myself up, I'm confronted by a highly amused smile, tugging lightly on a silver ring.

Motherfucker!

Rising to full height, I turn around quickly to wash my hands in the small sink behind me. I push on the soap dispenser too many times and lather up a crazy amount of hand wash. As I rub my hands together and watch the water turn red, I can't help but think about another time I stood at a sink, washing red off my hands.

I shake my head, hoping to dispel such thoughts.

I've exhausted my stay because if I spend a second longer washing my hands, anyone would think I have a serious case of OCD. Turning off the water, I dry my hands on the paper towel, totally delaying facing the person standing patiently behind me.

Taking a deep breath, I scold myself. This is ridiculous—he's just a guy.

Spinning on my heel and meeting his amused expression, I try not to notice the brightness of his vivid eyes or how hot he looks in a Johnny Cash T-shirt, which highlights all the sharp contours of his upper torso.

"Can I help you?" I ask, finally finding my voice.

Quinn's mouth twitches as he leans forward and braces both hands on the edge of the counter, taking a closer look at me.

Of course, I take a step back.

"It *is* you. I almost didn't recognize you with your clothes on and all," he replies with a smirk.

"Ha-ha, very funny. What are you doing here?" I cross my arms over my chest in defiance.

Quinn grins, tapping a menu on the counter with his long finger.

Of course, he's here to eat.

"Okay, pick a booth, and I'll be with you shortly," I say, picking up the menu and slamming it into Quinn's stomach.

He just smirks, and I practically run, making sure to sidestep the spilled ketchup before I embarrass myself further. I bolt through the double doors leading to safety, away from that smirk.

Taking two deep breaths, I stop and wrap my arms around my middle.

What was that? I don't understand why I react to a stranger this way. Is this what being normal is like? A complete freak in public? Because if so, I was doing that all on my own before conforming.

Putting my game face on, I grab my pot of coffee and stalk out, ready to face the world head-on.

Looking around, I see Quinn has taken a back booth, away from the two remaining customers who seem content to chew on their meals quietly. I will my feet to move, and my heavy boots clunk on the floor with each step I take. As I reach his table, I tell myself no eye contact.

In and out, and then this is over.

Reaching for his coffee cup, I flip it over to pour him a cup, which mercifully, I don't spill.

He has the menu propped up on the table and flips through it, wiggling his mouth from side to side in contemplation. He casually slouches back into the red booth, and as his hair slips over his brow when he bends forward to take a closer look, thankfully shrouding his eyes, he can't see me all but salivating over myself.

"So?" I ask after I finish mentally undressing him.

His eyes, which are still partially covered by wisps of hair, snap up to meet mine. He lowers the menu and folds it up, resting it on the table.

"So?" he repeats, settling into the booth and casually interlacing his hands behind his head.

And then, there is silence.

I'm used to these moments of silence as that's all I got dealing with strung-out people most of the time. But this silence is not uncomfortable. It is anything but.

But I have a job to do.

"What do you want?" I cringe when I realize that's not how you address a customer. "What can I get for you?"

Quinn's eyes never leave mine as he bites back a smile, but he thankfully doesn't say anything smart.

"Can I please have Bobby Joe's bacon burger, extra cheese, no onions or tomato, onion rings, and a Coke?"

He watches me as I nod after each word.

"Do you want to upsize your onion rings for a dollar?"

Quinn nods with a slanted grin. "Sure. Why not."

I reach for the menu, but his hand covers mine in a lightning-fast move.

A startled breath escapes my parted lips, but I don't give him the satisfaction of seeing me have a slight case of hysteria as my skin feels like it may be on fire under his hand.

"Don't you need to write it down?" he asks, his long fingers still enclosed around my wrist.

I shake my head, and the movement unfastens some of my hair, which spills around my face.

Pulling my hand out from under his—because I can't deal with the feelings swimming around in my chest right now—I tap my forehead with my finger and reply, "Nope, it's all up here."

Quinn arches an eyebrow, unbelieving.

Just to prove a point, I decide to recite his order.

"Bobby Joe's bacon burger, extra cheese, no onions or tomato, onion rings, and a Coke. By the way, what's with no onions on your burger, but onion rings?"

Quinn laughs. The deep, throaty chuckle sends a chill throughout my body.

"What can I say? I like to live life on the edge," he jokes, pulling on his lip and drawing the piercing into his mouth. "So you're new here?"

I stand immobile, transfixed on his mouth.

"Ah, yeah," I finally reply, snapping my eyes to his, embarrassed to be caught staring.

"Where are you from?"

A simple question to most is impossible for me to answer truthfully, so I don't.

"Thanks for fixing the shower," I counter instead, hoping

he gets the hint. "Hank told me you're the handyman. That's real nice of you to help him out."

Quinn nods, and once again, that mysterious grin hugs his cheeks. "I like hanging out there, so I'm happy to help whenever I can."

I feel an inexplicable pull toward Quinn, and by the way he's gazing at me with a cocked eyebrow and a constant smirk marring his flawless features whenever I see him, I dare say he reciprocates the feeling.

"How long have you been working there?" I question, hoping I don't come across as nosy, but I need to know all there is about him for some reason.

"Um," Quinn replies, his eyes lowering to his coffee as his pointer finger skirts around the rim quickly. "For a few years now." His finger is still doing laps around the cup. "It's just my brother and me, and well, my parents, they weren't really around." His finger ceases with the whirlwind of movement as he meets my curious stare. "So Night Cats was kind of my sanctuary when I was a kid, and still is."

Quinn's guarded response has me even more intrigued.

"Where were your parents?"

Quinn chuckles, but it's not a pleasant sound. "Let's just say my parents are selfish assholes, and my brother and I are better off without them."

I nod as his comment is one I can sadly relate to.

"Aren't they all," I reply in a faraway voice, hating the vulnerability in my response.

Quinn's brow furrows as if attempting to decipher my comment. But I have revealed too much, and I need to be more careful in the future.

"So if you ever need anything, when I'm at the motel, I mean, please let me know," Quinn says after a moment of silence, watching me closely.

However, before I can answer, the bell above the door chimes, announcing the arrival of customers. And judging by how loud they are, there are a lot of them.

"Thanks. I'll be right back with your Coke. Food won't take too long."

When I see the group who just strolled into the diner, the hair on the back of my neck instantly rears up. I immediately don't like them because one of them is the dick who nearly ran me over in the Jeep.

There are four of them. Two boys and two girls.

The girls wear red-and-yellow cheerleading outfits that could be deemed inappropriate. I'm pretty sure I can see their hoo-has if they move the wrong way. They're both platinum blonde, and their perfect hair sits in high, slicked-back ponytails held in place with red and yellow ribbons.

I think I just vomited in my mouth a little as I hear them giggling, fluttering their fake eyelashes to the two jocks.

Swallowing my disgust, I grab four menus from the counter and walk over to NFL Ken, the driver of the Jeep, and Cheerleader Barbie, while pinning my name tag back on.

"Hi, grab a seat, and I'll be with you shortly," I say, handing them menus.

I'm so proud of myself because the sentence didn't end with profanity.

"Who are *you*?" sneers cheerleader number one rudely while hooking her manicured fingers through the arm of the beefy-looking guy, who is *definitely* the driver.

She's giving me a serious evil eye as she pulls him to her side protectively, and I roll my eyes, tapping my name tag sarcastically. I walk off before I say something that will surely get my ass fired.

Where the hell is Tabitha? Looking at the clock, which thankfully reveals half an hour is nearly up, I give myself a pep talk.

You can do this, Mia. Only a few more minutes and then Tabitha can deal with them.

The party of four giggles and whispers not so softly when I approach their booth.

The cheerleader, who gave me serious attitude, sits in the middle of the group and eyes my face with disgust as I look at them, waiting for them to order.

"What can I get you?" I ask casually.

"Where's the carrot top?" asks the driver.

I look at him, and my lip curls. He is so…big and brawny and…rude.

"Who?" I ask, knowing all too well he's referring to Tabitha.

"You know, the redhead," he clarifies, slouching back into his seat and throwing an arm around the other cheerleader.

She giggles. "Brad."

Okay, meathead number one is Brad—the fucker who can't drive.

"Ooh, you got a thing for her?" mocks cheerleader number one, throwing an empty straw wrapper his way.

Brad pulls back, horror-struck. "Fuck no, Stacey. If I wanted to slum it, I wouldn't be doing it with a redhead."

And cheerleader number one is Stacey.

Stacey cackles and looks at me pointedly. "What about freaks?"

I bite the inside of my cheek to stop from flying over the table and pulling out her fake hair.

Ignoring Stacey, like she didn't just insult me, I ask, "Are you ready to order?"

Stacey crosses her arms over her bust, obviously pissed she didn't get a response out of me. It will take a lot more than a bunch of spoiled, rich college kids to get me riled up.

Jock number two gives me a small smile. "Can I please have a Coke?"

I give him a small nod, acknowledging his order.

"Gimme a Coke, too," says Brad, throwing the menu onto the table, unhappy with the food selection.

"Can I please have a Caesar salad, no ranch dressing, and a diet Coke?" asks cheerleader two.

Nodding, I then move my eyes over to Malibu Stacey, waiting for her order.

She's wearing a snide smile on her painted lips as she cocks a thin, fair eyebrow.

"I'll have a cheeseburger with no cheese, extra pickles, and I want the little diced onions, not the big ones you get on the double cheeseburgers. I want a skinny chocolate shake, no whipped cream, but lots of chocolate syrup." She taps her chin and adds, "Oh, and a basket of chili fries and a diet Coke, no ice."

I know what she's doing.

She's doing this because I haven't written any of it down, and she's trying to be difficult in what she orders so I muddle things up.

"Right, that's all then?" I ask, my smile dripping with sarcasm.

Stacey looks taken aback that I've remembered everything, but nods.

Turning my back to them, I mumble, "Bitch," under my breath.

When I enter the kitchen, I see Tristan reaching overhead to place three big boxes on a high shelf. His shirt rides up, exposing a sliver of toned flesh.

I quickly avert my eyes, embarrassed that I'm blatantly checking out the light dusting of hair on his tummy.

"Hey, everything going okay out there?" he asks, wiping his hands on his baggy shorts.

"Yup, fine," I reply while writing down my orders, failing to mention the asswipes out there.

"Whatcha after? I'll get it for you."

I haven't really figured out what Tristan's role is at Bobby Joe's. He hired me, but I know he's not technically the owner or chef. But he seems to do it all.

I rattle off the orders, and after I'm done, his dimple makes an appearance.

"Did you remember all that? Without writing it down?"

I nod like it's no big deal because to me, it isn't.

"Wow, watch out, Tabitha," he jokes playfully.

Speaking of which.

"I better get back out there. Tabitha is due back, and I don't want her to think I'm slacking off, talking to the boss. Oh, and *boss*, I spilled ketchup everywhere," I say teasingly.

Tristan tosses a bag of fries into the deep fryer, which makes a loud, sizzling hiss.

"Please—the boss? As for the ketchup, I won't take it out of your pay this time," he says, trying to mimic a deep, commanding voice but ends up just breaking out into a grin.

As I find my lips tipping up, I quickly excuse myself before I overanalyze the smile. And why I feel so comfortable around a complete stranger.

I'm about to push through the double doors but get barreled into by Tabitha.

"Oh shit, sorry," I apologize quickly.

But when I see her face, I know something is wrong.

"Tabitha, are you okay?"

I know that's a stupid question as she throws herself into my arms, crying hysterically.

I'm totally taken off guard and don't know how to react to a situation like this. She just keeps sobbing, and the more she sobs, the harder she grabs me.

"Tabitha?" I ask as she wraps her arms around my middle, squeezing the air out of my lungs.

I'm standing awkwardly with my arms straight by my sides and head pulled back, shying away from her touching me.

This isn't the right way to comfort her. It's not how I've seen friends console friends in the movies. And my current stance most certainly does not resemble that in the slightest.

"There, there," I say, trying my best to sound sympathetic.

The gesture just makes her cry louder, and I cringe.

"Tabitha, what's the matter? Did…your cat die?" I ask. I once saw a girl on TV crying this way when her cat died. Maybe that's what's wrong with her?

The kitchen door swings open, and out strolls Tristan with a milkshake in one hand and a Coke in the other.

He stops abruptly when he sees us in the hallway. "Is everything okay?"

I shrug, but the movement doesn't deter Tabitha because she's still holding on for dear life.

"I think her cat died," I say stupidly when an uncomfortable silence lingers with Tabitha's sniffles.

Thankfully, her cries cease, and she muffles against my chest, "I don't have a cat."

I shrug because that's all I got.

Tristan bites back a small smirk when he sees how rigid and awkward I look while consoling Tabitha.

"What's up, Abi?"

Tabitha sniffs, and thank the Lord, she lets me go.

"Brad," she replies.

Brad? As in asswipe, can't drive Brad?

Tristan's jaw clenches, and he looks toward the double doors.

"He's out there?"

Tabitha's lower lip trembles, and I'm afraid she's about to launch herself at me for round two of tears.

I quickly step to the left and nearly knock into Tristan.

"Here, I'll take those," I say as I take hold of the drinks and make a quick exit, leaving Tristan to deal with the tears.

As I see the table of four, I realize I would rather deal with the tears than them. I quickly peek at Quinn, who's still sitting at his table, talking on his phone. As I look at him a little longer than expected, he meets my gaze as he hangs up, and I almost trip over my feet.

Quickly lowering my eyes, I make a beeline for Brad's table.

I slide the Coke to Brad and the chocolate shake to Stacey without a word and turn my back, ready to hightail it out of there, when I hear a throat clearing.

"Excuse me, *Paige*," Stacey spits out, saying my name like it's a disease.

Closing my eyes tightly, as my patience is about to snap, I take a deep breath before I spin around and reopen my eyes, trying my best not to glare.

"Yes?" I say curtly, looking at Stacey pursing her lips.

"I didn't order this." She slides the milkshake to me.

My hand slaps around the tumbler, my silver rings clinking on the glass loudly. She pushed the milkshake with enough force it would have fallen off the table if I hadn't caught it.

"Yes, you did," I reply, and this time, I can't keep the irritation out of my voice.

"No, I didn't," she mocks, shuffling up in her seat and crossing her arms over her chest daringly.

"Okay, what did you order then?"

The table looks back and forth between Stacey and me, and I can sense a fight brewing.

"I ordered a strawberry shake," she replies, examining her fingernails like this conversation bores her.

My anger begins to bubble to the surface, and I'm scared of what will happen when it boils over. I take a visible breath and remind myself why I'm here.

I'm only here short term. I can deal with this snooty-nosed little bitch.

"No, you didn't. You ordered this," I state and slide the milkshake back to her with as much force as she did.

She quickly catches it, as it would have spilled all over her cheerleading outfit if she hadn't.

With that visual, I smile a big, sarcastic smirk, daring her to challenge me.

She pushes the milkshake aside and sits up, glaring at me.

"How would you know? You didn't even write it down."

"I didn't need to," I reply, and I can feel my face reddening in rage.

"What? You expect me to believe you remembered it?"

"I don't care what you believe," I retort complacently.

"Prove it," she says, smirking sinisterly.

The table looks at me, and everyone, bar Brad, looks mighty uncomfortable with this conversation.

"Prove what?" I spit out, knowing all too well what she wants.

"Tell me what I ordered."

Deciding to humor her, I twirl my finger around my hair, attempting my best bimbo impersonation as I say, "Cheeseburger with no cheese, extra pickles, the little diced onions, not the big ones you get on the double cheeseburgers. Skinny chocolate shake, no whipped cream, lots of chocolate syrup, basket of chili fries, and a diet Coke, no ice."

I say all this in my best mimicking voice, mocking the harlot in front of me.

The whole table bites their lips, embarrassed I have called Stacey out on her bluff.

"So can I go do my job now?" I ask cockily.

Stacey only nods and sips on her shake, humiliated, not meeting my eyes.

I turn on my heel and feel my lips slant up into a smile. A real, genuine, happy smile.

My eyes snap up to meet a pair of highly amused emerald eyes, biting back a big smirk as he obviously heard the exchange.

This time, however, I don't lower my eyes. I meet his gaze, and I don't know what comes over me when I return his smile, but it doesn't feel wrong.

It feels normal.

The rest of the day passes without another lick of drama.

Tabitha was right. The lunch rush is nothing compared to the dinner rush. I'm run off my feet, and by the time my shift ends at nine o'clock, all I can think about is showering and falling into bed.

I throw my dirty apron into the wash and am collecting my bag when Tabitha enters the locker room, looking as exhausted as I do.

"Wow, I'm beat," she says, slumping onto the lone plastic chair sitting near my locker. "Where are you off to now?"

"Home," I reply, not wanting to confess my home is actually a motel room.

"Do you want to get a coffee? I know that sounds stupid, seeing as we serve it all day. But there's a little coffee shop up the road open twenty-four hours, and they have the best pie selection," Tabitha asks, hopeful I'll say yes.

I don't know what to say. I've never been invited anywhere before, and I'm touched she would ask. But I can't. What would I say? I'm not good in social situations. And what if she starts crying again?

"I wish I could, but I can't… I have a few things I have to do. Sorry." I shut my locker door, hoping I don't sound impolite or ungrateful.

When I turn to meet her disappointed eyes, I suddenly feel terrible, so I add, "But maybe next time."

Even though I know that won't happen.

She nods happily. "I'd like that. I'm sorry about today."

I look at her confused, so she clarifies, "You know, about the crying all over you."

"That's okay, no problem."

And it's funny because I mean it. Yes, I was hopeless in how I dealt with her tears, but I didn't mind her leaning on me. It felt…nice.

Tabitha looks at me, and I know she wants to discuss why she was crying.

I give in.

"So Brad upset you?" I ask, pulling out my ponytail and

fluffing up my hair.

"Yes," she answers, her lower lip trembling. "He and I… we…"

"You what?" I ask, confused and a little curious.

What would a nice girl like Tabitha be doing with a jerk-off like Brad?

"Well, we, you know…" Squirming in her seat, she looks at me with big eyes.

"Huh?" I question again, not following.

"We…" she mutters.

As I witness her freckled cheeks color to a bright red, understanding dawns.

"*Oh*? You and Brad?" I ask, surprised that she would sleep with a douchebag like him.

Tabitha sniffs and looks slightly offended as she stands and reties her long hair. "Yes, me and Brad. Is it that hard to believe that someone like Brad would want to have sex with someone like me? I mean, is it because he's the sheriff's son, and I'm just…me?"

I don't get why she's upset. And who would have thought an asshole like Brad, who can't drive, has the sheriff as his dad.

As Tabitha uncomfortably rearranges her T-shirt, which hugs her beautiful curves, I get it.

"No, Tabitha," I say, taking a small step toward her. "I just meant, why would someone as nice as you want to have sex with a fuckface like Brad?"

Tabitha looks at me, her green eyes bulging out of her head. Her mouth falls open, and a loud laugh slips past her lips as she breaks out into a fit of laughter.

I didn't think my comment was funny, as I meant every word, but as long as she's laughing and not crying, then I'm happy.

"Thank you, Paige, I really needed to hear that." Before I know what she's doing, she throws her arms around me and hugs me—again.

This time, however, I'm not so rigid and slowly raise one hand, patting her on the back softly.

She pulls out of the embrace, clueless about how much of a step I made in returning the simple gesture.

"Well, see you tomorrow," she says over her shoulder.

I grab my belongings, and before leaving, I look at myself in the mirror above the small sink.

My eyes are still sunken in, and I still resemble the living dead, but I look different. Is this what being happy looks like?

Whatever it is, I hope it sticks around.

Taking one last look at myself, I decide I need to visit a general store to buy red hair dye.

With that on the agenda for the evening, I leave the locker room on a mission to find the closest store.

I bump into Tristan out in the hallway, hands filled with glasses.

"Hey, Paige," he says, smiling. "How'd your first day go?"

"It went great," I confess because it's the truth.

"That's awesome. So I'll see you tomorrow then?"

"You bet!" I say with enthusiasm. I'm surprised to find I mean it.

"Okay, cool. Well, have a good night," he says, slipping past me toward the kitchen.

"Hey, Tristan!" I call out, taking a few steps toward him.

"Yeah?"

Under the bright hallway lights, I can't help but notice the gorgeous color of his eyes, and I'm surprised I haven't noticed them sooner.

Totally embarrassed because I know I'm staring, I quickly

recover. "Do you know where the closest general store is?"

Tristan smirks, and I instantly see the similarities between his smirk and Quinn's.

Quinn.

After rushing around today, I didn't even see him leave, and I felt kind of bummed because I like him being around.

"Sure, it's just up the street. Turn left and walk about three blocks. You can't miss it."

"Okay, cool, thanks."

"Hey, if you like, I can drive you. I've only gotta do a few more things," he says like it's the most natural thing in the world.

What's up with the people in this town? Why is everyone so friendly? I still can't wrap my head around it. But going anywhere with Tristan, for some unknown reason, unsettles me.

And as I look into his eyes, I know the reason.

I find him attractive. I did from the moment I met him.

But the thing is, I really don't have time to be finding anyone attractive because I won't be here long enough to follow through with it. Besides, guys like Tristan are way too nice for girls like me.

"No, it's okay. I don't mind walking."

But as I look down at the glasses he's carrying, I scold myself for not offering to help him.

"I can give you a hand, though?" I offer, gesturing to his full hands.

"Thank you for the offer, but I've got it. Go enjoy your night. You've earned it." He smiles, giving me a small wink. "Good night, Paige."

"Good night, Tristan," I reply and hightail it out of there as that wink just punched me straight in the guts.

The cold air knocks some sense into me as I walk briskly down the sidewalk, shrouding my face with my hood and sinking into anonymity.

What was I thinking back there? I shouldn't be gazing into anyone's eyes dotingly. Especially someone I work with.

What the hell is wrong with me?

Maybe I'm not cut out for this whole normal life. Maybe I'm better off doing what I know best, and that's detachment. Not only detaching from people but also detaching from reality. It's what I do best and stops me from…feeling.

Thankfully, I see the store up ahead. The wind has picked up, and my thin sweater and shorts don't offer much warmth from the breeze.

The door dings as I enter, alerting the security guard that someone has arrived. He looks at me, and I give him my best flirty smile, hoping he won't ask to check my bag once I leave. I don't want him finding the illegal items stowed away in my backpack.

He happily returns the smile while adjusting his gun belt as if his pitiful weapon is going to impress me. Batting my eyelashes as I walk past, I know I'm off the hook as he hungrily licks his full lips, eyeing me.

Men are so stupid. You can bat your eyelashes or show off a bit of leg, and all sense of intelligence goes flying out the window—and what's left ends up in their pants.

I learned this little trick while dealing blow to a corporate hotshot at one of those high-rise buildings where security was mega tight.

I never walked around without my gun, knife, or pepper spray, and whenever security asked to check my bag, I had to ensure I wasn't carrying. And well, that doesn't work for a fifteen-year-old female drug dealer walking the dangerous, seedy streets at one o'clock in the morning.

So I learned how to flirt and talk my way out of being detected for what I truly was.

A con.

I came to realize quite quickly that this world is full of perverts. And no matter where I went or who I met, this fact never changed.

That's another reason I never got caught.

I was street-smart.

But socially smart? Put me into a situation where I had to act normal, and I was far from clever.

Today is a perfect example of this.

Cruising down the cosmetic aisle, I grab a hair dye that is on sale. I have a little money left over, so I decide to buy a heavier sweater.

With my black sweater and hair dye in hand, I make my way down toward the registers. However, when a big bag of nuts catches my eye, and it's on sale for ninety-nine cents because it's the last bag, I head toward the stand, wanting to buy it for Grandpa to say thank you.

I'm surprised that this gesture seems so natural to me, and I'm not second-guessing myself. Something about Hank makes me want to be a better person.

Reaching for the nuts, another hand snatches the bag out from under me before I have a chance to seize it.

No!

I'll fight, kicking and screaming for this last bag but curse the irony of life when I see who I have to battle.

Quinn.

"Seriously, are you stalking me?"

Quinn smirks that damn arrogant smile while tonguing his lower lip. His tongue passes backward and forward over his piercing, and I know he's doing this to distract me.

But I will not get sidetracked. Those nuts he's currently clutching to his broad chest are mine.

"So we can do this the easy way where you give me those nuts, and no one gets hurt. Or we can do it the hard way." I give him a sinister smile.

Quinn holds up a hand in surrender while the other hugs the nuts.

I take a step closer to him and don't fail to notice the massive height and weight difference between us.

But I'm street-smart, remember, and I know how to play dirty.

"Don't make me hurt you."

This, of course, just earns me a laugh from Quinn.

"I'd like to see you try, Red." He cocks an eyebrow at me daringly.

Red? I don't even question where this nickname originated because I have other pressing issues.

"Oh, you're so going to wish you didn't say that."

Quinn dips down to meet me at eye level, strands of his hair falling over his eyes. "Yeah?" he whispers, his breath caressing my cheeks.

"Oh yeah," I confirm with a nod, giving him big, innocent doe eyes while tugging on my lower lip.

Quinn's eyes drop to my mouth, distracted by the way I'm pulling on my lip.

Let's visit the point I made earlier. Men are stupid. You can bat your eyelashes or show off a bit of leg, and all sense of intelligence goes flying out the window—and what's left ends up in their pants.

And this time is no exception.

This time, however, the flirting doesn't twist my stomach

in knots because the person I'm flirting with is someone I actually find…attractive.

I emphasize my ploy, fluttering my eyelashes and looking up at him openly.

"So are you going to hand them over before someone gets hurt?" I say softly, trying my best to sound seductive.

Quinn shrugs, which emphasizes the broadness of his upper torso.

"Go on then, give it your best shot." He smirks, mischief reflecting in his amused eyes.

Pulling out the big guns, I slowly slide my hand up his chest and around his neck. At first, he looks shocked that I have touched him, and quite frankly, so am I as I have never really had to use *this* kind of tactic before. I don't usually touch. I typically just flirt more from afar.

I ignore the voice of reason, as it is screaming at me that touching him is just my hormones demanding I get my hands on him. But as I tighten my grip around his neck, my fingers lightly toying with the soft hair at his nape, we both shiver, and I forget this is all a ruse.

My hands wander of their own accord, and my fingertips begin tracing circles on the side of his neck involuntarily. I can feel his pulse quicken under my touch, and my heart matches his steady beat.

What am I doing? This response to him—is this normal?

My eyes flick up to his face, and I steal a minute to take in his soft, poignant eyes, knowing there is more to Quinn than he lets on.

I have never been this close to him…or anyone, and I want to take in every aspect of him. I'm not sure I'll ever get an opportunity like this again.

His nose is evenly sloped on both sides, complementing

his sharp, angular jaw, which is coated in dark stubble, shadowing the pointed planes of his face. He has three tiny freckles scattered sporadically around his right cheek. They only highlight that strong jawline and add to his appeal.

But I remain transfixed on his mouth. His lips are deliciously full, and I can't help but follow the movement of his mouth as he sucks on his bottom lip, drawing his small piercing into his mouth and sucking it lightly.

I know I'm staring, but I can't help it. His lips part, and I see a hint of silver glistening under the bright store lights.

It *is* a tongue ring.

Why does that just add to his appeal?

But holy shit, I have to mentally slap myself because I need his nuts.

Well, not *his* nuts, but the nuts he's holding.

"I'll make you a deal," he says. Standing this close to him, I can see the top of the stud sitting securely in his mouth.

"What deal?" I ask, his voice lulling me into a sleepy bubble.

"I'll give you this bag of nuts if you tell me your name."

"What?" Stunned, I cock my head to the side.

That's it? Surely, there's got to be a catch.

"You heard me," he replies, his eyes making me feel naked under his penetrating gaze.

"What if I don't want to?"

I can't tell him my name because…I don't want to lie to him.

Quinn shrugs. "Well, then I guess you go home empty-handed."

I don't know why, but the thought of lying to him doesn't sit right with me.

But as I look into his hooded eyes, I know it's because he

would never lie to me. He deserves the same respect from me.

I don't understand why I feel this way, so I decide I would rather play dirty than have to face the reason behind my decision.

My hand is still wrapped around his neck, and I know it's now or never. Slowly gliding my hand down the side of his throat and over his collarbone, I rest my palm on his chest, pretending to be deep in thought about his offer.

His heart thumps heavily under my hand, and it's good to know I'm not the only one affected.

"Why do you want to know my name? I mean, what would you *do* with that piece of information?" I ask, emphasizing the word *do* as I inch my face closer to his.

Quinn smirks, totally falling for it. As he opens his mouth, ready to answer, I make my move. With lightning-quick speed, I yank the nuts out of his grip and pull away, grinning stupidly.

Quinn is still leaning into the space I inhabited two seconds ago, his mouth moving wordlessly.

Like I said, men are stupid.

"You were saying?" I smile, chuckling softly at the expression on his stunned face.

Quinn tongues his upper lip and grins. "Touché, Red. I guess I kind of deserved that."

"You sure did. So how does it feel to be outsmarted?" I ask, grinning like a fool while hugging the nuts to my chest.

Quinn shrugs like it's no big deal. "It's all good. I got to look down your top, so we're even."

"What? When?" I inquire, mortified, my hands flying protectively to my chest.

When I see a small grin twitch at the corner of his lips, I know he's lying.

"You jerk!" I say, attempting to punch him on the arm playfully.

Quinn ducks out of the way. "Well, technically, you weren't wearing a top when I looked, so…"

My face flushes a deep crimson red because he's referring to when he walked in on me in the shower.

"Don't you dare say another word," I warn, cocking my eyebrow at him in caution.

He raises his hands. "Hey, a gentleman never tells, but…"

I turn around, beyond mortified that we're talking about my nakedness in public.

"Goodbye, Quinn," I throw over my shoulder as I practically run to the registers with my goods in tow.

I'm still in earshot when I hear him mutter, "I can't promise not to think about it."

I don't know why, but as I leave the store, I'm grinning from ear to ear.

Six

find my thoughts constantly drifting to Quinn as I'm cleaning out room 1, and I'm fairly certain I have vacuumed the same patch of carpet for the past five minutes.

What is wrong with me? I've let a handful of people get under my skin, and I don't understand why. This is the first time I've ever felt something other than…well, nothing.

I've only been here for three days, and I'm already happier than I have been in a very, very long time. But what goes up has got to come down.

Pulling out the polishing rag, I blindly commence dusting the bedside lamps, humming to a tune on the radio.

"Hey, Paige." I hear from behind me.

I jump, startled that I have company, and spin to see Grandpa standing in the doorway, looking around the room in awe.

"Well, goddamn, this room looks better than it has in years." He shuffles over to a potted plant I saved from shriveling into a sad heap, touching its leaves softly.

"Thanks," I say, and again, I feel my mouth tip up into a small smile.

"You've done a real good job."

I don't know why, but his words of praise, words I never received growing up, mean a lot to me.

I nod, embarrassed by my reaction to a simple thank you.

Thankfully, Hank changes the subject. "Would you have use for something like this?" he asks, pulling an iPhone out of the pocket of his gray trousers.

I eye the phone and then back up at Hank.

"Maybe. Why?"

"Well, my friend bought it for me, and I really don't need it. So I'd rather give it to you. Otherwise, it'll just collect dust in a drawer," he replies, his soft eyes revealing nothing but honesty.

"But I can't accept it. It's yours," I say, shaking my head.

Hank waves me off and shuffles over to me, placing the phone on my cleaning cart.

"Take it," he says like it's no big deal.

I stare at the phone, wishing I could accept it as I am currently without a phone.

"But…but I can't pay you. I mean, this is brand new and worth a lot of money. Why don't you sell it? You can get some cash for it."

"Paige, just make an old man happy and accept it." His crinkled eyes look into mine, telling me that it's okay.

"Thank you," I whisper, staring at the phone like it's a bag full of gold.

And to me, it is.

"Hey, that reminds me," I say, remembering the bag of nuts.

I was going to drop them off anonymously on my way out, so he's just saved me a trip.

Hank looks up at me, and I reach under the cart to pull out the nuts.

"This is for you," I mutter softly, kind of embarrassed to be giving him a bag of peanuts when he just gave me an iPhone.

His eyes light up as he looks at the nuts.

"You sure know the way to my heart." He chuckles, happily accepting the bag.

I give him a small smile and hate to admit that Hank is already embedded in mine.

It's just as busy in the diner, but today, I am finding things a little easier and breezing through the stuff I found difficult yesterday.

I'm carrying a bunch of dirty trays when I walk past the noticeboard and see a flyer advertising a new twenty-four-hour gym that has opened up not too far from here. As I'm programming the number into my phone, I feel someone looking over my shoulder.

I know it's Tabitha because I can smell candy. I know that sounds ridiculous, but every time I'm around her, that's all I can smell. And it's actually a nice scent.

"Whatcha doing?" she asks, putting her head on my shoulder, looking at the noticeboard.

Tabitha obviously has no problems with intimacy since she hugs or touches me every chance she gets.

"Going to check out this gym," I reply, pointing at the flyer on the wall.

Tabitha moves to stand next to me and rips it down from the board.

"Hey, this isn't too far from here. Would you mind if I tagged along?"

Is this some weird girlie bonding thing? I'm so confused. I thought girls' nights involved makeovers, popcorn, and pillow fights.

"Sure."

Every day, I seem to be learning more and more, but I bet I haven't even begun to skim the surface.

Nine o'clock rolls around quickly, and the dinner rush has kept Tabitha and me on our toes.

As I make my way out of the locker room, I see Tabitha waiting for me.

"Hey, whatcha up to now?" she asks, her car keys in hand.

"Just going home."

I didn't get a chance to dye my hair last night after my run-in with Quinn. Speaking of, I was a little disappointed I didn't see him today. But I brush those childish thoughts aside, as they're juvenile and petty.

"Do you want to hang?" she asks, looking at me optimistically.

"Hang where?" I question nervously, as I don't want her seeing where I call home.

"I don't know. What plans did you have for the night?"

"Um, I was going to dye my hair," I confess hesitantly,

not sure if that's the right answer. The box of dye is in my backpack.

Tabitha claps her hands and jumps up and down on the spot excitedly.

"Can I do it for you?" she asks, interlacing her fingers into prayer hands.

"Um…okay, sure," I reply, scrunching up my face.

I didn't realize dyeing one's hair was so exciting.

"Where are you staying? I can drive," she says, jingling her car keys in front of her face.

I nearly choke on my breath as I quickly make up some lame excuse. "Would it be okay to go to your place? My room is a real mess at the moment."

Tabitha begins fidgeting as she chews on her bottom lip, her finger lightly tracing over her car key quickly.

I'm about to tell her to come over because she looks torn, but she answers, "Um, yeah okay, sure."

I wonder what Tabitha has to hide.

Not that I can talk.

I bet her secret is nothing compared to mine.

We say goodbye to Tristan and walk to Tabitha's car—a brand spanking new BMW.

Looks like working at the diner has paid off. But I have a sneaking suspicion that has nothing to do with it because as we keep driving farther out of town and into suburbia, the houses become ritzier, and the level between the middle and upper classes is clearly drawn.

As we pull into a long driveway with big iron gates, Tabitha reaches out her window and buzzes the intercom.

After a few seconds, a snooty, nasal voice answers.

"Hello?"

"Hi, Mom."

Mom? This is *her* house?

As I look up and see past the gates, this house could easily be labeled a palace.

"Can you open the gate for me, please?" asks Tabitha nervously.

"Where's your remote?" the annoyed voice asks.

"Um, at work," admits Tabitha, biting her lip.

"Oh, Tabitha! For goodness' sake. What is the matter with you?"

The intercom goes dead.

Tabitha shyly glances at me while we wait for the gate to slowly slide open.

"My mom…" She pauses, and I can see the torn expression on her troubled face.

"Is a bitch," I add when she seems to be at a loss for words.

Tabitha's mouth twitches, and I can't determine if it's in rage or humor.

Either way, I must remember to use my mouth filter from time to time.

"Sorry. That wasn't nice of me to say," I apologize, hoping I don't lose the only friend I've made.

Tabitha is quiet for a moment, watching the gates groan open.

But suddenly, I see her eyes twinkle, and then she does something I never expected.

She laughs.

She laughs so hard, tears fall down her plump cheeks, and she slaps the steering wheel in delight.

I bite my lip, confused. Is she going to flip out?

"You're right," she pants between cackles. "She *is* a bitch." She accelerates, speeding up the driveway faster than I think she ever has before.

She parks on the gravel in front of the house and switches off the car, but we don't get out right away.

"I want you to know…my mom probably won't like you," she admits, looking at me sympathetically.

"That's okay. Not a lot of moms do," I reply, shrugging. "No biggie. One look at the piercings, hair, and tattoos, and it's usually a deal-breaker."

"No, it's not that," she says, shaking her red locks. "It's just…she doesn't even like me, her own daughter, so you don't stand a chance." She stares blindly up at the white mansion.

Looking at Tabitha, something inside me softens. How could anyone *not* like her? Especially her own mother.

"Well, that's her loss," I reply in all seriousness.

If I felt comfortable with the whole touchy-feely crap, I would reach over and give her a hug or something, but she'll just have to settle for a nod and a half smile.

"You think?" she replies, biting her lip. "Because she's my mom, and if your own mom doesn't like you, what hope do you have for strangers to like you…or want you?"

As I look over at Tabitha, I mean really *look* at her, past her happy smiles and forthcoming nature, I know underneath lies a scared, insecure girl, wanting anyone's approval.

She just wants to belong.

Holy shit, she's just like…me. Under her facade, she's just as scared and lonely, and she just wants to be normal.

Just like me.

"Paige, are you okay?" she asks because I've totally spaced.

"Yeah, I'm fine," I reply, not wanting to admit how similar Tabitha and I really are.

Well, it looks like everyone has secrets, and I think I've just made a friend who gets it.

"Okay, let's go in the back way." She smirks with a

mischievous twinkle in her eye.

I hop out of her car and cock an eyebrow.

"Why do I have a feeling you've never used the back way before?" I ask as our shoes crunch over the gravel.

Her bright, beaming smile under the moonlight answers all my questions.

We walk through the manicured greens, past a fountain spilling water out of the mouth of a dolphin, and arrive at the back of the white house, which is lit up with bright lawn lights.

She leads me to a short stairwell and waves me down when I hesitate on the top step.

"Are you sure you're not going to get your ass kicked for this?" I whisper. Everything is amplified in the silence.

Looking from left to right to ensure the coast is clear, I suddenly hear a bug chirp. That's all it takes to have me running down the stairs in a hurry, an inch away from latching onto Tabitha's back to save me from the loud, buzzing noise.

Tabitha gives me a small smile and quietly turns the doorknob, which creaks in protest. She looks ecstatic that she has broken some unspoken rule, and I go along with it as she ushers me in quickly, quietly shutting the door behind us.

I can't see jack shit, so I wait until Tabitha turns on the light.

"Do you have your phone?" she whispers.

"Yeah," I whisper back.

"Can we use the light on it? I don't want to turn the light on. Otherwise, Mom will know we're in here."

Ha, who would have thought little Tabitha was a sneak. I'm starting to like her more and more.

I switch my phone on, and it gives us some light. I move it from left to right, and from what I can see, we're in a basement.

Suddenly, my hands get clammy, and I can't breathe. The last time I was in a basement was with my dad. I can still remember the ear-splitting noise made by the gunshot.

And what I can also remember is the blood. There was so much blood.

"Mia."

That was the last word out of my dad's mouth as he lay dying on the cold, hard floor.

My heart begins pounding out of my chest, and I begin hyperventilating.

I need to get out of here.

Using my phone as a flashlight, I move it around the room, frantically trying to find an exit. Seeing a wooden staircase off to my left, I fly up it, kicking the door open as I reach the top step.

I take a deep, panicked breath and breathe it out through my nose to stop myself from having a full-blown panic attack.

"Paige, oh my God, are you okay?" asks a frantic Tabitha, putting her hand on my shoulder as I am crouched low, my hands splayed out on my knees.

Holy shit, what was that about?

That's the first time in days that a vivid memory has hit me to near debilitation.

"I'm fine, Tabitha, sorry," I mumble, rising to my full height after I've nearly folded my body in half.

The look in her eyes scares me. She actually cares. She actually *cares* if I'm okay.

"I'm just claustrophobic," I reply when she gawks at me, waiting for an explanation.

That's a total lie, as I was once locked in a broom closet for two hours, hiding from the police. But I can't tell her that, can I?

Her face drops, and she covers her hand over her gaping mouth.

"I'm so sorry, I didn't know."

"It's okay. I'm fine now," I say quickly, not wanting her to feel guilty for something she isn't responsible for.

But am I? I feel far from fine.

"Do you want a drink? You look a little pale."

I nod because it's all I'm capable of doing.

"Okay, no worries, follow me," she says, heading down the hallway, looking behind her to ensure I'm following.

I follow but cringe when my heavy boots thud on the pristine white tiles.

"Sorry, I think I ruined our smooth entrance," I apologize softly, clutching my hands around my middle to stop myself from throwing up.

"Don't worry about it," she says, waving me off. We round the corner, entering the kitchen, which is the size of my entire motel room.

"Wow," I breathe as I run my finger along the marble kitchen top.

Tabitha gives me a strained smile as she stands on her tippy-toes to reach for a glass in a high wooden cabinet.

The glass is one of those fancy goblet-looking things, and the bright lights bounce off the flute, reflecting rainbow speckles across the room.

She places the glass under a nozzle in the double-door stainless-steel fridge. As she pushes down on a lever, a few ice blocks shoot down and slide into my glass. She then pushes again, and a steady stream of water begins pouring into the glass.

I've seen these fridges in the condos of the rich folk I dealt blow to, and I think now what I thought then—totally unnecessary.

"Tabitha Jane Henderson!"

I twirl to see a slender lady wearing a cream tunic dress with navy heels and a matching belt, facing us with her hands planted on her hips. Her red-painted nails drum on her narrow waist, and she has a nasty scowl on her wrinkle-free, painted face. Her fiery-red hair is done up elegantly in a chignon, and a set of pearl earrings and necklace sit daintily in her ears and around her throat.

"What were you thinking, driving so quickly up the driveway? You know I just got it redone!" she snaps, her fingers continuing to drum.

Tabitha shakily hands me the glass, and I can feel the embarrassment pour off her.

My chest squeezes as I instantly feel sorry for her, and I can't just stand here while her ostentatious mom chews her ass out.

"I'm sorry, Mrs. Henderson, it's my fault. I wanted to see how fast her car could go, as I've never been in a BMW," I say quickly, stepping in to defend Tabitha.

Both Tabitha and her mom look at me like I've lost my mind, and I, too, am a little shocked at myself.

"Well, that doesn't surprise me. Tabitha has always been weak-willed. So who are you, then?" her mother questions, glaring at me.

"I'm Paige. I work with Tabitha," I reply, trying my best not to throw my glass at her scowling face.

She looks me up and down, and makes it quite obvious she wouldn't look twice if she ran me over with her shiny new Mercedes.

"Hello," she says dismissively with a wave of her hand.

I can feel the disapproval rippling off her, and I have an

urge to poke my tongue out at her.

"Paige, let's go up to my room," Tabitha says quickly, pulling on my arm and leading me away from her glaring mother.

"It was a pleasure meeting you, Mrs. Henderson," I say in a sickly-sweet voice, not meaning a single word of it.

Of course, I don't get a reply.

As we make our way through the foyer and up the polished staircase, all I can smell is citrus cleaning spray and loneliness.

No matter how much money these rich snobs have, it's never enough, but as the old saying goes, "Money can't buy happiness." But it can buy artificial happiness, which is the reason snobs like Tabitha's mom were my best customers.

"My room is at the end," Tabitha says as we reach the top of the staircase.

I look down the long corridor and can see many doors that lead off from the red-carpeted hallway. The place may be rich in possessions, but it certainly isn't rich in love. This place is sterile and loveless.

We finally reach her room, and when she opens the door, I like Tabitha all the more. This is the only room in the house that shows personality and isn't cold or barren.

"Sorry it's so messy." She throws clothes off the long, red sofa onto the floor.

She zips around the room, collecting strewn items of clothing and packets of candy, as I look around the huge bedroom, which is decorated in burgundies and golds. Tabitha has decked the walls with posters of her favorite bands and pictures of different holiday destinations around the world.

I wonder if she stares up at these pictures, wishing she was anywhere but here.

With her hands full, she tosses the goods into the

bathroom and closes the door behind her, looking frazzled.

"Tabitha, don't worry about it," I say as I plonk down onto the sofa.

Tabitha follows suit as she leaps onto the bed, landing on her tummy.

She places her chin in her open palms and swings her legs in the air behind her while looking at me apologetically.

"Sorry about my mom," she says, embarrassed, her cheeks flushing slightly.

I wave her off, tucking my legs underneath me.

"We can't help who our parents are."

Tabitha sees my reaction and pauses before she asks apprehensively, "Do you like your mom?"

I lower my eyes, not wanting to lie to her. It's bad enough she thinks my name is Paige.

"I don't know." I know I need to shut up, but after what I just witnessed downstairs, I owe Tabitha the truth.

Well, as much as I can tell her.

"You don't know?" she asks gently, her eyes softening.

I raise my eyes to meet hers. "No. She left when I was three, and it was only my dad and me."

"Oh, I'm sorry," Tabitha replies. I couldn't bear it if she looked at me any differently.

"Don't be." I don't want her pity.

"What about your dad? Are you close?"

I know she's only trying to get to know me better, but these questions are beginning to make me uneasy. I yank the sleeves of my sweater down over my fingers as the room has dropped fifty degrees.

"No," I simply reply as she awaits my answer.

"Oh, Paige…that sucks. I'm—"

I interrupt before she finishes. "Don't say you're sorry," I bark, meeting her eyes. "Because I'm not."

Tabitha nods. "Well, it's their loss because I think you're awesome."

I look at her, innocently swinging her legs, unaware of how much her comment means to me.

If I could cry, I would, but for now, this tearless feeling is enough.

"I love it!" Tabitha squeals as I'm bent over her basin, looking up at her excited face as she examines the red in my hair.

She carefully washes out the dye with a candy-smelling shampoo, which I recognize as her distinguishable scent.

"So what do you think about Tristan?"

"He's nice," I reply as I close my eyes to keep water from going into them.

"Do you think his looks are also nice?"

I think this classifies as girlie talk, so I play along.

"He's nice," I say again lamely, totally uninformed of the right protocol for talk such as this.

Tabitha laughs. "Well, I *know* he thinks you're more than nice."

"He what?" I ask, cracking open an eye to look at her.

She's nodding briskly, her red hair slipping into her eyes.

"How do you know?" I ask out of sheer curiosity.

"He told me," she replies while massaging my scalp.

My stomach turns, and I wonder if they've been talking about what a freak I am.

"It's all good, Paige." She giggles. "Anyone would think

you've never had an admirer before."

Well, that's because I haven't. Well, not someone like Tristan, anyway. Not someone who's nice to me for no reason other than just being a sweet guy.

"You have, haven't you?" she asks when I close my eyes, trying not to look too obvious. "Seriously? You haven't?"

I slowly shake my head.

"No way! I can't believe it! A hot, cool chick like you would have guys all over you, right?"

I open my eyes because surely I haven't heard her right. But the disbelieving look on her face confirms I heard her correctly.

"Don't be so surprised. I see guys checking you out when you're not looking," she says with a smile, giving me a small wink, and returns to washing my hair.

I return her smile, but it's only a half smile, as I feel uncomfortable talking about this.

"Okay, all done," Tabitha says, grabbing a big towel and wrapping it around my head.

I hold the front of the towel and sit up, thankful the grilling has stopped.

"Thanks, Tabitha," I say, rising from the stool.

"We're not done yet. Would you mind if I dried and styled it?" she asks, reaching for a comb behind me.

"Sure."

I think this is another girlie bonding thing.

Tabitha jumps up and down, clapping. "This is gonna be *so* fun."

I let Tabitha do her thing, and twenty minutes later, she smiles.

"Okay, gimme a sec, and we're done."

Tabitha wasn't happy with just playing hairdresser; she

also wanted to try some different makeups. She sugarcoated the fact I look like death warmed over from how washed out I am. She said she could give me an instant tan without leaving the house. I told her I wasn't interested in looking like Malibu Stacey, which she found hilarious, but I noticed her frown at just the mention of Stacey's name.

What would the reason be for her to frown? I rack my socially daft brain, hoping to find an answer.

Brad.

"Why were you upset the other night? About Brad?" I ask, hoping I don't sound too abrupt.

Tabitha stops applying powder to my face, her hand poised with the makeup brush near my cheek.

"Like I said, Brad and I, we…you know," she says, her pale skin tinting a bright pink.

I think back to a comment he made to Stacey about him not doing redheads.

Liar, liar, pants on fire.

"So why were you crying when you saw him?"

"Because…" She sniffs, dropping her hand onto her lap. "Because after we had sex, he treated me worse than before we slept together…which was bad. Every time I see him, it just reminds me of what an idiot I am for losing my virginity to him."

My mouth pops open.

"You lost your virginity to that dick?" I ask, just in case I didn't hear her correctly.

She nods, biting her lower lip, close to tears.

"Sorry," I apologize. "I didn't mean for it to come out so harsh."

"No, it's fine. He is a dick. I hated every minute of it. And if I could, I would take it back."

And let me revisit my point of why I'm a virgin.

It's stories like Tabitha's that I don't want to relate to. I could think of nothing worse than having an uninspired, sexual romp just for the sake of losing my V-card.

I'd rather wait till I'm ready. I'm not sure if I ever *will* be ready, but if the time never comes, then I'd rather that than the alternative of regretting something I can never undo.

Unlike other aspects of life, who I decide to give my body to in the most intimate way possible is solely my decision, no one else's.

"What about you?" Tabitha asks, wiping her eyes with the back of her hand. "Had any regrets?"

I wonder how long we've got. But I know she's asking about something entirely different.

I shrug, and my hair springs up, thanks to all the primping Tabitha has done to it.

"You *have* slept with a guy, haven't you?" Tabitha inquires, her bright eyes opening wide.

When I don't reply, she lightly slaps my upper arm. "Shut up!"

"I didn't say anything," I reply, totally confused.

"No, silly." She chuckles. "I just meant like, no way."

"No way, what?"

I am so lost in translation.

"That you're still a virgin," she replies, giving me a small smile.

"Why is that so hard to believe?"

She must read the baffled expression on my face as she quickly stutters, "I just meant, I mean…look at you…you're beautiful."

If I could cry, tears would prick my eyes. I've never once been called beautiful. And I never actually cared. But now, hearing it…it feels nice.

"Okay, well, enough of this," Tabitha says, brushing it off. "I'm all done. You can look at my creation."

She spins my chair around to face the square mirror sitting above the double sinks.

"Ta-da! What do you think?" she asks when I sit motionless, staring at my reflection.

I raise my hand slowly, and the reflection follows.

I wiggle my nose, and the reflection follows.

I touch my face, and the reflection follows.

The person looking back at me with soft blue eyes and skin that isn't deadly white is really…me.

Running my hand through my hair, I'm amazed at its softness and fullness.

"You have amazingly thick hair, so I just styled it a little differently to shape your face a little better. I hope that's okay?" Tabitha asks, worried when I still haven't said a word.

I nod, and my eyes widen when my hair bounces—yes, *bounces*.

Then I notice my eyes look blue, like really *blue*. And big.

"Why are my eyes so bright? And big?" I ask, leaning forward, nearly falling off the edge of the swivel chair to get a closer look.

"I just made them a little more natural with not so much black." Tabitha stands behind me, looking at my reflection in the mirror.

"Thank you, Tabitha," I whisper, still staring at my reflection in awe.

"That's okay, anytime. That's what friends are for."

Seven

All I can smell is death.

And that smell radiates from my dad.

His white T-shirt, which once fit him snugly, now hangs off his gaunt frame because it's two sizes too big. He's unsteady on his feet like he's eighty-five instead of forty-five. He hasn't showered in days, and I can't remember the last time he ate.

But none of these things matter to a drug user. The only thing that matters is when they'll get their next fix. That's the only thing they focus on. Life be damned.

My birthday was yesterday, not that it matters. I haven't celebrated a birthday since my mother left. But as each year passes, I promise myself, *"This is it. I'm out."*

But every year, I seem to fall deeper and deeper into desolation, and it's getting harder and harder to crawl my way back out. I spend the whole year psyching myself up, trying to get my dad cleaned up, and as another year ticks over, I realize what a waste of a year it was.

This year has been no exception.

"Have you got it?" my dad asks as soon as I enter the small, dirty kitchen.

My kitchen was once filled with cookies, orange juice, and fresh fruit. Now the only thing that litters the benches are lighters, beer bottles, and unpaid bills.

"Hi to you too, Dad," I sarcastically retort while opening the fridge and grabbing a beer.

I should be used to this by now, but it still fucking hurts to know drugs come first.

I'm exhausted after doing a last-minute drop-off for Phil in town, and I really need a drink. Popping the cap off the Budweiser, I take a long sip and close my eyes, savoring the taste.

"Don't be a smart-ass!" he says from behind me, the desperation clear in his shaky voice.

My hand clenches around the bottle in rage.

Smart-ass?

Smart-ass would be tipping his stash down the sink and telling him to go score his own drugs. Smart-ass would be me calling the police on his sorry ass. Smart-ass would be me dragging him off to rehab. So I truly doubt he knows the true meaning of smart-ass because from where I stand, I am far from it.

"Here." I reach into my back pocket and throw the clear baggie onto the table.

My dad launches at it, hovering over the substance like he's about to perish without it.

I curl my lip up in disgust.

This year is it.

I'm nineteen, and I quit.

No more.

I'm weaning myself off this destructive lifestyle because I don't think I'll survive another year.

As I am deep in thought, something on my dad's face changes. I can see it.

His beady eyes narrow, and he looks at me with cruel intent.

The sinister glare actually makes my stomach turn, and I have to look away, totally on edge. What is he planning?

"We need to talk," he mumbles while rubbing his chin. "I need you to do something for me, Mia."

My skin instantly chills, and I'm eight years old all over again.

"What?" I ask, my skin crawling at the thought of what he wants me to do.

He shakes his head, his greasy hair sticking to his brow. "Not now. I'll talk to you about it tomorrow," he says, taking his stash and licking his lips greedily for his next fix.

But tomorrow never came because in two days, I shot my father dead.

I jump out of bed like it's on fire and race blindly to the toilet, heaving up my dinner. My body shudders as I puke until nothing is left to throw up.

The cold tiles feel frosty under my knees, but I can't move as I'm afraid I'll topple over if I shift a muscle. So I stay cradling the toilet, hoping this bout of hysteria will pass.

I hate dreaming.

These are such hard-core memories, and I wish I could just forget them. But I have a feeling I'll never forget them for as long as I live.

I don't know what the fuck happened at Tabitha's last night. The memory of the day I shot my dad is one I haven't revisited, and honestly, I thought I was okay. Maybe I have some delayed grief button that's only now been switched on. Either way, I want to switch it back off.

I don't want to feel this.

Flushing the toilet, I wash my mouth out and brush my once bouncing hair off my sweaty brow.

The clock in the darkened bedroom reads one forty-eight a.m., and I know I'll never get back to sleep.

Frustrated, I slump onto the end of the bed, my head resting in my palms in annoyance.

I need to set my plan in motion, and I need to focus on why I'm here.

I need to find my mom.

That's the only thing that makes sense to me.

I need to find her and ask why the fuck she left me with him. How could she leave her three-year-old daughter in the hands of a monster? Once I get these answers, I hope to close that chapter on my old life and start my new life. One without drugs, or fear, or hopelessness.

Shooting my father was never planned. I was backed into a corner, and the only way out was to come charging, guns blazing. But now I have to live with my actions because there's no coming back from this.

I can never go back to LA since I'm sure I'm a suspect in my dad's murder. My decision has left me with no option but to live my life on the run, but it's better than my life back home. I may have been *free*, but I never felt it. I always felt I was a prisoner, sentenced to life without parole.

But no more.

My plan is simple.

I'm going to find my mom.

I have limited information on her—just her name and an old photo—which is the only memory I have of her. But I have to start somewhere.

I know it's a long shot, but as they say, "The hardest part of the journey is taking the first step."

And in my case, it's better than not moving at all.

I decide to go for a walk. It might help clear my head.

Once dressed, I quietly slip outside.

I've never been afraid of the dark because I know what goes bump in the night, and I know how to kick its ass.

So as I'm walking down a deserted stretch of road, I'm not concerned in the slightest. I think it's peaceful at this time of the night, and everything always seems calmer when no one is near.

The only sounds I can hear are leaves skittering along the road, and the occasional hoot from an owl, watching me with its attentive eyes.

Due to my insomnia, I've decided to check out the twenty-four-hour gym in town as the alternative to sitting in my room waiting for the sun to come up.

A flashing sign indicates the gym's location is just up ahead, and looking around the empty streets, I wonder why a sleepy town like this would need a twenty-four-hour gym. Either way, it's a win for me, as I know I'll be here often into the wee hours of the morning, running away from my nightmares.

Peeking into the glass window, I can see no one is

working out—even better. I take a step inside and see a girl in a purple polo shoving a handful of candy into her mouth while watching TV. She's sitting on the bench, enthralled by whatever's on the screen.

As I approach the counter, I can hear Brad Pitt telling his fellow disciples what the first rule of Fight Club is. I wait about a minute, not wanting to be rude, but the girl is totally oblivious I'm here.

"Hi," I mutter when she still hasn't looked over from the TV.

Her eyes tear away from the screen, and she looks shocked that she's not alone.

"Oh, sorry!" she says, wiping her hands on her black shorts, placing the bag of candy onto the counter as she jumps down.

"Brad Pitt," she says, pointing at the screen as if that explains everything.

I give her a small, stiff-upper-lip smile, really just wanting to work out and not make idle chitchat. I really just need to kick the shit out of something.

Thankfully, she gets it.

"Right, well, welcome to Punch It. I'm guessing you're new because I haven't seen your face here before. Any questions, please gimme a yell," she says happily as she reaches under the counter for my membership papers.

As she's typing away at the computer, inputting all the fake information I just gave her, I ask, "I do have one question."

She looks up from the computer screen, happy to answer my question.

"Where is your boxing equipment kept?"

My body aches, and the sweat pours off my torso, but I can't stop.

My muscles feel alive and alert, and my brain is switched off.

This is why I love boxing. You can get a workout by punching the shit out of something that doesn't talk back.

I've been at it for about twenty minutes, and with each kick or punch I deliver, I come back twice as hard the next time.

I know I'll be sore later, but it's so worth it.

"Night of the Hunter" by Thirty Seconds to Mars blares through the speakers, and I'm concentrating on the beat to time my kicks and punches with the upbeat tempo.

My hair sticks to my sweaty brow, and my clothes mold to every curve of my clammy body. I don't own any gym clothes, so I have made do with my black cotton shorts, red tank top, and black high-tops.

But I don't care how I look. This is the first time in a long time I've felt alive.

I deliver a roundhouse kick and nail it dead center into the red bag, which sways from the force of my power.

"What did that bag ever do to you?" a husky voice asks from behind me.

My skin prickles as I turn around to meet a smirking Quinn, wearing black sweatpants, a tight Skid Row T-shirt, and black skater sneakers. He looks too good to be working out.

His scruffy hair appears to be a shade darker than usual,

and I realize that's because it's wet, sweat collecting at the corners of his brow. It sits messily and obstructs me from completely seeing his vibrant green eyes. He has a heavier growth from when I saw him last, but it suits him as it highlights all his sharp angles and slopes.

I need to stop obsessing over this guy. He's smug, a smart-ass, and totally bad news, yet that's why I can't stay away from him.

"Good to see you're up to your old stalking ways again," I reply smartly, turning back to the bag and kicking it—hard.

I hear Quinn chuckle, and I hate that my body reacts in a way that it never has before. It wants to hear it again.

"Ah, you know, a man's gotta have a hobby. Besides, you're the one who's stalking me."

I let out a sarcastic laugh. "How do you figure?"

"Well, I was here first. And same goes for the other night when you stole my nuts."

"I didn't steal anything," I retort, punching the bag twice. "It's not my fault you're slow and easily distracted."

I can see him standing off to my right side in my peripheral vision, watching me closely with his arms crossed.

I show off a little as I throw out a left jab, thrust my left hip forward to give me some extra power behind the punch, and quickly finish off with a right uppercut. My toned arms execute the move, and I pull back, slightly breathless.

"Where'd you learn to fight?" Quinn asks, picking up a pair of focus pads from the floor and walking over to me, palms raised.

"Here and there," I reply, opting to leave out the streets of LA and dealing drugs.

"You're good. Wanna fight me?" He dares me to accept his challenge.

"You think you can handle me?" I retort, shaking my hands to stretch them out.

Thankfully, I've taped them, as I've gone harder than I normally would.

"Give it your best shot, Red." He smirks cockily, putting up the focus pads and steadying himself with a balanced stance.

He's serious? Okay, bring it on, because dealing with my response to him…I can't do. But fighting him…I can do.

I arrogantly walk up to him and look him in the eyes before focusing on the pads and delivering the combination of a right-left-right, and then the opposite left-right-left, ensuring my weight shifts correctly. My entire body is involved because that's where my power comes from.

I make sure to put all my force behind it, and when I'm done, I pull away without even breaking a sweat.

I raise an eyebrow at Quinn proudly because I know that looked good.

He lets out a big yawn and smirks. "Oh, sorry, are you done? I thought that was a warm-up." And I'll be damned, but a dimple appears on his left cheek. *Smug bastard.*

I launch forward and deliver a six-series combination using all punches, but quicker this time. And also with a lot more force. I add a front kick since he's taking my punches with ease.

The kick pushes Quinn back a fraction, and I can't help the smile that spreads across my cheeks.

And this goes on for five minutes, nonstop.

My body aches, and perspiration pools at the base of my lower back, but I can't stop. It feels too good. His eyes watch my every move, and I feel alive under his vigilant gaze. I know I'm pushing him, but he doesn't tell me to stop. He just lets me go until I almost collapse into a fatigued heap.

"Now…I'm done," I say breathlessly, wiping the sweat from my brow.

Quinn pants as he removes the pads and shakes his hands, stretching his fingers out.

"I'm impressed," he says between breaths. "Remind me not to piss you off anytime soon."

He tosses the focus pads onto the floor and stretches his arms above his head, cracking his neck from side to side.

He holds himself with an air of confidence, and I would even go as far as to say an arrogance, but that just makes him all the more attractive.

"Feel better?" he asks as I lean down to take a long drink from the water fountain.

Wiping the water spilling over my lips with the back of my hand, I look at him, confused.

"You know, 'cause you have some serious pent-up anger."

"I do not!" I snap angrily.

The corners of his lips begin to pull up into a tight smile. "Think you do, Red."

"Well, isn't it lucky I don't care what you think?"

I need something to do with my hands before I strangle him. Or have an urge to pass my fingers through his mussed hair—which frightens me more than the strangulation. I begin unraveling the white tape from around my hands, avoiding his eyes, and also, my reaction to him.

"Hey, it's not a bad thing. It's far from it, actually," he adds, and I know he's smiling that smug smile. "I'm just calling it as I see it."

"Oh yeah? So what do you see when you look at me?" I'm frustrated as my hands fumble, and I can't get the stupid tape undone.

"Here, give me that."

I look up and see him holding his hand out, gesturing with his chin for me to give him my hand. I know my fingers shake in rage…or something else.

I pull my hand back, but he's lightning quick as he reaches for it and pulls me and my hand toward him.

We are standing toe to toe, and my hand and heart feel like they're both on fire.

What is wrong with me?

My eyes focus on Quinn's chest, which rises and falls in quickened breaths. Lifting my eyes to meet his, I can see his slightly clenched jaw. But other than that, he gives nothing away. He has the perfect poker face.

"I see," he says as he gently unravels the tape from around my hands, "a young woman who isn't like everyone else. She's different. She's witty. She doesn't take shit from anyone and doesn't flinch when a stranger walks in on her while in the shower."

His mouth tips up as if recalling the memory.

He reaches for my other hand, resting motionless by my side. This time, however, I don't resist.

"I see bravery. I see naivete," he says softly as he continues untying the tape with expert care.

And in the small space between us, I can feel an invisible pull toward him, a longing to be near him.

He raises his eyes to meet my wide ones. "But most of all…I see a survivor."

The word survivor comes out of his mouth like a forceful punch.

The cool breeze on my hand alerts me that Quinn has finished, but a warmth spreads up my arm like a forest fire.

I lower my eyes and am hypnotized by the sight of Quinn's index finger caressing the tattoo on my inner wrist.

He doesn't speak, but his touch fills the silence with a million words.

"So, you got all that just by watching me box?" I ask lightheartedly, because I can't explain what's passing between us.

Quinn's mouth slants into a lopsided grin.

"No, Red. I got all that by watching you when you didn't think anyone was looking and let your guard down. It may have only been for a second…but it was enough."

My knees begin to tremble at the thought of those inquisitive eyes dissecting my every move. Judging by the accurate description, he must have been watching very closely.

"Do you have any?" I ask quickly, needing to change the subject.

"Any what?" He smirks, picking up on my discomfort.

"Tattoos," I reply, looking down at where his fingertip scores my skin open with each stroke.

"Oh," he says, looking at my wrist as if he only just realized he's been touching me this entire time.

He releases his hold on me, and I don't know why, but I suddenly feel cold without his touch.

He pulls on his lip ring, and I can't help my eyes as they follow the movement.

"If I tell you, I'm gonna have to kill you."

I know it's only a saying, but the word "kill" sends a shiver down my spine so intense I jolt.

Quinn sees my reaction, and his eyes soften.

"I was only kidding, Red."

I know he was, but the feeling I experienced down in Tabitha's basement begins creeping over me, and I need to get out of here before I have another meltdown.

Stepping away from him, I quickly grab my backpack

from where it's slumped against the wall.

"I gotta go. Thanks for the workout," I lamely say, all but running for the exit as I shrug the straps over my shoulders.

"I'm sorry, I didn't mean to make you uncomfortable," he says, chasing after me.

When I keep walking, he reaches for my arm. The contact on my skin feels like a thousand knives stabbing me, and I yank my arm back.

"Please…don't…touch me."

He instantly lets go, his hands raised in surrender.

"I'm sorry. Please look at me," he says anxiously as my eyes are glued to my scuffed shoes.

His breathing is as rapid as mine, and I feel horrible that I have freaked out on him for no apparent reason.

I raise my eyes and meet his, which search my face for answers.

"Talk to me, Red. What happened to you?"

He knows. How does he know?

I hiss in a deep breath, and suddenly, swallowing is a chore.

I can't tell him because he doesn't want to know what I did.

I don't even want to know what I did.

I killed my father.

I'm a murderer.

What I did suddenly overwhelms me, and I have five seconds to get out of here before I break.

I meet his gaze for the final time because I can't do this.

Quinn makes me feel…normal. He makes me want things I can't have.

Things a murderer doesn't deserve.

"I'm s-sorry," I stutter, barely holding back my hysteria.

The look on his face is one of worry and concern, and as he opens his mouth to reply, I charge out the door before he has a chance to utter a single word.

Eight

'm so tired, but the thought of going to sleep before my shift at the diner sends me into a panic. If I sleep, I'll dream, and I can't deal with that right now.

So *this* is what guilt feels like? Looks like I'm not the cold-hearted bitch I thought I was. I actually prefer the not caring as opposed to this. Now I feel like a meltdown is just around the corner if I, or anyone else, so much as breathes the wrong way.

That's what happened last night with Quinn. I feel like an idiot for running out on him when he was trying to be nice. I don't know why he's wasting his time on someone like me as I'm sure he isn't short of admirers. But I would be a liar if I didn't confess I feel alive in his company. Something I have never felt before when in the company of another individual. I don't know what it is about him. Maybe it's the way he holds himself like he doesn't have a care in the world. Maybe I envy his carefree nature, and when I look at him, I see someone I want to be.

Or maybe it's just my hormones reacting to the fact he's the hottest guy I've ever seen.

Kicking off the bed, which I collapsed onto after my shift this morning, I decide to go to the library before I'm due at the diner. I have other important issues to deal with, like finding my mom.

I grab my backpack and sweater, and pay Grandpa a quick visit before I leave. It's funny how I've only been here five days and already feel more comfortable here than I did back home. I guess LA was never my home; I was only there because I had nowhere else to go.

"Hank?" I call out as I pop my head into the office. I don't see him sitting behind the counter, reading the paper like he usually does.

Hearing the faint hum of the TV in the background, I duck behind the counter and push past the curtain, hopeful not to find Hank atop any ladders.

Thankfully, he's grounded and carefully reading over some paperwork. He's as blind as a bat, so he holds the paperwork mere inches away from his face, and I can see he's trying desperately to read the fine print.

"Hank?" I ask again because he hasn't heard me call out to him.

He jumps, startled as his tired eyes meet mine.

"Oh, Paige, sorry, I didn't hear you come in," he says, lowering the document.

"That's okay," I reply, concerned when I see his usual happy face looking troubled and worn.

"Everything okay?" I ask, looking at the piece of paper,

hoping he might share its contents.

He folds up the document and places it into the front pocket of his flannel shirt. It looks like what he was reading is not up for discussion.

"Yes, everything's fine." His strained smile doesn't reach his eyes.

Whatever the matter is, I don't press. He has been respectful of my situation, and I owe him the same.

"So you off to work?" he asks, nodding toward my backpack.

"Yeah. I thought I would check out the library before I start my shift," I confess, shuffling nervously at the fact that I'm about to search for my mom's whereabouts.

"Oh?" Hank questions, looking at me to elaborate. When I don't, he continues. "Paige, you can tell me to mind my own business, but have you had any luck locating your mother?"

I knew it was coming, but hearing him say it makes what I'm about to do all the more real.

"No, not yet. That's why I'm going to the library. I have to start somewhere," I declare, and saying it out loud wasn't as scary as I thought.

"Atta girl. Take my truck." He reaches into his back pocket and extends the keys out to me.

I look at his keys and back up at him. "No, Hank. I can't keep taking your truck. What if there's an emergency, and you need it?"

Hank lets out a cackle. "Oh please. If there was an emergency, I'd be calling the police. Here, take them." He jingles the keys.

I'm tempted by the offer because it will give me more time to spend at the library.

"Are you sure?" I press, not wanting him to feel I'm

ungrateful or taking advantage of his kindness.

"I insist." He reaches for my hand and places the keys in my palm.

I don't know what I did to deserve such kindness from Hank as God knows I've done a lot of bad things. But the day I met Hank was the day the universe decided to give me a break.

"Thank you, Hank. This means so much to me."

"I know, Paige," he says, his old eyes full of wisdom. "Go now. Time waits for no man. I should know."

I wish I wasn't so awkward at hugging and physical contact because right about now would be the appropriate time to give Hank a big thank-you hug. But I settle for a smile, which is more than I could offer five days ago.

I'm good at being quiet, so being in a library is like being at home.

I have been looking at the same computer screen for the past five minutes, unable to hit Enter. I have found an online Canadian phonebook because I thought it would be easiest to start with something simple, like her name.

But what if I hit Enter, and it comes up empty? Then what would I do? I have no real recollections of my mom besides the photo of her and me that I hastily grabbed when leaving my old life behind.

I've propped up the photo in question on the keyboard. My mother's kind blue eyes stare down at me lovingly while I cling to her neck with a big smile on my pudgy, rosy cheeks. I look so happy, and it's funny because I can't even remember what I was smiling about. You'd think a memory such as this would stay embedded in my mind forever, but I didn't know this moment would be one of the last happy times of my life.

I was three.

I know this because the pink unicorn birthday cake has three lit candles shining brightly in front of me. This was the last birthday I would ever celebrate, hence the nostalgia behind this photograph.

I just wish I could remember it.

Looking at the time at the bottom of the screen, I know it's now or never because I'm due at work in ten minutes. I take a deep breath and peer at the Enter button like it's my worst enemy, and in a way, it is.

This button has the power to change my life forever.

With my finger poised over the key, I take one last look at the picture and tap it quickly. My heart is about to claw out through my rib cage when my search reveals I have a match.

I stare at the screen, and the words *Cynthia Penny Lee* are in big, bold letters with an address and a phone number listed beside it.

I can't believe it.

I did it.

I found her.

Staring at me blankly in the face is my future.

Frantically searching for my notebook, which of course, is squashed at the bottom of my bag, I rip it out, tossing the other items aside, and flip to a blank page.

With shaky fingers, I write down the address and phone number of my mother. I can't believe it was that easy.

The thought sits uneasily in my gut because nothing thus far has been easy in life.

I just hope this is the one and only time that it is.

I ignore the fact I should be typing in another name.

My father's.

One step at a time, I tell myself, as I know I'll put off that search for as long as I can.

I admit I have a little skip to my step as I'm zipping around at work, waiting tables. And it doesn't go unnoticed by Tabitha.

"What are you on today?" she asks happily as I whiz past her in the hallway, nearly taking her out.

Normally, I would flinch or recoil from a comment relating to drugs since it is obviously a touchy subject for me.

But it doesn't bother me as much today as it normally would.

"Nothing. Just feeling happy, that's all. Thank you for doing my hair and makeup the other night," I say with a small smile. I have taken her fashion tips on board, and I must admit I like them.

Tabitha returns my smile, her bright eyes shining in happiness. "Oh, no worries. I probably had more fun than you!"

Tristan strolls past, carrying a crate of beer.

"How are two of my favorite ladies?" he asks with a big smile.

Tristan's happiness surprises me because I have never met anyone who is always so…happy. It's actually refreshing, and I find myself smiling voluntarily when I'm around him, which confuses the hell out of me.

"Hey, I'm thinking of having a party after work. Just a few

people," Tristan says, shuffling up the heavy crate as he looks at Tabitha and me. "You girls in?"

"I'm there! Paige?" she asks, looking at me, hopeful I'll say yes.

Tristan also looks over at me, his head cocked to the side, awaiting my answer.

I feel comfortable around Tabitha and Tristan, and I dare say, even safe with them. I don't feel I need to carry my knife with me constantly, which is a big thing for me.

I can't help but soften slightly when Tristan looks at me with a big dimpled smile.

"C'mon, I promise you'll have fun."

"And if I don't?" I shoot back quickly.

Wow, I just made another joke. What about him allows me to drop my guard?

"If you don't," he replies, chuckling deeply, "then I owe you a fun night out."

I don't know how to react to that. Looking at the attractive man standing in front of me without a malicious bone in his body, I can't help but comply.

"Okay, count me in."

I can't believe those words just slipped past my lips.

Tabitha squeals and claps excitedly, her hair bouncing with the momentum.

"Awesome. Now, let's get back to work. The quicker we get this over with, the quicker we can have some fun." He looks at me, giving me a small wink before backing into the kitchen.

"I think someone likes you," Tabitha whispers in a singsong voice, gesturing with her eyes to the kitchen.

I scoff playfully at her and quickly busy myself with collecting clean silverware to set the tables. I really don't want to deal with that possibility right now.

Like I said…one step at a time.

I wonder if my attire is okay. I never thought I would be in a position to worry about such trivial things, but here I am, standing in my tiny bathroom, wondering just that.

I don't own nice things, so I've made do with what I have.

I want to be comfortable, so I decide my black skinny jeans, white tank, and combat boots are the best option for a small gathering.

Thanks to Tabitha, I've tried my best to mimic her makeup techniques from the other night, and I think I've done okay. She threw numerous makeup products my way, insisting I take them. I refused, of course, but she wouldn't hear of it. Now I'm kind of glad I stopped being so stubborn and accepted them because the makeup helps hide the terror behind my eyes.

I've been to parties, but the only reason I was ever there was because my party favors were the main attraction for the happy patrons. I've seen what goes on. I mean, there are some parties I wish I could burn from my retinas, while others were just college kids wanting to get lit for the night.

But I have never actually been *invited* to one before.

In high school, I was considered a social leper. Therefore, no host would dare invite the freak to attend their pretentious gathering. Not that I ever wanted to go.

Slipping my flick knife into my boot, I tuck my jeans into them, not bothering to tie the laces. I need easy access to my knife, and tight shoelaces inhibit me from reaching for it quickly if I need it.

One last look in the mirror and I'm ready.

My shoes thud onto the long hallway as I make my way to the office to say good night to Hank. I don't know why I feel the need to say goodbye to him, but I feel better with him knowing where I am.

I cringe when I see him behind the counter, eating a microwave dinner that looks awful.

"That's not your dinner, is it?" I ask, curling up my lip while looking at his sloppy meal of God knows what.

Hank looks up from his meal, his glasses slipping down his small nose as he lets out a whistle.

"Well, look at you. You scrub up okay, young lady."

I run my finger over my stud nose ring, feeling a little self-conscious.

"Thanks," I mumble, trying not to sound ungrateful.

"Where are you off to?" he asks while wiping his mouth on a paper napkin.

"To Tristan's house. You know, Tristan who I work with."

Grandpa nods as he reaches for his glass of water.

"Ah, Tristan Berkeley. What a nice young boy. How're you getting there?" he asks, placing his glass on the wooden bench.

"I was going to walk."

Tristan has given me directions to his house, and although it's a bit of a walk, the fresh air and exercise will do me good.

"Oh no, you will not," Hank quickly replies while reaching under the counter, keys in hand.

I wave my palm in front of me, shaking my head swiftly. "No, Hank, I can't take your truck again."

"Who says?" Hank asks, standing slowly and shuffling to meet me where I stand.

"I say," I retort with a small smile.

"Paige, please take it. I don't like the idea of you walking alone so late at night. There are crazy people out there. If you don't take them," he says when I still refuse to accept the keys, "I'll drive you. I think you prefer the option of taking the truck, although, I wouldn't mind hanging out with you youngsters, maybe even stay for a beer."

I know he's pulling my leg, but I snatch the keys from his fingers as he chuckles lightly.

"I thought so. Have a good time. Don't do anything I wouldn't do."

I can't help but smile as I look at the frail old man in front of me. I don't think Hank is even aware of how much he has helped me…survive.

"Thank you, Hank."

And I do something I've never done before. I step forward and awkwardly wrap my arms around his delicate frame and hug him. At first, I feel stiff and rigid, but the familiar smell of him, mixed with the sensation of him calmly placing his fragile arms behind my back, allows me to relax into his embrace.

I can feel something catch in my throat, and my eyes begin to burn.

I pull away quickly, not wanting to be caught crying over a simple hug. That's not what normal people do.

"See you tomorrow bright and early," I say, attempting to cover how touched I am that he returned my hug without any reservations or uncertainties.

"If you come in late, you sleep in. I can clean the rooms. We only have three guests staying tonight." He smiles kindly, knowing how hard hugging him was for me.

"I'll see you tomorrow morning," I reiterate with a small smile.

"Okay. Good night then, child," he says, returning to his meal.

"Good night, Hank," I reply.

That burning sensation at the back of my eyeballs is back, and I quickly hightail it out of there, not wanting him to see how touched I am by his choice of words.

He called me child.

As I drive to Tristan's, I'm actually quite thankful I accepted because Tristan's place is farther than I originally anticipated. As I turn down a nice, clean neighborhood, I quickly scan the house numbers to find Tristan's. However, I don't need to look very far because the man running into a house wearing nothing but a red cape is a dead giveaway to where the party is.

I have no idea where to park. Cars already line the street, and I assume they're all here for Tristan.

So much for a small gathering.

I contemplate speeding down the street toward the safety of the motel when I receive a text message. I look over at the passenger seat to see who it is.

It's Tabitha.

> Where are you? It's no fun without
> u! ;)

I can do this.

Reversing into a tight spot down the road, I take a final peek at my appearance in the visor mirror.

My pupils are dilated, and my mouth is parched. I'm taking in steady gulps of air while my chest heaves in an unhealthy way. I look like a startled deer that has just spotted a hunter, and I'm preparing to run the hell away from danger.

> Paigeeeeee… I miss you :(

Taking a deep, steadying breath, I hop out of the truck,

hoping my legs don't give out from under me.

I hit the pavement, and the closer I get to Tristan's home, the quicker my heart beats.

A naked caped crusader comes bursting out through the front door and jumps down the three steps. He sees me walking up the drive, and I avert my eyes because I can see his junk bobbing with his movements.

"The party is in there. Save me a dance," he slurs, saluting me with a red plastic cup.

I give him a stiff smile and run up the three stairs faster than his cape whips in the wind.

The smell of beer, dope, and cheap cologne assaults my nostrils as soon as I enter the small hallway.

The house is so full I doubt my tiny frame could squeeze through the ocean of people in front of me without indecently assaulting at least half of them.

This was a bad idea.

I'm tempted to turn around, but when I see the top of Tabitha's red hair charging toward me, my plans of escape are futile.

"You made it!" she squeals, wrapping her arms around me and squeezing me tight.

My arms are trapped by my sides, so even if I were tempted to return her hug, I couldn't.

"Yup, I made it," I wheeze out. "Tabitha, you're choking me."

"Oh shit, sorry!" she says, thankfully letting me go. "I'm just so happy you're here!" She hiccups after she finishes her sentence.

I narrow my eyes, and notice the redder than red on her freckled cheeks and the slightly glassy look in her big green eyes.

"Tabitha, are you…drunk?"

"Maybe," Tabitha replies, letting out another hiccup. "Ooh, that tastes like beer."

I can't help the small chuckle that escapes me because I find drunken people hilarious. Yes, I have been drunk, but always in the privacy of my own home where I can't humiliate myself or end up running around naked wearing nothing but a cape.

"You made it."

Before I know what's happening, two big arms encircle my tiny frame, and I'm bear hugged into a burly chest.

Tristan smells awesome.

"Yup, I made it," I repeat, which comes out muffled as I'm pressed up against his hard torso.

Thankfully, he lets me go and gives me a sheepish smile. "Sorry for the PDA."

I return his smile and shake my head. "It's fine." Because it actually is.

The three of us stand around the cluttered hallway, Tabitha looking between Tristan and me with interest because I can't stop gaping at him.

He looks…hot.

He stands tall, and his snug V-neck navy T-shirt shows off his inked arm and tight black jeans emphasizes his height. His hair is flicked forward messily… Holy shit, he looks good.

"Soooo"—Tabitha giggles, interrupting my ogling—"whatcha drinking?"

I tear my eyes away from Tristan and shake away the fog in my brain.

"Um, nothing for the moment. I'm good," I reply, giving her a small smile when I see her sulk.

"But it's a party." She pouts, her bottom lip poking out

exaggeratedly. "Tell her, Tristan."

Tristan has his arms crossed over his chest and only shrugs with a dimpled smile.

"Oh, you two are boring!" She blows a loud raspberry, stomping her foot in protest.

Her juvenile action is hilarious, and I laugh. It's small, but it slips out before I can stop it.

I'm having a good time.

I can't believe I enjoy watching drunken idiots embarrass themselves while playing *Rock Band* on Xbox.

Tabitha is one of them.

As she's playing some rock tune that her short fingers can't keep up with, Tristan and I sit back on the sofa, watching her.

I haven't failed to notice Tristan hasn't left my side for the entire evening. I don't know why, but it doesn't creep me out or make me feel uncomfortable. I like having him close by.

A drunken girl with a dress that barely covers her pink bits walks past us and trips over her own feet. She lands awkwardly, and sadly, I break her fall. She's all but on top of me, and I push back, unable to move farther because the sofa restricts my escape.

Tristan can sense my discomfort immediately and yanks her off me by her upper arm.

"Watch where you're going, Amber!" he shouts to be heard over the noise.

Amber half stands, half wobbles, but thankfully remains standing upright. Her glassy-brown eyes rake over Tristan, and a wicked smile passes over her glossy lips.

"Hey, Tris," she slurs, her breath fanning out over his cheeks as she leans down to get a closer look at him. "You're looking yummy tonight."

Tristan pulls back, his lip curling in disgust. "Shame I can't say the same thing about you."

My eyes widen when I hear his comment. I can't believe Tristan, who has never said a bad word about anybody, just insulted someone.

I can't help but smile because it was a great comeback—kudos to him.

"Whatcha smiling at, ho?"

I look up and realize she's talking to me.

I can feel Tristan stiffen, but I can't help but find this whole situation comical.

This trashy brunette just called *me* a ho? I think she needs to look in the mirror.

"I asked you a question," she sneers, pulling back from Tristan and turning her attention to me.

"I heard you," I reply plainly, returning her stare.

"Well?" she asks, flicking her long, curly brown hair over her shoulder.

"Well, what?" I reply smugly, playing dumb.

"What were you smiling at?"

Her beady eyes narrow, and I can see how annoyed she's getting that I'm not playing along with her.

"Was I smiling?" I ask sarcastically.

She huffs out an annoyed breath, and her chest heaves in rage. "You know you were!" she shouts like a child.

I look at Tristan, who has a small smile pulling at the corner of his lips.

I could do this all night. "Was I smiling, Tristan?" I ask in mock horror.

Tristan can't stop his laughter as it bubbles out of his throat, and he covers his mouth to muffle his chuckles.

I look at Amber, batting my eyelashes innocently.

She rises to full height, straightening out her blue dress angrily.

"Oh, whatever, freak. Tris, where's your brother?" she asks, ignoring me.

Tristan's shoulders rise in a shrug. "I don't know. Probably upstairs, hiding from you."

I turn my head so quickly I nearly flick myself in the eye with my hair. Two insults in the span of two minutes—who knew Tristan had it in him.

Amber purses her lips and throws her head back, letting out a small "hmph" before she storms off, tripping over her ridiculous heels and falling onto some poor chump who's minding his own business.

Both Tristan and I look at her, then at one another, and laugh.

"So you have a brother?" I ask once we stop chuckling like schoolgirls.

"Yeah. He's older, twenty-two."

"How old are you?" I ask, realizing I know nothing about him and feeling slightly embarrassed I haven't asked him sooner.

"I'm twenty. Turning twenty-one in a couple of weeks, actually. How about you? I know you're nineteen." When I look at him, eyes wide, he chuckles. "I hired you, remember?"

Oh shit, that's right. My job application. I was beginning to think he looked me up or something. Not that he would find me, seeing as my name isn't Paige.

Tristan doesn't want to dig around in my past because he won't like what he finds.

"Have you got any brothers or sisters?"

Shaking my head, I can feel the walls closing in on me.

"Where're you originally from?" he asks innocently, sipping his beer.

Shit.

I can't lie to him. As I look into his honest eyes, I feel my mouth moving without my brain's permission.

"LA."

Tristan nods, oblivious I'm about to have a breakdown.

I tell myself to breathe.

In.

Out.

In.

Out.

Better.

"What about your parents? How'd they feel when you up and left the exciting streets of LA to come to the sleepy town of South Boston?"

I know he's trying to be friendly, but I'm seriously about to heave. I can't talk about my past—ever. To anyone. For a fraction of a second, I thought I could be normal.

I'm an idiot.

"Where's the bathroom?" I ask a little too animatedly as I jump up.

"Um, upstairs. I can show you," he says, slightly confused that I'm backing away from him like he's Jason Voorhees.

He makes a move to get up, but I stop him by basically yelling, "No! I can find it. You stay here, and um…I'll be back." That's the best I can do in my moment of crisis.

I push past a dude showing off his "dance moves" to a couple of unimpressed girls and am only confronted by more and more people. Shoving through the sea of unmoving bodies, I can feel sweat collecting on my brow and at the back of my neck. I need to get out of here.

Sadly, I'm running in the wrong direction of the front door and just farther into the hordes of people. I push random strangers out of the way, and others move to the side when they see me charging toward them with no intention of stopping.

Thankfully I see the stairs, and with all my might, I force my way, elbows out, through a couple making out in front of the staircase.

I hear a bang and know they have probably hit the wall, but I can't even vocalize a sorry since the next thing that comes out of my mouth will be vomit.

Racing up the steps two at a time, I get to the top in no time. However, as I look around, I have no clue where the bathroom is.

Four identical doors lead off the hallway, so I try my luck and run toward the closest door on my right. With so much force, I charge into it, tripping over my loose shoelaces and landing on my face.

Luckily, the carpet stops me from losing a tooth or breaking my nose.

Carpet?

I now know door number one is not the bathroom.

I'm lying on my belly, hands out in front of me, which thankfully broke my fall. I feel better being in a room away from people, noise, and...probing questions. Besides, it smells amazing in here.

Hold up, whose bedroom am I in?

My eyes scan the room and take in my surroundings. The dim room is lit with a few candles, and under the orange flickers, I can see band posters and art adorn the walls.

Abstract art. Stuff you would see in a museum and not get unless you studied all that Expressionism. I like it, though, as it seems perfect on these dark-colored walls.

A small desk sits off to the side, and books upon books are stacked in piles, littering the surface. I can't read the titles in the dark, but they look old and tattered.

Around me, I see a few discarded clothing items such as jeans, T-shirts, and socks, all tossed to the floor messily. Randomly sitting next to the garments is an open sketchbook. I can faintly see black charcoal lines but can't distinguish the drawings.

Finally, my eyes settle on the queen-size bed directly in front of me, and as I slowly rise on my knees, I see that I'm not alone.

My heart, which only just stilled, now begins beating wildly again because I've found the source behind that delectable scent.

He's sucking on his lusciously full bottom lip, tugging at his lip ring humorously while his emerald-green eyes twinkle in amusement.

I lower myself back onto the carpet because I can't deal with the sight before me. I close my eyes and will myself to disappear.

Sadly, I know I'm still here when a deep chuckle prompts me to the fact that I am lying facedown with my eyes closed in Quinn's room.

"So who's stalking who?" he asks, laughing freely.

Thankfully, he hasn't shifted off the bed, so if I don't answer him, maybe he'll believe I'm not really here.

No such luck.

"I can hear you breathing, Red."

"What are you doing here?" I foolishly inquire, which

comes out half muffled as my cheek is pressed up against the floor.

"Um…I kinda live here." He chuckles, amused.

Fuck, why *this* room? Why did I have to barge into *his* room like a crazy person?

"Oh, well…you have a nice room," I say, and wince at the stupidity of my comment.

"Thanks. It's even nicer when you're not lying on the floor," he replies, and I hear the bed shift, announcing he's gotten up.

Of course, my body doesn't listen when I will it to move. The only thing moving is my frantic pulse, pounding against my neck, demanding to break free.

Suddenly, I see a pair of feet in front of me.

"Are you going to lie there all night?"

I don't need to see his face to know he's smiling at me. "Maybe."

I hear him sigh, and before I know it, a pair of emerald-green eyes replace his feet.

With Quinn lying beside me, I can't help my eyes as they wander of their own accord and quickly appraise his chiseled face, thoroughly enjoying what they see.

Mercifully, he has left a reasonable space between us, so I don't feel crowded with him lying so close. But I have a sneaking suspicion that regardless of the distance between us, he could never be close enough.

I inadvertently shuffle a fraction closer to him, wanting to breathe in his exhalations. I want to breathe him in.

"You're right. The view is cool from down here," he says, his large eyes darting around the room, taking in his bedroom from a different angle.

I nod timidly, knowing Quinn is well aware of me staring

at him, but he doesn't seem to mind. A piece of hair falls over my face, blanketing my eyes, and I'm about to brush it away, but Quinn gets there first and sweeps it off my face.

When my vision is no longer impaired, I can see his eyes probing my face with apprehension, afraid I'll freak out again.

But I'm not moving a muscle since this moment is an unspoiled stillness between us.

I can't stop looking at his mouth. And when he begins tugging on his lip, sucking the hoop into his wet, luscious mouth, I wonder what it would feel like. Would the steel be cold, but heat the instant it was engulfed into his searing mouth?

"What are you thinking about?" he asks quietly, releasing his lip.

Shaking my head to expel the improper thoughts from my lust-filled brain, I meet his curious eyes as I ask, "You're Tristan's brother?"

Quinn smiles. "Yup. Well, technically, he's *my* brother 'cause I'm older than him."

His comment makes me smile.

"Someone was looking for you," I mutter, remembering my not-so-pleasant encounter with Amber.

"Oh yeah? Who's that?" he asks, his eyes never leaving my face.

"Amber," I reply, adjusting my hands to cushion them under my cheek.

"Oh fuck," he curses as he lifts his eyes to the ceiling. "Please don't tell me you told her I was up here?"

"Nope. But Tristan did." I smile smugly.

"Fucker." Quinn huffs, but I can tell he means no harm by his comment. "Serves me right."

"Why's that?" I question as I am totally mesmerized by

him and don't want him to stop talking.

"Let's just say there are some things I wish I could take back."

Yeah, like his dignity. I don't fail to see him pull up his lip in disgust as if reliving a nasty memory.

I lower my eyes and am kind of appalled that Quinn would touch Amber voluntarily.

The wheels in my head begin turning, and I can't help but wonder what role she plays in Quinn's life. From his detached response, I dare say he couldn't care less for her, but who knows? What I do know, for some unexplained reason, is that I need to find out.

"She's your…girlfriend?" I ask, hoping to sound casual.

Quinn watches me closely, and I match his inquisitive stare, subtly demanding an answer.

After a deep sigh, Quinn replies, "No, she is *not* my girlfriend. Amber is no one's girlfriend."

"What do you mean?"

Quinn smirks, and he seems amused by my eagerness to keep this ball rolling.

"Someone like Amber likes the attention of too many guys to remain faithful to just one person."

I nod, semi-satisfied by his response. "So she just happened to grab your attention one night, then?" I ask, needing to know if he and Amber are an ongoing thing.

Quinn nods, lowering his eyes, and he looks embarrassed for the first time ever.

"Yeah, and it's one night I really wish I could forget," he confesses, chewing on his lip.

Quinn doesn't seem like a one-night-stand kind of guy, so I can't help but wonder what possessed him to sleep with her in the first place.

As if reading my thoughts, he whispers, "It was a long time ago. My life at the time was messed up; *I* was messed up. Being with her was better than being alone for the night."

My mouth parts, shocked by his honesty, but I'm elated he has shared some of his story with me.

"Why were you a mess?" I question softly, hoping I'm not crossing any personal boundaries.

Quinn only shakes his head as if to expel the images from his mind.

"It's a long, tiresome story. One I won't bore you with."

I can read them loud and clear as mine are firmly in place every hour of every day. But I want to know the rest of his story.

"I want..." But I don't get to finish my sentence as Quinn softly places a finger over my lips to silence me.

"Tell me your secrets, and I'll tell you mine," he coaxes, his eyes searching my face for a response to his accurate presumption.

I lower my eyes, ashamed that I've pushed for personal information when I have no intention of sharing mine.

Quinn's pointer finger gently sashays over my trembling lips, and he smiles. "I thought so."

With my eyes still lowered, I let the subject slide because now that I know the truth, I am partially relieved. But unexpectedly, a barrel of different emotions passes over me, and the one standing at the forefront is jealousy.

As soon as Quinn slides his finger off my lips, and I'm free to speak, it's out before I can stop myself.

"Well, I hope you got checked for STDs since you're probably a poster child for VD after consorting with that tramp."

I quickly close my mouth, clamping my lips shut before I

can say another word.

My comment takes Quinn aback, and I'm afraid I might have overstepped.

But as he opens his sinful mouth, his laughter ruptures free, and I know I'm in the clear.

"Oh man. Beautiful *and* funny. Holy shit, Red," he says between fits of laughter, his hand covering his mouth to muffle his chuckles.

Did he just call me…beautiful?

To stop myself from passing out or overanalyzing, I hurriedly ask him, "What's with the nickname?"

Quinn shuffles a fraction closer, and his smell is mouthwatering.

"Well, I think it's fitting, seeing as you still haven't told me your name," he replies with a small shrug, rubbing his jaw.

I notice his fingers have a light coat of black substance. It looks like…charcoal. I then remember the sketchbook on the floor. Is Quinn the owner of those sketches I couldn't quite make out?

I'm still staring at his delicate fingers when I question, "But why Red?"

"Well, duh….'cause of your hair," he replies, chuckling in enjoyment.

I am in awe of his mouth. Every time he opens it wide enough, I can see a spark of silver, a reminder of the tongue ring, which is hidden away. This time is no exception because when he laughs, his barbell flashes me.

"Oh, of course."

"And your temper," he adds quickly with a lopsided grin.

"Temper?" I ask, eyes wide. "I do not have a temper."

Quinn bites back a smile. "Okay."

But I know he's not buying it.

"I do not," I repeat, pushing up on an elbow and looking down at him to emphasize my point.

"Hey, I saw you fight. I'm not arguing with you," he replies, playfully poking fun at me. "I'm still getting the feeling back in my hands, thanks to your ass kicking."

I can't believe it, but I laugh—again.

"Are you…laughing?" he asks in mock horror.

"Well, duh," I reply, mimicking his earlier comment.

"Wow. I'm shocked." Quinn chuckles deeply.

I cock my eyebrow at him. "What's that supposed to mean?"

Quinn chooses his words carefully. However, if his dimpled smile is anything to go by, his next words will earn him a beating. "It means if the wind changed, you'd be stuck with a permanent scowl, Red."

I move my mouth wordlessly. Did he just insult me with a smile?

"What? No smart-ass reply?"

I'll give him smart-ass.

I sit up promptly and punch him in the arm. It's a playful punch with no force behind it, but he gets the message. His mouth falls open as he's stunned that I hit him, but a cheeky grin spreads across his glowing cheeks a second later.

"You are so going to regret that."

I don't like the look in his eyes as he leisurely sits up, staring at me with a mischievous grin. I quickly push up and am on my feet within a second, backing away from him.

"Quinn," I warn, hands out in front of me. "Don't do anything you're going to regret."

Quinn's mouth tips up into a lopsided smirk as he pushes himself off the ground.

"Oh, believe me, I won't regret anything," he replies as he

stalks toward me sinisterly.

And suddenly, the thrill of the chase sends my heart into a quick pitter-patter of excitement.

I continue walking backward, my eyes never leaving his, and as I feel the heavy door push up against my back, foiling my plans of escape, I know I'm screwed.

"Quinn." I try to sound authoritative.

"Red," he parrots, continuing to stalk.

My hands are slung by my sides, flush against the door, and in a situation where I would normally flinch or fight to flee, I welcome him.

I'm anticipating his next move.

I don't understand my reaction to him.

But I like it.

As he approaches me, he stops within inches of my face and body.

He peers into my wide, animated eyes as he tugs on his lower lip, and I witness his gaze fall down my body in an obvious appraisal of my torso. My chest begins rising and falling quickly.

As he glides his hands up the door and places them by my head, imprisoning me within his strong frame, my heartbeat launches into a deafening thud.

Our bodies are a hair's breadth away from connecting, but he doesn't touch me. A charged static fills the air between our bodies, and this is the most erotic moment of my life.

He slowly slithers his hands down the door, inches away from my body, tracing my torso with the descent, but he never lays a finger on me.

And I realize...I want him to.

"Truce?" he whispers as he rests his hands by my waist, still denying me any contact.

I peer up at him, as he is easily six-three, and nod. "Truce."

The candlelight casts dark shadows over his face, veiling most of his features. But I can see a sliver of his bright-green eyes peering at me from under his lengthy dirty-blond hair, and the look leaves me breathless.

I have never seen *that* look in the eyes of another because of…me.

Is this what I've seen in the movies? Where boy meets girl, and they share a single moment, and nothing will ever be the same from that point forward?

I lower my eyes because I feel him indecently undressing me with his. My cheeks heat.

"You're an enigma," he whispers. It's barely audible, so I have misgivings about whether I heard him correctly.

But as he lifts his hand, extending his finger, and embarks on tracing a line across my cheek with barely a touch, I know I haven't misheard him.

I close my eyes, unable to stand still under his intense gaze. My skin feels like it's been torn open, bleeding out wanton need with his gentle touch. My breath catches in my throat, and I'm certain Quinn can see my heart beating out of my chest.

But he lets his hand fall before I can appreciate his touch.

I may be a virgin but *have* shared a few kisses. Nothing earth-shattering or anything I would want to experience twice. Well, that's not true. I have kissed only one person twice, and that's Justin Miller, the only guy who didn't treat me like a leper in high school because he, too, was a fellow freak.

But the other kisses I've shared are nothing like the ones I've seen in movies.

When they kiss…I *feel* it. I feel what you're supposed to experience when connecting with another.

The few lackluster kisses I've experienced have been disappointing and…indecent.

But as my eyes feast on Quinn's perfect lips, I know kissing him would be flawless.

I'm miles away, spellbound by Quinn's mouth and the way he's tugging at his piercing, when the door behind me suddenly flies open, interrupting my improper thoughts.

Falling forward, I tumble straight into Quinn, who steadies me by placing his warm hands around my waist. The moment we make contact, all I can focus on is the way his hands feel on my body. And although it may only be through my top, my skin is still on fire.

"Paige?"

I don't need to turn around to know that Tristan is behind me.

I miss the feel of Quinn's hands on me as he lets me go.

"Hi, Tristan," I reply and turn to face him.

"Is everything okay?" he asks, looking more at Quinn than me.

"Yup, all good, bro," Quinn replies as he steps away from me, but I can still see him out of the corner of my eye.

"You okay, Paige?" Tristan questions, making sure what Quinn has told him is the truth.

I wonder why that is.

"Yes, all good."

I feel like my insides are ready to explode.

"Cool. Did you find the bathroom?" Tristan asks, looking at me and then up at Quinn.

This whole conversation is nothing short of awkward. And I wonder what the creepy glances between Quinn and Tristan are all about.

"Nope, and speaking of…I better go find it." I want to get

the hell away from this uncomfortable situation.

"I'll show you," Tristan says quickly, still looking at Quinn, an unreadable message passing between them.

Their body language is a little standoffish, and I don't understand why.

Tristan gives Quinn one last look before he looks down at me with a strained smile. "Okay, let's go." He turns his back, hastily walking out the door.

Taking a step to follow, Quinn latches onto my hand, pulling me toward him abruptly.

My back presses to his front, and he still has a firm grip on my hand when he whispers in a quickened breath, millimeters away from the shell of my ear, "I like Red better."

And only then does he let me go.

I don't turn to face him, but I run out the door like a coward because if his face matches his heated words…then I'm not sure I would be able to leave.

I don't know what that was with Quinn, but I'm not naive and know I'm attracted to him inside and out. But this attraction is unreasonable. I don't even know him, but I desperately want to. The little insight he gave me was one I know well. It's one I face every day. He has his share of secrets, as do I, but is it wrong that I don't care?

I know it *is* wrong, so I need to keep away from him because Quinn is smart. I can see that about him. Sooner or later, he'll figure out my secret, and I don't want to be here when that happens.

I have to stay away from him.

But why will that be a lot harder than it sounds?

Nine

The vacuum cleaner scrambles my brain. After a few hours of restless sleep, I don't want to hear the loud buzzing noise.

But I promised Grandpa I'd be here, and I'm not going back on my word. And anyway, I'm not working at the diner today, so I can nap if I'm dog-tired later on.

I pat my back pocket, feeling the piece of paper with my mom's details written on it. I'm never letting it go. Just to be safe, I've written her details down at least half a dozen times in case I lose this piece of paper.

I can't believe I found her. It feels wrong that it was so easy, because nothing in my life has ever been easy.

But I'm not ready.

Not yet.

I've been here for close to a week, and I'm a day away

from receiving my first paycheck, so going to see my mom has to wait. And that's because I don't have enough money for a flight to Canada. And I'm also not turning up on my mother's doorstep sixteen years after she left me alone with my dad, presuming she'll welcome me back with open arms. She's the one who left me. I don't know *what* to expect when I see her again. But I'm not that naive to think it'll be an Oprah moment.

When I go see my mom, I'll have enough cash to leave if things get rough and be able to support myself because I rely on no one.

It's the only thing I know how to do.

"How was last night, Paige?"

Letting out a small yelp, I jump five inches off the ground when I see Grandpa waddle into the room, his arthritic hands full of mail.

"Holy shit! You scared me," I say breathlessly, clutching my chest and shutting the vacuum cleaner off with my boot.

"Sorry, child. I just wanted to give you this." He smiles, his wiry gray hair standing up at an odd angle like he fell asleep with it wet.

Narrowing my eyes, I notice he looks a little off color. I wonder if it has anything to do with the letter he read yesterday.

I look at his outstretched hand, which holds a white envelope.

"What is it?" I ask, eyeing it with suspicion.

"Your paycheck," he replies, moving the envelope from side to side playfully.

"But it hasn't been a week yet."

"That doesn't matter. Take it." He places the envelope into my palm.

I look down at it and then back up at him.

"Thank you, Hank…I really appreciate it," I say sincerely as this is my first step toward my new life.

However, as I take hold of the envelope, it feels thicker than it should be. Raising an eyebrow at him, I quickly open it up before he can dodge me. Staring back at me are a few extra green bills.

"Stop right there!" I demand as Grandpa subtly scuffles toward the door.

"Hank, this is too much. We never agreed on this amount. I can't accept it. Here, take this back." I shuffle through the bills, pulling out the extra amount and handing it over to him.

"No, I will not accept it. You earned that."

"No, I really didn't. This is way too much for a few easy hours of work, and you've given me a roof over my head. Please. I can't," I say, pushing the money out toward him.

But Grandpa, being Grandpa, raises his hands in protest. "You're not going to offend an old man now, are you?" he replies, his warm eyes shining with mischief.

"Oh, old man, my foot! I've seen you get around when you think no one is looking," I tease, knowing he won't accept the money.

He lets out a coughing laugh, and it echoes deep within his chest. Grandpa is not in the best of health.

I remember him mentioning a wife, but he spoke of her in the past tense. I wonder what happened to her, and I also wonder if they were happy together.

Looking at Grandpa with his toothless smile and warm gray eyes, I know he would make anyone happy.

"Whatcha doing tonight?" I ask casually.

Grandpa shrugs. "Just going to watch some TV. The game is on tonight."

"Please don't tell me you're going to eat that junk I saw you eating yesterday?" I ask, referring to the slop he ate for dinner last night.

"Nothing wrong with it," he replies gruffly. "It was on sale."

"That's because they couldn't even give it away."

Hank laughs heartily. "When it's just me, child, there's no point in cooking."

"Fair call and that's why I'm cooking you dinner tonight," I respond happily.

I couldn't think of a better way to spend my first paycheck.

"You don't have to do that." He waves me off. "You've got better things to do than cook an old man dinner."

"Actually, no, I don't, so don't argue. It's happening." I smile sweetly at him, making it clear this is not up for discussion.

Grandpa's eyes begin to water, but he doesn't cry. He understands that this is something I need to do to thank him for everything he's done for me in such a short period of knowing me.

"Thank you, Paige. I can't remember the last time I had a home-cooked meal."

"Don't thank me just yet, as I haven't cooked in, well… ever. So we may end up ordering Chinese," I tease.

Hank laughs. "Either way, it doesn't matter. It's the thought that counts."

"It's the least I can do. I owe you."

Hank doesn't realize how much his kindness has meant to me. Someone who never received an ounce of kindness from her own kin now receives it in bucketloads from a stranger.

Hank shuffles to me and places his soft hand on my shoulder, squeezing it lightly.

"You owe me nothing, child. You're a good girl, and I'd be

proud to call you my own."

My eyes water at his choice of words. No one has ever been proud of me. How could they? I haven't done anything in my life to *be* proud of.

But that's going to change.

I'm going to change.

I *am* changing every day. I'm changing into the person I've always wanted to become.

"Thank you, Hank," I reply softly, not able to meet his eyes.

I thank the day I got taken off destiny's shit list, and fate was finally kind to me, leading me to this remarkable man.

I'm zipping around the supermarket, checking my list of ingredients to make pork chops with apple sauce, green beans, and potatoes. Looking up and down the aisles of random shoppers making a simple chore look normal, I envy them.

How do they make this look so easy?

I have been looking at the ingredient *fresh nutmeg* scribbled on my list for the past twenty minutes, wondering where the hell it's kept. I have walked past the packet stuff about ten times, but I'm unsure if there's a difference between fresh and packet. So I decide to follow the ingredients, just in case.

Not looking where I'm going because I just want to get the hell out of here, I run over someone.

"Fuck!" I yelp, looking up from my illegible list, mortified that I have crashed into someone.

"I'm so..." I pause. "Sorry," I finish, looking up at my

victim and sighing.

"Oh, this is so getting into serious stalker territory." Quinn chuckles, his boot braced on the bottom of the shopping cart.

"If I knew it was you, I would have pushed a little harder," I reply smugly, raising an eyebrow.

Sarcasm is my friend and my way of coping with awkward situations like this one.

I can't stop thinking about our encounter in his room last night. Everything about it has thrown me into the deep end, and I'm afraid I'm going to drown.

He clutches at his heart dramatically. "Oh, Red. How your words wound me so."

"Whatever," I reply, ignoring the happy feeling building in my stomach at the sight of him.

I steer the cart around him, but he sidesteps so I can't go any farther.

"So whatcha doing?" he asks, placing his hand on the end of the cart so I can't push him out of the way.

"Trying to shop, but someone is in the way." I fake annoyance, but he sees straight through it.

"Whatcha shopping for?" he asks, not moving an inch, even when a shopper squeezes past us with a handbasket.

I give her an apologetic smile, but she turns her nose up, annoyed that I'm taking up the whole aisle.

I can see Quinn is as stubborn as he is hot. So the quicker I tell him, hopefully the quicker he'll leave me alone.

"I'm looking for fresh nutmeg, but I have seriously walked around this place twice and come up empty," I confess, blowing my hair off my face in exasperation.

Quinn chuckles, his Adam's apple bobbing with the movement. I tell myself to quit it because I need to stop focusing on bullshit like this.

"I just happen to know where that is. Follow me." He smiles and releases his grip on the cart.

"You can just tell me," I retort, not risking a glance at him as I push the cart up the aisle.

Quinn walks beside me with a skip to his step. "Where's the fun in that?" he replies, casually strolling with his hands buried deep in his jeans pockets.

I'm convinced Quinn takes pleasure in torturing me, as he seems to be finding this whole experience comical.

"So what's the special occasion?" he asks, reaching for a bag of Doritos and carelessly tossing them into the cart.

"What occasion?" I ask, looking at the Doritos and shaking my head.

"You cooking?" he replies, pitching a packet of beef jerky next to the Doritos.

"Why does my cooking classify as a special occasion? As far as you know, I might be Martha freakin' Stewart in the kitchen," I reply, turning a corner and walking up the next aisle, blindly following Quinn.

"That might be true, but surely Martha Stewart would know where the nutmeg is kept," he replies, pointing at a rack with a smug smile.

Trying not to look too humiliated as I grab what I need, I quickly toss it into the cart. Checking my list for the other items I require, I scratch my head, wishing I'd chosen a recipe that didn't have a billion different components.

"Here." He snatches the list out of my hand.

"Hey! Gee, rude much?" I playfully shake my head at him.

As his eyes widen and a small smirk tilts at the corners of his lips, I suddenly remember a few embarrassing personal items on the list.

"You're so annoying," I cry, snatching it back from him

while he's laughing his ass off.

I huff, pushing the cart down the aisle away from him. Of course, I can't escape him that easily. He sprints ahead of me, turns to face me, and begins jogging backward.

"Nah, I know you don't mean that," he says, tugging on his lip ring, his arms swinging high by his sides.

"Yes, I really do," I reply half-heartedly, reaching for a bag of apples.

He continues talking to me while running backward, totally blind to the shoppers behind him, but he doesn't seem to care.

"Well, how about you let me take you out so I can prove to you how unannoying I really am?"

"What?" I ask, stopping suddenly, nearly giving myself whiplash with the momentum.

"You heard me." He smirks, thankfully also stopping his backward jogging as he's about to smash into an angry-looking soccer mom.

"No," I reply, shaking my head.

I might appear cool and calm on the outside, but inside, my heart beats frantically against my rib cage.

"And why not?" he asks, cocking his eyebrow mischievously.

"Because I don't know you. You could be a creepy pervert, for all I know," I lamely respond, attempting to sound stern.

"Do I look like a creepy pervert?" he asks, turning in a circle playfully with his arms stretched out wide.

"No," I reply softly as I check out his butt.

"Well, what's the problem, then?" he questions as he takes a small step toward me.

The problem is, you don't want to take me out. The *real* me, that is. If you knew what I did, you wouldn't even want to talk to me.

Think, Mia. You need to shoot him down so he leaves you alone.

Married to Jesus? Ugh, Bible freak.

Genital herpes? Nah, gross.

I settle for the truth. Well, kind of.

"I can't. I have a date tonight," I reply, walking away from him slowly.

"Oh?" His cheeky grin slowly dips into a small scowl as he keeps in step beside me. "Who's the lucky fella?" he asks, and I swear I see his eye twitch.

"Oh, just someone I work with," I reply dismissively.

Blindly reaching for the closest shelf to distract myself from Quinn's probing stare, the first thing my hand passes over are condoms. Pulling my hand away like I've just been burned, I can't help the blush that inches over my cheeks as I bite my lip, totally mortified.

Quinn frowns.

"Well, I better leave you to it then." The playfulness in his voice has gone.

He reaches for his items, snatching them out of the cart as he gives me a stiff-upper-lip smile. "Well, have fun. I'll see you around."

I don't know why, but watching him walk away bothers me. But I have to let it be. This is for the best.

I can't let Quinn in because once I do, I know I'll never want him to leave.

Lugging in all the bags filled with the items I purchased

from the supermarket and plonking them onto my bed, I realize I may have overbought.

I don't cook, but it's not because I don't like to eat.

It's because I never had anyone to share my meals with. It got awfully depressing pretty quickly, sitting alone at age ten in a filthy kitchen, staring at the mac and cheese you prepared for your father, knowing he won't be conscious to appreciate your effort because he has passed out after a three-day bender.

After that, I just gave up.

As I got older, I always grabbed something on the road. Most of the time, it was bland, but it stopped the hunger pains and gave me enough energy to traipse around the streets delivering drugs.

However, after a while, I trained my body not to be hungry. Eating at the same cheap takeout places was like eating cardboard and probably as nutritious as eating dirt. So I ate only when I absolutely had to, and that's why I got so skinny, which I hate.

Changing into a loose Smashing Pumpkins T-shirt, I grab my shopping bags, ready to start on dinner.

I lock my door and trek down the quiet hallway toward the office. Hank said there's a little kitchenette behind the maroon curtain in the office, and I'm welcome to cook our meal there.

Gazing out into the green, grassy terrain, I can't help but think how my life has changed in the span of only a week. It's crazy, but I feel alive. Who would have thought coming here, to a place meant to be boring and quiet, could turn into a place I could happily call my home?

But of course, I can't.

Strolling into the small office, I hear the TV humming behind the curtain.

"Hank?" I call out, pushing the curtain aside carefully as I don't want to barge in, just in case he's sleeping, which I've found him doing on a few occasions.

This time is one of them.

I look around the dim room, which is simple in belongings. But fancy, modern equipment would look out of place in a classic room such as this.

A small TV is propped up on a wooden cabinet, flashing a rerun of *I Love Lucy*, and the ceiling has a few water stains spotted around the corners, but somehow, it seems to match the faded green carpet and white walls. An old wooden dining table for two, which has seen better days, sits in the center of the room and is set with a red tablecloth, which matches the tartan sofa that Grandpa lies upon, snoring softly.

As I watch his chest rise and fall with his soft breathing, I wonder if I look at peace, just like Hank does, when sleeping.

Somehow, I doubt it. My nightmares aren't what one has during a peaceful night's sleep. But I have no one to blame but myself.

Finding the remote lying on the floor, which has slipped from Grandpa's outstretched hand, I mute the TV and tiptoe into the kitchenette. I'm impressed that something so small can hold enough utensils and facilities to prepare a meal.

Scrolling through my iPhone, I find the recipe for tonight's dinner and begin pulling everything out of the shopping bags. Tossing everything onto the small white counter, I take a deep breath, slightly overwhelmed with the task ahead.

I take extra care in reading the directions, wanting everything to be perfect. This is the first meal I've cooked for someone who will appreciate it.

After a few hiccups and nearly slicing my finger in half, I think I've got the hang of this whole cooking thing.

I'm halfway through chopping the apples when I hear Grandpa yawn.

He's finally woken up. I've tried to be quiet, but I guess the clatter of pans and a few choice curse words are enough to wake the dead.

"Hello, child," he says from the doorway.

I spin around and hold back a laugh at the sight of him looking rumpled and fluffy from sleep.

"Good afternoon, sleepyhead."

Grandpa cackles, rubbing his eyes.

"Hey, how do ya think I keep my handsome looks? Gotta get my beauty sleep," he teases while stifling a yawn behind his palm.

I give him a small smile and turn around to continue my chopping.

"What're you making?" Shuffling into the kitchen, he looks over my shoulder but makes sure not to smother me.

"Pork chops with apple sauce, green beans, and roast potatoes. So far, so good." I laugh quietly. "I haven't burned the place down, so that's a start."

Hank chuckles and lets out another muffled yawn.

"Go sit down. Dinner shouldn't be too long." I smile, measuring the ingredients for the apple sauce.

"Let me set the table," Grandpa offers as he reaches into a cupboard against the wall and begins pulling out mismatched crockery.

"You're such a stubborn man," I say, shaking my head at him.

"You sound just like my Betty," he says with a sigh, and as I turn at the waist to look at him, I can see his eyes sadden at the mention of her.

"What happened to her?" I ask cautiously, hoping I haven't overstepped some line.

He holds the blue-and-yellow plates to his chest tightly, a faint smile tugging at his lips as he peers out the small window in front of him.

"She passed three years ago from a heart attack. Fittest thing you'd ever met. But one day, she just didn't feel like her normal morning walk. I thought she was coming down with a cold and was going to call the doc, but she insisted she was fine and told me not to worry about her. She said in her usual, teasing voice, 'Go do your chores, Hank, they ain't gonna do themselves.'"

Grandpa looks like this memory is a bittersweet one. I can imagine he revisits it often, as it's the last memory he has of Betty. But what a sad memory to have.

"I kissed her goodbye," he continues, "and that was the last time I saw her alive."

My hand flies to my mouth. "Oh, Hank, I'm so sorry."

"It's okay, child. The doctor says it was instant, and she didn't suffer. It was just like she went to sleep and never woke up," he replies, trying not to upset me.

"But still, that's a hard thing to deal with," I say, giving him a sympathetic look but not pity.

"It is. But I know my Betty, and she's up there, looking down at me and scolding me for slacking off, telling me to get back to work." He cackles as if he can hear her telling him just that.

"She sounds like an amazing lady," I say with conviction.

"She was. She was the heart of this place. She made sure every room had fresh flowers and chocolates on all the pillows. All those little things she did without a second thought. This motel radiated her love for the place. But now, it's just a sad withered shell of what it used to be."

My heart goes out to Grandpa. I may have never experienced that kind of love before, but I can imagine how much he misses her.

"But I go on, Paige. That's what we do. We have to live for the ones who can't. That's the only way to keep their memory alive."

Looking at the man in front of me, I can't help but wonder about Hank's life. After all the hardships and experiences that have led to this moment, to the here and now, was his life everything he hoped for?

I hope so.

A car door outside interrupts our conversation, and I subtly wipe my eye with the back of my hand. I'm not crying, but my eyes water. Listening to his story—anyone's would.

"I better go see who that is," Grandpa says, wiping his own eyes and leaving me to my thoughts.

Will I ever find anyone as special as Betty was to Hank?

I hope so.

It's not something I've thought much about, but it would be nice to have my own story about how someone touched me as much as Betty did Hank.

I shake my head and brush those nostalgic thoughts aside because I have a dinner to make.

I'm cutting potatoes into quarters when I hear Hank chatting with someone out in the office. I can't make out who he's talking to, but whoever it is, they're making him cackle, so this person is okay in my book.

"Paige?" I hear Grandpa call out. "Is there enough food for another person?"

Looking at the heap of food in front of me, I shout, "Yes, Hank, there's enough to feed a small starving nation."

Hearing him chuckle, he continues talking to whoever's out there.

I look out the small window in front of me and smile when I notice the lace curtains swaying lightly in the breeze. No doubt this was the work of Betty.

I wish I could have met her.

I'm just about to place the potatoes in the oven when I see Grandpa reverse his truck and park it near the shed.

What is he doing?

My questions are answered when I see who Hank was talking to.

Quinn.

The dish I'm holding nearly slips from my fingers when I see him sauntering over to Hank with an old aqua toolbox in hand.

I lean up on the edge of the sink and boost myself forward so I can get a better look at what Quinn is doing here.

Hank pops the hood and Quinn turns his black baseball cap around to prevent his long bangs from spilling into his eyes. He rests the toolbox on the engine and pulls out the tools he requires, then leans under the hood and begins fiddling with God knows what.

As he reaches farther underneath and his T-shirt rides up, exposing a sliver of skin, I find myself involuntarily advancing forward to check out the side of his torso because as he turns to fetch something out of the toolbox, I can see a hint of ink.

Tilting my head to the left to get a better look, it seems

like the tattoo is an extension of something running down the left side of his body and leading into the waistband of his jeans.

He ducks out from under the hood, peering around the side to talk to Hank, who nods, before the engine roars to life.

Quinn stands back, listening to the engine with his hands on his hips, deep in concentration. He motions with his hands to cut the engine, which Hank does. Scratching his chin briefly, he then pokes his head back under the hood, blindly reaching for a tool near him.

The farther he extends into the car, the more I can't stop staring at how good his butt looks and the way his back muscles ripple under his tight T-shirt with each of his movements. Inadvertently, I lean farther and farther over the sink until my forehead basically rests against the curtain to get a closer view.

Thanks to Betty and her knack for interior decorating, I can totally ogle Quinn without him knowing I'm so checking him out right now.

Or so I thought.

He slowly turns at the waist and peers over his shoulder, staring straight at me.

I'm pretty certain I'm cloaked behind the curtain, but now I'm not so sure as his green eyes flicker with humor, looking at the window.

My hands slip off the edge of the sink as I pull away quickly, and I push back from the window to drop into a squat. I'm breathless, and my heart begins beating quickly, doused in adrenaline from being caught.

I wait around thirty seconds, and then I do something silly. I evenly place my hands on the edge of the sink and pull myself up a fraction so the top of my head and eyes are the only things visible through the window.

But Quinn has gone.

His toolbox is still propped up on the engine, but he's not.

And that's because he's standing right behind me.

"Enjoying the view?"

Closing my eyes and cursing under my breath, I don't need to turn around to know that he has a huge, lopsided smirk plastered all over that ridiculously gorgeous face of his.

"I…I lost my nose ring," I reply quickly, lifting myself to full height and turning to face him.

I gasp as my eyes take in the sight of perfection before me.

He looks pointedly at my nose, his eyes shining in amusement as he leans casually in the doorjamb, arms and ankles crossed.

"I found it," I reply, raising a finger to my nose.

I turn my back to him and begin busying myself with dinner, placing the potatoes in the oven, hoping he gets the hint to leave me alone.

He doesn't.

"I thought you had a date," he says, no doubt with that damn smile on his face.

"I do," I reply plainly, not giving anything away.

"Ah, so where is he?" he asks as his boots thud against the kitchen floor.

Avoiding his question, I busy myself with wiping down the counter, but from the corner of my eye, I see Quinn standing a few feet away from me, leaning coolly against the edge.

"So is your date going to care I'm joining you for dinner?" he presses, watching me closely when I don't speak.

"Nope, not at all," I reply quickly, not meeting his eyes. My breath is coming out in labored puffs with him being so near.

"Really?"

"Yup."

Silence.

"When you said you were dating someone you work with, I began thinking of all the people at the diner. The only guy who is half decent and close to your age is my brother," he says after a minute of silence.

I turn quickly, panicked to tell him the truth.

"It's not Tristan," I say speedily, for some reason needing to defend him.

"I know," Quinn replies, wearing a smug smile.

"You do?" I ask, knitting my eyebrows together. "How?"

"Well, as much as I know my brother is dying to get into your pants, he's working tonight, so I know it's not him."

I blanch at his choice of words.

"I'm kidding, Red." He chuckles when witnessing my reaction.

"Oh," I reply, huffing out a relieved breath.

"About him working, not the wanting to get in your pants part," he adds with a wink.

I don't know how to respond, so I do so with sarcasm.

"Nice story. What are you even doing here?"

"That's not a nice way to treat your guest."

"You invited yourself," I retort. "And I'm still trying to figure out why."

He shrugs calmly. "Why not?"

Okay, I may not be in tune with the whole social etiquette thing. But I do know inviting oneself to dinner is normally considered rude. But looking at Quinn, standing in the small kitchen without a care in the world, I know the rules of society don't apply to him.

He's like me in a way. However, where I am new and naive to the dos and don'ts, he just doesn't give a fuck.

"My 'date' is Hank," I confess, making air quotes around the word date.

Quinn smirks, reaching for a sliced apple and popping it into his mouth. "Well, be kind to the old man. He'll have a heart attack dealing with a girl like you."

"Eww!" I slap his arm. "First, gross. And second, there's no one I would rather share a date with than him."

Quinn looks taken aback by my confession, but he quickly recovers with a joke. "I should be offended, seeing as I'm standing right here. But since it's Hank, I'll let it slide. If you're going to 'date' anyone, I'd rather it be Hank," he says, which throws me off.

"But not your brother?" I ask quickly for some stupid reason.

I regret the words as soon as they leave my mouth, and I hurriedly reach for an apple to distract myself. Quinn clutches my wrist softly, stopping me from moving…or breathing.

He leans forward and slowly inches toward my face while toying with his lip ring. "My brother couldn't handle you."

"And you could?" I whisper back with bated breath.

He looks me straight in the eyes and replies huskily, "You know I could."

He still has a firm but tender grip around my wrist and tightens his fingers to emphasize his point.

Why aren't I recoiling like I usually would? Why don't I have a smart-ass reply to knock him down a peg or two? Why does the thought of him "handling" me make me quiver?

"Everything okay, kids?" Hank asks as he shuffles into the kitchen, eyeing us curiously.

Quinn turns at the waist to face Grandpa, his hand still

searing my skin. "Yes. I was just telling Red to go easy on you."

Grandpa cackles. "Oh, Quinn Berkeley, you've always been a troublemaker. You need a good clip around the ears. I need to have a word with your mother," Grandpa says, not looking at us as he reaches for three glasses in the cabinet.

I feel Quinn's fingers stiffen on my wrist at the mention of his mom, and I wonder why.

He clears his throat, releasing my wrist abruptly before he says, "I better go finish checking out your truck."

So that's why he's here.

He's looking at Hank's truck because, knowing Grandpa, he wants to make sure it's safe because I'm driving it now.

Quinn pops a piece of apple into his mouth, licking the fallen juice from his lips. He steals one final look at me over his shoulder before leaving.

Only then do I breathe.

After placing everything in the center of the small table, I look at my handiwork and must admit it doesn't look too bad. The potatoes are a little burned, and the beans are a bit limp, but overall, it's not a total disaster.

I hope it tastes okay.

Grandpa is pouring himself a glass of cider when Quinn comes out of the kitchen, drying his hands on a dishcloth.

"Smells awesome, Red," he says, pulling up a plastic chair near me.

"Thanks. Hopefully, it tastes awesome."

Once we're all settled, Grandpa clears his throat.

"Would it be okay if I said grace?"

I've never been a big believer in God or religion…how could I? For my whole life, I prayed for my dad to stop getting high, and I prayed for my mom to return and make everything okay again. My prayers obviously went unanswered because the more I prayed, the worse things got. After a while, I just stopped altogether. He wasn't listening, so I stopped talking. I mean, how many times can you go unnoticed before you lose faith?

Quinn nods, and Grandpa looks at me for approval.

"Sure," I reply softly. It makes no difference to me.

Grandpa interlaces his hands and slightly bows his head.

"Thank you for this meal we're about to eat. And thank you for allowing me to share this meal with two wonderful people. But most of all, thank you for Paige."

My eyes snap up to meet Grandpa as I'm stunned by what he's thankful for.

"Amen," Quinn mutters softly.

We're all silent until Grandpa announces, "Let's eat." He reaches for the pork chops, oblivious that he just paid me the sweetest compliment of my life.

Quinn, however, is well aware of it, and he softly reaches for my hands twisting in my lap under the table, stilling them under his.

I risk a glance at him, and he greets me with a genuine smile.

A smile that tells me he knows.

We eat in silence, the TV the background noise we need.

Dinner turns out okay because twenty minutes later, Quinn and Hank have polished off everything I laid out on the table, and I hate to admit, the sight makes me feel good.

I think both Quinn and Hank know I'm running away from something, so they've kept the conversation light.

I'm elbow deep in soap suds when Quinn places a few dirty dishes on the counter beside me.

"I said I was happy to wash up," he says, grabbing a clean dish towel as he commences drying the dishes.

"It's okay. I don't mind."

This mundane chore is one that makes me feel normal, and I would wash a hundred more if it meant this feeling of normalcy remained.

We're quiet for a long while, both deep in thought, but the silence isn't uncomfortable, it's reflective. We work side by side, me washing and Quinn drying, and it's nice to just hang with someone. Only the low snoring of Grandpa in the next room breaks through the silence, but it's not bothersome. It's a nice sound as it reminds me that I'm not alone.

After I finish washing the last dish, Quinn tosses the dish towel onto the counter and reaches for my wrist.

I look up at him, stunned and confused. "What are you doing?"

Quinn, however, doesn't reply. He only pulls me away from the sink and leads me toward the door.

I shrink out of his loose grip and pull back. "Where are we going?"

My hands are still sopping wet and dripping onto the kitchen floor.

Quinn turns at the waist, smiling openly.

"Live a little, Red. Trust me?" he asks, extending his hand out toward me.

The simple gesture shouldn't leave me anxious and troubled, but it does.

"Trust me, Red."

This time, however, it's not a question. It's a promise.

I work my lower lip feverishly, eyeing his outstretched

palm fearfully. I have never trusted another human being in my entire life.

Can I trust Quinn? A stranger.

As my eyes meet his, I see nothing sinister or cruel in them, so I take a small breath and slip my hand into his.

Trust has never felt so good.

We walk silently hand in hand, tiptoeing through the living area where Grandpa has passed out on the couch, the TV flashing shadows across his relaxed face.

It must be nice to sleep so peacefully.

Stopping and slipping my hand out of Quinn's, I silently reach for an afghan thrown across the back of the sofa. I tuck it around Grandpa, and he stirs, snuggling into the blanket contentedly.

I turn back to Quinn, who's watching me with an unreadable look. I give him a small, embarrassed smile, and he returns it quickly before reaching for my hand again and tightly interlacing our fingers.

I look down at our union and then back up at him, and all I see reflected is warmth and sincerity.

Without a word, we walk through the small living room and out through the front door.

The cool night breeze is welcome against my cheeks due to the heat I feel from my palm sitting snugly in Quinn's. The air smells of rain, which is typical for fall. I've always been a fan of fall. Something is inspirational at the sight of big orange leaves catching on the breeze, swinging backward and forward until they can no longer remain attached to the branch they dangle from. As they tumble to join their fallen brothers on the frosty ground, you can smell new beginnings lingering in the air.

I wish it were that easy for me.

We're still silent as we hit the gravel, and the only sound that can be heard is the stones crunching under our sneakers.

With my hand enclosed in Quinn's, I allow him to lead me blindly to God knows where. But I'm not anxious or worried. I'm more curious as to where he's taking me.

He leads me up around the corner of the motel and begins trekking up a hill.

"Hey, where are we going?" I ask, holding tightly on to his hand.

Quinn chuckles. "You'll see. We're nearly there."

The farther we walk, the higher up we climb, the steeper the terrain. My worn-out soles offer me no grip, and I keep slipping. Thankfully, Quinn grasps his hand harder around mine to offer me support.

With my other hand, I inadvertently latch onto Quinn's wrist to stabilize myself when I slip.

"C'mon, Red, toughen up," he jokes, never faltering in his step.

Even though he appears nonchalant, I can see him peer over his shoulder every so often to make sure I'm keeping up and that I'm okay.

The sentiment, for some reason, touches me.

When we finally reach the top, Quinn releases my hand, staring off into the distance. I wonder what has captured his attention, so I turn and gasp when I see what he's looking at.

The lights of South Boston flicker before me, and the sight is quite beautiful. Being this high up, I feel like I have a bird's-eye view of the town. I can't make out one single person or event, but my mind fills in the blanks and begins envisioning all kinds of images, and I smile at the normality of it.

"It's amazing. We're so high up," I comment, my eyes still taking in everything before me.

Quinn doesn't speak but dusts off his hands and sits on the ground, his knees drawn up toward him. I feel silly standing, so I sit near him, my eyes never leaving the city below me.

Seeing the town from up here, at a different perspective, where everything looks so tiny and simple, I wish I could stay up here forever. I can almost forget that down there lays the truth of who I am and what I did. Up here, I can almost pretend I'm just a normal nineteen-year-old without a dark past that will catch up with me one day.

"Can I ask you something?"

"Sure," I reply, drawing my knees up toward me and hugging them.

"Do you ever think, what's the point?"

"What's the point to what?" I ask, resting my chin on my hands and turning to look at him.

The moonlight bounces off his reflective eyes as he weighs up his next sentence.

"The point to everything. To life. To why we try so hard when no one seems to give a damn. Looking down there," he says, gesturing with his chin to the town beneath us, "is a town full of people who smile and go about their daily lives like it's easy. Like living every day is effortless, and they don't go to sleep wondering what's the point to living when all it does is hurt."

I don't know what to say because Quinn has just summed up how I feel every second of every day. I know Quinn also has demons locked inside him, waiting to break free in a moment of weakness.

"I think we just go on because what other alternative do we have? Either we can give up or we can fight. And you don't look like a quitter to me," I say, studying him. "So we push on and we live the best way we can, hoping that one day we'll find the purpose to our existence."

Quinn nods, taking in everything I just said. "So have you found your purpose yet?"

I look back out into the starless sky, the only thing lighting it up are the lights below.

"No, but I'm trying. And I'll be damned if life gets the better of me a second longer than it already has."

This is the first time I have openly expressed how I feel to anyone. But I feel stupid for opening my mouth, and I begin closing in on myself.

"Hey, don't do that. Don't ever feel stupid for being honest. Especially with me," he adds with sincerity.

I don't know what it is about him, but I feel comfortable around him and trust him. The thought of trying to stay away from him fades little by little. I know I'm in trouble, but I just can't stay away.

"Red...what are you running from?" he whispers earnestly, afraid I'll blow up in his face or run away.

I sigh, surprised I don't flinch or break into a sprint when asked a question that weighs so heavily on me.

Peering into Quinn's deep-green eyes, I realize I have never felt this connection with a single soul.

"I can't tell you."

"Why not?" he asks. "We all have our demons. I would never judge you. I just want to..."

"You want to what?" I ask, suddenly curious about what he's about to say.

"There's something about you, and I just can't stay away. But I don't want to freak you out or push you too hard. But the more I get to know you, the deeper I fall. You're not like anyone I've ever met before, and I just want to get to know you, the *real* you," he confesses, and I know his admission was hard to make.

Call it intuition, but I know he has baggage, just like me. Fair to say his baggage is probably not as fucked up as mine, but that doesn't make it any less significant. But I can't do this. This wasn't the plan. I was to come here and be invisible, not make friends or feel…this. I don't even know what this feeling is, but I know it will only lead to trouble.

I stand quickly, feeling too exposed and vulnerable under his penetrating gaze.

"I've gotta go," I respond in quickened breaths.

"What? Why?" he asks, standing up promptly, afraid he's said something wrong.

"I just have to," I reply vaguely and make a run for it when I witness the sting in his eyes.

Of course, at that precise moment, the sky decides to open up and pour down on me as I attempt to maneuver down a hill and not break my neck. Quinn calls out behind me, but I don't stop. His echoing voice sends me charging down the hill faster, not caring that the rain impairs my vision and I have to squint to see.

"Red! Stop! Let me help you."

My feet have a mind of their own as they quicken in panic, afraid of what will happen if Quinn catches up to me. The rain pelts down around me, turning the grass into a slippery sludge, but I can't stop.

Thankfully, the ground becomes flatter, and I jump down, landing on the even ground, making a mad dash for my room. I can hear Quinn close behind, and that only sends my already thumping heart into a symphony of unhealthy, piercing beats.

Quinn's shoes crunch loudly over the gravel, and I smell him before I feel him pull me into his soaked, breathless chest.

"Stop running," he says, panting deeply.

And I know there's a double meaning behind his words.

He wraps a strong arm around my small waist, pinning my back to his front, stopping me from wriggling out of his grip. We are both sopping wet, and as the rain pounds heavily around us, Quinn doesn't let go. He doesn't move me under the safety of the walkway or shelter me from the punishing rain.

And because of that, I have never felt so protected, so safe as I do in his arms.

"Trust me," he whispers, his soft breath brushing along my neck and cheek.

I shiver with the sensation of his hot breath warming my cold, wet skin.

"I want to," I reply honestly, closing my eyes.

"Then do it. I promise you, I will never hurt you. I will fucking cut out my own tongue if I say anything to hurt you."

I can't help but soften at his words. No one has ever cared if their words have wounded me or caused me pain.

"Give me a chance…please."

And before I have a second to process what he's doing, I feel his wet lips press a light kiss over my frantic pulse. The kiss isn't seedy or presumptuous, it's chaste and heartfelt.

But I don't reply because this is all too much. And Quinn mistakes my silence for aversion.

"Get inside before you catch a cold." He sighs, not allowing me to comment on his previous admission.

And with that, he leaves me standing sopping wet in the pelting rain.

But I am not cold; I am far from it.

Ten

"Mia, get down here!" my dad calls out while I pace upstairs, waiting for him to tell me what the hell is happening.

When my dad told me to dress nicely because he had a surprise, I did what any daughter would do and listened.

I don't own anything "nice," so I settled for my short denim skirt and lace camisole. That's the nicest thing I own—how sad.

My heart is in my throat as I thump down the basement steps, unsure of what I'm about to be confronted with. Maybe, just maybe, he's about to tell me he's finally coming clean. I cross my fingers behind my back, hoping this is how our conversation will go.

Sadly, it doesn't.

As I peer around the basement, I raise my eyebrow in

confusion. The room has been converted into a makeshift bedroom, with a small, single dirty bed sitting off into the far corner of the room.

Maybe my dad plans to go cold turkey and sweat it out down here. Makes sense. I suddenly can't wipe the smile off my face.

"Daddy?" I ask when I see him standing ominously with his hands behind his back. "What's going on?"

I can't help the endearment that slips past my lips. The thought of my father sobering up and kicking the habit transforms me into a little girl wearing rose-tinted glasses.

"Mia, come here," he says gently, and of course I oblige.

Looking into his sunken eyes, I hope the next words that come out of his mouth will change my life forever.

And they do.

"Mia, I need you to do something for me."

"What?" I ask suspiciously as I look over at the bed and back at him.

"I need you to help me, Mia. I need you to take care of me."

"I do take care of you," I answer. Suddenly, my throat feels like I'm swallowing lead.

"I know you do, but Phil and I—"

As soon as I hear Phil's name pass through his lips, I know nothing good can come from this conversation.

"No. Whatever you have planned—no, Dad. I'm not doing it…I've done enough for you!" I scream, my hands shaking in fear.

My father cocks his head to the side and reveals what he has hidden behind his back.

A revolver.

"What the fuck?" I ask, my breath leaving me winded as I

eye the gun he's aiming toward my chest.

"This isn't negotiable. Phil will be here in five minutes with someone willing to pay big bucks for you. A virgin as pretty as you, Mia, will be very valuable to me and Phil."

Tears spring to my eyes, and I hate when one betrayal tear slips down my cheek and into my parted lips.

This is the last time I will cry.

"What are you talking about?" I ask, my chest rising and falling quickly.

My father takes a menacing step toward me, and it takes all my willpower not to buckle and show him fear. He slides the nose of the gun down my throat and dips it between my breasts.

I close my eyes in revulsion and swallow the bile creeping up my throat.

"Me and Phil, we made a deal. We both think you'd be a lot more valuable spreading your legs instead of using them to drag your lazy ass around the streets of LA."

The realization of what my dad proposes hits home, and I sway, having to hold the wall for support.

"How could you? I'm your daughter!" I sob angrily, not caring that I'm openly weeping and showing weakness.

"You are *her* daughter," he sneers. "Nothing but a whore, just like your momma!"

I sniffle, not understanding what he means by that, but I don't have time to think of anything but getting the hell out of here.

Think, Mia, get him talking. Distract him.

"What's in it for you?" I ask, wiping my fallen tears away with the back of my hand.

My father waves the gun as he explains.

"Phil can use the basement to conduct his business out

of…"

"You mean use it as a brothel!" I shout, trying to buy time.

"Call it what you want, Mia, but you're doing this. The sooner you get used to the idea, the easier it will be for everyone. You don't have a choice. You don't do this, then you cease to exist."

I stare at my father, my mouth agape. Did he just threaten to…kill me?

My father continues like he didn't just threaten my life. "Phil gets paid a lot more using your body than he would with you just delivering his stuff. And in return, I get an endless supply of all the dope I need and maybe make some money out of it, too."

In the end, it comes down to greed.

Both my father's and Phil's.

Over my dead body. There is no way I'm doing this.

No more.

"Don't worry, princess," my dad adds softly, totally flipping a switch. "You'll get paid too, baby. Phil will take good care of you. He can't have his number-one girl being a mess. You won't have to work late nights delivering dope and putting yourself in dangerous situations. Those days are over, baby."

I cannot believe it. My father is trying to justify prostituting me out to strangers, behaving like it's in my best interest to do this.

He is so far gone, and I haven't even realized it.

As I look into the eyes of the man I used to call my father, I know the man I used to love is gone and replaced with a sick, twisted monster. Or maybe he always was, and I just chose to believe he would change.

I have no other choice than to put him out of his misery.

"Okay, Daddy, I'll do it," I say in a small voice, trying my best not to vomit in revulsion.

I watch my father's face radiate happiness, but only because I've submitted to his sickening plan of using his daughter in a way no parent should.

He lowers his hand and opens his arms for me to hug him. I feel sick. I actually feel if I live through this, I'm going to be one warped, bitter individual.

I take a step toward him and pretend to trip over my feet.

It all happens in a matter of seconds, but those seconds, I swear, are in slow motion.

Pulling my Colt 911 out of my right combat boot with lightning-quick speed, I press the barrel into his chest before he can move.

My father's eyes widen, and he attempts to raise his gun, but I shove the barrel into his chest, shouting wordlessly that I'm not joking. I will fucking shoot him if he moves.

"Drop the gun, or I *will* shoot you," I say, never breaking eye contact with him.

"How could you? After everything I've done for you, you ungrateful little whore!" my father sneers, spittle coating my face.

I don't have time to explain that he has done *nothing* to help me. I've survived all of this because of me, no one other than me.

"Drop the gun!" I shout, cocking the trigger.

He raises a hand in the air in surrender and slowly lowers the gun to the ground.

He gradually stands and mocks me.

"What are you going to do now? You gonna shoot an unarmed man?" he spits, his eyes narrowing in rage.

I kick the gun, and it skids across the floor, away from my father's dangerous hands.

"No, I'm leaving. I'm doing something I should have done a long time ago. I was stupid to think you'd ever change and do anything for anyone other than yourself. No wonder Mom left you," I spit out, walking backward, my gun still aimed at his chest.

"Good, go. I don't need you!" he screams. "You're just like her." He grinds his jaw, and I know when he looks at me, all he sees is my mother.

"I would rather be like her than a pathetic excuse of a person like you." I snicker, still walking backward.

In hindsight, it probably was not the best thing to do in a basement since basements are usually filled with junk. Junk that one can easily trip over and lose one's balance, which is what happens.

I stumble over a discarded box and lose my footing for a second, but that's all it takes. In that second, my father dives for his gun, aims it at my head, and shoots.

Luckily for me, my father has always been a lousy aim, so he misses, the bullet embedding into the wall behind me. But as he lines up the gun, ready to pull the trigger again, I know he has a better shot. So I raise my gun and shoot.

And I don't miss.

My bullet rips into my father's stomach, and he stumbles back a few feet from the momentum. He stares down at his white T-shirt, a look of confusion spreading across his ashen face as the white material begins coloring to a bright red. He looks up at me, his mouth opening and closing slowly before he drops to his knees and crumples into an injured heap, bleeding out steadily.

I stare at the sight before me and freeze. Holy fuck, what have I just done? I never meant to shoot him. *Or did I?*

I have to get out of here because the neighbors were

bound to have heard the gunshots. And Phil is minutes away from turning up with my "customer." But before I leave, I have to ensure that what I did is real.

As I take two small steps toward my father, who lies prone, his eyes staring up at the ceiling, I lean forward and peer over him. The small shallow breaths he's taking and the way his chest jerks intermittently indicate he's dying.

A lone tear rolls down my cheek as I watch my father fade before my eyes. He turns his head toward me, meeting my eyes with pure wrath in his. And at that moment, I know I did the right thing because it was either me or him.

I give my father one final glance and back away from him. "Mia."

It's faint, but as I hear my name pass through the lips of the man I once called Daddy, I know that I too have died with him on that cold basement floor.

"Fuck you."

Well, today officially blows.

After my lack of sleep because of the worst possible nightmare, I'm stomping around room 4, ready to stab anyone in my way.

Of course, the couple I'm cleaning up after had to be the kinkiest fuckers known to humankind. Random condom wrappers are pitched all over the room, and bathroom, and... closet.

Last night still plays on my mind, and no matter how hard I try to stop thinking about Quinn, it just seems to have the opposite effect.

Did he mean everything he said? Can I really trust him? Do I want to? I think I need to figure out that answer before I get caught in the rain with him again.

I groan when I see a hint of blue poking out from under the green rug—another condom wrapper.

I don't get it. What's the big thing about sex? Fair to say, I've never had it, so I shouldn't comment, but it can't be *that* good, can it?

Thinking back to the way Quinn felt, holding my trembling body against his firm chest, and how that alone gave me dirty images I'm ashamed to revisit. Maybe with the right person, it really *is*. But I wouldn't know, and I'm afraid to ask. Who would I ask anyway?

I toe the rug, lifting it with the edge of my Chucks to slide the wrapper out, when suddenly, a bug comes lazily crawling out from underneath.

My eyes pop out of my head, and I hightail it out of room 4 on the verge of hysteria. In my panic, I bump into Grandpa carrying a stack of white towels.

"Where's the fire?" He cackles.

"Hank, you seriously need to do something about this bug issue," I say, trying to stop my voice from turning shrill.

Grandpa frowns and slowly nods. "I know, child, it's on my to-do list. I'll call the exterminators today."

"Great. Good. You should move it up to number one on your list of priorities."

He finds my phobia hilarious as he looks at me over the stack of towels.

"They're probably a lot more scared of you than you are of them."

"Well, they have a lot more legs and eyes than I do, so I think my fear is a little more warranted than theirs," I reply, shaking in revulsion at the thought of their endless legs and beady eyes.

"What time are you working today?" he asks as I creep into room 4 to make sure the bug is nowhere to be seen.

"I start at two. Why?"

"Because the motel will have to be vacated overnight if I get it exterminated," he replies, his keys jingling as he shuffles into the bathroom and places a new towel on the rack. "I'll see if they can come in a couple of days."

"It's okay, you just book a time and I'll sort something out," I reply, not wanting to put Hank out.

"You can always stay with my friend, Barry. That's where I'll end up," he says with a crinkled smile. "I'm sure Barry will love to brag to his friends how a young lady like you will be staying with him. Of course, he'll leave out the part where I'll be staying there also."

I can't help but laugh. "It's fine, really. I'll make some arrangements." Hank has done more than enough for me, so I refuse to let him worry about yet another thing.

"Okay, child. Have a good day at work. I'll call and let you know about the extermination."

Where can I stay? I could always find another motel, but I know how much they cost, and with money being as tight as it is, it just feels like money wasted.

This is just another reason I owe Grandpa so much. He has opened his home to me and given me so much more than a place to stay. He's given me a place I can call home.

My shift at the diner is crazy, as usual. I don't understand where all these people come from. Maybe they're just like me and passing through. However, the more time I spend here, the harder it is for me to remember that.

"What are you doing tonight?" Tabitha asks as I refill the sugar canisters.

"Um, not too sure yet," I reply, not wanting to let on that I may be homeless for the evening.

I still haven't heard from Grandpa, so I'm pretty certain he has stuck true to his word and scheduled the exterminators to come in a couple of days, giving me enough time to arrange a place to crash.

"Did you want to go shopping?" Tabitha asks, giving me big, puppy dog eyes.

Shopping? Really? I couldn't think of anything more torturous. But as I look at Tabitha, her full, lower lip pushed out in a pout, I crumple.

"Okay, could be fun."

Tabitha squeals, throwing her arms around my neck. I'm actually proud to admit I don't totally freak out now when she hugs me.

Who would have thought?

"Tabitha, this is kind of…pink," I say, looking down at the top Tabitha insisted I try on while she sits in front of me in the changing room, examining me closely.

I only did so to humor her, but now I wish I hadn't because I know she won't let me leave until I buy this or its bright-blue sister.

I straighten out the hem of the strapless top and scrunch

up my nose when it falls flat across my measly chest. "Um… is there something a little less pink and not so…revealing?" I ask, not wanting to offend Tabitha.

Tabitha cackles. "I never took you for a prude."

I open my mouth to protest but close it a second later because I guess I am a little prudish. I never had time to shop back home, and well, honestly, I would look ridiculous in a pink number like this while walking the seedy streets of LA.

"Okay, how about this one?" Tabitha asks as she flings another three tops my way.

Thankfully, they look a little less pink and not so booby.

Clutching them to my chest, I duck behind the curtain to try them on.

"This is so fun!"

I hate to admit it, but it is kind of fun. Every time I doubt Tabitha's idea of "fun," I'm proven wrong.

While I fiddle with some clip thing on the top and curse under my breath, Tabitha asks, "Everything okay?"

"Yeah, all good," I reply, not wanting her to barge in as I'm standing in just my bra and denim shorts.

I let another string of profanities fly out, and Tabitha giggles. "Watch out, I'm coming in."

Before I have time to decline or cover myself up, she comes storming in, sliding the curtain across the rod with serious force.

"Oh God!" I yelp, dropping the top to the changeroom floor and lamely covering myself with my hands.

"Oh, Paige, please. I have boobs, too." She looks at me and giggles, but stops laughing however when she looks down at my beige bra.

"Oh my God, please tell me you're wearing your laundry day underwear."

Wrapping my arms around myself tighter, totally embarrassed, I fess up. "I don't know what that is, but this is my only decent bra."

"Nooo?" she says, eyes wide and her mouth open in disbelief.

When I don't reply, she closes her mouth.

"You're serious? No offense, but my grandma has sexier underwear."

I shrug, not getting what the big deal is.

"Stay there," she says and ducks out behind the curtain, leaving a whoosh of wind behind her at how fast she exited.

I don't get it. Who cares what I wear underneath my clothes? I don't even care what I wear on the outside.

Tabitha is back within a minute and once again forgets all about personal space as she pulls the curtain open and strolls in, hands filled with all kinds of underwear.

She dumps them onto the bench seat and picks up the lacy red bra sitting on top of the mountain of goods.

"No way!" I say, shaking my head and waving my finger at her. "There is no way I'm wearing that. It's see-through!"

Tabitha laughs, caressing the soft material between her fingers. "C'mon, Paige, live a little."

I flinch when she uses the same phrase that Quinn did last night.

A surge of confidence sweeps over me, and I yank the bra out of her hands defiantly. "Fine, I'll try it on."

Tabitha claps her hands and takes a seat, watching me.

"Um, are you going to stay in here?" I ask, looking at her bashfully.

Tabitha finds my shyness hilarious and laughs loudly.

"Oh, okay, sheesh," she says after a minute of giggling and covers her eyes with her hand.

Good enough for me, so I quickly strip off my bra and toss it to the floor. I slip the fiery red number on, adjusting the straps and making sure I'm done up before I mumble self-consciously, "Okay, you can look."

Tabitha removes her hand, and it drops to her lap with a thud. Her mouth falls open, and she nods quickly, her eyes wide in excitement.

"Hot!" she yelps, clapping enthusiastically and bouncing up and down on her seat. "If you don't buy it, I'm buying it for you!"

I shake my head. "No, you will not."

I won't have her buying me underwear even though I know she can afford it; that's beside the point.

Looking at myself in the mirror, I don't look half bad, and my boobs…wow, I have some.

"Why are my"—I point down at my chest, still looking at them in the mirror—"so…perky?"

Tabitha cackles and holds her sides in laughter. "You are so fun to shop with! It's a maximizer bra."

"A what?"

"Never mind. Here, try this one on." She ruffles through the pile and pulls out a plain black satin one. "This one is a push-up bra."

"A what?"

"Trust me," she says with a sinister smile. "You think they look perky now? Just wait until you try this one on."

Thirty minutes later, I leave the store with three different bras, all with matching underwear. They didn't cost as much as they usually would because Tabitha had some store loyalty card, so I got twenty percent off everything. That's why I could justify buying all three pairs.

As we sit in the food court, Tabitha talking her way

through dinner, I realize what a good time I'm having. I never thought I would enjoy doing something as ordinary as shopping, but I am.

"We still have lots of other stores to visit," Tabitha says, waving her fork at me menacingly.

Giving her a small smile, I take a bite of my burger, as I have no intention of arguing with her.

We're silent for a moment, and my mind wanders to the condom wrapper I saw this morning and my thoughts about sex. Maybe I could…

"Spit it out." Tabitha smirks, her bright eyes shining with knowledge.

I shrug, suddenly feeling stupid and wishing I wasn't so transparent.

"Ooh, it's got to do with a boy!" Tabitha says, resting her fork against the rim of her plate and steepling her fingers excitedly.

"Not *a* boy," I reply. Well, it does, but not just him. "It's about all boys, and well, their…"

"Penises!" Tabitha shouts, filling in the blanks.

A table of older women turn to look at us, giving us serious stink eye, but Tabitha ignores them.

"What about them? Boys, not penises." She giggles, needing to clarify what she's referring to.

I playfully roll my eyes at her, and she suddenly gets all serious.

"I'm no expert, but I can try my best," she says sincerely. Suddenly, I feel like a total ass bringing this up since I know her experience with sex has been anything but pleasant, thanks to Brad, the a-hole.

"I don't know, how does it…feel or work?" I mumble, falling over my words uncomfortably.

Tabitha bites her lip to stop herself from laughing.

"Oh, never mind," I say quickly, waving off the topic and stuffing my face with fries to stop myself from further embarrassment.

Tabitha shakes her head, her long red hair swaying with the motion.

"No, I'm sorry. I'm not laughing at you, Paige. I'm just laughing because I'm happy."

"You're happy that I'm an uneducated moron?" I toss a fry at her.

Tabitha catches the fry and tosses it back at me.

"No, I just meant I have never had *this* before. I've never had a friend like you…ever."

Her confession touches me, so I decide to fess up.

"Want to know a secret?" I say, indicating with my fingers for her to come closer.

She nods, leaning into me.

"Me neither."

A big, dimpled smile spreads across her rosy cheeks, and she's quiet—a first for her.

After a few minutes of us finishing our meals, she whispers, "It hurts."

"What does?" I ask, swirling my fries into a pile of ketchup.

"Sex."

"Oh," I reply with a frown, kind of disappointed. "What's the hype about then?"

Tabitha shrugs. "I'm not sure. It might feel different with someone who cares about you, but for me, it hurt, and I hated it."

As I clench my fists, my blood begins to boil because I realize I'm actually angry for her. And I feel like using Brad's face as a punching bag.

And that gives me an idea.

"Tabitha, have you ever boxed?"

Tabitha shakes her head, looking a little afraid.

"Do you want to come to the gym with me and give it a go?"

Tabitha understands my train of thought and nods happily. "Fuck yeah!"

I can't help the laughter that bubbles out of my throat. Maybe this friendship thing isn't as hard as I thought it would be because I have the right person I want to be friends with.

"Here's trouble."

Tabitha and I both look up to see a smiling Tristan hovering above us.

Tabitha subtly fixes her hair, and I narrow my eyes at her as I witness her blush slightly. If I didn't know better, I'd say Tabitha is totally crushing on Tristan.

But who wouldn't? I mean, look at him.

Wearing black jeans and a tight charcoal T-shirt, with all that messy hair falling into those hypnotic eyes, who wouldn't have a major crush on this sweetheart?

"Hi, Tristan." I smile as he pulls up a seat, sitting near me.

"Whatcha girls talking about?" he asks, which sends Tabitha into a further blush.

I laugh and shake my head. "Oh, trust me, you don't want to know."

"Okay. So what are you doing now?" he asks, looking at me and then at Tabitha.

We both shrug, and Tristan smirks, and I swear, I hear about five girls sigh in lust, Tabitha included. How the hell have I missed this? Maybe it was there all along, and I just didn't know what to look for. Maybe I really am getting better at being normal.

"Well, did you want to come watch *Pulp Fiction* with me?" He smiles. "They're showing it as part of a Tarantino marathon."

Tabitha looks at me, nodding eagerly. I know she's asking me to please come along because she wants to spend every minute she can with him.

"Sure, why not."

Done with our food, we make our way to the movie theater.

As we're waiting in line to buy our tickets, I subtly check Tristan out from the corner of my eye. I'm only doing this because I can see the similarities between him and Quinn now that I know they're brothers.

I've been dying to ask where Quinn is, but I don't.

But fate, in a morbid way, looks down on me as Amber appears out of nowhere, latching onto Tristan's arm.

"Hey, hottie."

Tristan pulls his arm out of her claws and takes a step closer to me to get away from her.

She looks just as trashy tonight as when I saw her last. She's wearing jeans that are basically painted on. And the blue top she's wearing barely covers anything.

"Where's your brother?" she asks, eyeballing me.

I take a step closer to Tristan, ready to claw her eyeballs out if she says another word about Quinn, which is totally irrational.

"I don't know, Amber. I'm not his keeper," Tristan replies, making it more than obvious he has no time for her.

"What is with the Berkeley brothers being so untouchable?"

"Maybe we just don't want *you* touching us."

I choke back a laugh, impressed with Tristan's insults.

Amber ignores me, knowing what happened the last time we spoke.

"I didn't hear your brother complaining last night."

That wipes the smile off my face. Last night? That's impossible. I was with him last night. But I wasn't with him *all* night.

I haven't heard from him all day, and I admit, I was kind of hoping he would magically appear at work, especially after last night. Is the reason he's been MIA standing right in front of me? That thought turns my stomach, and suddenly, I feel like I'm about to hurl.

"Hey, guys," Tabitha says, walking over, phone in hand.

She looks at Amber, then at me with wide eyes. I just shake my head and subtly roll my eyes, hoping she gets my facial charades.

Luckily, she does.

"Anyway," Amber purrs, running a manicured finger down Tristan's chest. "Tell Quinn hi."

"Tell him yourself!" he says, smacking her hand away, giving her a nice view of his back.

She leaves in a huff, and we all kind of stand around awkwardly for a second or two.

"So I hate to be a wet blanket, but my mom wants me home, like now," Tabitha says, frowning.

I know her mother is the Queen Tyrant, and when her mother wants her home, Tabitha is not to keep her waiting.

"Sorry, Paige," she says, looking at me sheepishly. "But we gotta leave in like thirty seconds; otherwise, World War Three will break out."

"That's okay, Tabitha. I can just walk home. I'm out of your way, and I don't want your mom chewing out your ass over me."

Tristan looks back and forth between us and kindly offers, "I can take you home, Paige. If you wanted to, I mean, after the movie."

Seeing a movie is the last thing I want to do after Amber's admission, so I politely decline. "No, it's cool. I might split now anyway."

Tristan looks slightly disappointed, and Tabitha just looks plain guilty.

"It's fine, guys. I don't mind walking," I say, looking at them both with a small smile.

"No!" Tristan and Tabitha shout at the same time.

I hide a smile, and we exit the line so the people behind us can take our spot.

"You're not walking by yourself," Tabitha says, shaking her head quickly as we make our way to the elevators.

"I'll be fine," I stubbornly argue while pushing the call button in haste.

"No way, I'll take you," Tristan says as the elevator doors open, and we step inside.

"What are you doing? I thought you wanted to see the movie?"

"It's not important. Getting you home safely is."

I know this argument is not worth disputing. Judging by the hard set of Tristan's jaw, he's not changing his mind.

We quickly exit the elevator, and Tabitha gives me a big hug goodbye before sprinting to her car. I can hear her phone echo in the distance, no doubt her mother beckoning her home.

I follow Tristan closely as I have no idea what he drives, but his means of transport is the least of my problems as I can't stop thinking about Amber and Quinn.

Amber and Quinn…naked.

The thought makes me gag, and I begin coughing loudly, thumping my chest to swallow past the lump currently sitting in my windpipe.

"Are you okay?" Tristan kindly questions as he stops quickly, reaching for my arm to steady me.

"Fine."

We reach an old Ford pickup.

"Nice ride," I say, running my hand over the black side panels.

"Thanks. Wish it was mine. Quinn let me borrow it," he says, not knowing I have just secretly sighed at the mention of his name.

Tristan opens the passenger door, which eases open with a sexy smoothness—just like its owner.

As soon as I take a seat on the red bench seat, I am engulfed in the world of Quinn Berkeley. I reach forward and finger the miniature Jack Skellington bobbling from the rearview mirror. I smile as I imagine it bopping away with Quinn at the wheel.

Tristan hops in and starts the engine, which purrs to life, reminding me of Quinn fiddling under the hood of Hank's truck.

"So where to?"

I could lie and tell him I'm staying someplace else, but what does it matter. I'm sure he'll find out sooner or later that I'm staying at Hank's.

"Night Cats," I confess, looking over at him warily, which is ridiculous. It's not like I'm staying there forever.

Why does that thought leave a bitter taste in my mouth?

"Oh, you're staying with Hank. Awesome. I didn't know you were staying there."

I nod but don't speak as I nervously brush a piece of hair

behind my ear.

"Quinn works there," he says casually.

"Yeah, I know," I reply after I've calmed down enough not to embarrass myself with incoherent babble.

"Oh?" Tristan asks, looking over at me as we stop at a red light.

"I work there, too. I've seen him around." I try to appear carefree, but I look anything but as I begin fiddling with the frayed edges of my denim shorts.

"He's never mentioned it," he says, taking off as the light turns green.

I lift my shoulders in a shrug, not that he can see me.

"Hank knew my parents," Tristan confesses after a moment of silence.

I don't fail to notice his use of past tense.

"Oh?" I reply, not wanting to push and appear nosy.

"Yeah. Bobby Joe is my grandma."

"Oh."

However, when I say 'Oh' this time, it's with a lot more enthusiasm.

I remember Hank mentioning him knowing Bobby Joe. And that explains why Quinn helps him out. Hank is a friend of Quinn's grandma.

"Yeah."

Just when I think he's not going to elaborate, he continues. "My grandparents opened up Bobby Joe's in the fifties, and my grandpa named the diner after my grandma, being the old romantic that he was. Not long after, they had my mom, Donna. For her whole life, my mother was told that when she was older, the diner would be passed down to her. But my mom wanted to go to college and experience something new since she had worked at the diner all through her teenage years. Anyway, that's where she met my dad."

I instantly notice the animosity that rolls off Tristan's tongue at the mention of his father.

"My dad, Paige, he's a deadbeat. Always has been, always will be. Anyway, my dad saw a good thing in the diner as it had a great rep, loyal customers, and he knew all the hard work was done for him. So he convinced my mom to drop out of college and take over for my grandparents. My grandparents were happy to hand it over to her because they were ready to retire and enjoy the money they made after all the years of hard work they had put into the place. But they weren't thrilled when my mom told them my dad, Ben, had proposed to her and that she was pregnant with Quinn."

"Oh." That seems to be the only response I'm capable of tonight.

"My mom is the nicest person you'll ever meet, so I just dunno what she saw in my dad. Anyway, a couple of years later, I was born, and by the time Quinn and I were old enough to understand, we knew that my mom wasn't happy…but she stayed with my dad."

"Why?" I whisper. I can't understand why his mom would stay, and mine…wouldn't.

"Because of me and Quinn. She would never leave without us. She knew this was our home. Dad sometimes pushed us around when Mom was working fourteen-hour shifts at the diner, threatening Quinn and me with a beatdown if we told my mom. He was a mean drunk with a heavy hand and had a huge gambling problem."

Images of Quinn as an intelligent, emerald-eyed child, and Tristan, an innocent, younger brother, clinging to his older brother while their drunken father storms around in a rampage, breaks my heart.

What also is a kick in the guts is that no matter what, Donna stayed for her kids. She pushed through because that's what mothers do.

But mine didn't, and suddenly, I have an epiphany.

What if my mother didn't want to stay? What if she was leaving my dad *and* me?

Tristan continues, deep in thought. "When Quinn was ten, he stood up for me and my mom. My dad came home, drunk as usual, and started pushing my mom around. This was something he had never done before. I mean, he screamed at her and verbally abused her, but he never touched her until that day. And that was the day Quinn had had enough. He got into my dad's face, and he pushed him. I still remember the rage in Quinn's eyes, and my dad also saw it. He was stunned that Quinn would stand up to him and warned him to step down, but when Quinn wouldn't back down, promising to protect me and my mom, my dad hit him. And I don't mean a slap. He hit him so hard that he split Quinn's forehead open."

I cover my open mouth with my hands, my eyes wide.

Tristan looks over and shakes his head. "I dunno why I'm telling you all this." He gives me an apologetic smile.

"No, please continue," I whisper. Tristan needs to get this off his chest.

He nods, thankfully, because I need to know how this story ends.

"That day, my mom left my dad. She told him to leave and never to come back. And if he did, she would go to the police and press charges for what he did to Quinn. Dad knew she was serious, so he left, but I doubt he ever wanted to be with us, anyway. Mom raised us as best she could, but, well, something happened a few years later, something that changed us forever…" He pauses, looking sad about what comes next.

"I'm sure I'm boring you. Some stories are better left untold," he concludes, pulling into the parking lot.

I'm all but jumping up and down in my seat. His story has left me with so many questions, but I can tell we've pulled into Night Cats by the red flashes passing over Tristan's face.

I need to get out, but I am stuck to my seat.

"Thank you for listening," Tristan says, unbuckling his seat belt and turning to look at me. "I've never told anyone that before. I'm sorry to dump it all on you."

"Don't apologize. I'm glad you trust me enough to tell me something so personal. Sometimes, it's easier to tell a stranger your story than it is your friends," I reply, knowing all too well how he feels.

"I'd like you to be my friend," he says with a smirk, and I realize what I just said.

"Oh right. Well, we are. Friends, I mean."

"Good."

There is a silence between us, and just as I'm about to unbuckle my seat belt, Tristan confesses, "I guess I knew that deep down, you'd understand. You're not like all the fake girls here. You're real."

"Thank you," I reply softly, slightly embarrassed by his honesty. "That's a really nice thing to say, Tristan."

Tristan's smile lights up his handsome face. "Anytime. Here," he says, extending his hand out. "Give me your phone."

Funnily enough, I don't question him why as I slip it into his palm.

"Now, if you feel the need to bare your soul," he says with a chuckle as he begins tapping on the screen, "you've got my number."

He hands me back my phone, and I can't help but notice how gentle his fingers look. A stupid thing to notice, really, but I notice it nonetheless.

"Thanks, Tristan."

I know I should give him mine, but I can't. It just feels too personal.

"See you tomorrow," Tristan says, acknowledging my sudden discomfort.

I unbuckle my seat belt and give him a small nod goodbye.

"Good night, Tristan." I hop out of the truck, giving him a final wave before he drives off.

As I drag my feet over the asphalt on the way to my room, I'm deep in thought.

So many questions are plaguing me: Where are Donna and Ben now? Where are Tristan's grandparents? Why doesn't Quinn work at the diner? Where *does* Quinn work? What happened to Ben? And more importantly, what happened a few years later that changed everything? The list is endless.

I then realize that Tristan's past is also Quinn's past. Although he wasn't the one to give me the information, I now understand why Quinn is so guarded, as I have a sneaking suspicion Tristan doesn't know the whole truth.

Speaking of truths, I don't want to give too much attention to one truth, and that is about me and my situation. Donna stayed for her kids. Regardless of how unhappy she was, she sacrificed for her children.

So what does that say about my mom, who up and left a three-year-old in the hands of a monster?

For my whole life, I've put my mom up on a pedestal. She was my prize at the end of all this shit. But what if I'm wrong?

What if my mother left me and hasn't looked back?

Eleven

The diner was crazy busy, and I worked the late shift, which is good as it gave me a place to be. But now that it's closing time, I've got *nowhere* to be.

"You sure you got a place to stay?" Grandpa asked as I walked into the tiny office, hanging up the room keys.

"Yes, Hank, I told you, all good. I'll see you tomorrow." I felt like a total ass for lying to Hank.

"Okay, you call me if you need anything. You got the number I gave you?" Looking down his glasses at me, he pinned me with an authoritative stare.

"Yes, and yes. Stop worrying, I can take care of myself."

"I know you can, but…"

"No buts. I'll see you tomorrow."

"Whatcha up to now?" Tabitha asks, tossing her apron into the dirty laundry basket.

"I might hit the gym," I reply, tying back my long hair. "Did you want to come with?"

"Oh, I'd love to, but Mother needs me to watch her practice some boring speech she has to deliver tomorrow night at some charity event."

I try to hide my distaste but obviously fail miserably.

"Trust me, I'd much rather hang with you."

"Next time," I reply, and I can't believe I'm actually kind of disappointed.

"Okay, it's a date."

We say our goodbyes, and I bump into Tristan in the hallway on my way out.

"Good night, Paige. Thanks for tonight." He smiles, his dimples punching me in the guts with their cuteness.

After my chat with Tristan two nights ago, I've been looking at him differently. Not how I look at Quinn, of course, who still has been MIA. But after someone opens up and shows you a little of their soul, the way Tristan did, it's kind of hard not to see them in a different light.

"No worries. I'll see you tomorrow," I reply, still itching to ask him where Quinn is, but I don't.

I hit the gym, but after being on my feet all day, I have no energy to work out. I do some cardio, trying to burn a hole in my brain to stop thinking about Quinn. I'm slightly disappointed that he hasn't dropped past Hank's or the diner. He doesn't have my number, but he knows where I am.

But where is he?

After our talk, or whatever the hell it was a few nights ago, I thought I'd at least see him, but he's been a ghost. After his "Trust me" speech, I thought we might hang out or at least talk.

I still don't know what to make of these feelings I have for him, and even though I told myself to stay away from him, I can't. But the fact he's avoiding me is troubling, as I'm starting to believe there may be some truth behind what Amber said, which deep down hurts.

Using that as motivation, I kick the shit out of the bag for forty minutes, feeling slightly better, but the emptiness in my gut still lingers like a bad smell.

It's now midnight, and I have the whole night to decide what the hell to do.

Grandpa insisted I take his truck, which I'm so grateful for, as I would be walking the streets aimlessly otherwise.

Hopping into the truck, I look over the steering wheel, drumming my fingers against it and contemplating where to go. I decide to wing it, but I don't want to drive around too far because I don't want to use up too much fuel.

I'm getting my next paycheck in a few days from the diner, as they pay every two weeks, which is great—my money from the motel is running thin.

After dinner, small supplies, and my unplanned shopping spree with Tabitha, I don't have as much left over as I thought I would. But why doesn't that thought worry me like it should? I guess because deep down, I know it means I'll have to stay here longer, which doesn't sound so bad.

I decide to drive around, park somewhere inconspicuous, and sleep in the truck for the night.

I've slept in worse.

South Boston is really beautiful. The farther you drive out, the greener and more isolated it becomes. A perfect place for one to get lost in.

The conversation with Tristan has been playing on repeat the whole drive. This is the problem with not being busy—I have time to think about things I don't want to. Like my mom, my dad, my life—things I can usually drown out with noisy restaurants and vacuum cleaners.

The only thing I can hear out here is, well…nothing. That is, until I hear a gunshot.

I yelp in surprise as it seemed to be amplified out here in the silence. I know it came from behind me, so I pull a U-turn and drop my speed to a crawl while looking out my window to determine where the noise came from. I don't have to look far.

My headlights illuminate a black-and-white Border Collie running for dear life toward my truck. I slam on the brakes, put the truck into park, and jump out.

The dog looks petrified, his pink tongue flopping out the side of his mouth as he runs toward me at full speed. Wide-eyed and shaking, he charges into me, knocking me back with the force of his jump.

He lets out a small whimper as I pat his head and crouch down to meet him face to face.

He's emaciated, hollow-eyed, and scared—I know the feeling too well, and I wonder what monster he's running from.

My question is answered as I see a man wearing blue overalls over a dirty white T-shirt way too tight for his heavy frame. He hobbles up the road, shotgun in hand and a mean scowl plastered all over his dirty face.

Mine and the dog's hackles rear up when we see him limp up the rocky road, eyeing us both.

I hate this asshole the moment he opens his mouth.

"You fucking mutt, get back 'ere!" he shouts when he sees the dog backing away from him.

I instantly stand in front of the dog, protecting him.

"Move outta the way, bitch. That dog ain't good for

nothin'," he spits out the side of his mouth and glares at me when I don't move.

Nor do I intend to.

I look down at the shotgun and know if I make a sudden move, he will blow my head off without thinking twice about it, so reaching for the knife out of my boot is not going to work.

With no other choice, I use my street smarts.

"How much do you want for him?" I ask, my hands raised, showing him I mean no harm.

"You wanna buy him?" His eyes widen at the prospect of making some money.

We live in a sad, sad world, where the universal language of money is everybody's first spoken language.

"Yes. I'll give you fifty dollars."

"A hundred," he pipes up, leaning on his shotgun and scratching his round belly.

"Fine, one hundred it is."

Whatever you offer, they always want more and will barter with you so they feel like a "Big Man" when they make the deal.

Little does he know, I was willing to pay anything for this little guy.

"My money is in my boot," I say, hands still raised in the air.

He nods and points the gun at me. "Slow."

Crouching slowly, with one hand still raised, my eyes lock with his as I drop the other hand to pull the one-hundred-dollar bill out of my boot. My fingers skim over my blade, offering me comfort by knowing it's there.

I stand quickly, showing him the note in my hand as I hold it above my head.

"Walk it over," he shouts, gun still aimed at me.

"Fine. Let me put the dog in the truck." I'm not going to give him the money, and he shoots the dog anyway.

He nods, his brown, greasy hair catching in the wind.

"Here, boy," I say, walking backward to the passenger door, my eyes never leaving the shotgun as I open the door for the dog.

The dog can't get into the truck quick enough, but I notice him limping just before he jumps in. He lies on the seat, head resting between his dirty paws, and he looks at me with big chocolate eyes, wanting to get the hell out of here.

I take a few steps forward and look down the barrel of the gun and shiver as it brings back a memory I wish I could just forget.

Throwing the money at his chest, I see that his name is Jimmy, which is printed on the front of his overalls. I walk away hastily. I need to get away from him because the closer I get to him, the more and more I can see Phil.

The smell.

The look.

Everything reeks of greed.

Thankfully, I hear his boots crunch over the gravel, his footsteps echoing away from me.

Rounding the car, I practically sprint, and the door whines in protest as I yank it open. Only when I close the door and lock it behind me do I let out a relieved breath.

Looking over at the little dog near me, lying on the bench seat and gazing up at me with big, puppy dog eyes, I now know where the saying came from.

The engine roars to life, and I hightail it out of there, leaving a cloud of smoke behind me.

After my hands stop shaking, I realize I need to give this

guy some food. Sadly, after the asshole took all my money, I've only got about six dollars to my name, but as I look into the dog's chocolate eyes, I know it's so worth it.

He edges closer to me, laying his small head against my knee, and my heart skips a beat at the gesture.

"I know. You would have done the same thing for me."

With no other choice, as I don't want this little guy sleeping in the truck as he's covered in sores, and he looks dehydrated and hungry, I pick up my phone, punching out a text. Within a minute, I receive a reply.

Sure :)

"So I bet you regret giving me your number," I say as Tristan opens his front door.

He greets me with a sleepy smile, and I feel like a jerk for asking him to help me out. But I didn't know who else to call.

"Don't be silly. Come inside, it's cold out." He yawns while rubbing his arms.

The dog stays close to my heels as we enter Tristan's house, which looks a lot less crowded than when I saw it last.

Tristan notices the dog limping as he closes the door behind us.

"Oh, poor guy," he says, his mouth dipping into a frown as he leads us into the living room.

He pulls a rug out from the cupboard, laying it on the floor in front of the mantel. The dog lies down on it and lets out a contented sigh while I crouch, rubbing between his ears.

"What's his name?" Tristan asks, crossing his arms across his broad chest, looking down at us.

"I'm not sure. I don't think he had one."

"How about Lucky?" a deep, familiar voice resonates from behind Tristan, and my heart kicks up a pace at the sound.

Quinn strolls in, looking like he's just woken up as his hair is fisted into messy peaks and his eyes are lidded and sleep-worn.

Tristan looks back at Quinn and smirks.

"Lucky? Totally unoriginal and completely corny—I like it."

Quinn catches my eye and gives me a small wink over Tristan's shoulder when he turns back around to look at me.

I bite my lip and busy myself with patting Lucky between the ears.

"Where'd you find him?" Quinn asks, walking into the living room and bumping playfully into Tristan on his way past him.

Quinn drops to his knees near me and looks at Lucky.

"He's skinny. Tris, get him some water and see if we have anything dog friendly in the house. Preferably not beer or chili."

"Sure," Tristan says, giving me a small smile before heading into the kitchen.

Now that it's only Quinn and me, the static in the room begins to tingle around us, and I can't meet his eyes even though I'm happy to see him.

I continue running my fingers through Lucky's matted fur, watching his eyes drift closed.

"Where'd you find him?" Quinn asks again, breaking the silence.

"Down by Maple Grove," I reply softly. "Some asshole named Jimmy was about to shoot him. I couldn't just stand by and let that happen."

"I'm guessing Jimmy made you cough something up?" he asks, and I finally meet his eyes.

I wish I didn't. Quinn does things to my heart that I don't understand. From the first moment I laid eyes on him, I've been sucked in. I just don't know what to do with these feelings.

"I paid him a hundred dollars."

Quinn's jaw clenches, and he huffs out a small breath. "Motherfucker."

"It doesn't matter. He's worth every penny."

Silence.

"I'm sorry I've been MIA."

I cringe, not because of the truth behind his words, but because he just spelled out my name. That's the closest he'll ever get to saying my real name and the thought is a kick in the guts as to why I cannot pursue this, whatever *this* is between us.

"Hey, look at me. Are you okay?" He tips up my chin with two fingers.

I give him a small nod, and he releases me.

"Where have you been?"

Quinn sighs deeply and stills my hand from patting Lucky. "You want the truth?"

When I nod gently, my hair slips into my face, shielding my eyes.

He squeezes my hand. "I've been purposely trying to stay away from you."

"What? Why?"

"Because it's for the best," he replies as he gently interlocks his fingers through mine.

His simple gesture of holding my hand is not the action of someone who wants to stay away from me, and I wonder where this has come from.

"The best for whom?" I inquire, trying to decipher the look on his face.

"For everyone, Red. You and me, we're cut from the same cloth. We'll just end up hurting each other."

What the hell does that mean, I ask myself. What about his whole 'I'll cut out my tongue' speech?

I berate myself for thinking that maybe I could trust him and that he *was* different.

"Well, if that's what you want."

"It's not what I want, but it's for the best," he answers, squeezing my hand and looking a little conflicted with his response.

"Do you always have to be so ambiguous?"

Quinn's eyes sadden as he lowers them.

"There's nothing ambiguous about it, Red. In time, you'll thank me. Everyone will."

Why do I have a feeling that *everyone* is Tristan?

His eyes flick up as Tristan walks in, and he quickly lets go of my hand.

Now I know this definitely has something to do with Tristan.

"Okay, all we got is Spam and this," he says, holding up an unidentifiable can as he walks into the room.

Quinn smirks at his brother, holding out his hand. "I'm pretty sure this little guy would eat just about anything."

Tristan hands Quinn the tin of Spam and a bowl, and as soon as Lucky hears the tin open, his ears perk up. He sits obediently, his long tail wagging frantically at the prospect of being fed.

Both Quinn and I let out a small laugh at his eagerness while Tristan heads back in the kitchen.

Quinn bangs the tin on the edge of the bowl, loosening up the meat, and it slides into the bowl with a wet plunk.

It looks absolutely disgusting, but Lucky licks his lips, eyeing the bowl patiently. Quinn places his dinner in front of him, and Lucky dives into it without delay.

"Make sure you…" He pauses as he looks at the empty bowl. "Chew it."

Lucky looks up while licking his lips in delight, sniffing the air for more food.

This dog has stolen my heart. I've always wanted a dog, but having a pet back home was unfair to the animal. I didn't even want to be there, so I'd never torture another living creature to the same fate.

Tristan returns with a bowl of water and raises an eyebrow at the empty dish.

"He eat that already?"

I nod, giving him a small smile.

"I saw him limping before," Tristan says as he places the water in front of Lucky, who happily gulps it up.

"I know. I saw that, too," I reply, looking up at him. "Are there any vets I can take him to?"

Quinn leans forward, and with a gentle grip, he feels Lucky's front paws and then moves onto his hind legs. The whole time I watch his elegant fingers move over Lucky's body with care, I can't help but feel slightly jealous of Lucky's examination.

"He's fine. Nothing is broken. He probably strained it when running away from that asshole, Jimmy."

"Jimmy who?" Tristan asks quickly.

"Jimmy Redfern," Quinn replies, curling his lip in disgust.

"Motherfucker," Tristan mutters, taking a seat near me.

Quinn nods.

The way Quinn and Tristan move in sync with one another is actually really nice to watch. It's blatantly obvious that they're close, and after Tristan's confession about Quinn standing up to his dad to protect his mom and Tristan, it makes me think that he never stopped.

Is that why he believes it's for the best to stay away from me? Because of Tristan? Both he and Tabitha have mentioned Tristan liking me.

What if Quinn is doing this because he's being the big brother and protecting Tristan? But this time, he isn't protecting Tristan from his dad. This time, he's protecting Tristan from himself.

Sitting between Quinn and Tristan has suddenly taken on a whole different meaning.

This whole situation gives me a headache, and I wish I could take a hot shower and crawl into bed.

Sadly, I can't do either.

Lucky has curled up into a ball and fallen asleep against my foot, and the instant trust he feels for me warms my heart.

"Did you want to crash here?" Tristan asks, looking at Lucky, who has no intention of moving.

I look over at him sheepishly.

"Would that be okay? Hank is getting the motel sprayed for bugs. Otherwise, I would have taken Lucky there."

Quinn exhales loudly. "Why didn't you say anything? You're always welcome to crash here."

"I can take care of myself," I reply, narrowing my eyes at him, suddenly angry with his protectiveness.

He reads it for what it is and nods.

"Take my room. I'll stay down here," Quinn says stubbornly, his eyes never leaving mine.

"No, I can't do that. Thank you for the offer, but no."

"And why not?"

"Because it's not cool you sleeping on the couch while I take your bed."

"We could always share," he adds with a smirk while I nearly choke on my tongue.

Tristan gets up quickly.

"Paige, take my room. I don't mind sleeping down here."

My eyes are still glued to Quinn's but drop to his mouth as he begins toying with his lip ring.

"No, Tristan," I say, my eyes never leaving Quinn's face as I flick them back up to meet his challenging stare. "I'll stay down here. It's totally fine."

This stare-off between Quinn and me is getting heated.

"And besides, I should stay down here with Lucky," I add, finally snapping out of my Quinn obsession.

I have no doubt Tristan can see my reaction to Quinn, and I need to stop it because it's not cool and probably making him uncomfortable.

"Thank you, Tristan. But honestly, I'd feel more comfortable down here."

Tristan steals a peek at Quinn and then nods. "Okay, if that's what you want."

"It is," I reply, rubbing Lucky's belly, which is rising and falling softly.

Tristan runs a hand through his hair.

"Well, can I at least get you something to eat? Drink?"

"No, I'm good. But could I trouble you for a shower?" I can't imagine I smell too good after the gym.

Tristan smiles, and by God, he is handsome. He has the face of innocence as he extends his hand down to me, which I gratefully accept.

As I stand, Tristan pulls me into him, and the space

between us leaves me slightly claustrophobic. As he stares into my eyes, I can see something I can't pinpoint reflected on his face. It leaves me feeling a little self-conscious.

"Good night, Red," Quinn says, and I take a step back from Tristan at the sound of his voice.

I turn to look at him and stifle a sigh because he looks fucking hot. Slightly pissed off is a good look for him.

"Good night, Quinn," I reply, wishing I could figure out what the hell he was thinking.

"Night, bro," Tristan says, looking at Quinn, who nods.

Tristan leads the way to the bathroom, and I follow a few steps behind, thankful to be away from both brothers in the same room.

Quinn is confusing as all hell with his "I need to stay away" speech, then giving me flirty eyes and doing that thing with his lip ring.

"Here's a towel." Tristan hands me a big, fluffy blue one that he pulls out from the hallway cupboard.

"Thank you, Tristan," I reply, standing in front of the bathroom awkwardly as I accept it. "Thank you for letting me crash here and looking after Lucky."

Tristan smiles his lopsided smile. "Don't mention it. It's not like I'm giving you the most comfortable place to sleep."

"I've slept in worse," I answer softly, hugging the towel to my chest.

Tristan nods but doesn't ask me to explain.

"Good night. Call out if you need me. My room is down the hall from Quinn's."

I try not to heat under the mention of Quinn's room.

"Good night, and thanks…again."

Tristan does something that surprises me. He reaches forward, placing a warm hand on the back of my head, and kisses my forehead lightly. It's over before I even know what to think, and as he pulls back, his eyes search mine, smiling warmly.

I know my mouth is agape, but he doesn't make me feel stupid. He just walks away like kissing me is the most natural thing to do.

As I watch him enter his room, I all but dive into the bathroom and lock the door with my back pressed up against it. What was that?

Not wanting to think about this a second longer, I strip out of my clothes, leaving them in a neat pile in the corner. I turn the water tap all the way to hot and step into the shower, which is relatively clean for a boys' shower. The hot water feels like heaven, and I only turn the water to cold a smidge, as standing under the scalding heat feels good.

I stay in the shower till my fingers have turned into little prunes and the bathroom has turned into a steam room. Switching the water off, I realize I left my change of clothes in the truck.

Looking down at my pile of dirty clothes, I cringe at the thought of putting on unclean clothes and underwear over my clean body. It seems wrong, not to mention gross especially when I smell like Quinn.

There were two body washes in the shower, and as soon as I smelled that musky sandalwood one, I knew which one was Quinn's. And like a total stalker, I used it. Imagining his broad hands lathering up the body wash and rubbing it all over his body is a vision I hope to fall asleep to.

Wrapping the towel tight around my body, it engulfs my tiny frame as I've decided to make a run for it and grab the set of clothes out of the truck. I make sure the towel is tucked in around me and not going to fly open and embarrass me when

I open the door.

As I turn the handle slowly and poke my head out a fraction, the coast looks clear. Taking a step out, my foot lands on something soft, and I jump back onto the cool bathroom tiles, noticing two T-shirts sitting neatly in front of the door.

I crouch down, my knees cracking in protest, and scoop up the two garments. The first I finger is a T-shirt I've seen Tristan wearing, and is a picture of Tim Burton's *The Corpse Bride*. My fingers move over to the other T-shirt, brushing over a print of Johnny Cash flipping the bird. Quinn's T-shirt.

So here I am faced with a dilemma. Which do I choose? No doubt, Tristan set his shirt down by the door first, as he would never leave his shirt if Quinn's was already there.

But Quinn would.

Faced with a decision I don't fail to see the significance of, I stand in the bathroom with Tristan's T-shirt in my right hand and Quinn's in my left. But there is no choice to make because it'll always be Quinn.

I slip on his T-shirt, and I only just refrain from burying my nose into it, taking a big whiff.

His shirt sits mid-thigh, and the material feels soft against my skin. I hate to admit the feel of it pressing up against my naked skin sends a jolt of excitement through me.

Looks like I'll be sleeping well tonight.

So much for me sleeping well.

I have tossed and turned, and it's not because the couch is uncomfortable. Far from it. Every time I try to close my eyes, Quinn's fragrance engulfs me.

And I also feel risqué wearing nothing underneath his T-shirt.

The clock on the mantel reads just after two, and I'm hoping I get some sleep since I have to be back at the motel by eight. Snuggling under the soft brown blanket so it sits just under my chin, I squeeze my eyes shut, willing sleep to overtake me.

It doesn't, and that's because I know I'm not alone.

I can't see much as it's pitch black, and the heavy curtains are doing a good job of keeping most of the moonlight out.

Sitting up and ensuring the blanket is still sitting under my chin, I squint, hoping to make out who's standing a few feet away.

"Hi," he says in barely a whisper.

What is he doing here?

"Hi," I reply, matching his tone.

"Were you asleep?"

"No."

"Why not?" he asks, slinking closer and closer with every word.

I shrug, which is stupid because he can't see me.

"I'm not much of a sleeper."

"How come?" he presses, and I feel the sofa dip beside me.

"Because I don't like to dream."

"What are you afraid to dream about?"

I slowly lower myself down by my elbows. As I descend, I feel him inching toward me, pushing me down with his presence because all of his weight is held up by his palms, which are resting alongside my waist.

"What are you afraid to dream about?" he questions again, so close to me that I can feel his long hair tickling my cheeks.

"You," I reply breathlessly, not able to stop myself.

Quinn releases a deep breath that fans over my cheeks and down my neck.

I am so turned on, a feeling I have never really felt before. And I want to kiss him more than anything, but I'm afraid to move.

Quinn's body hovers over mine, and he still won't allow me to feel his full weight. As I shift my legs, the blanket glides off my thighs, and he slips between them, fitting perfectly. I bite my lip when I feel the soft material of his sweatpants brush over my naked legs.

He slowly glides his hands up beside me and rests them on the pillow by my head. But he still won't press into me, allowing us to be chest to chest.

"What are you doing down here?"

"I couldn't sleep knowing you were down here. It was too much of a temptation. *You* are too much of a temptation."

His words do amazing things to my core, and I scissor my legs, unable to keep them still.

"But you said it was best to stay away from one another."

"There's always tomorrow."

"And tonight?" I question, almost afraid to know his answer.

"Tonight is ours."

The moment his lips trail slow, hot kisses along my jawline, my skin breaks out into tiny goose bumps. When his stubble softly sweeps across my face, a heat begins to build low in my belly. I arch my head back, my eyes slipping shut, relishing in the feel of his gentle lips on my skin.

His lip ring grazes over the shell of my right ear as he takes the lobe into his mouth, sucking deeply. It feels just as I imagined it would, cold and warm all at the same time.

I'm close to exploding as he begins kissing down the side of my neck and lazily licking over my burning flesh, the barbell in his mouth sending a chill through my entire body.

"Holy shit."

My neck has been kissed before, but never like this.

"Are you okay with this?" he asks huskily as he places a kiss at the edge of my mouth but never my lips.

"Yes."

Wisps of his hair brush over my cheeks as he moves onto my left ear, giving it the same treatment as my right. And when he finally lowers himself onto me, the feel of his bare chest against mine is like nothing I've ever felt.

We moan softly in unison, and I'm glad I'm not the only one affected by our union.

With his left hand still resting by my temple, he sashays his right thumb along my bottom lip, spreading the moisture over my full lip. I slip my tongue out apprehensively, and when the tip touches his thumb, he exhales softly. Thumbing the middle of my lip, he slowly slides it down my chin, under my neck, and between my breasts. I'm well aware that my heart beats uncontrollably, and I have no doubt he can feel it beating wildly against his thumb.

As he snakes it lower, his forearm brushes over my nipple, and it instantly pebbles in response to his touch, the other joining in quick succession. I know he can feel them both pushing into him, but he doesn't grab them and is the perfect gentleman.

"Can I?" he asks as his delicate fingers start a dance of the devil when they begin grazing over my belly.

I moan in response.

As his hand slides lower and touches bare skin, I jerk in shock and in pure desire. He exhales heavily as his hand inches higher and higher up my leg, but when I remember I'm royally naked underneath, I freeze.

"Are you all right?" he asks, his hand stilling on my upper thigh.

My eyes are still closed, but as I open them, a sliver of the moon has crept through a section of the curtain, lighting him up before me. The look in his eyes is one of pure desire, but I know he would stop if I asked him to.

I bite my lip, and his eyes instantly follow the movement. I want him to touch me, but I'm afraid.

"It's okay, I'll stop," he says, moving his hand back up to rest on my tummy. "You should get some sleep anyway. I heard your boss is a slave driver."

I smirk and hope he's talking about Hank and not Tristan.

He rolls off me, and I miss his weight instantly. But he surprises me as he rolls onto his side, pulling me close into his embrace.

We are nose to nose, and our breaths mingle into one. And it feels…nice.

"Good night, Red," he whispers, pulling me even closer so we are flush against one another.

"Are you staying down here?"

He nods, his hair brushing my cheeks. "If that's all right with you. If you're going to dream about me, the least I can do is be here for it."

"I'd like that."

I've never slept with anyone before. I've never slept beside anyone before, either.

"Maybe I can keep those nightmares away," he whispers after a minute of silence, wrapping his arm loosely around my waist, his hand resting on my lower back.

"That'll be nice," I reply sleepily, my eyes drooping

drowsily, not even asking how he knows I have bad dreams.

As I close my eyes, I drift off and experience the first dreamless night in years.

Twelve

I wake to my face getting licked continuously.

I lazily open one eye and am greeted by morning breath.

Lucky's breath.

My eyes snap open as I realize where I am.

And that I'm also alone.

Where's Quinn?

I know I didn't dream last night as I can still feel his lips and hands all over my body, and I'm slightly disappointed to wake up without him. Falling asleep in his arms was the best feeling in the world, and it's something I could quickly become addicted to. I slept through the night without a single nightmare or waking up in a cold sweat.

I don't know what it is about Quinn, but whatever it is, I want more. We haven't even kissed, and he turns me inside out.

We both know it would be smart to stay away from each other, but after last night, I don't think I can.

My eyes drift to the coffee table, and I notice my backpack sitting on the floor beside it.

Quinn.

I have no doubt he did this as he didn't want Tristan waking up and seeing me in his T-shirt.

Deep down, I know my attraction for Quinn will get someone hurt. And I have no doubt that Quinn knows it, too. But after last night, I'm powerless to stop it.

Lucky nuzzles my hand, wagging his tail and looking at me with those eyes.

"Okay, let me get dressed, and then I'll find you something to eat," I say, rubbing his head.

Creeping up to the bathroom with Lucky in tow, I quickly change and fold Quinn's T-shirt, giving it one final sniff. I neatly place it on top of the sink with Tristan's and sigh, wishing I never had to take it off.

Once satisfied I look okay, I make my way to the living room to tidy up the sofa before I leave. As I fold up the blanket, I hear plates clanging in the kitchen. Eager to catch Quinn before Tristan is up, I cross my fingers and duck my head around the corner, hoping it's him. But it's not.

"Good morning. How did you sleep?" Tristan asks, cracking two eggs into a red frying pan.

"Great," I reply, failing to mention why.

"Oh, that's awesome. Looks like the lumpy sofa isn't too bad after all."

I return his smile, and Lucky nudges my hand when Tristan opens a package of bacon.

"Don't worry, little guy, I have some for you, too. Take a seat," he says to me, pointing his spatula toward a chair.

Lucky sits happily, waiting patiently by my side as I sit at the kitchen table, fiddling with an empty beer bottle.

"Whatcha got planned today?" he asks because it's Saturday, and I'm not on the schedule to work at the diner.

"I have a shift this morning at the motel, then I was thinking of giving this little guy a bath," I reply, looking down at Lucky.

Lucky looks up at me, and both his ears drop in disapproval.

Tristan smirks. "Good luck with that. Would you like some?" he asks, pointing at the breakfast popping away on the hotplate.

I shake my head as I've never been a big breakfast eater.

"Red looks more like a coffee drinker than an eggs and bacon kinda girl," says Quinn as he saunters into the kitchen with a smirk.

I'm glad I'm not currently eating or drinking because I would have choked at the sight before me.

Quinn has obviously just stepped out of the shower as his wet hair curls up at the nape and is slicked backward, like he's combed his fingers through it, tousling it just the right way so it falls rebelliously. His ripped black jeans are tucked into military boots, and he's wearing the Johnny Cash T-shirt I sported only twenty minutes ago.

"Morning." He grins when he sees my jaw hit the table.

I half grunt, half choke in response.

Why is he wearing *that* T-shirt?

The thought that his naked skin rubs the piece of fabric that my naked skin was all up in last night has my stomach somersaulting in happiness.

Quinn pulls two mugs out from a cupboard above his head, pouring a cup for himself and another for me.

"How'd you sleep?"

He passes me the mug, and our fingers overlap when I reach for it. No doubt he's done this on purpose as he gets his kicks out of watching me squirm.

"Fine," I reply, unable to meet his eyes as I accept the mug, cautious not to touch his hand again.

He chuckles and takes a seat near me while Lucky shifts to sit near him.

"Traitor," I mumble under my breath, but Quinn hears me and smiles.

"You working today?" Tristan asks Quinn, who nods while sipping his black coffee.

"Where do you work?" I ask casually, tracing the circular pattern on my coffee mug.

"In hell." Tilting his head to the side, he watches me closely.

What's he doing? I feel naked under his gaze, and as I remember how close that was to happening last night, my body shivers in delight.

"He works at Gary's Garage downtown," Tristan replies with a grin as Quinn is more interested in having a stare-off with me than answering my question.

"Oh. That explains you tinkering around on Hank's truck."

"Yeah, that thing isn't safe with you behind the wheel," he comments with a full grin.

"What's that supposed to mean?" I retort, folding my arms over my chest.

"I've seen you fight. I can only imagine you'd give the poor Old Girl a beating."

I open my mouth in protest, but Tristan joins in, chuckling along with Quinn.

"It's true, Paige. I've seen you zip out of the parking lot at work," Tristan pipes up, holding back his laughter.

"What?" I spin around to face him. "I do not."

"Tris told me he almost lost a leg when you reversed out the other day," Quinn jokes from behind me.

"Oh, fuck you both!" I cry out, but suddenly, I'm joining in with their laughter.

Lucky barks excitedly and spins in a circle, enjoying the chatter filling the kitchen, and I can't help but reflect how normal this is. I never thought sitting in a kitchen on a Saturday morning with two brothers and a dog could make me so…happy.

Quinn stands, gulping down his coffee and giving Lucky a pat on his head.

"Later."

I try not to pout or make it obvious I'm a little disappointed that after last night, he's not even going to acknowledge that something happened between us.

"See ya, bro," Tristan says, turning his back to us to serve his breakfast.

Quinn takes this stolen moment to reach down and lay the briefest of kisses on my forehead. It's so quick I barely feel it, but the feel of his lips transports me back to last night.

As he pulls away, I meet his eyes, and I don't like the look reflected in them.

I see finality.

So it looks like he meant what he said.

This can't be the end.

Can it?

Tristan isn't working today and has kindly offered to help me wash Lucky.

"Okay, on the count of three. One. Two. Three!"

Nice try.

Lucky bolts in one direction while Tristan and I go in the other.

Hank cackles hysterically while leaning against the doorframe of the office, eating a bag of nuts. Tristan huffs out a breath, which shifts his messy bangs off his forehead, and I can't help but bite back a smile.

We've been trying for the past twenty minutes to coax Lucky toward us to give him a much-needed bath. But the bright-green hose Tristan holds is obviously a dead giveaway as to what we're planning.

Lucky stands a few feet away, ready to dart away if we come anywhere near him.

Tristan looks at me, raising his eyebrow. "This isn't funny."

"Yeah, it kinda is," I reply, covering my mouth to stop the laughter from escaping.

Tristan narrows his eyes at Lucky.

"It's gonna happen, dog. Stop fighting me." Lucky barks at him, wagging his tail, thinking this is all a big game of chasey.

"Paige! Catch!" Grandpa tosses me a tin of dog food.

As I catch it, I look at the label.

"Ooh, roast chicken. Where'd you get this?" I ask as it's extremely random for someone to have a can of dog food without owning an actual dog.

"It was left behind in one of the rooms."

I scrunch up my brow. "When did you ever allow dogs in the rooms?"

"Never," he replies with a wrinkled smile.

"So either someone snuck in their dog, or they were into some fucked-up kinky shit," I reply seriously.

Both Tristan and Grandpa break out into loud fits of laughter while I shiver at the gross images passing through my brain.

"Okay, Lucky, you want some?" I ask in a high-pitched voice, hoping to spark interest as I open the tin.

And it does.

Lucky walks toward me, eyeing the food and nothing else. I give Tristan a slight nod, and when Lucky is within reaching distance, Tristan dives for him.

Lucky doesn't flinch because he's still eyeballing the food.

"Good boy," I coo, patting him on the head as I scoop out a handful of food and place it in front of his mouth.

Tristan eases the hose on and begins rinsing Lucky's matted coat while I hand-feed him. I can't help but watch the way Tristan's fingers brush through Lucky's fur with gentleness and care. This man before me has a heart so pure and real that I can't help but feel blessed to be in his company.

But I have to tread cautiously as I haven't failed to notice his longing glances when he thinks I haven't been looking. I don't want to give him the wrong impression because I don't like him in *that* way. I shouldn't be liking *anyone* in that way, but I do. And I don't know what to do about it.

The look in Quinn's eyes this morning keeps playing on my mind, and I'm afraid he'll keep to his word. I know it's for the best, but why do I feel so empty inside at the thought of never feeling his hands on me again?

Lucky nudges my hand, snapping me out of my blackout.

"Sorry, boy," I apologize while scooping out more food with my fingers.

"You know, there are things called silverware you could use," jokes Tristan while soaping up Lucky's back.

I shrug. "I've had my hands in worse."

"Yeah?" Tristan asks, raising an eyebrow.

"Yeah."

"You know you can trust me, right?"

I nod, giving him a small smile. "I know."

This is one of the many things I like about Tristan. He doesn't push.

"So I was thinking of having a party for my birthday," Tristan says, rinsing the soap off Lucky.

"Yeah?" I remember him mentioning his birthday was coming up soon. "When is it?"

"Next weekend."

"Awesome. You should totally do something. You only turn twenty-one once."

Something suddenly passes over him.

"What's wrong?" I ask, surprised I can see his mood shift before my eyes.

"It's my dad."

"What about him?"

He pauses and releases his lip.

"He splits for the whole year, but for some fucked-up reason, he always seems to turn up on my birthday and ruin it."

"What a jackass."

Tristan chuckles, and the sound reminds me so much of Quinn. "That he is."

"You wanna know what I think?" I say, scraping out the last of the dog food.

"Sure."

"Fuck him. Don't let him ruin another birthday. Your dad being a dick is an even bigger reason to have an epic birthday party. And if he turns up, you'll have a group of people ready to kick his sorry ass," I add with a smirk.

Tristan nods, his face lighting up in a big smile. "You're right. Here's to a birthday like no other." He releases Lucky because he finished washing him.

Lucky breaks into a sprint and does a circle of the parking lot, the wind catching in his wet fur. Then he comes back, charging toward us, stopping a few feet away, and begins a big shake down, drenching Tristan and me.

I stand frozen with one eye closed and mouth open, dripping wet. Tristan decides I'm not wet enough and squirts me in the chest with the hose. The water spray is cold, and I screech in shock, turning my back to him, which he takes as an invitation to spray me further.

"No fair!" I cry, running away from him, which is pointless since the range on this thing is huge.

Lucky joins in, bouncing up and down, barking happily as I run around the parking lot, squealing like an idiot.

"Tristan, stop!" I yelp with my hands out in front of me, and my body twisted at an odd angle to shield myself from the spray.

He's laughing hysterically and finally stops, happy with his handiwork.

I look like a drowned rat with my long hair plastered to my cheeks as I trudge over to him, my Chucks swishing with each step I take. I try to appear mad, but as I get closer to Tristan's bright eyes, I can't help the smile that spreads from cheek to cheek.

"You're lucky I needed a shower," I joke, gathering my hair

in my now clean hands and wringing out my soaked locks.

"Sorry, it was just too perfect an opportunity."

"Oh yeah?" I say, pursing my lips, eyeing the hose hanging loosely in his hands.

"Yeah," he replies, unaware I'm about to beat him at his own game.

I make a mad reach for the hose and easily snatch it out of his grip. Tristan's eyes widen, and before he has a chance to speak, I direct the hose at him and hit him square in the face. He splutters, closing his eyes, but I don't stop. I instead aim a little lower and run backward while spraying him in the chest.

"Oh, you're so paying for that." He chuckles while flicking back his hair and rubbing the water from his eyes.

"You have to catch me first," I mock, turning the hose off and standing my ground.

I can't help but admire the way Tristan's white T-shirt highlights his upper torso, emphasizing his hard chest and sharp collarbones as he stalks toward me.

But I feel wrong looking at him that way and avert my eyes while turning the hose back on, spraying him some more to distract myself from ogling him.

"Paige!" He laughs, turning his head away, but he continues pursuing me.

Suddenly, the water dies off, and I see that Hank has turned off the tap with a big cheeky grin on his face.

"Traitor!" I yell at him, giggling.

Tristan quickens his pace, and before I know it, he wraps me in his strong arms and lifts me off the ground.

"Put me down!" I yelp, swatting him on the back. I wrap my legs around his waist because I'm about to fall face-first.

But he only does the opposite and shifts me farther up his body. With no other choice, I wrap my arms around his neck to gain my balance. We're at eye level, our chests rising and falling quickly, still pumped with adrenaline. Suddenly, my position becomes awkward, and I wriggle free because I feel like I'm doing something wrong by being in his arms this way. Thankfully, he lets me go, but I don't fail to see the heat in his eyes.

"You play dirty," he says with a smirk.

I return his smile but realize things are about to get complicated.

Thirteen

For the next week, I quickly fall into the routine of going to work, going to the gym, and hanging out with Tristan. I don't know how it happened, but I don't question it because I enjoy his company.

Of course, Quinn has been absent all week, and whenever I casually ask Tristan where he is, I get the same response of "I dunno."

Lucky has been staying with Tristan since the motel has been booked. I have a feeling Hank is in some financial trouble because I walked in on him having a heated argument with someone on the phone, and I could tell it was about him owing money. When I asked him if everything was okay, he brushed it off as nothing, but I know better. Hank is no liar, and it's written all over his face that something is up. I really want to help in any way I can, but it's hard to help when you don't know what's wrong.

I came here for a reason: to work, stay to myself, and leave when the time is right. But the more time I spend here, the harder it is for me to picture myself anywhere *but* here, surrounded by my friends. I haven't even thought about my mom in over a week, which scares me because I can't allow myself to get too attached. Hank, Tabitha, and Tristan know Paige, not Mia. The question is, if they knew Mia, would they like her? After everything she's done, would they still want to be her friend?

The thing that scares me the most is I think they would.

"Do you think he'll like it?" Tabitha asks, holding up a T-shirt with a *Superman* logo.

"Definitely. He's a total nerd, and he can live out his superhero dreams wearing that." I smile when Tabitha rolls her eyes.

"You're so right," she replies, tucking it under her arm while we walk toward the register.

It's Friday night, and it's Tristan's birthday tomorrow, so Tabitha and I are cramming in some last-minute shopping. I had to wait until I got paid. Money is running a little low, and to be honest, I haven't saved anything. I thought I would be beside myself, but I'm not. The things I've spent my money on have been money well spent. I know I'll be staying in South Boston longer than planned, and I'm okay with that. I think the hard part will be leaving.

Once Tabitha pays for the T-shirt, we decide to visit the food court because we're famished.

"I think I'm going to order a salad." Eyeing the menu, she makes it clear she'd rather have the burger and fries.

"You have whatever you like. You know we'll just burn it off at the gym when hitting Brad, sorry, I mean the bag."

I chuckle at the intentional slip. We've been calling the punching bag Brad to inspire Tabitha to bash the shit out of it.

"What are you going to have?" she asks with her back turned to me while perusing the menu on the board.

"Yeah, Red. What do you want?" a voice whispers in my ear.

My whole body becomes taut, and I hold my breath as Quinn presses up against my back. His warm breath tickles my throat, and I can't stop the goose bumps that spread across my arms, which I fold around my waist nervously.

"Paige?" Tabitha questions when I don't answer her, but I can't.

I feel like my tongue is stuck to the roof of my mouth, and swallowing is slowly becoming an issue.

She turns, and her eyes widen when she sees Quinn standing behind me. Her eyebrows rise into her hairline, obviously confused about why I'm piggybacking Quinn.

"Um, hi, Quinn," Tabitha says, looking at me instead of him.

"Hi, Abi," he replies, and goddamn him, he's so close to me, I want to die.

"What are you doing?"

She extends her hand to me as I seem to have forgotten how to move. Thankfully, she spins me around to face Quinn as I slip my hand into hers. But I wish my back was still turned because my memories of him have not paid him justice.

He's wearing ripped jeans, navy Chucks, and a faded The Cure T-shirt. His hair sits messily, slipping over one emerald eye while the other makes it obvious he's checking me out.

"I'm here to get Tristan a birthday present."

"Uh-huh," Tabitha says, totally unbelieving.

As Quinn brushes his long bangs out of his eyes, I notice

his red and scabbed knuckles.

"What happened?" I ask, looking down at his hands.

Quinn shrugs and toys with his lip ring playfully.

"Where have you been?" I ask, trying not to sound too miserable.

"Here and there," he replies vaguely.

Does he not remember what happened between us on the sofa? Did it mean nothing to him? Looking at him, I know that the answer is probably no. I'm sure Quinn is not short of female attention, and I'm yesterday's news.

The thought doesn't sting as much as it pisses me off, and the wall I've built up around me suddenly erects.

"Well, how about you go back over *there* and leave us alone?" I say with a bite of venom behind my words.

Tabitha gasps, and Quinn's mouth turns up into a small smile.

What the hell is wrong with him? That was meant to be an insult, not amusing.

I turn my back to him and pretend to busy myself with the menu, and not how I'm shaking in rage because of the feelings he evokes in me.

Tabitha gives my arm a supportive squeeze while I exhale in anger.

"Red, don't be mad at me," he whispers against my ear as he presses into me. "I told you, it's for the best."

I'm about to spin around and give him an earful, but he adds softly, "You think it's easy for me to stay away from you, especially after the other night? You're all I can think about, all I can smell…all I can taste."

An intake of air gets caught in my throat, and I think I'm about to choke. Tabitha watches our exchange with wide eyes, but I can't pull away.

"You deserve to be happy, and you'll get that with Tristan. With me, you'll only end up getting hurt."

I freeze as soon as he mentions Tristan. This is the first time he's openly confessed that he's staying away because of Tristan.

"How do you know? You won't even try."

"Because, Red, being with you would possess every single inch of me, and you're not ready for that."

"You don't know what I'm capable of."

"No," he replies, kissing the shell of my ear. "*You* don't know what *I'm* capable of."

I have no idea what he means, but I hear an ominous message behind his words.

He gives me one final kiss on my neck, just below my ear, which sends an inferno from head to toe as I feel his lip ring dig into my skin, and then, he's gone.

I take a deep breath, and a tsunami of emotions rolls over me.

"Paige, are you okay? Here, sit," Tabitha says, linking her arm through mine and plonking my comatose ass into a seat.

"*What* was that?" she asks, her eyes wide, looking over my shoulder to where Quinn went.

I shake my head, biting my lip.

"Has something happened between you guys?"

I know by *something,* she means sex.

"No, nothing like that," I reply, finally finding my voice.

"Then what?" she asks, reaching out over the table and rubbing her thumb over my hand comfortingly.

"We, I don't know…fooled around a little," I reply, shrugging uncomfortably.

Tabitha's mouth opens wide. "When?"

"The night I got Lucky."

"Oh my God, you got lucky?" she shouts, misunderstanding me.

I let out a small chuckle as she has no volume control when excited. "No, not lucky, lucky. I mean Lucky, my dog."

Tabitha nods, her mouth forming an O, and she gives me her full attention.

"I crashed there that night and stayed on the couch. Quinn came downstairs and said it was best if we stayed away from each other."

"From what I just saw, that *definitely* does not classify as staying away from each other."

"I don't know what to think. We haven't even kissed. This is ridiculous." I sigh, covering my face with my hands.

Tabitha reaches for my hands and removes them from my face.

"What just went on between you two was explosive. I have a feeling the tables would have had to be cleared if you guys *had* kissed. You obviously have a connection. I mean, sheesh, I felt like I was intruding on a private moment." She gives me a small smile before she continues. "I don't think you guys *can* actually stay away from each other. It'll only be a matter of time before you succumb to the inevitable."

Is there any truth to what Tabitha is saying?

Deep down, I know there is.

I toss Tristan's birthday gift onto my bed, grateful I purchased it before bumping into Quinn.

I pace the room because I can't sit still. I feel edgy, but most of all, I'm confused. I'm so confused by everything

Quinn-related. The way he touches me is not the action of someone who wants to stay away from me. I know for certain he's doing this chivalrous act for Tristan's benefit, but it's not Tristan I want. I knew from the first moment I laid eyes on Quinn that he would be trouble; I just didn't know how much.

I flop onto the bed and sink into the spongy mattress, raising my eyes to the ceiling angrily. This is why I never got involved with anyone back home. I had enough crap to deal with and didn't need relationship woes to add to the shit pile. But now that I've opened up Pandora's box with Quinn, I can't shut it. And I don't want to. I want to experience all the hype that comes with a relationship, and I only want to do so with Quinn.

When I turn to look at the nightstand to see what the time is, my eyes fall on a one-hundred-dollar bill instead of the digital clock. I sit up quickly and brush my fallen hair out of my eyes. I snatch the note off the table, wondering where it came from. I certainly haven't left it here. And it didn't appear out of thin air.

Turning it over, I notice it's smeared with a spot of blood. I cock my head to the side, deep in thought, fingering the corner of the note.

Then I remember Quinn's knuckles. Could it be? Did he pay Jimmy a visit and get my hundred dollars back? I recall how mad he got when I mentioned I paid Jimmy for Lucky, but I never thought he would go get it back for me. I never *expected* him to.

This is a total mindfuck.

Falling back onto the bed and squeezing my eyes shut, I hope to fall into a dreamless slumber where a pair of emerald eyes won't be the main attraction in my dreams again tonight.

Fourteen

"**A**re you sure this dress looks okay?" Tabitha asks, standing in front of me shyly in a blue babydoll dress. Lying on my bed and sucking on a raspberry licorice swirl while swinging my legs in the air, I mull over her outfit. "You look awesome."

It's funny that I have no qualms about her being here. When I told her I was staying at Night Cats, she just smiled and asked if it would be okay to hang out here rather than at her place. I knew it had to do with her mother, and quite frankly, I prefer it here where we both can be ourselves.

"You think? I don't look overdressed or—"

I throw the end of my licorice at her and sit up.

"Stop that. You look fucking amazing. I'm sure Tristan will think the same."

Tabitha blushes. She bashfully confessed she's sweet on

him, but she's adamant she doesn't stand a chance against me. She knows I'm not into him that way but said Tristan will never look at her the way he looks at me, which freaks me out. I don't want him to be looking at me other than as a friend.

"Let's go," I say, rolling off the bed.

"Wait!" Tabitha shouts, running over to me.

She pulls out a wand of lip gloss and paints my lips with a fine coat.

"Better. Now you're all ready to pucker up for Quinn." She smiles, nudging me in the ribs playfully.

"Quit it." I chuckle, swiping her hands away.

But deep down, I am a little excited to see Quinn. I need to ask him if he did indeed leave the money I found last night, and if he did, then why.

"Uh-oh."

"What?" I ask, my gaze snapping to hers.

"You've got the Quinn Look," she replies, her eyes lighting up.

"The what now?" I ask, raising an eyebrow.

"The Quinn Look," she repeats. "It kinda looks something like this."

She places both hands over her heart, tilting her head to the side with a faraway look plastered on her face while fluttering her eyelashes.

"Oh, I do not!" I retort, slapping her on the arm playfully.

Tabitha chuckles.

"You keep that up, and you'll be walking tonight." I'm the designated driver for the evening because I'm not much of a drinker.

That zips her lips shut, but she still gives me a small smile.

"Paige?"

"Tabitha?"

She looks at me seriously, though slightly embarrassed. "Thank you…thank you for being my friend."

I don't know what to say to her, so I do the only thing a friend should do in a situation like this.

I'm the one to initiate the hug, and it doesn't feel weird.

We leave the motel, and it doesn't take long to get to Tristan's.

We have to park about three blocks away, though, as Tristan's street is filled with cars and people mingling on the road, alcohol in hand, with no intention of moving.

Tabitha and I hit the pavement, and I can tell by the way she's pulling at her square neck collar that she's nervous.

"Abi, you'll be fine," I say, using her nickname with ease.

"I know, I just feel weird. It's so stupid. It's just Tristan, but he gives me butterflies."

I give her a sympathetic smile.

Thankfully, no naked caped crusader threatens to blind me and Abi with his junk this time around. We ascend the stairs and both look at each other when we see the number of people inside.

"Wow, I didn't realize Tristan knew this many people," I say to Tabitha as we begin squeezing our way through the crowd of people milling in the doorway.

Tabitha shrugs, looking over the heads of random strangers for Tristan.

We don't have to look too far as we both see Tristan leaning against a wall, cornered by a not-so-subtle girl wanting to give the birthday boy a big smooch.

I have to laugh at the uncomfortable expression on his face. I feel it's my duty as his friend to save him. Reaching for Abi's hand, I yank her over to where the girl claims she can make all of Tristan's dreams come true.

"Happy Birthday!" I shout a little inappropriately, but it works as she backs off to see who has just deafened her.

"Thank God you're here," he whispers, ducking around the girl and pressing a warm kiss to my forehead.

He pulls me to his chest and encloses me in a loose embrace. This is how Tristan usually greets me, even at work, and I'm starting to get used to it. But it is purely innocent. Well, it is on my behalf.

"Hey, Abi," he says, letting me go and giving Tabitha a warm hug.

I can tell she has died and gone to heaven being wrapped in his arms, and I give her a small wink over his shoulder.

Thankfully, the girl got the message loud and clear, and has latched onto some poor chump to the left of me.

Tristan lets Tabitha go and huffs out a deep breath.

"Thanks for the save."

I notice a lot more as he looks amazing. He's in tight black jeans, black motorcycle boots, and a white shirt, which he has rolled the sleeves up on. A sliver of his chiseled chest is on display since he has two buttons undone on the fitted shirt that hugs his narrow waist. His hair is styled to look unkempt, but it totally works with the dark stubble on his strong jaw.

I swear I see Tabitha's jaw hit the floor, and I bite back a smile. I'll have to remember to show her *her* Tristan Look when we get back to the motel.

"So who's driving?" Tristan asks, looking back and forth between me and Tabitha.

"I am," I reply. Tristan looks a little disappointed that I'm not drinking, but he quickly recovers. "Come on, Abi, birthday shots," he says, linking his arm around her shoulders and leading her toward the kitchen.

It's been about an hour, and I have scoped out the entire house, bar Quinn's room, and there's no sign of him. Where is he? I'm not ashamed to admit that the fact he is once again MIA is more than upsetting. It's fucking frustrating.

I would be pounding on his door right about now, but I have to keep an eye on Tabitha. She's extremely intoxicated, and Brad, the douche, is here, loitering around her. His little sidekick Malibu Stacey isn't around, so he obviously considers Tabitha suitable to flirt with when he's on his own. I'm proud that Tabitha has pushed his advances away and continued having fun.

Tristan has been one popular birthday boy. Every girl in attendance has given him a birthday kiss, but I can tell he's not interested in any of them.

I don't want to think about who he is interested in.

Lost in thought, I fail to notice the sofa cushion beside me dip until I hear his voice.

"Having fun?" Quinn asks into my ear.

Damn this response I have toward him. I will not keel over.

"Yup," I bluntly reply, refusing to make eye contact with him.

There's a small silence between us, and I make no attempt to break it. As childish as this makes me, I just continue to sit vacantly.

"Are you going to ignore me all night?" he asks, shuffling closer to me while I shift away.

I lift my shoulders in a nonchalant shrug. "I'm just playing by your rules, Quinn. You're the one setting the pace, not me."

Quinn seizes my chin and coaxes me to meet his eyes. His hold isn't rough, just more of a forward act to get me to look at him. Begrudgingly, I move with him and try not to melt when I do.

"Don't."

"Don't what?" I scorn, pulling out of his grip. "You tell me it's best if we stay away from one another, but every corner I turn, you're there. If that's not a clusterfuck of contradiction, then I don't know what is."

I look down at his hands, which are still scabbed and red.

"What happened?" I ask, gesturing with my chin to his knuckles.

Quinn is silent, allowing me to totally tear him down since he knows I won't stop.

"Would it have anything to do with this?" I raise my hips off the sofa, reaching into my pocket and pulling out the one-hundred-dollar bill.

I throw it into his lap and cock an eyebrow, daring him to challenge me.

"That money is yours," he says, eyeballing the bill.

So I *was* right. I wasn't certain if my theory was correct because it was just too ridiculous to fathom. But now that he confirmed it, I'm even more confused by what the hell is going on between us.

"I don't need you to fight my battles for me. I'm not some damsel in distress who needs your saving. And this chivalrous act of yours is pissing me off," I retort, unable to stop. "I don't know what about me makes you think I need your help, but let me clarify, I don't. If you don't like me or whatever, fine. But this whole 'I will only hurt you' speech"—I lower my voice to poorly mimic his—"is a total cop-out." And then I take a breath.

"You done?" he asks with that stupid smile tugging at his lips.

"Oh, not even by half," I reply, shoving up my sleeves as I'm suddenly burning up.

One minute, I'm sitting on the couch, and the next, I'm straddling Quinn's lap.

As I look down at him, my chest pushes out into his face embarrassingly close while I'm about to hyperventilate, but his eyes never leave mine. He has one thumb hooked into my belt loop, which he used as leverage to pull me onto his lap so quickly. And the other is slung low on my waist, the tips of his fingers grazing my ass.

"Don't go quiet on me now. I'm all ears." He raises an eyebrow, mocking me.

"Let me go," I say in a rushed breath as he hardens underneath me, which scares and excites me all at the same time.

"No. You want this, Red, then you need to know what it feels like." He slowly lifts his pointer finger, resting it on my lower lip.

He begins stroking it back and forth, dipping it into my mouth and rubbing my wet inner lip leisurely. "Being with me will consume parts of yourself you never knew existed. Are you ready for that? Can you give me everything even though you know I will push you until you're ready to break?"

My eyes droop to half mast, and I am all but rocking on his lap. I'm so turned on.

He stops stroking my lip and leans in, pressing his mouth to my slack lips. My eyes open in alarm, but he doesn't open his mouth or kiss me. It's a simple but deliberate unity of our lips. He pulls away, inches from my face, and I gasp when I'm confronted head-on with such beauty.

"You see," he whispers. "I would break you."

I can't believe the words that slip past my lips. "I want you to. Better to feel pain than nothing at all."

Quinn raises an eyebrow, surprised by my admission.

That makes two of us.

Quinn runs the back of his fingers across my cheek. He watches me closely, but I don't waver. I want this. Sadly, our moment is ruined by a hysterical Tabitha.

"Quinn!"

We both turn to see her, red-cheeked and panting out of breath.

"It's Tristan," she says, hands on knees, catching her breath.

I can feel Quinn stiffen under me.

"What happened?" He lightly pushes me off him, eyeing Tabitha closely.

"He's outside. He's fighting." Tabitha takes another breath. "With your dad," Tabitha concludes, eyes wide.

Quinn is up in a heartbeat and charging out the front door. Tabitha and I follow him quickly, pushing the mingling crowd out of our way.

It takes us double the amount of time as it does for Quinn to get outside, and when we do, the sight before me is not a happy one.

The moonlight reflects off Quinn, standing between Tristan and a man who is clearly their father.

Ben Berkeley is a tall man, and I can see the similarities. But where kindness and warmth radiate from Quinn's and Tristan's eyes, nothing but hatred is reflected in Ben's.

"You little pussy, get back over here. Still getting your older brother to fight your battles for you? Nothing ever changes!"

Ben slurs, trying to get past Quinn, who is like a brick wall, preventing his father from taking a step toward Tristan.

"Back the fuck off!" Quinn spits, getting into Ben's face. "Leave before someone gets hurt."

I push past the spectators, cheering and loving the spectacle before them. I want to punch them all in the face, but I need to get to Quinn.

I jump down the front steps and cautiously stand a few feet away, ready to help Quinn if need be.

"Always the smart mouth, weren't ya, boy? You'll never learn your lesson. You think you can take me? C'mon then, give me your best shot," Ben snarls, pointing at his chin, taunting Quinn to hit him.

Quinn clenches his jaw and exhales a deep breath through his parted lips.

"You're pathetic. Go crawl back to whichever hole you came out of. No one wants you here," Quinn snarls, inches away from Ben's face, and I can see him shaking in rage.

"Oh, my boy, that's where you're wrong. I think no one wants *you* here, seeing as you drove your mother away," Ben says, shoving Quinn in the chest.

The shift in Quinn's eyes is clear as day, and by the hard set of his jaw, I know he's about to snap, so I take this opportunity to break into a sprint. Tabitha calls out to me to stop, but I can't, and I don't until I latch onto Quinn, stopping him from charging his father.

"Quinn, don't. He's not worth it," I whisper into his ear, interlacing my fingers through his.

I can feel the rage pouring out of every fiber of his body, and I'm actually frightened of the anger building within him.

He grinds down on his jaw and squeezes my hand so tightly it's borderline painful. But I don't flinch because I'm here for him in any way he needs me.

"Oh, you little pussy. Now you've got a girl fighting your battles." He laughs malevolently, sipping his beer with most of it running down his chin, staining his gray T-shirt.

Quinn pushes me behind him, but I stand rigidly.

He turns his head slightly; his eyes remain focused on his father, who sways drunkenly.

"Red, go inside. Take Tristan with you."

I can hear the desperation in his voice, but I just can't leave him alone out here with this maniac.

When I don't move, he squeezes my fingers. "Please."

With no other choice, I regretfully let his hand go and walk toward Tristan, who looks terrified. The look in his eyes is actually painful to watch, and I need to get him inside because I don't know what he's thinking.

"Tristan, let's go inside. Quinn has got this, okay?"

Tristan's eyes finally meet mine, and I can tell by their glassiness that he's drunk.

"Come on, Tristan," I say, holding my hand out to him. "Let's go inside. I wanna go see Lucky. He's probably lonely, cooped up in your bedroom all alone." I feel like the lamest person for saying something so stupid, but I don't know what else to say.

Tristan looks down at my hand and then back at Quinn, who I can hear still getting abuse from his father. I have to try to block it out because all I can think about is charging over there and headbutting Ben.

Finally, he nods, gingerly taking my hand and giving it a small squeeze. I lead him around the back because I don't want him going anywhere near his father. He leans into me, wrapping an arm around my neck to balance himself as we sway up the stairs.

He bangs into the wall just before we enter his bedroom, and I slam the door shut.

I let out a breath and watch Tristan collapse face-first onto his unmade bed. I run over to him and sit on the corner of the bed, not really knowing what to do. When he groans, which comes out muffled with his face squished into the mattress, I hesitate before I run my hand lightly over his back.

"Are you okay?" I whisper, rubbing a circular motion between his shoulder blades.

All I get in response is a grunt and a groan.

"Tristan? Can you hear me?"

Another groan.

I stand and crouch beside the bed, running my fingers through his silky hair.

"Tristan? Can you flip onto your back for me?" I say, wedging my hands underneath him, forcing him to roll over.

With a little coercion, I get him to comply, and he awkwardly rolls. His arm is twisted at an odd angle underneath him, so I reach for it and slowly slide it out and rest it on his stomach.

When I hear a knock on the door, I jump up, hoping it's Quinn.

"Paige?" Tabitha pokes her head around the door.

"Hi, Abi," I whisper, standing and walking over to her quickly. "You okay?"

She shakes her head, her face paler than usual.

"Would it be okay if I went home with Alice? I know you probably want to stay and talk to Quinn. But I'm really not feeling too good."

I nod hastily. "Yes, of course. Sorry I can't take you, but I don't want to leave Tristan alone."

Tabitha completely understands and gives me a small

smile. "No need to explain."

"Is Quinn okay?" I ask nervously, biting my lip.

Tabitha shrugs. "His dad left when he threatened to call the police."

I let out a breath I didn't even realize I was holding.

"Thanks. Fuck," I mumble under my breath. "Where's Quinn now?"

Tabitha shakes her head. "I'm not sure. He just stormed off after his dad took off."

Shit.

"Okay, thanks, Abi. Be safe," I say, hugging her goodbye.

She looks over at the bed and makes a pained face.

"I hope he's okay. Stay with him, Paige. He needs you."

She kisses me on the cheek before softly closing the door behind her.

I pinch the bridge of my nose and close my eyes to center myself, but it doesn't work. My legs begin to tremble, so I walk over and plonk onto the bed near Tristan.

Looking around his room, I take in the books that litter his messy desk and see posters of obscure movies I have never heard of before hanging on his walls. And on the side table near me sits a photo of Quinn, Tristan, and a lady I'm guessing is their mom. I quietly pick up the silver frame and look at the faces of three people who look so much alike.

There is no doubt Donna loves her boys, as she has both arms wrapped around Quinn and Tristan lovingly. There's nothing extraordinary about her; she looks like an average, middle-aged lady posing for a photo with her sons. But it's what I *can't* see that makes her exceptional. I know that inside this woman lies a fighter, someone who would sacrifice her own happiness for her children. She's someone who would stand up for her kin when they were threatened and not think twice about it. She's what every mother should be, and *that's* what makes her extraordinary.

I think back to what Ben said about Quinn driving his mom away and wonder what happened. What is the Berkeley family's backstory?

"Paige?" I hear Tristan groan.

I silently return the frame to the bedside table and look over at him.

"Hey," I whisper. "I'm here. Are you okay?"

Tristan moans, and I can't help the chuckle that slips past my lips.

"Will you stay with me tonight?" he asks, eyes still closed.

I hesitate, not sure if that's such a good idea.

"Please," he says softly.

I can't say no to him, especially when he looks like death. "Of course."

His shoulders sag in relief, and I know I've made the right choice.

Tristan tries to kick off his boots but fails miserably. I edge down the bed to help him because this will take all night if I don't. I unlace his boots and slip them off, smiling to myself when I see his Batman socks.

He blindly fumbles with the buttons on his shirt and gets frustrated when they remain fastened.

"Here, let me," I say, stilling his fingers.

He drops them to his side, and slowly, with trembling fingers, I undo each white button.

As the buttons pop through the eyelets, I descend his chest, and my eyes follow the movement because as each button comes undone, it reveals a sliver of creamy white flesh. My eyes wander down his torso, appreciating the sight before them. But I feel wicked for even checking him out because it's wrong, and he's passed out.

Untucking his shirt and pulling it out of his pants gently, I try not to look at his chest as I somehow manage to maneuver his shirt off without breaking his arm. Taking in the sight of Tristan, helpless and topless before me, and his arm of ink, I quickly drop my gaze to his pants.

No way are they coming off.

I toe off my boots and slip in beside him, fully clothed. My back faces his front, and I rest my head on the pillow that smells so much like Tristan.

Curling into myself, I process everything that has happened. Not only tonight but since my arrival close to three weeks ago.

I'm no closer to getting to Canada than when I first arrived, but I'm not too sure if I'm in such a hurry to leave anymore. My priorities have shifted. And that's all because I have met a bunch of people who have made me feel at home. My eyes grow heavy, and I can't stop them from slipping closed as sleep overtakes me.

I wake in the middle of the night, aware of two things.

I am overheating, and someone is in pain.

Number one is because I'm wrapped up in Tristan's arms. His body heat warms me from head to toe, and it's a nice feeling as opposed to waking up in a cold sweat.

Tristan's exhalations tickle my neck since my back presses snugly into his front, and the rise and fall of his chest soothes me back to sleep. But then I hear that pained noise again, coming from the room down the hall, which is Quinn's.

Quietly slipping out of Tristan's embrace, I creep across his carpeted floor and get to the door without too much noise. Turning the handle softly, I tiptoe out into the hallway toward the noise that woke me.

The light is off, and I feel like a total stalker, creeping down the hallway in the dark. But as the pained noise turns into something more of a pleasurable scream, I feel my stomach drop. I should just turn my feet around and go back down the hallway to where I won't see a sight that will tear me in two.

But I don't.

My feet continue their path until I stand a few inches away from Quinn's room. I am flush with the wall as I close my eyes, sickened when I hear the sound of flesh slapping flesh and the unmistakable sound of someone being pleasured beyond belief.

The sound belongs to a female.

I need to see this to get him out of my head, and I know when I witness this one act, Quinn will be out of my system for good.

Inching myself toward the door, I peek through the tiny sliver left ajar. But it's enough to send my stomach roiling with nausea.

The bedside lamp illuminates Quinn's naked body, pumping into a girl from behind, who is spread out on all fours, bucking backward onto him. My eyes lower to Quinn's tight ass, which is clenching as he thrusts into the girl viciously. But she seems to like the force as she moans and buckles from Quinn's violent strength.

This act is not how I imagined it would look; it looks fast, vicious, and mean.

My eyes drop to his tattoo, and I can see it is a side piece starting from mid-chest, wrapping across his ribs and flowing down his lean hip. The colors are bursts of orange and red, and even though I can't make out what it is, I can see script writing is meshed into the coloring.

As Quinn shifts slightly, the light catches off the nipple ring which is hanging loosely from his left nipple, and the sight before me is one of pure dominance.

Quinn has one large hand clenched around the woman's hip, which he's squeezing forcefully, steadying himself as he pushes into her. With her long brown hair wrapped tightly around his other fist, he pulls her head back painfully with each thrust.

As he slams into her, she cries out, "Fuck me harder!" and I can see her ample breasts dangling beneath her, her nipples grazing the sheet underneath her.

My skin pricks in revulsion when I recognize her pained face and voice.

It's Amber.

I cover my mouth to stop the vomit from creeping up my throat, yet I don't move.

Quinn looks fierce, and there's no love in this act—this is cruel and almost punishing.

This must be what Quinn meant by him breaking me because this isn't heartfelt or kind. It is cold, animalistic fucking. The sounds coming out of his parted lips are raw and pleasurable, and I can tell by his harsh breathing that he enjoys every second of it.

I've seen enough, so I creep back to the safety of Tristan's room.

I slip back under the covers and don't shift away when he wraps a kind arm around my waist, hugging me to his chest. I listen to the thumping of his heart, which lies under my ear, drowning out the sound that chills my blood cold.

Fifteen

For the next few days, I keep to myself.

All I can think about is Quinn and Amber. I try to decipher why he would sleep with someone he obviously dislikes, but I come up empty.

I keep busy working at the motel and diner, and thankfully, I don't see Quinn.

As the days pass, I convince myself I'm glad I saw what I did because now I can get back on track and focus on what I originally came here for.

I can't believe how two brothers can be so different. I could never imagine Tristan engaging in an act so aggressively like Quinn.

Nothing about Tristan is like Quinn, and I know he's the right brother to obsess over, but he's not.

I have no doubt Quinn left the door open, knowing I

would hear him consorting with someone who encompasses all I despise in another human being.

Quinn doesn't do anything without thought, and I'm sick of this roller-coaster ride with him. He's made it loud and clear where his feelings for me lie.

I'm just a fool for thinking he was any different.

"Everything okay, child?" Grandpa asks while we're sitting on the couch, watching TV.

We've just shared a bowl of spaghetti. I've fallen into a routine of cooking for Hank and myself, which is great, as I've put on five much-needed pounds.

"Yeah, why?"

"You've been awfully quiet these past few days," he replies, sipping his tea.

"Have I?"

He only nods but doesn't push.

After a minute of silence, I mumble, "Sorry, Hank."

"Whatever for?" he questions, his brow crinkling.

"For being a social pariah."

I wish I could open up and tell him everything. I wish I could tell just one person what I have to live with every day, but I can't. I would never burden him with my problems.

"Paige, we all have our secrets," he replies seriously. "But I want you to know you can talk to me. Whatever it is, I promise I'm here."

The sincerity in his eyes is clear as day, and I appreciate the sentiment. But I can't risk him knowing the truth because the less he knows, the better.

Last night, I dreamed Phil was chasing me, and when he caught me, it was bad—really bad.

I woke myself up, screaming hysterically, the feel of his sweaty palms on me feeling all too real.

I never factored Phil into this equation, and I really hope the dream isn't a premonition.

I love working at the diner. It's a great distraction from the real world. It's always so busy that I never have time to think about anything other than what table 22 ordered or which table ordered the gluten-free sandwich.

There's no time for thoughts about my life or where I'm headed.

Backing out of the double doors while carrying my lunch tray, I nearly bump into Tabitha, who is off to the side talking to Brad.

She looks extremely uncomfortable and trying to wedge past him, but he won't budge.

"Everything okay, Abi?" I ask, standing near her, eyeballing Brad.

She sniffs, and my back stiffens at her response.

I'm so sick of this jackass having this effect on her.

"Abi, can you take this to table 15?" I ask, handing her my tray, my eyes never leaving Brad's.

Tabitha nods and accepts it with a sigh, meeting my eyes with a thank you reflected in hers.

As she walks away, Brad tries to push past me, but I stand my ground.

"Brad, I'm giving you one warning, and consider yourself lucky you're getting it. Stay away from Tabitha."

"What're you gonna do?" he mocks while getting in my face.

"I will fuck you up," I reply, meaning every word.

"Oh, I'm so scared," he says in mock horror. "I think once I'm done playing with that little redhead, I'll move on to you."

I push my chest into his and raise my face to meet his in challenge.

"Try it. I dare you." I raise an eyebrow defiantly.

My face contorts in pure rage, and Brad can see the change as he shrinks back, unsure of what to do.

"Whatever, freak," he spits out. "You haven't seen the last of me." He walks off, eyeing me over his shoulder before he sits at a booth.

When the door dings, announcing we have a new customer, I see Malibu Stacey enter and frolic over to Brad, planting a disgusting, pornographic kiss on his lips. I shake my head, repulsed that Brad would hit Tabitha up when Stacey isn't around.

Tabitha is over within a second. "Are you okay? I'm so sorry I just left you. I didn't know what else to do."

I take a few calming breaths and realize my fists are clenched by my sides.

"It's okay, Abi. You shouldn't be anywhere near that guy. He's poison," I reply, still eyeing him and Stacey canoodling together.

"What did you say to him?"

"I told him to stay away from you. Otherwise, he has to deal with me," I say with half a smile, downplaying what I actually said to him.

Tabitha's lower lip trembles, and tears pool in her big, innocent eyes.

"Thank you. No one has ever stuck up for me before," she confesses, a tear running down her rosy cheek.

"Well, that's because they're all idiots."

Who would have thought I would defend someone's

honor so strongly that it leaves me shaking in rage?

Tabitha throws her arms around my neck and hugs me tightly.

"Thank you, Paige. You're my best friend."

I still, slightly shocked by her admission, but I return her hug, her candy scent engulfing me.

I've never been anyone's friend, let alone anyone's *best* friend. When the time comes for me to leave, I'm going to really miss being Tabitha's best friend.

"What's with all the tears?" Tristan asks, ducking his head out from behind the double doors.

Tabitha quickly wipes away any evidence of her tears and tries to smile, but Tristan isn't buying it.

"We're going out tonight. Just us three," he says, looking down at me. "Besides, I owe you for the other night."

I know he's referring to his birthday, but I shake my head.

"You don't owe me anything, but you know what? Fuck it, let's go out."

Both Tristan's and Tabitha's eyes light up, and Tabitha claps excitedly.

After the past few days, scrap that, after the past few years, I need to go out, get drunk, and forget who I am.

We pull up at Tristan's place, and Tabitha beeps twice. I eye the driveway, noticing that Quinn's truck isn't there. I don't know where he is, and quite frankly, I don't want to know. The scenarios I have placed him in over the past few days all involve him naked and sweaty and fucking whatever bimbo he can find.

Tabitha notices my reaction, and it scares me that she can read me so well after knowing me for such a short time.

"Still haven't heard from Quinn since you saw a little *too* much of him?" she says in disgust. I told her I saw him and Amber together.

I shake my head. "Nope. And it's for the best."

Great, now I sound just like him.

Tristan bounces down the front stairs, and both Tabitha and I swoon.

"He's so hot."

I nod because he is, but looking at him reminds me of Quinn. And then I begin thinking about Quinn fucking Amber, and then, well, then I start to feel nauseous.

"Ladies," Tristan says, opening the back door and slipping into Tabitha's BMW gracefully.

"Hi, Tristan," she gushes.

I almost laugh at her reaction but don't because mine isn't any better when I see Quinn.

"Hey," I say, turning over my shoulder to say hello.

His mouth parts slightly, and his eyes widen.

"Wow, you look amazing," he says in awe.

"Um, thanks. I have Abi to thank," I reply, turning away embarrassed as I gaze out my window at the night lights.

"Well, you both look amazing," he adds when he picks up on my discomfort.

Tabitha beams while I look out into the star-filled night, my thoughts drowning me whole.

It takes about forty minutes to get to the club.

The line to *Revolt!* extends all around the block, but Tabitha has connections. Well, her mom does.

I feel awful for cutting in line, but it will take forever if we don't. I give a few apologetic nods to disgruntled patrons as a big, beefy security guard by the name of Surly escorts us to the front of the line.

We don't get carded, and again, I think the connections factor comes in handy.

We pay the cover charge and enter the glass doors, and as I look around the bar, my mouth is agape at the sight before me.

Revolt! is a chic bar filled with an assortment of people who I never thought would congregate together in one place. A mix of preppy jocks to old-school rockers, everyone seems to be having a blast, bopping to some happy tune playing over the speakers.

Our feet automatically take us toward the bar, and I slip past a couple making out against the brick wall.

"Who wants a drink? My treat," Tristan says, looking between Tabitha and me.

"I'll have a Salty Chihuahua and a shot of tequila," I say with a smile because the name always cracks me up.

Tristan raises his eyebrows at me. "Watch out! Someone is out to get drunk," he jokes, waiting patiently to be served.

Tabitha offered to drive tonight as she not-so-subtly said I must drown my sorrows in tequila.

So who am I to argue?

However, after my eighth drink, things become fuzzy and a little uncomfortable. Tabitha chats with an old high school friend while Tristan and I play the drinking game, Animal.

Numerous shot glasses litter the sticky tabletop in front of me because I suck at this game. On the other hand, Tristan is a pro, making me look like a total amateur.

"You suck!" I laugh, slapping my palms against the table and downing my shot of whatever sits before me.

"Now, don't be a sore loser." He grins while I scrunch my

face up in disgust after tossing back a drink that tastes like gasoline.

"Oh"—I blow out a raspberry at him—"to you!"

He laughs while I'm attempting to breathe after my potent cocktail.

"This game blows. Next!" I chuckle, swatting him in the arm.

"Guys, I'm going to go dance," Tabitha says, smiling. "Wanna come with?"

Both Tristan and I shake our heads in disgust, and she laughs.

"Okay, I'll be back soon." She shuffles out of the booth, dancing down to the dance floor.

Tristan slides two shot glasses out in front of us.

"Next game. Truth or dare."

I know better, as my truths will get me into trouble, but I stupidly nod when my brain screams no.

"Okay, you first."

"Hmm, truth," I say foolishly.

I am obviously drunk, as sober Mia would avoid the truth like the plague.

"What's the most embarrassing thing you've ever done?"

That's easy.

"I fell asleep while skinny-dipping and woke up giving a Boy Scout his first erection."

Tristan laughs hysterically while knocking back a shot. I'm not too sure of the rules, but I'm guessing if the answer to the question is acceptable, then the person who asked the question has to drink.

"Okay, my turn."

I really want to ask him about his family, but I don't.

"Who was your first crush?"

Tristan smiles and replies without thought. "Jessica Rabbit."

"The cartoon character?"

Tristan nods and bites his lip playfully. "Yes. Isn't she every eight-year-old boy's fantasy?"

I splutter out a laugh and take a drink of my tequila.

This goes on for about ten minutes, and I'm enjoying myself as I get to know Tristan through the silly questions I'm asking.

Tristan spins his empty shot glass, obviously thinking of a question to ask me.

"What's the worst thing you've ever done?"

My laugh dies down when I think about how I would answer that question, and I'm sure it shows on my face.

"Dare!" I quickly cry, nearly jumping out of my seat.

Tristan cocks his eyebrow.

"Are you sure? I'm giving you one last chance to back out."

I shake my head, my hair swishing with the movement.

"I'm no quitter, Berkeley. Give it your best shot."

Tristan inches toward me, dipping his face to meet mine.

"Kiss me," he whispers, his blue eyes focused on mine.

I lean forward to kiss his cheek, but he backs away.

"Not there. Here," he says, pointing at his full pink lips.

My eyes drop of their own accord, and as he licks his plump lower lip, my heart begins beating frantically.

I can't kiss him. It's…wrong. But how the hell am I going to back out now? I need a distraction and like now.

"Hey, kids."

Crisis averted.

I pull away so quickly, my head spins, and I smash into Quinn, who sits beside me. As soon as my flesh touches his, my skin is alight.

He looks perfect, as usual, in a tight white T-shirt, black jeans, and a leather jacket.

He pulls in his bottom lip, his white teeth tugging at his piercing reflectively. I don't know what he's thinking, and it pisses me off. Everything about him pisses me off, but I can't stay away.

Tristan clears his throat, and I shrink away since I have inadvertently almost climbed into Quinn's lap. Then the nasty image of Amber and Quinn assaults my brain, and I inch away from him.

"What are you doing here?" Tristan asks with an edge to his voice.

Quinn smiles boldly. "Hello to you too, brother." He reaches for a shot glass and throws his head back, downing it quickly.

I'm fixated on the way his throat moves, swallowing down the liquor, his Adam's apple moving as the liquid goes down.

Mentally slapping myself, I refocus.

"How are you, Red?" Quinn asks with a frown as he stares disapprovingly at my face.

"Peachy," I sharply reply, trying not to decode his frown.

"You look…" He stops, searching for the right word. "Different."

Well, *fuck* him. I don't need his approval, and who is he to judge, as he had no qualms fucking Amber.

"Oh, I'm sorry, I didn't realize you cared what I looked like. But isn't it lucky I don't care what *you* think," I spit out heatedly.

Quinn looks taken aback by my outburst, and I suddenly feel about to suffocate.

"Let me out."

I stand abruptly, trying to push past Quinn, who blocks

my escape.

Both he and Tristan stand, but thankfully, Quinn steps aside, and I race past him, storming off, looking for Tabitha.

I need to get away from Quinn because my traitorous body responds to him in a way it shouldn't, especially after what I saw.

Where is Tabitha? She'll know what to do.

Scanning the packed place, I can't see her anywhere. She's not on the dance floor or at the bar, so that leaves the bathroom.

I enter the black-painted room and try not to heave at the smell. Kicking off a stray piece of toilet paper that has stuck to the bottom of my boot, I call out to her.

"Abi?"

There are five cubicles, and as I look under the door of each, I hear a groan in the end stall.

Quietly, I knock on the door.

"Abi, is that you?"

"Paige?" she asks, followed by her throwing her guts up.

"I'm coming in," I warn and push open the door, slipping into the small cubicle.

Tabitha is hunched over the bowl, grabbing onto the sides as her body shudders with the force of her heaving. I brush back her fiery red hair to stop puke from getting into it.

"What's the matter? Is it something you ate?" I ask, holding her hair in a loose ponytail.

After one last heave, she shakes her head loosely.

"No, I don't know what happened. One minute, I was dancing, and then the next, I felt dizzy, disoriented, and couldn't even stand upright. I felt like I was drunk, but I only had one drink."

That sparks my interest.

"What did you drink?"

"Don't get mad, but Brad bought me a drink. He said he wanted a truce and that he was sorry. I didn't see the harm in it," she says with a slur that echoes off the toilet rim as her head is buried into the porcelain.

"And you got sick not too long afterward?" I ask, my heart beginning to pound.

She lazily nods

"Abi, look at me," I say, and she weakly lifts her head, which flops as she's unable to support herself.

"I can't see you properly, Paige," she says with difficulty as her eyes slip shut.

"Abi, can you stand?"

She shrugs, which results in her slipping forward and smacking her head against the wall. She tries to move but has limited muscle control.

"Son of a bitch," I mutter with rage. I'm going to kill him. "I'm going to go get Tristan, okay? Don't move."

She nods, tears slipping from her frightened eyes, begging me to help her.

I squeeze her shoulder softly, giving her a reassuring smile.

"I'll be right back."

I sprint out of the bathroom, almost slipping on the tiles as my body pulsates in rage. I search for Tristan but don't have to look far.

He and Quinn stand a few feet away from the girls' bathroom, talking animatedly. They stop as soon as they see me approach, and I don't have time to question what they're discussing.

"Tristan, Abi is sick."

Tristan's eyes soften. "What's the matter?"

I look from him to Quinn, who looks as serious as I've ever seen him.

"Brad roofied her," I spit out.

Both brothers' faces reflect the other's identically.

"What the *fuck*?" Quinn snarls, his strong jaw clenching.

I blow out a breath and shrug.

"Brad is a dick, and he'll pay for what he did. But for now, can you help me carry her out? She can't stand. She…"

Before I finish my sentence, Quinn is stalking into the ladies' bathroom, unconcerned if it's occupied. He's out a second later with Tabitha cradled in his arms, her hands wrapped around his neck and her head tucked under his chin.

"Where's her car?" Quinn asks, rearranging his hands under her knees, holding her tighter into him.

Tristan searches for Tabitha's keys in her shoulder bag.

"Follow me," he says as he fishes them out.

He and Quinn turn to leave, but there's no way I'm letting Brad off.

"You guys get Abi to the car. I have to grab my bag and stuff. I'll be with you in a minute."

Quinn looks at me, his eyes narrowing, but he doesn't argue. "C'mon, Tris."

Tristan gives me one last look, and I nod, hoping he follows Quinn. Thankfully, he does.

As soon as they are out the door, my eyes search the room for Brad. He's not at all hard to spot with his ridiculous college football jacket. He's flirting with some girl at the bar.

Pushing my way through the sea of people and reaching into my top, ensuring my push-up bra is doing its job, I reach Brad in less than a minute.

I shove my way between him and some blonde, twirling her hair between her fingers.

"Hi, Brad," I purr, running my finger down his clean-shaven cheek.

The barfly takes the hint and storms off, leaving me alone with this disgusting individual.

Brad looks taken aback, but as I wet my lips and push out my chest, an air of confidence passes over him.

"Hey, babe," he breathes, looking down my top. "Not that I'm complaining, but what are you doing?"

I lean forward, my red lips grazing his cheek as I whisper, "Hopefully you, in the next two minutes."

I actually feel sick being this close to him as his cheap cologne suffocates me, and so is the predatory look in his beady brown eyes.

"Couldn't stay away?" he says cockily, running a big, rough hand down my hip.

"Something like that. Follow me," I say over my shoulder, making sure to wiggle my ass as I walk away.

It works, and he's following in hot pursuit.

We exit, and I round the corner, looking for a dark, seedy place. Perfect. I spot an alleyway and head for it.

"Where're you going?" he says, grabbing my ass.

I quicken my step, and as we're halfway down the alley, Brad grabs my arm and slams me into the wall. The bricks scratch at my bare back as I have on a short camisole, but this is good. I want him to hurt me because it just fuels the rage I have burning inside me.

His hands roughly take hold of my breasts, and he kneads them forcefully while I faux giggle.

"Brad, baby," I say huskily. "Let me take care of you."

Placing my hand on his chest, I push him back, switching positions so his back is now pressed up against the dirty wall.

He licks his thin lips and eyes my breasts with hunger.

"Come on, then. It's not going to suck itself," he says with a shit-eating grin.

Taking a deep breath and utilizing my street smarts, I run my hands down his muscled body, and he groans as I unbuckle his football-shaped belt buckle.

I seductively look up at him as I drop to a crouch and purr, "I'm about to blow your mind."

He leans his head back and closes his eyes, moaning.

"Oh, you fucking crazy bitch."

I take this moment to reach into my boot and pull out my flick knife. With lightning speed, I dig the knife into his throat, and his eyes open in alarm. I thrust down onto his windpipe as he pushes off the wall but stops as he feels my blade cut into his throat.

His wide eyes look down at me as he spits out, "You're so fucking dead."

Scoffing, I push my arm across his chest, tilting the knife up and nicking his Adam's apple.

"Funny, seeing as I'm the one with the knife. You're *going* to stay away from Tabitha," I sneer, eyeing him angrily.

"You're both dead," he declares, trying to push forward.

Looks like the knife isn't making my intentions clear, so I quickly reach down, grab his balls, and twist.

He lets out a pained yelp, and his eyes instantly water.

"Like I was saying, you will stay the fuck away from her because if you don't…" I twist a little harder. "This disgusting thing will become aquatinted with my knife. And next time, I won't be so forgiving."

Brad's face is turning red, and he's gasping for air, so I let him go, but my knife stays poised at his neck.

"We clear?"

Brad nods, unable to speak.

I pull my knife away as I'm pretty certain Brad is now paralyzed in the groin area.

But I'm wrong.

As I turn away, he grabs me by the shoulder, slamming me backward, and I hit the wall—hard, my knife falling from my hand. A rush of wind leaves my lungs, and I'm stunned. But when he comes toward me, his fist aimed for my head, I duck low and punch him in the abdomen. I've winded him, as I've hit him in the solar plexus, and he pulls away, clutching his side, struggling to breathe.

I deliver a right hook to his face, and his head snaps back with a sickening snap. He looks stunned that I have the balls to take on a two-hundred-pound quarterback, but I've taken on worse.

He licks his bleeding lip and charges me, but I sidestep him and knee him in the groin. He drops to the dirty ground, howling in pain.

Dropping down to eye level, I spit out, "You go near her again, and I'll finish what I started."

Brad's face is contorted in rage and pain as he holds his junk in his cupped palms.

Standing up and knowing I'm running out of time, I don't pay attention to my surroundings, and this is what costs me. Brad is clearly on something because he should be down, but he grabs my feet, pulling them out from under me. I fall face-first, my wrists breaking my fall, which crunch on impact.

I wince as my forehead hits the concrete, and I see stars.

Before I know what's happening, Brad crawls onto my back, using his heavy weight to crush me, which presses my chest into the dirty ground that smells of garbage and piss.

I try to buck him off, but he pins me with a knee in the center of my back, his whole weight resting on my spine. I kick out like a crazy woman, but I'm not going anywhere. His hands violently reach for the waistband of my jeans, trying to yank them down.

Anger overcomes me, and I know I need to get him off because his intentions are made clear as I feel his arousal digging into my back.

"Get off!" I snarl, kicking my legs, trying to dislodge him, but he's not going anywhere.

He wraps my long hair, which has come loose from my ponytail, around his hand, pulling my head back all the way and exposing my neck.

"You fucking whore! I'm going to fuck you till that tight pussy bleeds…and then, I'm going to fuck it again and again." He pulls my camisole roughly, tearing it in two.

I need to come up with a plan in two seconds before Brad makes good on his word.

I am so angry with myself; I know better than this.

I'm about to fight with all my might, using what I learned on the streets, when I feel Brad being yanked off my back, and the unmistakable sound of a fist connecting with flesh echoes off the alley walls.

Everything is a little blurred, but I can make out Brad being beaten to a pulp by someone.

I push up and wince as pain shoots up my arms, but I need to get off this dirty ground before I throw up. As I stand, I realize my top hangs off me, my lacy red bra exposed for the world to see.

But that's the least of my concerns as I see that *Quinn* is my Superman. And he's currently kicking the shit out of a prone Brad, who's lying in the gutter, each kick hollowing in his chest.

I limp over as my back feels bruised, holding my hands to

my chest to stop my shirt from falling to the ground.

"Quinn." It comes out hoarse.

But he doesn't stop. He looks like a warrior, blood splashed across his face and knuckles—Brad's blood.

Quinn continues kicking him in the ribs, and when I hear Brad splutter up a mouthful of blood, I know he won't stop until Brad is either unconscious or dead.

"Quinn, stop!" I cry, reaching for him, but he's deaf to reason as he continues his assault on a non-moving Brad.

Only when a wailing siren can be heard does he stop. He pulls back, his emerald eyes eaten up by pure black irises consumed with rage.

His eyes drop to my bare chest as my ruined top plummeted to the ground while I struggled to restrain Quinn.

Quinn's lip curls, and he snarls before kicking Brad in the ribs one last time.

He shrugs out of his jacket and slips it around my trembling shoulders.

"Red, we gotta go," he says, linking his fingers through mine, his eyes wild.

I look down the alley and make out red and blue lights flashing against the walls.

Nodding, I grip his hand, and we make a mad dash for the other end of the alley.

I blindly follow the man who just saved my ass.

The moment we jump into his truck, Quinn cranks on the heater, his eyes never leaving the road as he zips in and out of traffic.

I am bundled up in his jacket, and being surrounded by his smell and the heat sends some of the chill away, but not all of it.

I can't stop thinking about the way Brad's body felt digging into me, and I feel sick. I cover my mouth with my hand and swallow it down.

"Are you okay?" Quinn asks, looking at me quickly, his eyes darting between me and the road.

"I just want a shower," I whisper because I can smell Brad and the alleyway all over me.

Quinn nods, his hair slipping into his intense eyes. "We're almost there."

"Where're we going?"

"To Night Cats," he answers, his brow crinkling, and I know he's still fuming.

"Where are Tabitha and Tristan?" I ask bravely, afraid he'll yell at me for getting into such a stupid situation.

"Tris took Abi back to our place. I'm sure her mom wouldn't appreciate seeing her daughter in the state she's in."

I nod because he's right.

We pull into the parking lot, and the sight makes me feel better. I can't get out of the truck quick enough and practically run to my room, in desperate need of a shower.

Quinn follows, and I turn to look at him over my shoulder.

"You don't have to come in. I'm okay."

Quinn doesn't reply and only keeps close behind me as I dig into my bag for my keys. My fingers tremble as I try to unlock the door, but I can't maneuver the key into the lock.

Quinn reaches over my shoulder and softly pulls the keys from my hand, unlocking the door easily.

I enter, and the familiar space is one I never thought I would be so elated to see. Quinn follows, softly closing the door behind him.

As I turn around, the realization of what almost happened to me hits home, and my legs begin to crumple beneath me. But I won't show Quinn I'm about to crack.

Instead, I shrug out of his jacket.

"Thanks." I smile, slipping my arm out of the sleeve, but Quinn stops me, placing his hand on my arm.

"Go shower. I'll be here when you get out."

I don't bother arguing with the utter conclusiveness in his voice.

Nodding quickly, I make my way into the bathroom and kick off my ruined clothes. I can't get into the shower fast enough, and the scorching water spray burns my skin, but I don't care. It returns some feeling back into my shivering body.

Thinking back to everything that happened, I brace my hands on the tiles, my head dropping low, trying to steady myself. How could I have been so stupid? I know better than to be so careless.

After twenty minutes, I step out of the shower, combing my wet hair and brushing my teeth—twice.

Looking down at the small towel barely covering my body, I curse because I've forgotten to bring in a change of clothes. I could slip on Quinn's jacket, but it still wouldn't cover enough of me not to blush crimson.

Sucking it up and taking a deep breath, I open the door and see Quinn sitting on the bed, resting against the headboard with his legs crossed, remote in hand, watching TV.

His eyes snap up to meet mine as I shyly step out into the room, tugging at the towel.

"I forgot my clothes," I say stupidly, explaining why I'm standing in front of him in an indecent towel.

He gives me a strained smile, and I place his jacket on the back of a chair.

Now that I've calmed down and hysteria isn't clouding my vision, I can see Quinn has speckles of blood on his hands and face.

"Did you want to use the bathroom?" I ask, trying not to make a big deal out of Quinn's war paint.

He nods, and his silence worries me as he has an unreadable look.

I sidestep him to allow him to pass, and as the bathroom door closes behind him, I dig through my dresser and pull out a pair of sleep shorts and a tank.

Switching off the light as the bright fluorescents give me a headache, I slip under the covers, which don't feel as scratchy as they usually do. I flip on the bedside lamp, not wanting Quinn to think I'm trying to set a romantic feel with the dimmed lighting.

The bathroom door opens, and as Quinn switches off the light, stepping out into the room, I can see he's topless. I'm curled in a fetal position facing the bathroom, and as Quinn takes a step toward me, my body responds in a way it shouldn't.

The tiny room suddenly got a lot smaller, with his commanding presence filling any vacant space.

I lower my eyes as I check out his hardened chest, abs, and sculptured V-muscle. He has a light dusting of darkened hair painting his belly button, and it slithers down into his low-slung jeans.

The light flickering off the TV draws attention to his nipple ring, a silver hoop with a small ball hanging off the end of it. My eyes stop at his tattoo, which I still can't quite read, but the sight before me is one of pure perfection.

Quinn can see me totally checking him out, but he doesn't shift uncomfortably.

"Sorry about the shirt. It had bl—" He pauses. "It was dirty," he says instead.

I nod and bite my lip as suddenly, the air is charged with… something, and all I can think about is him lying next to me.

"You can come lie down. If you want," I add when he stands awkwardly in the middle of the room.

I should be incensed with him, as images of him and Amber flash through my mind as I invite him into my bed. But after what happened tonight, it all seems so trivial. He saved me, and I hate to think where I would be if it wasn't for him.

So all my anger subsides because all I want him to do is comfort me and make me feel safe.

He tongues his lip ring before he nods and prowls over to the bed. I try not to ogle how his lean body radiates pure dominance with every step he takes.

He toes off his boots and sits on the bed, kicking his legs so they lay on top of the blanket, but he never slips underneath.

He shuffles up the bed and rests against the headboard, crossing his arms over his chiseled chest and looking down at me. I raise my eyes to meet his, and a swarm of emotions overwhelms me.

"Thank you," I whisper, biting my lip. "For everything."

Quinn shakes his head, his hair slipping into his fiery eyes. "What were you thinking, going out there after him by yourself?"

He's mad at me. He has every right to be. I'm mad at myself. But I won't sit back and be scolded like some naughty child.

"I got in a couple of good shots before he got me down. He should have stayed down."

"I'm sure you did, but he didn't stay down, did he? What would have happened if I didn't come find you? You would just be another statistic," he says, grinding down on his jaw.

"You weren't even scared. You were angry! Do you have no fear? You could have been seriously hurt. For fuck's sake!"

Suddenly, I feel defensive.

"I never asked you to come find me. No one asked you to be my knight in shining armor. I can take care of myself," I snap, glaring at him. "Something I have mentioned before."

Quinn exhales, running a hand through his hair. "Why do you do that?"

"Do what?" I ask heatedly.

"Pretend you don't need anyone in your life. It's okay to be vulnerable, to need help. It's not going to make anyone think less of you. Stop acting like you're goddamn invincible!"

"Oh, you're one to talk!" I snap, sitting up and meeting him head-on. "You're a walking conundrum, and at the possibility of connecting with someone, you run or hide...or fuck someone else's brains out."

"What are you talking about?" he asks, his eyes narrowing.

"I saw you."

"Saw what?" he asks, clearly puzzled by my outburst.

"I saw you...with Amber," I confess, repulsed by the memory.

Quinn is stunned by my revelation, which makes me think that his leaving the door open wasn't intentional.

He rubs the back of his neck, and I watch the way his hardened stomach ripples with the movement.

After a moment of silence, he confesses, "I'm sorry you saw that."

"Why? You didn't look sorry when you were fucking her!" I retort, suddenly feeling hot and kicking the blankets off my legs.

Rolling onto my back and placing my hands behind my head, I stare up at the ceiling, deep in thought.

The bed dips beside me as Quinn lies down near me. I don't turn to face him because I don't know what I will do. I'm a ball of emotion, and I don't know if I want to hit or kiss him.

I can hear Quinn sucking on his lip ring before he says, "You're right. I do shut people out because I'm sick of letting people in and then them leaving. What's the point?"

Why do I have a feeling he's talking about his mom? And maybe…me?

When I turn my head to look at him, his face is mere inches away from mine.

"I was only with Amber because I saw you and Tristan sleeping together, and you looked so peaceful, so happy, and no matter how much I want you, Red, because I do, I don't deserve you…but my brother does."

My breathing begins increasing, and I try to will my pounding heart to stop. But the more I try, the faster it beats.

"Quinn…I'm *not*…a good person. Tristan deserves someone better than me."

"Bullshit," he whispers with a shake of his head.

"If you knew what I did…you wouldn't say that." I declare my fears for the first time to another living soul.

"What did you do that's so bad you can't allow yourself happiness? What are you running from?" he asks softly. "Tell me, Red."

I shake my head, wanting to back away from him. "No. I can't."

"Why not?" he pleads, his eyes beseeching me to tell him the truth.

Here goes nothing. "Because if I tell you…" I pause. "If I tell you what I did…you won't look at me like the way you do now."

Quinn inches forward, licking his bottom lip. "How do I

look at you?"

"Like I'm *worth* looking at. Like I'm worth *something*," I admit, lowering my eyes.

Quinn reaches forward, tilting my chin to look into his insightful eyes.

"You don't realize how much you're worth."

"That's not true," I murmur, my chin still enclosed in his grip. "If that were true, you wouldn't have shared your bed with another person other than me."

A stunned gasp passes through Quinn's lips, and I lower my eyes, hoping he doesn't freak out, as there is one thing I need to know.

"Amber said you and her…" I whisper, thinking back to her mentioning she had been Quinn's little bed buddy while he was MIA.

"What did she say?" Quinn questions, his eyes searching mine when I raise them timidly to meet his.

"She said you guys have been together," I confess, feeling sick at the admission.

Quinn curses under his breath, his jaw straining. "Together?" he asks, his eyebrow arching in confusion.

"Yeah," I nod. "She implied she's your go-to girl, when you need to…go."

"She's lying. I've only been with her twice. And both times had me wishing I was anywhere but there, with her. I'm a fucking idiot," he says, looking ashamed. "I meant what I said about her."

"So why did you sleep with her again if you don't like her?" I question, afraid something has changed since the last time we spoke about her.

Quinn sighs, closing his eyes briefly before reopening them. "You don't have to like a person to have sex with them.

And that's all it was—mindless, numbing sex."

Lowering my eyes once again, I believe him, but it doesn't make me feel any better.

"You wanna know why I slept with Amber?"

Not really, but I nod.

"Because, Red, I have tried *everything* to get you out of my head, but nothing has worked. The only thing I hadn't tried was *fucking* you out of my system." I blush at his admission. "But that was a complete mistake. One I wish I could take back. And knowing you saw it, fuck me, I hate myself more than I already do for doing something so fucking stupid. I'm so sorry. Please forgive me."

"It looked like you enjoyed it," I sadly confess, thinking back to the memory.

Quinn looks at me intensely, searching my eyes feverishly.

"I felt *nothing* for Amber…and the only time I could come," he whispers seriously, "is when I imagined it was *you* I was buried deep inside. It doesn't matter how many girls I'm with. They'll never be you."

I open my mouth, stunned, because I really don't know what to say. But he silences me by inching forward and closing the distance between us, physically and emotionally.

At first, I don't move, stunned to feel his soft lips on mine. But as he coaxes me to open my mouth with his tongue, my lips part willingly, and I explode.

I can't describe what I'm feeling as the sensation of Quinn's mouth on me, kissing me with a fierce need, is like nothing I've ever experienced before. He gently rolls on top of me, resting his weight on his hands as he deepens the kiss, his barbell searching out every crevice of my mouth, causing me to shiver in desire. As he angles his mouth over mine, kissing me deeper and harder, his lip ring bites into my lip, the sting of it hitting me straight between my legs.

I raise my hands apprehensively and glide them up his lean sides, feeling the bump of each rib, and then move up over his biceps, encircling his neck. When I rake my fingers into his hair, the strands feel like silk as they slip between my fingertips.

I can feel Quinn hardening against my leg, and after tonight, you'd think I would recoil or be afraid, but I'm not. I welcome it as I open my legs for him, and he settles between them naturally, like he was created to be there.

My fingers never leave his hair as he breaks our kiss and begins softly biting my neck. I've never experienced this before, and a heavy feeling is building in my belly.

Quinn kisses leisurely over my throat and continues down to the top of my chest, rising and falling in breathless anticipation. As he swirls his tongue in the valley between my breasts, I arch my back, needing to get closer to his skillful tongue.

My nipples instantly harden when his naked chest presses down on me, warming every inch of my skin. I tighten my grasp in his hair, my fingers flexing as his hand snakes down my torso and rests on my bare thigh. He squeezes my leg to match his mouth's rhythm, sucking my lip softly.

A moan escapes my parted lips, and Quinn slides in his tongue, kissing me until I pant.

I can't stop my legs from scissoring because the ache between them is almost painful.

"What's wrong? Am I hurting you?" Quinn asks, pulling away, his eyes searching mine.

I shake my head with bated breath and whimper when he shifts between my legs, pressing into my core.

Quinn's eyes widen in understanding as he sucks on his

lip ring smugly.

"You wanna get off," he whispers, and it's more of a statement, not a question.

I bite down on my lip because that's exactly what I want.

"Do you want me to get you off?" he asks huskily, sucking on my bottom lip, dragging it away from my teeth.

I moan as he glides his barbell along my bottom lip. And images of what that piercing could do to me…down there plague my mind, and I almost come thinking about it.

The hand resting at my thigh slowly slithers higher and higher until it reaches the apex of my thighs. As he presses the heel of his hand against me, I jolt off the bed, ripples of pure need rocking my starving body.

Quinn hisses in a breath through his clenched teeth. "What do you like?"

I don't know what I like as I've never been asked this question before. Yes, I've gotten myself off, but never by somebody else.

Quinn sees my apprehension and kisses the corner of my mouth.

"You've gotten off before, right?"

I nod, feeling my cheeks burn.

"So what do you like?" Quinn asks once again, brushing my hair off my brow softly.

"I…I don't know," I reply, feeling like a total idiot.

"You don't…oh," Quinn finishes, slipping his hand away from my core, thankfully understanding what I mean.

"Are you sure you want me to?"

I nod, silencing him.

"As long as it's not what I saw you do to Amber," I admit as I am so not ready for that.

Quinn looks as if I've slapped him.

"Not with you, Red. Never with you. I meant what I said. We do this, and I will possess every part of you. Do you want that?"

My hand timidly slides up his rocky abs, and when I reach his nipple, I tug on the piercing lightly, which earns a quick hiss from Quinn.

"I want you."

Quinn's chest exhales in relief, and he swoops forward, kissing me fiercely. His hand lazily walks up my leg, and ever so softly, his fingers begin rubbing over my center through the soft cotton of my pajama bottoms.

I rocket off the bed as I feel his wicked fingers on me.

"Are you okay?" he asks softly, his hands stilling, his eyes searching mine deeply.

"Yes," I croak, my body shuddering with every stroke.

He bites my lip and slowly glides his fingers down the waistband of my shorts, his two fingers gliding up and down my slippery entrance lightly.

My eyes sink to half mast because if I look into his eyes, I will explode before he even seeks refuge inside me.

Quinn kisses my chin as he inches a finger into me, and I choke back a sob of pleasure. He begins moving in and out, slowly at first, but as I reach down and grab onto his wrist with a death grip, encouraging him to move faster, he obeys.

I am shamefully riding his hand, my mouth parted in ecstasy, and I'm not embarrassed of this moment of vulnerability because it's with Quinn.

"You okay?"

I nod, as I can't speak.

He then inserts another long finger, stretching me, and my back bows off the bed as I'm about to detonate. When his fingers dance over me, I can see why people get addicted to this feeling because I am now an addict—a Quinn addict.

Quinn leans forward, consuming my mouth with his, his soft hair brushing my cheeks, and everything is too much. I am close, and Quinn knows it. He can read my body like he's done this a million times before, and as he brushes over my clit with a quick flick, I explode in a thunderous scream. I slump into a messy, noisy heap, my heart beating wildly.

It isn't until I feel Quinn kissing my cheeks softly do I open my eyes, coming down from my post-orgasmic heaven. I watch him carefully as he brushes the hair off my brow, his chest rising and falling quickly, and I realize he probably also needs some kind of release.

But I don't know how.

He must be able to read my worry as he traces my eyebrows with the finger that was seconds ago buried deep inside me.

"That was the hottest thing I have ever seen. You coming because of me, because of what I was doing to you, holy fuck. I could make you come ten times a day, and I still wouldn't get enough," he confesses hoarsely.

My legs go weak at the thought, and I hate to admit that it still wouldn't be enough for me either, as this feeling is surreal.

We are quiet for some time, and I can't stop thinking about how this changes things between us. Well, it changes things for me; I just hope it does the same for Quinn.

I wince when he brushes over the graze on my forehead. His eyes darken, and I know he's reliving tonight's memory.

"You need to report what happened to you," he says seriously, ruining my bubble of bliss.

There's no way I can do that. Going to the police will require me to divulge personal info, which will turn me into the culprit.

"No way."

"Would it have anything to do with the Colt you're carrying?" he asks, waiting for my reaction.

"What? How do you know I'm carrying?" I ask, my voice rising slightly. "Not that there is anything wrong with carrying a gun. A girl can never be too sure when she may need it for protection."

I know I should be concerned that he's been snooping around in my things, but funnily enough, I'm not.

Quinn's mouth twitches as he doesn't fail to see the significance of my comment.

"That's true," he replies, but I know those inquisitive eyes will figure out what I'm hiding sooner or later.

Hopefully, it's later rather than sooner.

"Go to sleep, Red."

"Will you be here when I wake up?"

But when he kisses my forehead, I don't stand a chance and slip into a welcomed slumber.

# Sixteen

only wake because the bright sun streams through the sliver between the curtains, which conveniently hits me dead center in the face.

It takes a minute for my foggy, sleep-deprived brain to scan through the events of last night. And I can't help but blush when thinking about what happened between Quinn and me.

I remember how gentle he was, something I never thought he'd be after seeing him and Amber together. But he did say it would never be that way between us. Now, I'm totally curious as to how things *would* be between us.

"Mornin', Sleeping Beauty."

Lost in Quinn thoughts, I fail to notice him in my room. He's obviously had a shower because his hair is wet and tousled from towel drying, and I feel a little self-conscious about last night. I flush when I notice him smirking at me.

"Nice shirt," I say, my eyes dropping to the Alice in Chains T-shirt he is wearing. Although it looks amazing on him, I prefer him topless.

He smirks while slipping his belt through the loops on his jeans. "Thanks, I own one just like it."

I cock an eyebrow and notice the hem is frayed in the same spot as mine.

"Hey! That's mine," I say, mouth agape as I sit up in bed, the blanket pooling around my waist.

Quinn's eyes drop to my chest, and a small smile tugs at the corner of his lips, his hands stilling on fastening his belt.

I look down at what has captured his attention and roll my eyes.

"My eyes are up here."

His eyes are still fixated on my chest as he replies, "I know where your eyes are."

I can't help but smile since this is the same conversation we had when we first met. Who would have thought we would be having another three weeks later?

I stretch and wince to distract myself when I realize I'm a little sore. Funny how I felt nothing but pleasure last night.

Quinn notices my reaction and sighs, finally quitting with the ogling.

"Red, I wish you'd change your mind about going to the police."

I shake my head stubbornly. "Not gonna happen."

"Why not?" he questions, sitting at the end of the bed, tugging my little toe, which is peeking out from under the covers.

Because I'm a fugitive, I ad-lib.

"Because Brad's dad *is* the police. What would be the

point?"

"They'd only have to take one look at your face and know you weren't lying," Quinn says, eyeing my forehead, his nostrils flaring with each heavy exhale.

"And they'd only have to take one look at *his* and see what a great job you did of it, and he could claim it was self-defense. That we both jumped him, and he was only protecting himself."

Quinn is quiet as he knows there's truth to my words.

"I just hate that he's out there walking around after what he did to you and Tabitha."

"I don't think he'll be walking around for the next few days," I say with a small smile, thinking how he was lying in a bloody heap when we left him. "Anyway, I've been through worse."

Quinn traces light circles over my ankle, and I shiver under his touch.

"One day, you'll tell me what's going on in that pretty little head of yours."

"Don't hold your breath," I reply softly, wishing it could be different between us.

Thankfully, he lets it go.

"Let's go raid the kitchen," he teases, lightening the mood.

"Sounds like a plan, seeing as I'm"—I look at the clock on the wall—"late for work!" I throw off the covers and run into the bathroom, Quinn's chuckles sounding behind me.

I quickly shower and get ready in record time, and both Quinn and I are out the door in fifteen minutes. It feels weird walking alongside him after everything that's happened. I don't believe in fate or destiny, but as I sneak a peek at him, my mind might be swayed into thinking otherwise.

From the moment I saw him, I knew he would create a

splash, but I never thought he'd cause a fucking tsunami.

His hands are dug deep in his pockets, and thankfully, his attitude hasn't changed too much toward me because I don't think I could deal with too much, too fast.

"Whatcha thinking?" Quinn asks with a chuckle.

"Nothing," I reply, embarrassed.

"That didn't look like nothing."

When I don't reply, and the only thing that can be heard is a few squawking birds and the gravel crunching under our shoes, Quinn laughs. "You can admit you want me."

"Oh, shut up."

Quinn toys with his lip ring, his eyes narrowing from the early morning glare.

"It's okay, Red. I know I'm irresistible." He ducks out of the way when I try to playfully punch him.

I know Quinn is doing this to lighten things up between us after last night.

It works.

We both stroll into the office chuckling, but stop as we hear Grandpa talking on the phone, his back turned to us.

"No, you cannot come here to view the property. I said I would get the money to you."

Both Quinn and I freeze. We've never seen Hank so riled up.

"You can't take this place from me. It's my home."

My heart drops into my stomach, and I look at Quinn, who looks just as taken aback.

After a few choice words, Hank slams down the phone and rubs the back of his neck.

"Hasn't anyone ever told you eavesdropping isn't polite?" Grandpa says with a small smile, turning to face us.

How can he be smiling right now?

"Hank, what's happened?" I ask, stepping toward the counter and reaching out to touch his arm.

I don't even question my actions anymore because they feel natural. I'm here for Hank, just as he has been for me.

"It's nothing for you to worry about," he replies, his eyes softening when he notices my distress.

"Bullshit! Stop being so stubborn and tell me."

Both Grandpa and Quinn let out a chuckle.

Grandpa rubs his crinkled brow, and I can see how this situation has weighed heavily on him.

"I'm behind on my payments. I've got ninety days to come up with twenty-five thousand dollars. Otherwise, the bank repossesses the motel."

I gasp, and that heavy feeling in my gut returns. I also feel like a total ass for accepting money from him. He paid me, even when he couldn't afford it, and my heart constricts at the sentiment.

"That's not going to happen," Quinn says, snapping me back to reality.

Hank smiles, but he doesn't believe a word Quinn is saying.

"Thank you, son, but I don't have that sort of money floating around."

Quinn shakes his head, his long hair slipping into his eyes.

"We will get you that money."

"How?" I ask, intrigued, turning to look at him.

"We're going to fix this place up, and you're going to be so busy, you won't know what to do with yourself."

I like his way of thinking and turn to Grandpa, nodding.

"I'm sure if we did the place up a bit, just like how Betty had it"—I hope I'm not overstepping a line by mentioning her—"you'll be busy again and be back in business."

Tears well in his eyes, and he shakily brushes them away. "You're both good kids, but—"

"No buts," I interrupt, shaking my head. "This is happening. And you won't be paying me any more money."

"But—"

"No buts," Quinn says, beating me to it.

Grandpa looks between Quinn and me, and I can see the appreciation reflected in his kind eyes.

As he clears his throat, he says lightheartedly, "Well, looks like I don't have a choice in the matter."

Both Quinn and I reply in unison, "You don't."

Quinn has offered to drive me to work, but the closer we get to the diner, the more anxious he becomes.

Finally, I break.

"What's wrong?"

His eyes are focused intently on the road ahead as he shrugs.

"Cut the crap," I say, stopping him from pulling that excuse with me.

His mouth dips into a lopsided smile.

"It's just…what we did last night. Can you not tell Tristan until I talk to him?"

"Well, I wasn't planning on divulging the details of you having your hands down my pants, so we're good."

Quinn smiles. "I know that. I just meant; I don't want him to see us together…until I explain."

I turn to face him, adjusting my seat belt, which is choking me all of a sudden.

"Are we? Together?" I clarify shyly because I have no idea what last night means.

Quinn scratches his stubbled jaw, his eyes focusing back on the road.

"I dunno. What do you want?" he asks after a pregnant pause, turning to look at me again.

"I…like you, Quinn. You're annoying as all hell and not very nice to me most of the time." He chuckles at the stab. "But I like you. I dunno what that means…but I know I'd be sad if—"

"If what?" he asks when I clam up.

"If I didn't give this a chance. But there are things about me, Quinn…things that I can never tell you. Stuff that you don't want to know."

"How do you know that?"

"Trust me on this. I know. *I* don't even want to know," I say, closing my eyes briefly, wishing things could be different.

"We've all got skeletons in our closets, Red," Quinn says, and I try not to recoil at the accurate description of what's lingering in mine.

We pull into the parking lot, and things get awkward.

"When will I see you again?" I ask, trying not to sound clingy or possessive.

Quinn hesitates, and my stomach drops.

"Tonight, Red. I promise you. I won't go MIA on you again."

I really wish he would stop using that phrase.

I exhale softly. "Cool."

My hand is braced on the door handle when Quinn reaches over and pulls me toward him. I slide across the bench seat and end up pressed against his firm side. The warmth radiating from his body heats me in an instant, and I try not to hyperventilate, thinking about the prospect of kissing him again.

"Have a good day," he says, inches away from my face.

"Y-you too," I reply, falling over my words.

He thumbs my bottom lip, his eyes engrossed on my mouth. "I don't know what it is about you." He leans forward, kissing me until I almost pass out from lack of oxygen.

Quinn doesn't just kiss, he devours, and I can't get enough.

After a minute of making out, he pulls away. "You better go."

Nodding with scarlet cheeks, I hop out of the truck, not looking back.

Quinn's engine roars out of the parking lot, and I don't think anything is sexier than a guy who can handle a truck.

As I open the glass door, I see Tabitha waits for me by the counter and looks like hell. Poor thing, coming down is never fun. She runs toward me and throws herself in my arms.

"Oh, Paige! Thank you. I can't thank you enough."

"You okay, Abi?" I squeak as she cuts off my oxygen supply.

She nods, her soft hair tickling my cheeks. "I am because of you, Tristan, and Quinn. Tristan said Brad *drugged* me," she says, pulling away, whispering the word "drugged."

Nodding, I dip my mouth into a frown. "He did, Abi. He's a lowlife jerk, and he can get away with this shit because his dad is the sheriff. I'm so sorry you went through what you did."

"It's okay. *I'll* be okay because of friends like you guys," Tabitha says, wiping her red-rimmed eyes.

I've decided not to tell Tabitha or Tristan what happened with Brad since I just want to forget it.

"Are you busy tonight?"

Quinn said he would see me tonight but didn't stipulate where or when.

"Nope," I reply, knowing Tabitha needs some company after last night.

"I wanted to take you, Tristan, and Quinn out to dinner," she says as we walk down the hallway, arms linked.

"Abi, you don't have to do that."

We both turn to see Tristan behind us, looking very businesslike with a pencil behind his ear.

As soon as I see him, I suddenly get a serious case of the guilts and lower my eyes.

"How are you feeling?" Tristan asks, trying to grab my attention.

"I'm okay," I reply, my voice wavering as I meet his eyes.

"Quinn got you home safely?" he questions, his eyes narrowing, confused by my sudden jumpiness.

"Yeah, he did," I reply, brushing my hair over my forehead, hoping the thick makeup conceals the bruise I have hidden underneath.

There is an uncomfortable silence, and Tabitha immediately picks up on it.

"Okay, so…" She claps her hands. "Dinner tonight will be fun."

I breezed through work without my mind wandering to Quinn too often. And that's because it felt wrong every time Tristan smiled at me or pulled me in for a hug.

I feel like I'm deceiving him somehow, and I hope Quinn talks to him before dinner because I don't know how long I can keep this up.

Finally, our shift ends, and because it's Sunday, we close up early.

Tabitha and I are freshening up in the locker room, and she huffs when she hears me sighing while touching up my makeup.

"Spit it out."

I'm only touching up my makeup as I don't want my foundation to rub off, revealing the cause behind my shocking headache.

"Spit what out?"

"Why are you so jumpy?" Tabitha asks, taking a step toward me.

"Quinn and I kissed last night, and…I like him, Tabitha. He makes me feel…alive," I confess, bashfully.

Tabitha's eyes are wide, like she's trying to decipher why that would be the reason behind my erratic behavior.

"So what's the problem then?"

"Tristan," I reply, lowering my voice.

"Oh." She nods in understanding.

"Quinn wants to talk to him before we…I don't know. I don't even know what we are."

"You guys don't have to put a label on what's going on between you. Just let nature take its course," she says like this isn't rocket science.

"I just don't like lying to Tristan. That's all."

"I know. But Quinn knows his brother, and if he thinks this is for the best, then I'd listen to him," she replies sympathetically.

She's right.

"Now tell me, did Quinn put that tongue ring to good use?"

I immediately blush and zip up my hoodie, ready to hightail it out of here before I start to reminisce.

I ride with Tabitha, and when she parks in front of a pizzeria, the delicious smell has my stomach rumbling.

When we pick a table toward the back of the restaurant, Tristan goes to pull out the chair next to me, but Tabitha pats the seat near her.

"Come sit near me, my superhero." She smiles innocently, giving him a small wink.

Tristan hesitates but thankfully doesn't argue and sits near her.

I give her thank-you eyes, and she nods.

We're waiting for Quinn, who I am afraid won't turn up. But a part of me hopes he doesn't because I don't know how I'll get through this meal without choking on it.

As I look over the menu, my mouth waters as everything sounds pretty delicious and also not too pricey, which is great, seeing as I'm running low on cash again. As I'm no longer working at the motel, but volunteering instead, I need to find another job. I could ask for more hours at the diner, but that would mean more time spent with Tristan, and I'm not sure how things will be between us after he finds out that Quinn and I are…whatever we are.

I scoff at the thought. It's not like Tristan is in love with me. I'm sure he'll be totally fine.

Well, I hope.

"Kids," Quinn says, addressing the table while taking a seat near me.

I bury my head further into the menu, fake studying it with acute awareness. I'm trying not to make a scene but am failing terribly, especially when Quinn places his hand subtly on my knee under the table, squeezing it lightly.

"Hi."

Quinn chuckles beside me, and I envy how calm he can be.

"How're you feeling, Abi?" Quinn asks, reaching for a menu with his right hand, his left still torturing my knee.

"Better. Thank you for last night," she replies sincerely. "If it wasn't for you guys…" She leaves the sentence hanging.

Quinn shrugs it off, shaking his head. "I'm just glad you're okay."

I can't meet Tristan's eyes, and I know he can sense my weirdness from across the small table.

"Everything okay, Paige?"

Nodding quickly, I bury my nose further into the menu futilely since I know what I want to order. Quinn senses my anxiety and rubs his fingers across my bare knee as I'm wearing my denim short shorts.

A server zips over, taking our orders, and I don't fail to notice her eyeing Quinn. Suddenly, a wave of…something passes over me, and I want to punch her in the nose.

Quinn, being Quinn, flirts back, giving her a small wink when handing the menu back to her. Now I want to punch them *both* in the nose.

I shift my knee away promptly, and his hand slides off. I want no part of him touching me when he's flirting with some bleached-blonde bimbo.

This is getting really awkward, really quickly, and I know it's my fault, but how do I put a lid on my feelings? I've never felt this way before, so I'm unsure how to deal with this situation. I wish I did because right now, I resemble a crazy person.

Tristan's phone rings, and when he looks at the screen, he groans. "Great, it's Anna. She better not call in sick tomorrow.

I'll be right back," he says, excusing himself. He walks outside to take the call.

My shoulders depress as I exhale the breath I've been holding. Tabitha looks at me sympathetically and also excuses herself, faking a trip to the bathroom.

I shuffle uncomfortably and fiddle with my silverware nervously. Quinn looks at me and my fidgeting hands, and stills them under his big palm.

"What's the matter?" he asks in a hushed voice.

"Nothing," I reply, my hand sweating under his.

"Don't lie to me. Are you uncomfortable?"

I shrug, not really knowing what I feel.

"I'll leave," he says, making a move to stand.

"No!" I almost yell, then flinch when I realize how loud I've spoken.

"I just…have you talked to Tristan?"

He just gets hotter and hotter each and every time I see him. He hasn't shaved and has quite a heavy growth covering his face, and the darkness of it highlights the pinkness of his full lips. Of course my gaze falls to his lip ring, which I am obsessed with, more so now as I know how it feels moving against my lips.

Quinn sucks on his piercing before answering. "Not yet. I haven't had a chance to. I'm sorry. I probably shouldn't have agreed to come tonight. I just, well, I wanted to see you," he confesses, making a face. "What a pussy, huh?"

I can't stop the smile that spreads from cheek to cheek at his admission, and I almost forget his little flirty display with the server.

"Can you not…flirt in front of me? It makes me uncomfortable," I confess, hoping I don't sound like a jealous girlfriend.

Quinn looks guilty as he frowns. "I'm sorry, Red, I wasn't thinking. I just, er, you know," he says vaguely, scratching his brow.

I raise an eyebrow because I most certainly *don't* know.

When he sees my confusion, he clarifies, "It's just what I would usually do, and seeing as I don't want Tristan knowing something is up…"

He's going to behave like a manwhore, I finish for him silently. It makes sense, but it doesn't make me feel any less uncomfortable.

"Fine, whatever. But do you think you could refrain from fondling my knee while your brother is sitting opposite me?"

"I could fondle something else if you like," he says with a chuckle, leaning in subtly and kissing behind my ear.

My long hair shrouds him, and I try not to whimper as his hot lips sashay across my flesh with exact precision.

"Ha, very funny," I reply breathlessly, trying not to combust.

"Who said I was joking?" he replies, his hand returning to my knee.

This needs to stop now before I blow my cover. Thankfully, Tabitha clears her throat before sitting down, and Quinn pulls away quickly.

I look over at her guiltily, but Quinn, on the other hand, is cool and collected. Tristan arrives a second later, and I realize being around Quinn is hazardous to my health. It's like no one else exists when I'm near him, which is dangerous. What happens if I let my guard down and he finds out who I *really* am?

Dinner passes smoothly enough, and I manage to keep my food down as it's delicious. Quinn thankfully stopped with the flirting, and Tristan didn't seem to catch on to anything being off between Quinn and me. But after tonight, Quinn has to tell Tristan about whatever is going on between us. Otherwise, I will. I can't lie to Tristan, who has been nothing but honest with me. I owe it to him. There are some things I can't be honest about, but this, I can.

As we make our way to our cars, I automatically make my way to Tabitha's car because I came with her, but Quinn stops me.

"Red, I'll take you back to Hank's."

The silence can be cut with a knife…

But Quinn is blessed with brains as well as beauty as he nonchalantly explains, "We were going to talk about the plans for Night Cats, remember?"

I look at him, my mouth slightly agape, but I nod. "Oh yeah, of course. I forgot."

Tristan looks just as confused as I am.

"What plans?" he asks, turning to look at Quinn.

"Hank will lose the motel if he doesn't come up with some serious money. So Red and I have come up with a genius plan to stop that from happening."

Tristan looks stunned, his eyes widening. "Why didn't you say anything?"

Quinn shrugs. "I just did."

I feel like stomping on Quinn's foot because he doesn't have to be so rude to his brother. Tristan huffs, and I can tell he's not happy at the prospect of me being alone with Quinn. But seeing as it's got to do with Hank, he'll let it slide.

"What do you guys have planned?" he asks. Tabitha also listens eagerly, slipping a piece of gum into her mouth.

Quinn explains our plan, and when he's done, both Tabitha and Tristan want in.

"I'm in."

"Me too," pipes up Tabitha, the small frown on her freckled face a sign of how devastated she is to hear the news. "I wish I could give it to him 'cause God knows, my family can afford it, but…"

"No one expects you to, Abi," I say, giving her a gentle smile. "Wanting to help is generous enough."

"So when do you want to do this?" Tristan asks.

"Tomorrow," Quinn replies, "so on that note, good night." He places a hand on my arm, directing me to his truck.

I practically dig my feet into the pavement and lightly remove my arm from Quinn's grip, glaring at him. I turn around and hug Tabitha goodbye.

"Good night, Abi. I'll call you tomorrow and let you know what's going on."

Tabitha nods and pulls away with a wink.

"Have fun." I know she's not referring to this alleged planning that Quinn and I are supposed to discuss.

"Good night, Tristan," I say, feeling awkward.

He gives me a small smile and, just like usual, pulls me in for a hug. I hug him back loosely as it almost feels like a betrayal to Quinn, which is ridiculous as it's just a hug.

Tristan's arm tightens around my back as he murmurs, "Good night."

I subtly pull out of his embrace when he holds on for a little too long, and the look reflected in his eyes is that of uncertainty. I feel awful, and a pang of guilt stabs me in the chest. I hope I never see that look mirrored on his face ever again.

Quinn waits for me to reach his side and mercifully doesn't grab me as we walk to his truck in silence. We both get in, and Quinn adjusts the heater, seeming to know I'm always cold.

The silence continues for the next few minutes, me looking out the window, deep in thought, while Quinn drives wordlessly. The only noise is the heater blowing softly, warming the truck. But somehow, it can't thaw through the sudden coldness between Quinn and me.

We pull up at Night Cats, and I unbuckle my seat belt as this silence suffocates me.

Quinn kills the engine and opens his door, stepping out. Unsure of what he's doing, I too step out, and he meets me as I turn to shut my door. He stands in front of me, watching me closely. Feeling self-conscious, I squirm, pulling the sleeves of my hoodie down over my arms to cover my fingers.

I need to say something. Anything. But what? I know the silence between us is because of Tristan, and how we're going to tell him, but the question is, *what* are we going to tell him? It's not as if Quinn has declared his undying love for me.

Deep in thought and still standing motionlessly, Quinn slowly reaches forward and links his fingers around my waist, pulling me toward him. I don't resist and follow the movement, and before I know it, I'm wrapped in his arms.

This is the first time I've been in his arms this way, and it feels different from when I am in Tristan's embrace.

It feels effortless. And it feels right.

We hug for a few moments, and as I nestle closer to his chest, surrounded by his smell, I know I'm in trouble. I have feelings for someone who will be really, really hard to say goodbye to when the time comes. But when did this happen? When was the exact moment my world got tipped on its axis and shaken up beyond repair? I should have stopped it, but who am I to stand in the way of something inevitable?

The sound of Quinn's heart beating steadily against my ear is comforting, and if I close my eyes really tight, I can pretend I'm just a normal girl, being wrapped up in the arms of her normal…boyfriend? But make-believe is for dreamers, and I'm a realist. I will enjoy the here and now because I don't know what tomorrow holds.

Quinn pulls away first, but he reaches for my hand, interlacing his fingers through mine while silently leading me toward the hill we climbed all those nights ago. The terrain is still rocky and steep, but this time, Quinn is behind me the whole way, steadying me so I don't fall, and I don't fail to see the significance behind his gesture.

As we reach the top, the incredible view before me still takes my breath away.

With my hand still enclosed in Quinn's, he lowers me down onto his lap as he sits on the grassy terrain. I don't hesitate to let him lead me, and for once, it's nice having someone I trust to make the decisions for me.

We sit unmoving, both enjoying this stillness as opposed to the one between us earlier. It isn't until Quinn leans forward, kissing my neck, that I snap out of my daze.

"Quinn, I'm…when I leave, what happens then?" I whisper, afraid of his reply.

He takes a moment to answer, his heavy breathing an indication of him weighing up his response.

"Red, no one knows what happens next. That's the mystery of life and all that philosophical shit. But the here and now, that's what we *can* control. Each day is a test, it's a lesson, and it's a future memory we will return to when we feel sad or lost." He takes a deep breath and continues. "I can't promise you flowers or romance, but I can promise you loyalty, honesty, and most of all…" He pauses, brushing my hair off my shoulder, skimming his fingertips along my exposed neck. "I can promise you me, the real me. I won't hide from you because I know there's no point. Behind those intelligent, beautiful eyes lies a gifted, remarkable woman who sees past my bullshit and still wants to be around me. Still *wants* me, and I can't figure out why."

My heart breaks hearing Quinn confess his insecurities because under his punch lines and wit lies a wounded, insecure being—just like me.

I want more than anything to confess my sins, to be upfront with him, but I just can't.

"Quinn, I have secrets. And the things I have done…I can't take back. Things I wish I could, but I can't. So if anything, I can't figure out why *you* want *me*," I admit, being as honest as I can without divulging too much.

Quinn's chest falls on an exhalation, and he draws me back so I'm lying flush with his chest.

"I don't care what you've done," he whispers into my ear, my body shivering as his lips graze my outer shell. "We both have secrets, things we both wish we could take back but can't. And that's okay because those secrets don't rule me when I'm with you. They don't define me. And I hope you feel the same with me."

I pause. How can it be? How can someone illustrate the daily battle I fight within myself so articulately and so accurately? Could it be that I have found someone who understands me better than I do myself?

"I do," I reply sincerely.

And that's why I find myself slipping further under Quinn's spell, and I'm scared it's only a matter of time before I'm fully bewitched.

"Then just ride it," he says into my ear. "We both have a past, but let's not let it rule our future."

I nod, my eyes slipping closed as his lips kiss my neck,

focusing on my rapid pulse fluttering under his mouth.

"You're unlike anyone I've ever met before, Red," he says, his hands tightening around my middle, holding me close, but it's still not close enough. "We're both broken, attempting to become unbroken, but somehow, together, we fit."

And he tilts my chin, smashing his eager lips to mine, kissing me with a passion that steals my breath away.

This is the beginning of the end.

The end of Paige Cassidy because Mia Lee is back.

The real Mia Lee.

The real me.

Seventeen

For the next few days, Tabitha, Tristan, Quinn, and I sweat our butts off, working at the motel day and night, and that's because it will take a team effort to get the motel back into business.

We have started from scratch, gutting everything and giving the place a totally different feel. It's still old school, but we've modernized it so it will suit all patrons—from businessmen to families to honeymooners. And I must say, it's coming along fantastically.

The colors we've chosen to paint the rooms are brighter, warmer, and welcoming. And once we finish buying new amenities, you won't recognize the place.

So that's what leads Quinn and me to the linen aisle of a department store in the mall, picking out the necessities.

I needed to get away from both Berkeley boys being in

the same room as one another because the tension could be cut with a knife. Quinn still hasn't told Tristan we're seeing one another, and it's just plain awkward being anywhere near Tristan when Quinn is around and vice versa.

When Tristan pulls me in for a hug, I can feel Quinn eyeballing us, and when Tristan isn't looking, Quinn will pull me away for covert kisses and hugs. I don't know how much more of this sneaking around I can take. But I'm too afraid to stop because it feels so good.

When I ask Quinn why he won't tell Tristan, his reply is always the same. *"It's complicated, Red."* And my response is always the same. "Then make it uncomplicated."

"How about these?" Quinn asks, holding up a packet of fire-engine-red curtains, distracting my thoughts.

"Yeah, that would be great if we were running a brothel." I smile, snatching the packet and placing it back on the shelf.

Quinn laughs, smacking me on the ass.

"Don't be a smart-ass. This isn't really my forte, and I'm only tagging along for the view," he says as I am mid-bend, reaching for a packet of white pillowcases off the bottom shelf.

Embarrassed, I quickly snap back up while he chuckles, pulling me in for a one-armed hug.

Things between us have become quite intense, and we've made out—a lot. But our kisses are usually stolen moments when Tristan isn't looking or before work. I'm not complaining, but it'd be nice to spend an evening together without hiding who we are.

I pull away before we get no shopping done. Even standing in a paint-splattered T-shirt and ripped jeans, he looks gorgeous.

"You're so checking me out." He laughs, crossing his arms over his broad chest while cocking a smug eyebrow.

I instantly blush at being caught and busy myself by placing big, fluffy green bath towels into my hand basket.

Quinn's confident chuckle is not helping the situation, and I turn around, pretending to look at a stand of sheets on sale.

He slips both hands around my waist and presses his chiseled front to my back, his nipple ring pushing between my shoulder blades.

"It's okay, Red. I like you looking at me. Especially when you give me those sexy bedroom eyes."

"Bedroom eyes? What? I do not!" I screech, on the verge of hiding my head in shame.

As I hear him chuckle, I know he's only teasing.

"Oh, isn't this just sweet?"

Quinn turns, and I turn with him as I'm still wrapped in his arms. I feel his body stiffen as we're faced with a sight that turns my stomach.

Brad and Stacey.

Stacey looks ridiculous, sporting tight jeans and a hot-pink tank, with her shiny hair piled high on her head. Her makeup is so thick, I'm actually surprised she can display any facial expressions under the impenetrable layers of gunk.

Brad, on the other hand, looks as if he could use a coat of her makeup, as there is no mistaking the yellowing bruises marring his face. The bruises Quinn put there. And my pulse begins to quicken at the memory of that night.

I involuntarily shrink into Quinn, who tightens his hold around my waist, protectively shielding my body with his.

"Well, as the saying goes, freaks of a feather flock together," Stacey says, staring at me icily while pursing her lips.

"As interesting as this conversation is," Quinn says over my shoulder, "we have someplace better to be."

I can't help but notice the way Brad eyeballs me. And not in a "fuck you" kind of way. It's more of a sordid, undressing me kind of way.

I feel sick.

I shuffle my Chucks uncomfortably and instantly my eyes drop to the floor. Quinn picks up on my discomfort and squeezes my waist comfortingly.

"You keep looking at her, and she'll be the last thing you see," Quinn spits out, and I believe every single word.

"Ha! That's rich!" snarls Stacey, taking a step toward us, cheeks blazing a blistering red.

I'm wielding the handbasket like a weapon, and if she takes a step closer, I'll smack her in the face with it.

"She's the one who came onto *my* boyfriend, and you're the one who got all jealous and took it out on Brad. *You're* the one with the reputation of being a psycho, not Brad."

Quinn chuckles, which enrages Stacey further.

"Sweetheart, if your boyfriend is so innocent, why didn't he run to Daddy and press charges?"

Stacey stops her rant and takes a step back, realizing the truth behind Quinn's words. Brad grabs her arm and pulls her toward him.

"Come on, babe. They're just lowlife losers. Don't waste your breath."

My eyes are still glued to the floor, but I can feel my body begin to shake in rage as soon as I hear his voice. I need to get out of here.

"This is an all-time low, even for you, getting someone to fight your battles. When you man up, come see me," Quinn mocks and thankfully turns, never letting me go.

Only when we're a few feet away does he release me, but he ensnares my hand in his, and we begin walking.

"Don't worry, this is only the beginning," Brad calls after us, and my skin instantly pricks, not liking the determination behind his words.

We leave empty-handed, but I don't care because I need to get as far away from the store as possible. Quinn opens the truck door for me, and I all but dive into the seat, curling in on myself. I have a premonition that there will be severe repercussions with what happened to Brad. And I have no one to blame but myself.

We drive silently, Quinn not smothering me or asking if I'm okay, because I'm not. Not paying attention to where we are going, it isn't until Quinn parks the truck do I realize where we are.

"We're not going back to Night Cats?" I ask, looking at his humble home through the windshield.

Quinn shakes his head and gives me a secretive smile.

"Nope, I'm giving you the night off."

I follow suit and trail him as he opens the front door. We are instantly greeted by Lucky, who seems to have become the third member of the Berkeley household.

"Hey, boy," I coo, crouching down and rubbing his head affectionately.

He looks so much healthier than when I first got him, and I know he has Quinn and Tristan wrapped around his little finger or paw.

Quinn silently strolls into the kitchen, leaving me in the hallway with Lucky, and both of us follow his movements, wondering what he's up to. He returns a second later with two beers and a doggy treat, which has Lucky turning his head toward Quinn, instantly following him as he takes the stairs, two at a time. I'm left crouching in the hallway, wondering what's going on.

I follow and am filled with curiosity as to what Quinn is up to. His bedroom door is left open, and I duck my head in, trying not to think about the last time I was at his bedroom door.

Lucky chews happily on his treat, settled in a wicker basket near Quinn's bed while Quinn slips out of his Chucks.

I casually look around his room, and even though the only time I really had a chance to look around was when I was lying on the floor, it's still amazing.

"That's beautiful," I say as my eyes land on a charcoal sketch, pinned to the wall above his desk.

It's of a woman nursing an infant at her breast, her head bowed as she looks lovingly at the child. I can tell by the attention paid to detail that Quinn would have sketched this while watching from afar. It is stunning, the strokes done with precision and care. I can imagine him watching closely, his shadowy hair slipping over his brow as he outlined his subject onto paper.

Quinn walks over to where I'm standing and looks at the drawing, sucking his lip ring, deep in thought. We haven't discussed his drawings in great detail, but I know it's something he loves doing, and something he's exceptionally gifted at.

The charcoal under his fingernails is yet another thing I find attractive about him. The thought of his fingers, the fingers that have touched me with such care, working over a piece of paper with such artistic talent adds to the conundrum that is Quinn Berkeley. I have seen those fingers also turn cruel, but never with me.

"It's something I did the other day. I haven't drawn in ages, but lately, I've been inspired," he confesses, still gazing at the picture.

"You're really good. If you want to show me, I'd love to see some of your other stuff."

He turns to me with a smirk. "You really want to see more?"

I nod enthusiastically. "I'd love to."

Quinn's eyes soften, and he hands me the beer he has loosely hanging from his fingers.

"You might need a beer for what I'm about to show you."

He chuckles as he walks to his desk, opening up a drawer while I sit on the end of his bed, kicking off my shoes.

He returns with a tattered sketchbook he holds with care and sits near me.

"This is my most recent stuff," he says, placing the book onto my lap and reaching for the other beer on the bedside table.

I run my hands over the smooth black cover, and picture how many times it has been Quinn's savior. Inside will give me an insight into Quinn's mind, and suddenly, I'm a little nervous to see what's inside.

Flipping open the cover, the first picture I see is that of a small boy. The boy in overalls looks up into a cloud-filled sky, watching a plane, and the smile on his young face is unmistakably happy. His chubby little finger points toward the plane, and in the other hand, he holds an ice cream cone. Again, the meticulousness paid to this drawing takes my breath away because I feel like I'm there, watching this boy through Quinn's eyes.

"It's amazing," I say after staring at it for a full minute, my eyes taking in every detail.

"Thanks."

I turn the page and the next picture is of Night Cats. But not of Night Cats the way it is now; it was Night Cats when

Betty was alive. It is fresh, vibrant, and full of life. I skim over everything, my eyes not wanting to miss an inch of what he's drawn. I think I've just found our blueprint to how we should model Night Cats.

The next drawing is of Grandpa, and I can't help the breath that leaves me. It looks as if Grandpa has come alive on paper. I brush my finger inches away from his cheek but never making contact, not wanting to smudge the picture.

"Have you shown Hank?" I ask, looking up to meet Quinn's guarded eyes.

He shakes his head and smirks. "No way. Can you imagine what the old man would say?"

I flip through page after page, viewing pictures of people I know and places I've been. It isn't until I get to the last page that I get to my favorite picture.

"Quinn," I gasp, looking at the picture before me, my mouth agape.

He bites his lip and almost looks nervous as I gently run my fingers along the picture.

It's a drawing of me at the diner, elbows braced behind me, leaning on the counter, looking lost. I'm staring vacantly ahead, and my mouth is dipped into a small frown. The diner is filled, and the tables around me are occupied with people none the wiser that I am bleeding before their eyes.

My knee is bent, and my sneaker is tucked behind me, resting on the wall under the counter for support. My hair has slipped free from my messy ponytail.

"It's beautiful," I whisper, my eyes never leaving the drawing.

"It's because you're beautiful," he replies, matching my tone.

This explains our conversation at the gym when he

pinpointed who I am just by watching me when I let my guard down. I am so out of my element and don't know how to respond. So I do the only thing that feels natural, I kiss Quinn.

I put as much passion and appreciation into the kiss to show him the words I cannot speak. And he returns my passion, my appreciation, kiss for kiss.

Placing a warm palm on my cheek, he cradles my face closer to his, kissing me like I'm his salvation and he'll expire without me. I place the book beside me, not wanting to damage it, and I do something I have never done before—I take charge.

As I gently push into Quinn's hardened chest, he watches me as he falls backward, and I climb his body slowly. He looks up at me with wild eyes as I straddle his waist, my denim skirt riding high up my legs. I don't shy away because this feels instinctive, and I feel like a goddess as his eyes worship every inch of me.

When I lean forward, my long hair shrouds us in a cloud of darkness as my lips meet his, and we devour one another. The kiss is filled with want and infatuation, and it's messy, and it's frantic, and it's perfect. The tiny moans that slip past my lips as I kiss Quinn get louder and louder as he glides a hand up my thigh, my skin burning with his touch.

I'm rocking against him, and the harsh denim of his jeans scratches me in just the right way. I think I might explode. I feel him harden beneath me with my movements, and I want to feel every inch of him because I have elicited this response, and I am fucking proud.

Timidly, I walk my fingers between us, gently rubbing over the huge bulge in his pants. Breaking the kiss, I moan softly, surprised at how it feels. Quinn hisses while sucking down on his lip ring, eyes untamed. I gain a little more confidence and begin rubbing over his hard-on quicker, wanting to touch him in the flesh. I bravely inch toward his belt buckle, but his hands still mine from moving any farther.

I meet his eyes, confused, afraid I've done something wrong.

"Red, you're not ready for that," he whispers with a catch in his voice.

I can feel myself pout, but he's right.

"Will you let me touch you?" he murmurs, eyes searching mine carefully.

I nod timidly, and he smirks while flipping me onto my back. Now that the roles are reversed and he's looking down at me, I feel a little vulnerable, but I know he won't hurt me.

He begins by kissing me, but softer this time. The passion is still there, but the urgency has simmered to a slow, languid pace. I like it.

He dominates my mouth as he works his barbell over my lower lip, seeking refuge in my mouth and battling with my tongue. My body begins to tremble, and the pressure builds between my legs once again.

Quinn kisses down my throat, sucking my neck; a beautiful balance of pleasure and pain. He descends my body, his mouth touching any bare piece of flesh he can find. But it's not enough, so I push up and shyly slip my T-shirt over my head, revealing my lacy black bra.

Quinn watches me, and as I lower myself back onto the bed, I bashfully cover my hands over my breasts, suddenly embarrassed at my nakedness. But Quinn softly removes my hands, his eyes filled with need as he rakes his heated gaze across my chest.

My nipples instantly harden under his examination, and his eyes follow the motion immediately.

He lowers his mouth and latches onto my left breast through the silky material, pulling my nipple deliciously slow. I whimper, and as he circles his tongue, I arch into his mouth, wanting more.

His hand lazily rubs over my thigh, but I want it higher, so I shamelessly slide my hand over his and move his fingers until he brushes over me.

My heart begins beating in time with the rhythm of his fingers as he starts rubbing me languorously, and I'm going to come from this sensation alone.

Quinn pulls his mouth away, eyes lidded and mouth parted, exhalations coming out in loud breaths.

"I really want to be between your legs," he whispers, still working me over with his hands.

"You are," I manage to choke out, my eyes meeting his.

"No…with my mouth," he replies, pulling at his lip ring.

Just the thought of that is enough to leave me soaked. But I have never had someone do that to me before. And I've never wanted them to…until now.

Quinn can see me mulling it over. He keeps his fingers from moving but never removes them from between my legs.

"Do you want me to?" he asks, never pushing.

I would be a liar if I didn't admit I've thought about how it would feel, especially with his barbell.

"I'm…embarrassed," I reply, mortified by my admission.

"Don't be. Don't ever feel embarrassed around me, okay?"

I nod.

"We don't have to do anything you're not comfortable with. I could kiss you all day, and that would be enough. Just being this way with you and you trusting me is more than I could ever ask for."

His sentiment touches me, and I believe every word he

just said. But this is big. This is a big thing for someone who has never allowed another to get close to her, let alone get close to her with their…mouth. But I don't know if I'll ever get another opportunity like this, especially with someone like Quinn.

What if I never feel *this* with anyone else ever again?

So with that in mind, I sigh softly. "Okay."

Quinn raises his eyebrow, ensuring my response is in relation to his question about going down on me.

I nod shyly, and he removes his hand from between my legs, placing both palms on my hips. He unclasps my button and shimmies my skirt down my legs until it pools at my feet, and I kick it onto the floor.

Quinn takes his time examining my body, lingering on my belly, and then down to my lacy black underwear, which doesn't cover a whole lot.

My legs shift in nervousness and also in excitement.

Quinn leans back on his knees and reaches for the light switch behind him, shrouding the room in darkness. He is so considerate, knowing this will make me feel more comfortable in a shadowy room. But I want to see him; I want to watch him. So I reach toward the bedside table and turn on the lamp, hoping Quinn won't mind.

He doesn't.

He skims his hands over my belly, his fingers circling my belly button, and then he slowly hooks his thumbs into my underwear, slipping them down my legs. He drops them onto the floor and turns to gaze at my nakedness.

"Holy fuck," he whispers, his eyes remaining on my sex.

I feel so exposed, so vulnerable, but instead of sealing my legs, I shift them and part them slightly wider, liking the desire I can see in Quinn's bright eyes.

He doesn't waste a moment longer as he settles between them, laying three velvety kisses up my inner thigh before he licks my entrance in one wet, hot lick. My back bows off the bed, and I don't think I can come back down. I clutch at the bedsheets, fisting handfuls tightly as Quinn softly grasps both my thighs. With a firm grip, he pushes them wider apart so he can gain access to *every* part of me.

He's gentle at first, testing to see what I like, what makes me cry the loudest. But everything he does feels amazing, and I don't want him to stop—ever. I cry out each time he sinks into me with his skillful tongue. The smooth metal piercing penetrates parts of me I never knew existed. This is like nothing I have ever experienced before.

Plunging his tongue deeper, he circles his barbell around my core. I whimper and break out into a fine sheen of sweat, trying to calm myself down as I don't want to come, not yet. I reach down, yanking onto his hair, needing something to grab when I ride my wave of pure ecstasy.

The noises coming from Quinn's mouth are beyond erotic. They are filled with obsession and are utterly dominating. He enjoys the effect he's having over me, and as he slips a finger into me, working alongside his tongue, I am so close to coming that I can taste it.

He places his free hand under my lower back, arching me farther into his mouth and licking me so deep, I feel wonderfully violated. He slips his finger out of me, and his big hand clasps my hip, angling me to shamefully ride his face.

At this angle I can watch him, watch what he's doing to my body, and even though I feel depraved doing so, I can't tear my eyes away. I watch in awe as his pink tongue laps at me like I am his reason to exist.

"You feel and taste incredible," he says, his warmth breath

spreading a chill through me. "I want you all over me, Red."

"Oh God." His words, coupled with his actions, are sending me over the edge.

"Does it feel good?"

All I can do is nod.

But it's not enough for Quinn. "Tell me."

"It feels like every part of me is coming alive," I confess breathlessly. "You're everywhere…but it's not enough."

He groans, clearly pleased with my description.

He rubs his face from side to side, slathering my arousal all over his mouth. If that isn't the hottest thing I've ever seen, then I don't know what is.

"No one has ever done this to me before."

A possessive growl slips past Quinn's lips. I know he likes that he's the first.

"I like that you're the first," I manage to say because I'm so close to coming, it's hard to think straight. "I like that you're the only man who will make me…come."

"Oh, baby," Quinn groans, increasing the tempo of his devilish tongue.

His hold on me is firm, but I like it. I like that I can feel him barely holding on and losing control because of what I'm doing to him.

"I like that too," he confesses, biting over my clit softly.

My back arches, and a guttural moan leaves me.

"I like that this…pussy belongs to me."

His dirty words are not sordid. They are filled with possession and obsession, and I want it now and always.

"Say it, Red." He pulls back, watching me. "I want you to say it."

At this point, regardless of my embarrassment, I will say anything so long as he continues. "My…pussy…it belongs to you. Quinn."

"So fucking hot."

Before I know what he's doing, he flips us so he's on his back. I have no idea what's going on until he grips my wrist and coaxes me to climb his body. Or, more specifically, his face.

I follow his lead and rest my knees on either side of his head. He places his hands on my hips, grinning up at me.

"What a view."

Before I have a chance to blush, he gently encourages me to sit…on his face. A sated moan escapes me the moment I do because this is something else.

He works his mouth and tongue, driving me wild, and my body begins rocking on instinct. I want to come.

Forgetting my embarrassment, I close my eyes and grip the headboard, losing myself to this exotic moment. I rock against Quinn as he holds me tightly around the waist and guides my unsure movements. His mouth and tongue lick, suck, and pull, and I can't help but rock faster because everything feels so good.

I understand why Quinn switched positions, as this allows me to be in control. It allows me to call the shots and dominate him. And I like it.

I bounce and rock against him, each movement heightening the building tension. He eats me out with passion and desire, ensuring he holds me tight against him.

I pump my hips, and his piercing, his stubble, only adds to the pleasure, and when he lifts me, only to slam me back onto his face, I lose control. I ride his face hard and fast, and he takes everything I give.

Gripping the headboard, I lift my hips and peer down at Quinn, and when the light catches off his barbell as he flicks over my clit, before biting it—hard, I scream and detonate in a way I have never done so before. I'm coming so hard, but he won't stop; he continues coaxing my body with his hands and mouth, and I throw my head back, eyes squeezed shut, my body shaking in immeasurable pleasure.

My heart gallops madly, and the aftershocks rock my body until Quinn lets me go, his wicked mouth stilling. He lays a tender kiss on the inside of my thigh.

When I think I can move, I roll off him and collapse onto my back, breathless and spent.

I am all floppy legs and arms, and I doubt I can move. Thankfully, Quinn places the soft blanket over me and tucks me into his side, allowing my quivering muscles to relax.

I'm nearly asleep, sated in a way I never thought possible, when Quinn whispers, "Are you asleep?"

I groan an incoherent reply, which earns me a chuckle from Quinn.

"Are you happy to spend the night?"

I nod as I doubt my legs are capable of walking right now.

"Good night," he says softly, tucking me closer.

"Good night," I reply with a yawn.

Before I drift off, I am certain I hear Quinn whisper, "I'll never let anyone hurt you. I promise."

And his words send me into the deepest sleep I have had in…forever.

Eighteen

The next month we get Night Cats looking the best it has looked in some time. The fresh coat of paint has transformed the motel, and even though we aren't finished, Hank is busy. People driving along the highway don't recognize it as the run-down place it once was, and Hank is booked before long.

The reason we can afford all the supplies for Night Cats is because of Tabitha. Her family is more than rich, they are filthy rich, and Tabitha, who wants no part of their wealthy lifestyle, has funded everything with her allowance. Quinn, Tristan, and I have contributed as much as we can, but Tabitha has taken charge, and I think she has found her calling.

It makes me feel so good that I have been part of something like this, helping someone who has been there from the get-go. My plans to visit my mom in Canada seem to be less and less important as I have found a bunch of people I consider family.

Tomorrow is Thanksgiving, a holiday I never celebrated because I had no one to celebrate with. But this year is different. I have a group of people who want to share it with me. And one person, in particular, has insisted we go all out.

"You better get some sleep, Red. Tomorrow you have a big day slaving in the kitchen, making me some turkey," Quinn teases, pulling me into his arms as I yawn, tucking the blanket around us while we watch *Halloween*.

Tomorrow, we're having Thanksgiving lunch here, and I'm a little nervous because I've never cooked for a large group of people before. Well, it'll only be the five of us, but still, that's the biggest audience I've ever catered for.

I pinch his nipple ring playfully, and Quinn half groans, half yelps. After the night he went down on me, we have been fooling around, but it's been quite tame. And I think that has got to do with Tristan, who is still in the dark about us.

Whenever I question Quinn why, he still gives me the whole 'the time isn't right' speech, but I know he's putting it off because he doesn't want to hurt his brother. And by the way they interact with one another, I can see Quinn loves his brother dearly.

I'm pretty certain Tristan knows something is up between Quinn and me, but I don't think he wants to acknowledge it because that would make it real.

"Can you wake me up if I fall asleep?" I whisper, not wanting Tristan to hear us.

I have slept over a few times, but all times have been unintentional because we've watched a movie and I've fallen asleep. And Quinn not having the heart to wake me, has let me sleep through. But when I wake, I sneak out in the early hours, not wanting to be caught by Tristan.

All this sneaking around isn't cool, but I have become addicted to Quinn, and the alternative of not seeing him is one I don't think I can do. So for now, this will do.

Quinn sighs, bundling me into his naked chest. "Yeah. This sneaking around sucks, and I'm sorry, it's just…"

But I silence him. "I know, and it's okay. Being with you… it makes it all worth it."

I pause, hoping I haven't freaked him out with my overshare.

But Quinn exhales, and I feel his lips pass over my hair softly.

"I feel the same, Red. You make everything worthwhile."

My heart somersaults with his confession, and I try not to grin from ear to ear, but my efforts are futile.

The dining table is filled, and I haven't even set the turkey down yet.

Tabitha turned out to be a whiz in the kitchen, and I'm not ashamed to admit I was more of an apprentice than the head chef. But it looks amazing, regardless of who prepared it, because it was prepared with love.

"Hello, baby," Quinn says into my ear as he slips his hands around my waist.

I squirm a little because I hate being openly affectionate with the risk of Tristan walking in at any moment.

Quinn didn't wake me up like he promised, so I spent the night, and now I feel like a total ass. Thankfully I had a change of clothes in the truck so I could shower and not have to slip out and risk being caught by Tristan.

"He's talking to Hank," Quinn says, reading my body language immediately.

Instantly sagging in relief, I allow his lips to kiss up and down my neck while I liquefy at the feeling of being in his arms.

"I'll tell him tonight," Quinn says, laying a final kiss on the tip of my shoulder.

I turn around quickly to face him, my eyes wide.

"I don't like you sneaking out of here, like some secret. It's not fair on you or Tristan. He's going to hate me, but he'll get over it," he says, running a hand through his wet hair as he's just stepped out of the shower.

I nod and try to hide my smile but fail. I'm elated he feels this way because I don't want to be a secret. I have enough of them.

"You know what this means, though, right?"

I shake my head, confused.

"It means you're stuck with me now," he replies, attempting to sound playful, but I know he's asking this to gauge my reaction.

I shrug and take a step toward him, threading my finger through his belt loop and pulling him toward me.

"That sounds horrible. I better take the first bus outta here." I smirk, reaching up on tippy-toes and kissing his lips softly.

Quinn growls and pulls me into a tight embrace, deepening the kiss until my legs grow weak.

"You're not going anywhere," he whispers between kisses, biting my lip.

I can't form a response because, deep down, I know he's right.

I'm here to stay.

Quinn helps me carry the last of the food, including the huge turkey, into the dining room.

Everyone sits around the table, talking about Night Cats and teasing Hank, saying he'll be able to retire a millionaire in a few months' time. Things are looking up for Hank. He may be only paying back a small dent in what he owes, but it's a start.

As Quinn sets the turkey down, I look at the table, and it's perfect. This is perfect.

The best Thanksgiving ever.

Quinn ensures I sit near him. Being near him and him being in my life has made everything seem okay. Maybe, just maybe, I can do this.

Maybe I *can* live a something-like-normal life.

"Would it be okay to say grace?" Hank asks, looking around the table.

We all nod, and this time, I believe it. This time it makes a difference to me because whatever is up there, watching over me, has finally cut me some slack and given me a chance to be me.

"Thank you for this meal we are about to eat. Sitting around this table with a group of people who have changed my life, I realize how grateful I am to be alive. After so many years of living in the dark, I have finally found the light. Amen," Hank says, and I smile because I feel the same way.

Quinn has found my hand under the table, giving it a light squeeze. I sit, staring at a table filled with misfits. And me, the biggest misfit of all, has found a place I want to call home.

I'm stuffed, and we haven't even had dessert yet.

Tabitha prepares coffee while I'm clearing the table. The boys are in the living room watching TV, and I can't help but revel in this feeling of normality. Is this what it feels like? Because if so, I want in. Tabitha hums to herself while preparing the coffee, staring out the window with a small smile. It looks as though the feeling is mutual.

I excuse myself as I need to use the bathroom and climb the stairs with a skip in my step. I'm so happy. This feeling is one I have never felt before, and everything in my life is how it should be.

Everything is perfect.

Well, it was until the doorbell chimes.

I wonder who it is and poke my head around the corner, looking down the stairs to see who's at the front door.

I wish I hadn't because it's the police.

I duck behind the wall, but peep around the corner, remaining unseen.

"Can I help you?" Quinn asks casually, his hand braced against the doorframe as he addresses the police officer.

My heart begins beating frantically, and my palms begin to sweat because I know the next few minutes will change my life forever.

"Do you know a...Mia Lee?" the police officer asks, flipping through a small notebook.

"Nope," Quinn replies offhandedly.

"Are you sure? We've had reports that she's been seen here and at Night Cats."

Fuck, how does he know?

Tabitha answers my question.

"Hello, Mr. Davidson," she says, and I instantly recognize the surname as Brad's.

So this is what Brad meant by it only being the beginning. It serves me right for picking a fight with the sheriff's son.

"Hello, Tabitha. So you're sure you haven't seen this woman?" He holds up a photo.

It's a photo of me.

"Hey, that's—"

But Quinn cuts Tabitha off. "Nope, like I said, Sheriff, never seen her before in my life."

What's he doing?

"You do realize, son, with a reputation like yours, covering for someone who is wanted by the police will get you into a whole lotta trouble you can't afford," warns Sheriff Davidson.

Quinn shrugs. "Well, isn't it lucky that I don't know her, then."

I can see Tabitha fidgeting nervously, and I feel horrible for putting her in such an awkward position.

"What did she do?" Tabitha asks softly.

This is it, the moment my lies finally catch up to me.

"She has a rap sheet a mile long. But we need to speak to her about what she did to her father."

"What did she do to him?" Tabitha asks.

"She shot him."

My heart drops into my stomach, and I'm going to be sick. I cover my mouth to hold in my lunch but swallow it back down because I have to do what I do best.

I have to run.

I tiptoe down the hallway as I hear Sheriff Davidson still talking to Quinn and Tabitha, which buys me a good ten-minute head start. Slipping out of Quinn's window and shimmying down the drainpipe, I thankfully drop to the ground without breaking a leg.

My long legs have never run so fast, and I have no sense of where I am running to. I just know I have to get away from my past, which is biting at my heels.

It's now well past two o'clock in the morning, and I'm hiding in an abandoned home on the outskirts of town. The first car I could flag down I jumped into, and they took me as far as they were going. I didn't care where that was as long as it was away from the people I betrayed.

No doubt by now the police are out looking for me. But that's not what troubles me the most. It's what my friends, my *family* think of me, now that they know the truth.

I have switched my phone off. Besides being scared the police can trace me through it, I also know that Tabitha and Tristan are blowing it up with endless phone calls and text messages.

But it's Quinn who I'm most afraid of. I can't stand to see the hurt in his eyes now that he knows what I'm capable of.

I have hurt every one of them, and for that, I deserve to be caught and punished. So I bravely switch it back on, waiting for the endless sea of messages to register on the screen.

I receive nonstop texts from Tristan and Tabitha as expected, but nothing from Quinn, which is no surprise. I know he'll never forgive me, and I never expected him to. But it still fucking hurts.

There's one voice message, and I decide to listen to it, but

I wish I didn't.

"Child, come home. Whatever you did…it doesn't matter. I know there's a reason behind it, and we're here for you. Don't run. Please, just come home."

I listen to Grandpa's message over and over, chewing the inside of my cheek to stop myself from crying because I don't cry. I'll never cry ever again.

But the hurt and sorrow in his voice kills me, and I just can't leave…without saying goodbye. If I get caught doing it, so be it because I'm sick of running from a past that won't let go.

So I flag down a passing car and head back to the motel.

I arrive just after three, and I mold myself to the wall, shrouded in darkness by the rain clouds rolling in.

I want to grab my belongings because as meager as they are, they're mine, and they remind me of the times when I could pretend my life wasn't a fucked-up mess.

Silently slipping the keys out of my pocket, I enter without a sound. Too afraid to turn the light on, I scamper around in the dark, using the moon as my only light.

I have nothing of interest in the bathroom, so I head straight to my closet to get what I need. But mid-travels, I yelp when the lamp on the bedside table switches on.

I turn defensively, my heart thumping out of my chest, my breath leaving me in loud gasps.

"What are you doing here?" I ask after finally finding my voice.

"Looking for you," Quinn replies as he sits casually on my bed, leaning up against the headboard with his ankles crossed.

"Why? To turn me in?" I ask, backing away from him.

I can't translate what's going on behind his green eyes, and I'm afraid to find out.

Quinn chuckles, but it is in no way a happy sound. "You think I'd do that to you?"

"I don't know. Why wouldn't you? I'm a fugitive."

Quinn closes his eyes and braces both hands behind his neck, squeezing tightly. His chest rises and falls rapidly, and I can hear his jaw grinding.

"I don't care what you are, Red. It makes no difference to me." He kicks his feet off the bed, coming to a stand.

"You should," I reply breathlessly, walking backward as he slowly stalks toward me. "You know what I did, yet you still don't care?"

Quinn brushes his tousled hair out of his tired eyes.

"The only thing I care about is the fact that you ran. After everything, you think I would just turn away and let you deal with this on your own?"

I shrug and bump into the wall while retreating from him.

"It's a lot to deal with! This isn't some minor issue I can just sweep under the rug. My actions will follow me and haunt me for the rest of my life. And I don't expect you to stick around because I would never expect that of you. I should have never let this happen. Now you're all involved in my bullshit," I confess sadly, looking up at him with wounded eyes. "I am so selfish to do this to Hank, to Tabitha, to Tristan…to you."

Quinn swoops forward so our faces are inches apart. "You don't get to decide that! You are a part of our lives. You are a part of *my* life, and I'll be damned if I let you run away from me again."

I open my mouth to talk some sense into him, but he lunges forward and kisses me with such passion, I almost forget to breathe. How can he want to kiss me? After everything he knows, how can he still *want* me?

He wraps both hands under my ass, lifting me onto his

waist, his mouth never leaving mine. I comply and wrap my legs around his hips, holding on tight, never wanting to let go. My head bangs on the wall with the force of his mouth on mine, and I can taste blood, knowing his lip ring cut into my lip, but I don't care. I suck it into my mouth, pulling with a delicious tug because I want to devour him with my last breath.

We kiss until I can no longer breathe, and I pull away breathlessly, needing to steady myself and also to figure out what the fuck I'm going to do.

Quinn's eyes are frenzied, and as he rests his forehead against mine, he whispers, "Promise me you won't run, Red."

I shake my head, placing my hand against his cheek. "I can't promise you that, Quinn. I'm wanted for murder. I can't stay here."

Quinn pulls back, a confused look on his face. "Murder?"

"Yes," I reply, matching his expression. "I killed my…dad."

"No, you didn't," he replies. "You shot your dad, but he didn't die…he's still *alive.*"

"What?" I whisper, sliding down his body, unable to hold myself up.

My shaky legs crumple beneath me, and I sag to the floor as my world shatters.

Quinn drops to his knees, searching my face. "This is good news, right?"

But I shake my head, unable to vocalize how far from the truth that is.

If my father isn't dead, then that means…I am.

I have no doubt that now I'm not only running from the police but also from my father.

And Big Phil.

"Talk to me, Red!" Quinn pleads as I feel myself going

into shock.

There is no way he can be alive; I saw him, but I saw him what? I didn't see him die before me, so Phil saved him since he was minutes away from arriving when I took off.

Everything just got a whole lot worse. And I need to run.

I mentally slap myself and focus on what's important—I need to get out of here.

Standing quickly and wavering on my feet, I grab my backpack and toss it over my shoulder, heading for the door. But Quinn grabs my arm, spinning me around violently.

"Stop! Tell me what's going on!" he yells, and I've never seen him so angry.

"I can't!" I scream, trying to pull out of his grip, but he won't let me go. "Let me go, Quinn! I have to go!"

"Why? Talk to me! What did he do to you?" Quinn screams, shaking me evenly. "Tell me!"

My heart beats ferociously, and I'm afraid it's about to burst free from my rib cage and plummet onto the ground before me. As I look into his hard-set eyes, I know he won't let me go until I tell him the truth. I'm running out of time, so I do the only thing I can. I tell him who the real Mia Lee is.

"Quinn…I shot my father because he wanted me to do something no father should ask of his daughter. He's a drug addict, and since the age of eight…I've been a…drug dealer. I have destroyed countless lives because I was too chickenshit to stand up to my dad and tell him no."

Quinn's grip loosens, and his eyes widen, horrified by my confession. But now that I've started, I can't stop.

"Big Phil, he was my dad's drug dealer, made a deal with my dad. I was to be his little drug bitch, delivering drugs to all the lowlifes of LA, and my dad could have all the drugs he wanted. No one questions an eight-year-old who looks to be on her way to school, so it was the perfect ruse. I was eight fucking years old! I didn't know what they wanted me to do. I just thought I was doing something for my dad to make him better, make him the father I remembered before my mother left me, left me alone with that monster."

Quinn is silent, hanging onto every word but never judging.

"But the older I got, I knew what I was doing, and that it was wrong. But when it came to my father, I was still that innocent, scared little eight-year-old, yearning for her dad's approval. The things I have seen, the things I have done," I whisper, meeting his eyes, "I hate myself for."

"You were just a kid," Quinn says, trying to shield me from the horrible reality of my life.

"That's no excuse, Quinn. I knew what I was doing when I was an adult. I knew I was destroying lives, but I just didn't care. I was selfish because I wanted my dad back. He was all I had, and I thought by doing this for him, one day he'd stop. But he didn't. He just got worse," I acknowledge, my body beginning to tremble with the memories I've tried so hard to repress.

"What happened? Why did you...shoot him?" Quinn asks, rubbing my cheek softly with his thumb, encouraging me to continue.

"Because he...the day I shot him...he pulled a gun on me and told me I was to pay for his drug debt in another way. And that was something I could never do," I whisper, a tear sliding down my cheek.

This is the first time I've allowed myself to cry; the first time I've allowed myself to feel.

Quinn gasps, understanding what "another way" entails, and he takes a visible breath.

"It was either you or him. And you chose yourself. Don't you see, you had no other choice," he says, brushing away my tears.

"We all have choices, Quinn, and I made the wrong one. I should have stopped it before it got out of hand. I deserve whatever I get. I may not have killed my father, but I had a hand in killing every person I dealt to. Hit by hit…I was killing them, and I didn't stop. If that doesn't make me a bad person, then what does it make me?" I ask, pushing him away.

I need to get away from him because now that he knows my ugly truth, he'll look at me like the horrible person that I am. I reach for the door handle, but Quinn steps out in front of me and attempts to restrain me, so…I slap him. I can't stop myself as I need to hurt something, anything, and he's just in the way from me achieving that.

However, he doesn't falter. He simply stands his ground, clenching his jaw, his eyes narrowing at me, daring me to get past him. I push at him with all my might, but he crosses his arms over his chest, not moving an inch. His actions enrage me, and the years of abuse at the hands of my father come lashing out of me like a volcano of emotions.

I slap, punch, bite, kick, pull, scream, and curse at Quinn until my body shakes in exhaustion and my voice is hoarse. My rage blinds me, and I am also blinded by the uncontrollable tears pouring from me, and I fear they may never stop.

It isn't until I have slumped against Quinn's chest do I realize what I have done. I have hurt the one person who has every right to walk away and leave me to deal with my mess on my own, but he hasn't. He's still here, cradling me into his arms, telling me that everything will be all right.

I sob so hard my chest heaves with excruciating pain, and I collapse onto the floor, my legs too weak to hold me up. Quinn catches me, and we fall to the floor together, him rocking me, holding me like he'll never let go.

I pull away, my tears running freely, and I know I look like a mess, but I can't stop.

"Why? Why are you still here? I don't understand…how can you not hate me?"

When he replies, I see the damage I have inflicted on his face by my punishing fists, and I gasp. What have I done?

"Quinn, I'm so s—"

But he silences my apologies as he grips my cheeks roughly in his palms.

"Don't you see? You've had the balls to do something I've only dreamed about. You took control of your life, Red, and you didn't allow your father to belittle you a moment longer. How can I hate you when I *admire* you for doing what you did?"

I sniff, my sobs racking my body when I hear his confession. I know he's talking about his father, and I guess he's right…we *are* cut from the same cloth.

I shakily pass my finger over the blood pouring from a wound on his lip, the wound I inflicted on him.

"I'm sorry…I'm sorry I lied to you. I'm sorry…for everything."

"Shh, you've got nothing to be sorry for."

"I don't know where to go. And I'm…scared."

Quinn wipes away my tears, his eyes leveling on mine. "We'll figure it out, okay? I promise you, you'll never be alone."

I nod, touched by his words, and finally calm down enough to think relatively straight.

"I can't stay here; I have to go. My dad and Phil, they'll be looking for me. And I can't put you all in danger."

"I'm coming with you."

"No! I'll come back for you. I promise."

Quinn stands up, flinching a little, and I know his ribs are sore because of the beatdown I just gave him.

"You're insane if you think I'm just going to let you split on your own," he says, extending his hand to me.

I accept and don't feel as shaky on my feet after my purge.

"Give me your things. You go say goodbye to Hank, and I'll wait for you in the truck," Quinn commands.

Without arguing, I hand him my backpack and grab my Colt out of the bedside table. Reaching behind me, I slip it into the waistband of my jeans—old habits die hard.

Nodding, I take a final look at my surroundings, of the place I called home.

We both exit the room silently, and as I head toward the office, Quinn grabs my hand.

"Promise me you'll meet me at the truck," he says, his eyes searching my face desperately.

"I promise." And I mean it.

With one final look, he turns and leaves me to do something that will be one of the hardest things I've ever done.

My feet crunch over the gravel, and as I look around at the familiar landscape, I realize how much I don't want to leave, but I have to. I make my way to the office and find it unusual that Hank has the TV turned up so loud that it's blaring outside.

However, as I get closer, I realize it's not the TV I can hear.

I recognize the voice instantly.

It belongs to my father.

My blood chills to an arctic temperature, and a million and one thoughts clog my brain. But only one is crystal clear—I need to help Hank.

I silently tiptoe to the office, my back pressed to the

wall, hoping to be cloaked by the darkness. I peek my head through the window, ensuring I remain unseen as I watch my nightmare become a reality.

"Just tell me where she is, old man!" my father shouts, waving a gun in Hank's face.

My father looks like death, and you'd think after all this time of not seeing him, I would feel…something for him, but I don't. The only thing I feel is remorse for not shooting straight.

But my heart yearns for the man who has been more of a parental figure than my own biological father. The man currently staring death in the face and not cowering in fear or ratting me out.

Hank sits behind the counter casually, seemingly undisturbed to have a pistol waving violently around in his face.

"I don't know who you're talking about," he says calmly, lying through his teeth.

"Don't lie to me!" my father yells, pointing the gun at Hank's chest. "I *will* shoot you."

Hank shrugs, popping a peanut into his mouth, his shaky fingers the only sign that he's afraid.

"You're going to shoot a defenseless old man?" he asks, shaking his head shamefully. "I don't know no Mia Lee, nor have I ever seen her. Now, if you'd be so kind to step off my property before I call the police."

"You're lying!"

Watching this terrifying scene play out in front of me has my heart kicking against my chest, pounding in sheer terror. But my whole existence is put on hold when I hear the voice of a man who still, to this day, scares the living shit out of me.

"Of course, he's lying," says the voice from behind Hank.

Phil.

Phil looks just as I remember, and the reaction he elicits in me is the same—I want him dead.

Everything at this moment is heightened, and my flight or fight instinct takes over. I have to fight.

I creep closer to the door, reaching for the gun at the small of my back, and pull it out silently. I watch and wait to catch them off guard because one wrong move and Hank is dead.

"Do you know that she's a cold-hearted criminal? This girl who you're protecting"—he waves his gun in my dad's direction—"shot her father and left him for dead." Phil takes a menacing step toward Grandpa, his bald head gleaming under the lights.

Hank only shrugs, his brave eyes never wavering from Phil's predatory stare.

"And you'd still protect her? A stranger? You would risk your worthless old life for someone you hardly know?" Phil asks, perplexed, scratching his temple with the barrel of his gun.

I bite my lip, ashamed, as there is some truth in what Phil has just said. I *am* a stranger to Hank. But as I look at him, his familiar face, and his wrinkled, kind hands, I see not a stranger but family. But regardless, I *have* risked Hank's life by coming here, and my selfish need to be normal has put him in danger.

I have to make this right, and I will.

Hank only cackles, stubbornly crossing his arms over his chest, infuriating Phil.

"This is your last chance," Phil snarls, one hand filled with a paper bag, the other holding a Beretta.

The two men who ruined my life stand before me, and the rage I feel cannot be put into words. It's now or never, so I creep closer, my finger poised on the trigger, ready to aim and shoot, and this time, I won't miss.

Hank steadily stands his ground and shakes his head.

"Get off my property, you lowlife scumbags!" he shouts, standing and walking toward Phil.

My breath gets caught in my throat as Phil cocks his gun, raising it to Hank's temple, hoping to intimidate him. But Hank just turns his weary face to meet Phil's confidently.

"She ain't no stranger. She's family. And I would be *proud* to call her my daughter," Hank spits, and I gasp as he's about to get himself killed. "That child brought nothing but warmth into my life, and because of that…I will *never* tell you where she is."

My heart stops beating because Hank has just sacrificed himself for me.

I have no doubt Hank knows that I'm watching him, urging me to run. But I don't because surely Phil wouldn't… but he does.

My body reacts before my brain can catch up, and I lunge forward, pointing my gun at Phil, but I'm too late.

"Wrong answer." Phil snickers and pulls the trigger.

The next few seconds pass by in slow motion, and I will be permanently scarred from seeing Phil shoot Hank in cold blood.

My entire body freezes as I watch Hank drop to the ground with a nauseating thud while my father and Phil laugh as they begin raiding the cash register to make this look like a robbery gone wrong.

"Stupid old bastard," my father chides, looking down at Hank, who wheezes, gasping for air. "You deserve to die for protecting that good-for-nothing little bitch."

The pain in my chest isn't from my father's venomous

words because his words mean nothing to me. *He* is nothing to me.

The pain is from watching the only person who believed in me and loved me die before my eyes.

My eyes hysterically drop to Hank, my gun hanging limply and uselessly in my hand, as I see him lay motionless, blood covering his kind, gentle face. His gaze is fixated on mine, and slowly, the light leaves his eyes because he's dying. He gives me one final smile, and as a small tear spills down his cheek, his eyes close, and just like that…he's gone.

NO…

This is surely a dream.

But as the metallic tang of blood hits my nostrils, I know this isn't a dream. This is my worst nightmare come true.

This is hell.

The rage that I feel can't be put into words, and a bloodcurdling scream comes tearing out of my throat as I charge toward the door, ready to dish out revenge on the two men who have killed an innocent man. A man who stuck by me until the very end. A man who died to save me. A man I loved.

I don't care if I go down. It'll be worth it. To watch those motherfuckers pay for what they have done to Hank will be worth any ramifications I receive.

But my scream and my attack are stopped when a strong set of arms wrap around me. One hand forcefully covers my mouth while the other yanks me up by the waist, lifting me off the ground and dragging me away hastily. I kick and scream, but it's futile. Quinn is far stronger than me, and he's running so quickly, the landscape blurs ahead of me.

He throws me into the truck from the driver's side because he knows I'll head straight back out there to finish them off if he doesn't hold me down.

"Stay!" he snarls when I make a move to open the passenger door.

He latches onto my arm and starts the car, pulling out of the parking lot so quickly that we slip and slide all over the gravel. Surely by now my father and Phil know that someone has seen them, but do they know it's me?

I don't care.

My brain desperately attempts to process everything that happened but simply can't. It cannot accept the fact that Hank is dead…because of me.

I didn't pull the trigger, but I may as well have. This is my fault, and only one thought in this whole clusterfuck of events is clear. And that is, they need to pay. Not tomorrow or the day after. But they need to pay now.

Quinn drives with one hand gripping the steering wheel while the other clutches my arm, stopping me from wriggling around and trying to break free. I still have my gun, so I do something stupid.

"Stop the car!" I demand, pointing the gun at him.

Quinn flicks his eyes toward me and looks down at the gun, smirking angrily.

"You're going to shoot me?" he asks, his eyes darting between me and the road.

I don't know what I'm capable of right now because my rage clouds any rational thoughts.

When I don't budge, he pulls the car over so abruptly, I nearly slam my head into the dashboard.

"Go ahead, do it, then! What are you waiting for?" he shouts, turning to face me as he seizes my hand and positions the gun at his heart.

My hand begins to shake, and tears spring to my eyes as I

see the rage and hurt contort his face into a snarl.

"Go on, Red, shoot me! Rip out my fucking heart!"

His words slap me across the cheek, and I sob as my hand goes slack, the gun dropping onto the seat near me. I cover my face with my hands, weeping into them uncontrollably. Quinn grabs the gun, and I hear him throw it into the glove compartment.

I'm howling, my throat sore from the screams bubbling from the pit of my stomach.

"They killed him!" I sob. "They killed Hank! He's dead! He's dead…because of me! I fucking froze! I choked when Hank needed me the most."

The realization of what happened hits home, and I'm going to be violently ill. I open the door and heave up the entire contents of my stomach, unable to stop until there's nothing left to give. But still, that's not enough. I force my body to expel the hurt and the anger inside me until I'm gagging and retching.

Quinn is behind me, rubbing my back, attempting to soothe me, but I shrug him off because I don't deserve any comfort. I don't deserve any sympathy because I'm the one who deserves to be lying in her own pool of blood, not Hank.

"Red, enough. We've got to get out of here," he says quietly, his hand still stubbornly caressing me.

"No," I choke out, my head still hanging out the door. "Turn back. I have to find them. They have to pay for what they did to H-Han…" But I can't get the words out because it'll make what happened tonight real once I say them.

"They'll pay, I promise you. Just trust me, please. But we have to get out of here." The urgency in his voice alarms me to the fact that he too, is now in danger if I'm caught with him.

I won't allow another person I care for to perish, so I

reluctantly pull myself into the truck, but I can't face him. When I turn my face to stare into the night sky, he reaches over me, then softly closes and locks my door.

"Red." He sighs, but I shake my head, cutting him off.

"Drive," I say, and thankfully, he complies.

I'm pretty certain I pass out because when I come to, I'm in Quinn's bedroom, bundled up in his bed.

"Quinn?" I croak, straining my eyes to see.

"I'm here, Red," he says, hands filled with clothes as he's packing a bag.

"What are you doing?" I ask, eyeing him curiously as I slowly sit up.

"Nothing," he says, throwing his clothes onto the floor and switching on the light.

"How're you feeling?" he asks, sitting on the edge of the bed.

His hair is wet like he has showered, but he still looks exhausted.

"Have you slept?"

He shakes his head and rubs a hand down his face.

I feel my heart break because he looks overwhelmed because of me. I have brought nothing but sadness and danger into the lives of people who have done nothing but care for me.

My lip trembles, but I pull it together because I've done enough crying.

Now is the time for retribution.

"We need to go to the police. We need to tell them what

we saw. What they did to Hank," he whispers.

I bite my lip, not being able to deal with the fact that Hank is dead.

"You're right. I owe that to Hank," I reply, my stomach turning as my mind replays the last memory I have of him.

"Red, you can't run. That's no life for you to live."

I nod.

Now that my father is alive, it's probably safer for me to go to the police and tell them everything. Because if I run, I'm as good as dead.

"I was thinking, if you tell them your story, what your dad and Phil made you do, you'll get off. You won't do any jail time," Quinn pleads, reaching for my hand.

"I don't care if I go to jail. I deserve to do time. I've been given a life sentence anyway for what I did to Hank," I say, tears stinging my eyes.

Hank is dead because of me, and I'll never forgive myself for killing an innocent man.

"Hey, stop that. You did nothing wrong." Quinn pulls me into his arms and hugs me.

I try pushing him away, but he's so strong, and I'm so fucking weak that I need his strength to pull me through this shitstorm that I've created.

Nineteen

I wake before Quinn, his warm body enveloping mine protectively. But I unfold myself from his arms as I feel dirty and am in desperate need of a shower. I tiptoe down to the bathroom and stand under the shower spray until the water turns cold.

Quinn is right. I have to turn myself in. A life on the run is no life to live. I've tried it, and if anything, I felt more imprisoned than I would be locked in a cell.

I quickly dress, wanting to talk with Quinn about my decision. He's slipping into a clean shirt, his hair tousled and sleepy-looking, and to me, he's the most beautiful person in the world. But I'm a realist, and I know this will probably be one of the last times I spend alone with Quinn.

Once I talk to the police, I'm sure the only time spent with him will be through a glass window, talking into a phone.

"Hey," he says, turning to give me a small smile.

"Hey," I reply, walking over to him quietly and stepping into his open arms. "Thank you for everything."

"This isn't goodbye," he says, his arms encircling my waist tighter.

I don't reply because I don't want to taint this last memory since I will revert to it when missing him.

We stand hugging, collecting our breaths after the whirlwind of the past twenty-four hours. We pull away, however, when we hear the front door slam shut, and a hysterical Tabitha screams out to us from downstairs.

Quinn and I are down the stairs in a heartbeat and confronted by a tearstained Tabitha.

"Abi?" I ask, feeling like a horrible friend for lying to her for so long.

"Paige!" She sighs, throwing her arms around my neck and hugging me tightly.

Her calling me by that name feels weird since she knows my real name now, but I let it be.

"Is it true? Hank is…?" she asks, tears running down her cheeks as she pulls away to look at me and Quinn.

As Hank's name passes Abi's lips, my bottom lip trembles, and tears threaten to fall from my bloodshot eyes. But I tell myself no more tears and look at Quinn, who only nods sadly, answering Abi's question.

She breaks into a sob, hugging me tighter, and I rub her back numbly.

She pulls away, wiping away her tears.

"It's not true! You wouldn't do that to him!" she sobs, and I freeze.

"Abi, what are you talking about?" Quinn asks, taking a step toward us.

Tabitha's sobs get louder and louder, and I pull her out of my embrace, meeting her eyes.

"Abi, we wouldn't do what to him?" I ask, trying to remain calm.

"Kill him," she replies, her lip trembling.

"What?" I wheeze. "Who told you we…did that?"

"I overheard my mom talking to the police this morning. They were looking for you," she says, looking at me, "and you." She then looks at Quinn.

"Why?" I ask her, my heart launching into my throat.

Tabitha takes a deep breath and rubs her eyes. "The police think you and Quinn…shot Hank. That you stole the money out of the safe, and when Hank found you, you shot him."

"Motherfucker," Quinn gasps, pulling his hair into dismay.

"Why would they think that?" I ask, trying to piece everything together.

"Anonymous tip," she replies.

Anonymous, my ass. No doubt this is the work of my father and Phil. That explains the bag I saw Phil holding when he shot Hank.

They did this so I would run and not go to the police. My dad and Phil are smarter than I gave them credit for and probably had the same idea as Quinn. They knew I would turn them in, and they would be the fugitives, not me. But now, by pinning Hank's murder on Quinn and me, they are hopeful we'll run. And then they'll follow and deal with justice their own way.

But I'm so tired of running.

Then my world comes crashing down. If they know about Quinn, then they know about…Tristan.

"Where's Tristan?" I ask, the panic clear in my voice as I turn to Quinn.

"Fuck!" he screams, bolting up the stairs.

Tabitha has her hands over her mouth like she's about to be sick.

"Abi, I'm so sorry I got you involved in all this shit. But I will tell them you had nothing to do with it. No harm will come to you, I promise." I pull her in for a tight hug.

"Paige…Mia," she corrects, and my real name has never sounded sweeter. "I don't care what you did. You may have lied to me about your name, about what you did, but I know you never lied about being my friend. I will do anything to protect you."

I can't stop the tears.

"Thank you, Abi. You'll always be my best friend," I whisper, truly understanding the meaning for the first time.

Quinn sprints down the stairs with his phone pressed to his ear. "He's not upstairs or answering his phone."

I notice Lucky isn't around and conclude, "He's probably walking Lucky. Keep trying his cell. I'll send him a message and tell him to come straight home. It's not safe for him to walk around. I have to go to the police."

Quinn turns to look at me, eyes wide.

"Red, we need to come up with a better plan. Now that we've been pegged for Hank's murder, things have changed."

I shake my head. "No, Quinn, don't you get it? My dad and Phil won't stop until I'm either dead or they kill everyone I care about. This is about vengeance, and they'll stop at nothing until they've had their fill."

"Don't you dare," he says, his jaw clenching. "Don't pull this martyr crap."

Tabitha looks from Quinn to me. "What is he talking about?"

I look at my friend, who has been nothing but kind to me,

and I'm so lucky to have met her.

"Red, no!" Quinn yells, grabbing my arm, trying to shake some sense into me.

"It's the only way," I whisper. "I confess to Hank's murder, and I go to jail. The police are already looking for me. It won't take much to convince them that I shot Hank because of a robbery gone wrong. It's the only way for you to be safe. That's all I care about."

"Mia, no! You can't." Tabitha's eyes widen, pleading with me not to do this.

"I have to. Otherwise, I'll be running from my dad and Phil for the rest of my life. What kind of life is that?" I say, reciting Quinn's words.

I hear him curse under his breath, but I continue. "But if I go to jail, they'll stop chasing me and leave you alone."

"But you'll go to jail for a long time," she cries, and her compassion for me touches me so deeply, a sob racks my body.

"It's the only way," I whisper, looking at Quinn with tears streaming down my cheeks.

The look in Quinn's eyes breaks my heart, but I have to do this. I owe him this.

When he sees I won't budge, he suddenly turns toward the wall, hitting it so hard the plaster crumbles around his fist. I flinch but try not to show any emotion as I pull my phone out of my back pocket, ready to end this.

But as the front door opens, the cool breeze slapping me in the face with its iciness, all plans of calling the police get thrown out the window as my phone falls to the floor, shattering on impact. Tristan slumps onto the floor, his hand braced on the handle, blood staining his white T-shirt.

Lucky comes running in after him, covered in blood and barking hysterically. The scene is pure chaos.

Quinn reaches for his brother and heaves him inside, slamming the door behind him, the look of panic reflected from head to toe.

"Tris! What happened?" Quinn yells frantically, his hands attending to every part of his body to find the source of his wound.

He doesn't have to look far.

Tristan has a knife wound to his side, blood seeping out quickly.

"Fuck!" Quinn roars, cradling his brother to his chest. "No!"

This can't be happening.

"Red, go get some towels, anything to stop the bleeding," Quinn says, his hands pushing down on Tristan's wound.

But the bright swirls of red running over his hands and down Tristan's side are not a good sign.

"Call an ambulance!" I scream, running over to him and dropping to my knees, ignoring the pain of smashing into the hard tiles.

I slip my hoodie off, bundling it up and pressing it to Tristan's side.

"No," Quinn says between clenched teeth. "Not until we're gone."

"What?"

Tristan's eyes flicker, and he tries to focus but can't.

"Quinn?" he whispers weakly.

"I'm here," Quinn says, trying not to break down, needing to be strong for his brother. "Didn't I tell you running with scissors is hazardous to your health?"

"Ha...funny," Tristan says breathlessly, attempting to smile but wincing.

"What happened?" Quinn asks, leaning forward, his hair

covering his eyes as he bends in to listen to Tristan.

"They…they were looking for…Mia," he gasps, his eyes searching for me.

"I'm here," I sob, latching onto his ice-cold hand and kissing his fingers. "Abi, call an ambulance now!"

Tristan squeezes my hand. It's soft, but I can feel the plea behind them.

"Run," he whispers as I meet his pained eyes. "I didn't tell them where…but your dad, they…coming…here." He begins coughing up blood, a sure sign his lungs have been nicked.

I wipe the blood with my shaky fingers. "No. I'm staying with you."

Tristan tries to shake his head, but the movement is unsteady.

"Run," he whispers again.

His eyes flick to Quinn. "Go. Take…care…of…our…girl," he breathes out, smiling at me.

"No!" I cry when his eyes slip shut, his head lolling to the side.

"Tristan! No!" I sob, laying my head on his chest, the pain I feel breaking me in two.

I hear this heart beating faintly under my ear, and I turn hysterically to Tabitha. "How long till the ambulance gets here?"

"They said f-five minutes," she stutters, looking down at Tristan, eyes filled with tears.

"Red, we gotta go," Quinn says, looking at Tabitha and gesturing with his chin for her to take his place.

"What? Are you crazy? I'm not going anywhere until the ambulance gets here."

"I'm not asking you; I'm *telling* you. I will not allow my brother to die in vain, so move," he says again with an edge to his voice.

I take one last look at Tristan. Fresh tears spill from my swollen eyes.

"He's not going to die," I choke out, my hand caressing his cold cheeks. "Thank you for saving me. Time and time again."

Tabitha has taken over Quinn's place, her hand caressing Tristan's brow, sweeping his blood-stained hair out of his face.

"Mia, get my bag," she says, indicating with her eyes where she dropped it by the door.

I don't question her and quickly reach for it.

"Take my wallet and cell."

"What? No."

"Don't argue with me. We don't have much time. Withdraw all the money from my credit cards. That'll give you enough money to give you a big head start and then destroy them. I'll report my bag as being stolen in two days, so make sure you withdraw the money as soon as you can before my mother cancels my cards. Destroy your cell. You too, Quinn. Take mine, use it to contact me, and also so I can contact you."

All this is too much, and I don't know what to say, so I throw my arms around her, hugging her tighter than I have ever hugged her.

"Thank you."

"C'mon, Red, we have to split," Quinn says, both our backpacks strapped to his shoulders.

I eye him, wondering when he had time to pack a bag, but then I remember him doing so last night. He knew that deep down, it would come to this. That we would be forced to run.

Standing up quickly and giving both Tabitha and Tristan one final look, I hope to see them again sometime soon.

Quinn grabs my hand, yanking me out the door, and we're both running toward the truck without looking back.

Lucky runs behind us barking, and my heart breaks.

I can't leave him behind.

"Get in," Quinn says to Lucky, reading my thoughts.

Lucky jumps in, and I follow quickly. Quinn has the truck rolling before I can shut my door. We fishtail it down the road, and before I know it, we're hitting the highway and leaving my nightmare behind.

We're both silent, lost in our thoughts, and I doubt I'll ever be able to pull myself out of this mess and remain sane. The lives I've destroyed because of my selfish need to find the real me has cost the people I love so much.

Love.

I get it now.

And it's all thanks to a group of misfits. It's because of them, because of their unconditional love, that I'm human again.

I look over at the man who has risked so much for me, who has secrets just like me, who is saving me from my past—a past that has cost *him* so much. And I bite back my tears because I have no right to cry.

He's in this mess because of me; *they* are all in this mess because of me.

And Hank is *dead* because of me.

I have to make it right.

So I promise myself, here and now. I will seek retribution on the individuals who have wounded the people I love.

Even if I die trying, they will pay.

I never really understood the saying, "I'd rather die fighting than die for nothing at all."

But now…now, I get it.

Subscribe to my Newsletter:
https://landing.mailerlite.com/webforms/landing/b4j1v6

Something Like Normal Playlist:
https://tinyurl.com/bddea5bp

About the Author

Monica James spent her youth devouring the works of Anne Rice, William Shakespeare, and Emily Dickinson.

When she is not writing, Monica is busy running her own business, but she always finds a balance between the two. She enjoys writing honest, heartfelt, and turbulent stories, hoping to leave an imprint on her readers. She draws her inspiration from life.

She is a bestselling author in the U.S.A., Australia, Canada, France, Germany, Israel, and The U.K.

Monica James resides in Melbourne, Australia, with her wonderful family, and menagerie of animals. She is slightly obsessed with cats, chucks, and lip gloss, and secretly wishes she was a ninja on the weekends.

Connect with Monica James

Facebook: facebook.com/authormonicajames
Twitter: twitter.com/monicajames81
Goodreads: goodreads.com/MonicaJames
Instagram: instagram.com/authormonicajames
Website: authormonicajames.com
TikTok: @authormonicajames
BookBub: bookbub.com/authors/monica-james
Amazon: https://amzn.to/2EWZSyS
Join my Reader Group: http://bit.ly/2nUaRyi